NIMISHA'S SHIP

Other titles by Anne McCaffrey
Published by Ballantine Books:

Decision at Doona
Dinosaur Planet
Dinosaur Planet Survivors
Get Off the Unicorn
The Lady
Pegasus in Flight
Restoree
The Ship Who Sang
To Ride Pegasus

THE CRYSTAL SINGER BOOKS
Crystal Singer
Killashandra
Crystal Line

THE DRAGONRIDERS OF PERN® BOOKS
Dragonflight
Dragonquest
The White Dragon
Moreta: Dragonlady of Pern
Nerilka's Story
Dragonsdawn
The Renegades of Pern
All the Weyrs of Pern
The Chronicles of Pern: First Fall
The Dolphins of Pern
Dragonseye
The MasterHarper of Pern

By Anne McCaffrey and Elizabeth Ann Scarborough:
Powers That Be
Power Lines
Power Play

With Jody Lynn Nye:
The Dragonlover's Guide to Pern

Edited by Anne McCaffrey:
Alchemy and Academe

ANNE McCAFFREY

NIMISHA'S SHIP

DEL REY

THE BALLANTINE PUBLISHING GROUP

NEW YORK

A Del Rey® Book
Published by The Ballantine Publishing Group

www.randomhouse.com/BB/

Library of Congress Cataloging-in-Publication Data
McCaffrey, Anne.
Nimisha's ship / Anne McCaffrey. —1st ed.
p.   cm.
ISBN 0-345-38825-9 (alk. paper)
I.   Title.
PS3563.A255N55   1999
813' .54—dc21   98-45500

Manufactured in the United States of America

First Edition: February 1999
10 9 8 7 6 5 4 3 2 1

To a courageous and generous young woman
For the greatest gift
One woman can give another

ACKNOWLEDGMENTS

Once again I am thankful to my first readers who keep me from making egregious errors or mistakes.

For *Nimisha's Ship*, I owe Harry Alm in his capacity of naval architect and my son, Todd J. McCaffrey, for their input, timely additions, and corrections. Marilyn Alm, Lea Day, and Mary Jean Holmes have all read and made suggestions for which I am truly grateful. To J. R. Holmes, a special thanks for his valuable contribution of PanSpermia.

An unknown number of online folks have inadvertently helped me name my characters. Syrona gave me permission to use her name as a main character and I ruthlessly borrowed others. And, as always, my gratitude to Vaughne Hansen in Virginia Kidd's office and especially to my editor, Shelly Shapiro.

NIMISHA'S SHIP

CHAPTER 1

<< ● >>

Lady Rezalla Boynton-Chonderlee was often bemused and puzzled by her body-heir, Nimisha Boynton-Rondymense, as the child began to develop a personality. She was, indeed, all and more that a womb-mother could wish in her body-heir: beautiful, gentian-eyed, intelligent, healthy, and obedient in almost every matter. Lady Rezalla considered the infrequent displays of temper and minor rebellions against necessary protocol only to be expected in the very young. Nimisha was certainly not as wayward or overindulged as some of the children of her contemporaries.

However, as Nimisha grew past the nursery stage and started the formal tutorial lessons, she showed decided preferences that were unexpected. She loved to take first mechanical and then robotic units apart, a hobby that struck her womb-mother as unusual. Lady Rezalla consoled herself that at least Nimisha showed an aptitude for something that kept her occupied for hours. Lady Rezalla knew that some of her social peers had . . . difficult . . . children with tendencies to be violent or abusive as the very young often were. Even in the best families. She privately admitted to some anxiety that Nimisha's mechanical avocation might be considered "quaint" for someone in the most prestigious social level of Acclarke City on Vega III. On the positive side, the Boynton-Chonderlee-Rondymense connection was sufficiently powerful to permit much that might have been censured or condemned in a lesser Family.

"It's in the genes she inherited from me, Rezalla," Lord Tionel Rondymense-Erhardt remarked on one of his visits to see the daughter he had contracted to provide Lady Rezalla. Though he would have been perfectly willing to have had a much longer contract with the elegant Rezalla, she had never given him the least bit of encouragement for an extension. This disinterest both annoyed and intrigued him since he was much in demand as a sire in the best Acclarkian circles. Still, he enjoyed her company and excruciatingly accurate remarks about their society and peers. She was not averse to his visits since she felt that *her* body-heir by him was quite the best of the lot he had so far sired. She was less sanguine about the way he encouraged Nimisha in her whimsical bent, happily answering her questions or giving her a pointer when she seemed at a standstill in reassembling what she had taken apart.

"It has obviously escaped your attention, my dear Rezalla," he remarked one day after explaining to Nimisha the function of the tiny chips she had spread out on the floor, "that she invariably *improves* the design and function of whatever she's tinkering with. I find that most ingenious of her. Most ingenious. If she continues to develop this aptitude, why I might just leave her my Ship Yard. No one else I've sired shows the least bit of interest in spaceship design. Much less doing any work of any description. I have grave concern that what nine generations have built up in the Rondymense Ship Yard GmBH might decline and disappear in the next one."

"*My* body-heir," Lady Rezalla replied, rather more dismayed than pleased by Lord Tionel's remarks, "will have no need for unsuitable bequests, Lord Tionel."

"You were happy enough to find ten thousand shares of Rondymense stock in her birth-gift portfolio," he remarked. Then he went on in his softest, most persuasive voice, his blue eyes dancing, though his face had assumed a properly repentant expression.

"Don't be angry with me, Rezie. There's nothing unsuitable about a firm that has been designing spaceships and in profit for over two hundred years. Surely the financier in you appreciates that!"

The point was well taken, Lady Rezalla had to admit in all fairness. She herself had increased her holdings and wealth due to a nearly infallible instinct for the profitability of new businesses. Tionel was not given to casual remarks. She knew very well that his body-heir, Vestrin, a decade older than her Nimisha, was a disgrace to his sire. He seemed to have no interest in anything that wasn't "thrilling, exciting, or totally new," which included dangerous hunts and rather nasty jokes on those who might be considered "close" friends. Tionel could do worse than sign the Rondymense Yard over to his girl child if he wished it to continue. Nimisha need not *do* anything in such a well-run establishment. Rezalla didn't know how much Tionel did in the administrative end of the business, but she was quite capable of instructing her daughter in the financial aspects sufficiently to keep the Yard in profit. Especially as many contracts from the Admiralty were awarded to Rondymense Ship Yard GmBH. It was always good to be "in" with the Admiralty, especially as she had recently acquired the controlling interest in a small freighter company.

"I have never faulted you on your business acumen, Ti," she replied, relenting as they both watched Nimisha's careful reassembly of a robotic toy, the gift of her Great Uncle Dahmison. While expressing appreciation for the gift, Lady Rezalla wondered if Uncle knew which sex the child was. But it was certainly the sort of thing Uncle would give: It made the most appalling noise. Children liked noise; Rezalla didn't. "You've always been lucky with your designers."

"*My* designers?" Lord Tionel looked insulted and gestured at Nimisha. "I'm my designer. I am responsible for all the innovations at the Yard. *And* half of what the Vegan Fleet uses."

It was Lady Rezalla's turn to be surprised, and despite her many years of schooling her expression to show only what she wished an audience to see, it was a full minute before she could respond with cool dignity.

"You never mentioned that, Tionel." It was as near a reprimand as she could bring herself to make. Members of the First Families had to set good examples to everyone, even their peers, but they *delegated* duties; they didn't *do* them.

"I thought everyone knew," Tionel replied with a properly cool indifference and a shrug of one shoulder. "Ah, very nice, Nimi," he said as his six-year-old offspring presented him with the repaired toy. He set it on the floor and pressed the activating stud. It began its series of acrobatics, making Nimi clap her hands. "What did you alter in its circuitry?"

"She's made it quiet!" Lady Rezalla said, her voice echoing her delight. So Nimisha had noticed her distaste for the sound it had made. "Such a dear child."

"Well done, Nimi, well done!" Lord Tionel clapped his hands and, without a glance at his former contractual spouse, held his arms out to the child. She promptly climbed into his lap and put her arms about his neck, a show of affection that caused Lady Rezalla to regard Lord Tionel with dismay. He noticed. "Nonsense, Rezie. I am her father and I like to cuddle my children."

"How . . . how exceedingly . . . old-fashioned of you," Lady Rezalla said, seething with a variety of emotions, the most dominant being envy.

Nimisha would never have dared to climb onto her mother's lap. But then, Rezalla had never indicated that such a display would have been acceptable. Lady Rezalla did not like her exquisite self handled. What with Nimisha's preoccupation with mechanical things, her fingers and hands were rarely as clean as they should be, though Nurse did the best she could. Oddly enough, Nimisha did not have even a smudge of dirt on her clothing.

If Tionel wished to have his fashionable tunic and trousers marred by dirty fingers, that was his choice. He had always been a tactile person. If she had once found this trait of his charming, she did not think unessential personal contact dignified. Certainly not in their social sphere. At least Nimisha was still very much a child, so such a display could be condoned. She and her sire seemed to have established a bond that was not entirely due to the child's interest in taking things apart. It did the child no harm to receive paternal caresses—if not carried too far. Lady Rezalla was fair-minded. She thought she and Nimisha had an excellent relationship; certainly she enjoyed her daughter's company whenever she chose to take her anywhere. For the first time, Lady Rezalla realized how odd her own behavior might look to others. Very few of her social friends bothered to have their child-heirs accompany them as much as Lady Rezalla did. But she genuinely liked the child and thought her occasional observations clever. Rezalla also thought herself quite broadminded in rearing Nimisha. The child's only flaw, as her mother saw it, was this fascination with dismantling and reassembling mechanical and chippy things.

She did remonstrate with Tionel when he started presenting Nimisha with birthday gifts of a construction nature; things to assemble even down to schematic drawings and instructions. To offset Tionel's influence, Lady Rezalla subtly began to emphasize the feminine instruction that all girls of their social level had to acquire and display suitably in Acclarkian society. She was quite successful in such tuition. By the time Nimisha was eight, she insisted on choosing her own apparel. As she displayed an innate good taste, as well as a sense of color and design, Lady Rezalla stopped fretting about her child's quaint preference for mucking about with greasy gears and engines and the chips she so enjoyed fooling with. What only Nimisha's Nurse knew was that her charge knew how to strike a balance that permitted her time to do what she really wanted—to examine things mechanical and improve them—

and time to satisfy a mother whom she genuinely loved and re-spected, at least in matters of dress and deportment.

"Actually, good design is good design anywhere," Nimisha told Nurse after a shopping session with her mother. "And choosing clothing isn't much different from choosing the right chassis for a sleek skimmer."

Such a remark merely proved to Nurse that her charge was cleverer than Lady Rezalla realized, a fact that Nurse proudly as-cribed to her own careful nurturing of her charge.

Because Nimisha's sire did show a marked interest in her—and the guidance counselors admitted that a friendly paternal regard generally contributed to the stability of a child, male or female—Lady Rezalla permitted Lord Tionel to take Nimisha on trips to the Rondymense Ship Yard. Since Nurse was agoraphobic and bluntly refused to leave the solid surface of Vega III even for Nimisha's sake, Lady Rezalla sent to the employment agency she patronized for a suitable female attendant who had experience in space travel. Five candidates were offered by the agency, and their prospective employer subjected each to a long and searching interrogation.

Lady Rezalla settled on twenty-one-year-old Jeska Mlan be-cause of her family's long and illustrious record as military and naval personnel. Mlan had trained and applied for Service as well, but sadly she was one centimeter too short and a half kilo too light to be eligible. So she had registered as a bodyguard. All her creden-tials were in order, her intelligence was above average, her manner pleasant, and her accent that of an educated Acclarkian (accept-able in any social circle). It was important that Nimisha did not pick up any "common habits." Lady Rezalla deplored the latest fad in her society—of using certain cant terms or resorting to archaic language and expletives that mystified her.

The young woman certainly didn't look like a bodyguard. Though not traditionally pretty, Jeska was attractive, her face showing good character, and she knew enough about dressing herself to enhance her appearance. She would look well in Lady Rezalla's stylish personal livery. But the telling factor was Jeska's interest in things mechanical.

"My father and brothers taught me how to keep a skimmer serviced, Lady Rezalla," she said, and then added with a slight smile, "and other equipment that I hope I shall not have to use."

"Then you are familiar with stunners?"

"I have been checked out by the Acclarkian Peace Guardians on hand weapons and carry permits for personal defense implements," Jeska replied.

"Do you have a current valid permit with the APG?"

"Not at the moment, ma'am, but my training has been registered with them."

"I shall apply for the necessary permit immediately. Do you generally carry two knives, Mlan?"

"Yes, m'lady," Jeska said without apology. The security arch on the main entrance had disclosed that the girl carried one sheathed between her shoulders and another in her right boot, a slender blade that the Residence Manager termed a "stiletto."

Lady Rezalla could approve of the quiet dignity of that response: consonant with her training, certainly, and a basic precaution for an attractive young female. There were parts of Acclarke where personal weapons would undoubtedly be required, though Mlan's address was not in one of those insalubrious areas.

While Jeska's primary duty was to accompany Nimisha on any excursions outside the Boynton-Chonderlee compound, she was also enjoined by Lady Rezalla to keep the girl physically fit. Mlan's résumé had included a list of the awards that she had received for gymnastic events. Rezalla herself used daily dance and an aerobics routine to keep supple, in addition to weekly sessions with a trainer. So many of her contemporaries resorted to surgical methods to maintain their figures, a practice that Rezalla found abhorrent and which she intended to eschew. Though one of her close personal friends, Lord Naves, specialized in body sculpture, she did not intend to use his skills. Good physical habits in childhood would result in a firm adult body that would need no surgical interference.

"So many children these days are content to have everything done *for* them," Lady Rezalla said, leading her new employee to meet her daughter. "I do not care to see my daughter become languorous and ineffectual. You will see that she is kept in top physical condition."

As Lady Rezalla did not specify what physical fitness program she wished her daughter to learn, Jeska passed on more of what she herself had been taught by older brothers and sisters in the services. Gymnastics provided a solid base from which to start. When Jeska saw how beautiful her young charge was, she included general self-defense moves in the exercise program. As Nimisha grew in height, weight, and strength, Jeska added offensive tactics, including the use of daggers, stunners, and hunting weapons, and how to turn seemingly innocuous objects into weapons in an emergency. While Jeska knew that many members of the First Families were ardent hunters and enjoyed pursuing very dangerous prey on those preserves set aside for such sport, Nimisha was uncharacteristically—for her social rank—devoid of any interest in the hunt. She ignored those of her peers who boasted of killing this animal or that predatory avian and waved aside details of such prowess. She was vitally interested in how the flitters, skimmers, and ground vehicles worked. And how to improve their performance—an interest that Jeska was certainly delighted to foster.

Like most scions in her rank of society, Nimisha was tutored at home, her mother deciding what subjects she should study. Languages, of course, and mathematics featured very early on, as well as a foundation in economics. She was also tutored at the appropriate age in astrography, galactic history, various branches of the physical sciences, the workings of the Vegan civic administrational structure, and basic legal precepts.

"Which means when to put in a hurry-up call to the family legal advisers," Nimisha said to Jeska with a droll grin. At ten she was far more aware of civic responsibilities than Jeska had ever been.

Jeska was quite willing to improve her own education, especially in useful areas like mathematics, legal codes, and statutes. So, since she had no duties during the morning tutorial sessions, she took to sitting quietly in the back of the room, acquiring knowledge that had not been available in the general curriculum of her school. Like any member of a serving family, she had learned phrases and words of many different languages, but not necessarily those appropriate for the ears of a First Family scion, so she was pleased to become acquainted with more socially correct usage. She was delighted when Nimisha emphasized more and more engineering concepts with the science tutor who was only hired to give her a basic general understanding of the profession.

Nimisha regretted that the schoolroom computer system did not have a tri-d display device sophisticated enough to allow her to design something more satisfying than gowns or interior decorations or the other programs available to a First Family scion of the female sex. However, her tutor did find a manual for a professional design unit and privately sighed over its seemingly unlimited virtual display factors. Although Lady Rezalla allowed her body-heir a great deal of leeway, Nimisha knew when discretion was required. It was enough to have Jeska permitted to join the lessons.

"It's much easier to review lessons with someone," Nimisha had confided in Jeska. "I'm glad you're not bored."

"That's highly unlikely in your company, Nimisha," Jeska replied with a grin. She had quickly grown fond of the bright, cheerful child in her care, and if she bent a few rules for Nimisha, the girl did the same for her.

As Nimisha grew older, she was invited on more frequent excursions with her sire, and these Jeska enjoyed almost as much as her charge.

The Rondymense Ship Yard occupied an area on the outskirts of the primary Vegan Fleet Space Yard, where new vessels were built and older ones underwent maintenance and refitting. While Lord Tionel never said anything to the point, Jeska Mlan was quick to realize that Rondymense was in such proximity to the big Fleet installation because it supplied the Fleet with a great many of its improvements, most of which originated in Lord Tionel's fertile mind. Jeska was thrilled: She might not have made the Service, but she became privy to a lot that her serving relatives would never know. Since discretion had been a facet of her early childhood training in an active service family, she had no trouble keeping what she saw and heard to herself. On her infrequent visits home, she often had occasion to smile quietly as she listened to her siblings raving about this or that improvement to the Vegan Spaceship 7890B, or the brand-new VSS 8650C—innovations she had watched from the design stage onward. She was also alert to the fact that Nimisha was equally discreet, though Lord Tionel had frequently discussed technical aspects that Jeska knew to be very top secret. But discretion was subtly inbred in any child of the First Families.

It didn't take Lord Tionel long to realize that his daughter's bodyguard was as eager to learn as Nimisha. So he equipped them both with tools and gave them projects to complete, all deftly geared to augment the larger educational program he now had in mind for Nimisha. When she appeared to have stopped growing, he had them both measured for space suits so they could accompany him and his crews on exterior investigations. Of course, they knew as well as he did that Lady Rezalla would have instantly curtailed these visits had she known that they'd accompanied Lord Tionel into the vacuum of space. But he had undertaken their instruction himself, been satisfied that they appreciated the risks and would adhere to the precautions. They were always safely linked to experienced EVA personnel.

Early on, Lord Tionel tested Jeska's piloting skills in a space skimmer as well as a ground vehicle and rated her competence equal to that of many pilots. He also taught Nimisha how to drive, preferring to be certain she was capable long before Lady Rezalla allowed her body-heir a personal ground vehicle.

"I may be usurping some of her birth-mother's prerogatives," he told Jeska one day without a trace of guilt, "but I prefer to oversee her education in such matters. I've no doubt Lady Rezalla instructs her as efficiently in the purely feminine skills in which she herself excels."

Jeska nodded, understanding completely what he had not said. "I am very appreciative, Lord Tionel, of the benefits I have received while in Lady Nimisha's company."

"You've an aptitude worth cultivating, my girl," he replied honestly. "When Nimisha no longer requires your . . . companionship, this Yard would consider you an asset." He smiled in his beguiling fashion, rubbing his hands together as if already anticipating the moment when he could make good on his offer.

"Small wonder you succeed so well with the Fleet types, Lord Tionel," she said, grinning impudently up at him. The current High Admiral of the Fleet was an attractive and highly efficient woman. Jeska knew he spent considerable time with her and her Design teams.

His smile broadened and he accorded her a slight bow. "I like to encourage talent wherever I encounter it. Now," he continued in a brisker tone, "what trinket would please my daughter when she receives her Necklace four weeks from now?"

"A skimmer, sir," Jeska replied promptly, sober-faced, though she couldn't keep the glint of mischief out of her eyes.

"A skimmer?" The uplift of his voice in surprised repetition made her grin.

"Even Lady Rezalla will agree that Lady Nimi, at fourteen, should have her own transport. Especially as she will promise to service it herself." Jeska paused, rather pleased that she had been able to astonish Lord Tionel. "That way no one but she and I will know the engine capacity, the optimum cruising range, or the versatility of the vehicle."

"Ah!" Lord Tionel's eyes lit up. He gave Jeska's back such an approving thump that only the girl's superb natural reflexes kept her from bouncing off the worktable in front of her. "Oh, sorry about that, Jeska. Caught me by surprise, you did. Excellent. Excellent." And he went off, chuckling to himself. "Capital idea! Just the thing."

Since Jeska had been Nimisha's companion for six years, she was permitted to attend the important Necklace Ceremony, traditional in First Family circles. She stood well behind those who were related by blood, of course, but she was there when Nimisha celebrated her minor majority, colloquially known as the Double M.

The adult majority was four years hence, but body-heirs were expected from the moment of their Necklacing to act in an adult fashion and leave childish practices and manners behind them. Beside Jeska, Nurse was sniffling, since this ceremony marked the end of her employment. That she was being munificently rewarded by Lady Rezalla and need never work another day in her life did not seem to compensate for leaving Nimisha. Since Jeska was fonder of Nimisha than she was of any of her own siblings, she quite understood Nurse's sorrow. She would continue in her duties to the body-heir of Boynton-Chonderlee House, but she and Nurse had been of one mind in keeping certain aspects of Nimisha's daily routines from Lady Rezalla. Once Necklaced, Nimisha was guaranteed more freedom from constant supervision. Indeed, during the festivities, other servants would be moving Nimisha's belongings out of the nursery and into private quarters in the west wing of the House.

Before relatives from both sides of the bloodline, as well as Lady Rezalla's particular friends and confidants, Nimisha was led in by her dam's mother, the Lady Astatine Boynton-Tatanovic, a formidable woman who had never approved of her own body-heir's friends or her deplorable tendency to dabble in "finance." But Lady Astatine knew what was owed to Family despite the fact that she deplored Nimisha's height, among other things that were beyond the girl's control.

"You make me look like a midget, young woman. Most inconsiderate," was the grandam's complaint. "Don't bruise my fingers. Gels are supposed to be delicate, not have the grip of a man. Did not your dam teach you *any* feminine arts?"

"Your couturier made my gown, Grandam," Nimisha murmured. She might not have gone through the ceremony officially allowing her to speak out to an elder, but she would not allow anyone to fault her birth-mother. Especially her grandam.

"That much Rezalla learned from me," was the haughty reply. "Who the most original designers are."

"And learned well, Grandam."

A muffled throaty growl greeted that courteous reply. Then Lady Astatine passed Nimisha's hand to Lady Rezalla for the rest of the ceremony and stepped back, deftly kicking the train of her elegant and fabulously expensive gown out of her way.

Nimisha was handed by her mother onto the three-level podium set in place for the ceremony, so that she was clearly visible to the assembled. Lady Rezalla, her eyes bright with tears of pride, advanced with Lord Tionel, equally bright-eyed and grinning widely with delight in his part of the ceremony. He held the case in which Nimisha's Necklace reposed. He had insisted on sharing the cost so, when he turned to display the magnificent jewelry, there were muted gasps and astonished oh's of approval.

The family of Tionel Rondymense-Erhardt was just fractionally older and more exclusive than the Boynton-Chonderlee, so the necklace intricately displayed the families' identification patterns, the same ones that had been indelibly tattooed on Nimisha's neck shortly after her birth. With the courtliest of bows, Lord Tionel presented the case to his former contractual spouse. Lady Rezalla lifted the glittering ornament by its ends and, standing on the highest level of the podium, deftly encircled her body-heir's neck and fastened the clasp. Using one finger, she gave a minute adjustment to the left-hand side to cover the tattoo beneath. Then she tapped Nimisha. Nimisha turned and her mother accorded her the six embraces required by the ceremony, the accolades of approaching adulthood. And for once the kisses were genuine touches of lip to cheek and lip to lip.

Moving gracefully, and as deftly as her grandmother with the train of her splendid gown, Nimisha then accepted the salutes from her sire, her grandam, and the relatives awaiting to applaud her entry into Society. She did a smooth and gracious circling, though she could have done without Great Uncle Dahmison's sloppy kisses. She wasn't the only one of the younger relatives in the auxiliary lines who disliked his tendency to slobber.

Then she made her way to Nurse and embraced her warmly, giving her the four kisses of extreme favor. She gave Jeska the two proper embraces allowed and squeezed her hands tight, covertly promising that they'd both try out the new skimmer that was parked behind the house. They might have to sneak out of the house at night to do so, but fortunately her Necklacing party would not be as prolonged as the one to celebrate her adult majority. That was four years away and there would be so much to do to reach that exalted state. Especially now that Nimisha would have more control over her daily activities.

The music started—since this was a Boynton-Chonderlee House affair, the musicians were humans, not mechanicals—and her sire requested the first dance, as was his right. Lady Rezalla watched, not quite beaming with pride at the elegant way father and daughter danced, but as close to such an expression as she allowed herself. She sighed once, rather pleased that she had picked Tionel to sire her body-heir. He had done well by her and was doing far more than most sires did for their offspring. Certainly more than he did for the oaf who was *his* body-heir. She spared a sideways glance at Vestrin. He was as tall as his sire and with the same nose and ears, but after that he resembled his dam, the insidious Lady Vescuya, far too closely. Fortunately Lady Vescuya was not among the invited: She had a previous engagement she could not cancel, for which Lady Rezalla was grateful, since she had as little use for Vescuya as did almost everyone else of the First Families.

When Lady Astatine brusquely waved off Tionel's offer to dance, as etiquette required of him, he more gladly took his former spouse onto the floor. At the end of that dance, everyone paired off to enjoy the music and the rest of the celebration.

Lord Vestrin did the obligatory dance with his blood-half-sister and spent the next hour, Lady Rezalla noted, on the sidelines criticizing the guests to Great Uncle Dahmison, whose hearing was minimal anyway. Then Vestrin abruptly departed, making the barest of bows to his hostess and birth-father.

When the last guests were well gone, Nimisha and Jeska slipped down the stairs, dressed in clothing appropriate for an early morning spin in a newly acquired skimmer. Nimisha spoke the security

passwords into the estate system, and the two walked quickly to
the garage area.

Jeska had her knife out a second before Nimisha did when a
shadow detached itself from the corner of the first parking slot.

"If you two thought you'd try it out on your own, you thought
wrong," Lord Tionel said, holding his arms widespread as he
emerged.

"Scare the life out of me, you would," Jeska said, sheathing her
knife. "I could have skewered you, Lord Tionel." She didn't sound
the least bit repentant.

"I know your reflexes by now, Mlan, so I was in no danger,"
Tionel said, chuckling.

"I could have sworn I saw you drive away, sir," Nimisha said,
after taking a deep enough breath to calm a fast-beating heart.

"Oh, I did, and doubled back around before the security net
was activated. I brought suitable clothing. And I can be Tionel, or
Ti, as you wish, m'dear, now you're Double M."

"Don't you have any faith in your training of me, Tionel?" Nimisha asked, quick to accept his offer.

"Oh, I do, but you haven't driven something as powerful as this
one, and neither has Jeska. In this test run, you'll drive with me until I'm sure you both have the measure of these engines. Get in."

As this was a two-seater skimmer, suitable for city and country
travel—or so Lady Rezalla would think—there were only two bucket
seats. However, behind them, there was a little space and a ledge
across the back, just adequate for someone as slender as Jeska, if
she sat sideways with her knees bent.

The skimmer purred into activity when Nimisha thumbed on
the engine.

"Slowly, my girl. Those engines could wake even your dam
from a sound sleep," Tionel said, raising one hand in warning.

"I can feel the power in them," Nimisha agreed, smiling. "You're
such a good father, Tionel."

Tionel sighed and Nimisha wished she'd phrased that some other way, for she knew how disappointed he was in his own body-heir. And really, she couldn't blame him. Vestrin was useless and he needn't have been. Once again Nimisha had cause to thank her mother for her upbringing and nurture. Vestrin's dam might have been the acknowledged beauty of her debut year, but that, seemingly, had been her one achievement. She had, however, presented four notable Lords with body-heirs, never once losing her elegant figure in the process and increasing her personal wealth each time. Three of them were as indolent as Vestrin. Only the fourth, young Lord Haricore, showed signs of being interesting, and he was such an active child that he required a full squad of bodyguards . . . more to rescue the victims of his never-ending pranks than to keep him safe.

Nimisha lifted the skimmer slowly, turning the lever to port once she was above the low garages and heading out the main entrance, which opened at the use of her password. There was no sense of movement, though the ground passed swiftly beneath them.

"Lights . . ." Her sire gave her a grin, for her finger was already depressing the appropriate panel.

"Light is more likely to wake my mother than noise," she said coolly. "I read the operating manual three times. So did Jeska."

"The manual and the operation are distinctly separated by hands-on experience," Tionel said. "Take us to the lakeside. I've cleared it with Traffic Control that I'm testing a new vehicle. There won't be any repercussions when we let this sleek motor out."

The two in the front heard Jeska's throaty chuckle. "You think of everything, don't you, Lord Tionel?"

"Well, that was an obvious precaution."

They reached the lake within minutes.

"Take it down to the end at whatever speed you feel you can handle to reach that destination," he said, sitting back and folding his arms.

Jeska took a firm hold of the conveniently placed seat tabs and willed herself heavier as she felt Nimisha increase the forward motion. The girl was cautious, possibly because it was so obvious that the skimmer possessed a very high-powered engine and she needed to get the feel of it. Nimisha executed a neat U-turn at the base of the lake. The geographical feature was actually an earth fault, one hundred and two kilometers in length and forty in width, that had been dammed to make a water-sports facility convenient to Acclarke.

Nimisha headed down the moonlit ribbon of water and began to increase the power, slowly at first, getting the feel of the controls and then speeding up.

"What's holding you back, Nimisha?" her sire asked teasingly. "The engine has been well broken in, you know."

"I will go as fast as I want to, Tionel Rondymense, and I'll thank you not to taunt me."

Tionel threw back his head and laughed. "Impudent scut!"

Jeska sighed with relief, but she really ought not to have doubted Nimisha's common sense. She did crane her neck to see what speed was being achieved and saw the gauge holding steady at three hundred kilometers. She saw the cliffs that bordered the north side of the long lake zipping by and then kept her eyes straight ahead. Moments later Nimisha eased back on the stick and, when it came time to execute a turn, the skimmer was doing a sedate speed of one hundred klicks.

"Now, let me see you handle a few basic maneuvers, Nimi," her father said. "The controls, as you will have noticed, are light to the touch. And you have no doubt noticed where the ejection controls are." He turned his head around. "There's one for the rear ledge, too, Mlan."

"I felt no need to look for it, milord," Jeska said in an amiable drawl.

When Nimisha had performed the aerobatics her father requested, she landed and looked back to Jeska. "Your turn," she said and, inserting herself between the two bucket seats, managed to cram herself into one corner while Jeska went forward.

With no desire to show off, Jeska did the length of the lake at the same speed that Nimisha had used.

"I'm disappointed in you, Jeska," Lord Tionel said, clicking his tongue.

"What's suitable for Lady Nimisha is so for me, too, sir," Jeska said dryly.

"I am reprimanded," Lord Tionel replied, one hand on his heart as he executed a bow in her direction. "Which of you will take the skimmer home?"

"I will, sir," Jeska replied promptly. "This has been an exciting day for Lady Nimi and she must not appear hollow-eyed from fatigue tomorrow—or, rather, later this morning, when she's formally allowed to take possession of her Double M day gift from you."

"Well answered," was his comment.

"Thanks, Jes," came from the back. "It's such a comfortable vehicle, I'm nearly asleep."

What neither young woman ever publicly admitted was that this particular skimmer was also spaceworthy, which made it much easier for them both to go to the Ship Yard. There they spent a great deal of time with the trainers that Lord Tionel had employed to teach his daughter the engineering skills she expressly wished to learn. Since these included advanced mathematics, she could honestly reply to her mother that she was applying herself to lessons that would be useful in her adult life. Having Jeska to work with her on the lessons made them more fun and provided a competition that had them both vying to be the best.

On their first trip to the Rondymense Ship Yard in the new skimmer, Lord Tionel celebrated by taking them into the Design section and introducing them to the methods by which he achieved exactly the right design for the ship that he wanted to construct.

It was a big empty room, which surprised both girls. Lord Tionel grinned and motioned them to the side.

"Lights off. Designer on," he said.

The lights obediently went off. "Designer on," a quiet voice said.

"We are to design an interstellar freighter, displacement tonnage thirty thousand, cargo tonnage eighteen thousand, cargo space to be sectioned off into freezer units, liquid or bulk."

"Did you want to start with an existing design?"

"No."

"Accepted. Do you have a basic shape in mind?"

"Yes, I'd like to see an ellipsoid."

An elliptical shape appeared in the room, lighting the darkness, along with lines that denoted scale. "Like this?"

Lord Tionel considered. "Mmm, no, let's go with a deltoid pumpkin-seed shape."

The shape changed. "This is similar to the StarStream hull in my database; would you like to use that instead?"

Tionel shook his head. "No, for the kind of freighter the client wants, this is a better starting point. Now, I want to push a new star drive through the back of the hull, taking up no more than five percent of the rear volume, to give the most cargo space."

A portion of the rear of the image changed color. "Like this?"

"Yes." Lord Tionel stroked his chin. "Now," and he pointed, though he needn't have with a voice-operated Designer, "extrude that through the hull for one percent of its length and flatten the new face."

The colored image bulged through the pumpkin seed. "Like this?"

"Exactly. Now, put in a standard ten-g star drive in that space, add tankage and plumbing, and tell me how it performs at top Interstellar Drive."

"Fully loaded?"

"Of course."

"Such a shape, fully loaded at maximum speed, would exceed the performance of the StarStream hull by two percent."

"Not good enough. Let's see what changes we can make with our pumpkin to improve performance."

"What about making it a plumper pumpkin, Ti?" Nimisha suggested. "After all, it's cargo space you want, isn't it? If she carries more than the StarStream hull and still exceeds performance without other modifications, you've already achieved an improvement."

"Designer, let's see a plumper pumpkin," Lord Tionel ordered with a chuckle.

None of the three in the Design facility realized that they had spent nearly eight hours working on a variety of modifications until Jim Marroo, who was night supervisor, buzzed through on the comunit. Lord Tionel frowned angrily, for they were about to solve a major difficulty in the drive coefficient.

"No one is supposed to interrupt me here," he said in a growl and then looked at his wrist chrono. "Lady Rezalla, or my name's not Tionel Rondymense-Erhardt."

"Lord Tionel, it's Lady Rezalla, or you may be sure I would not—"

"In this case, an interruption is quite in order, Jim. Tell Lady Rezalla I've had the girls helping me . . . helping me . . ." He turned to Nimisha and Jeska for assistance.

"Choose the color scheme for your new yacht," Nimisha said quickly. The information was repeated and Lord Tionel breathed an exaggerated sigh of relief.

"Designer, save the entire session under the password *decor*. Lights on, and open door," he added. He ushered the girls out quickly. "I'd no idea we'd been in there so long."

"It was a lot more fun than I've had since the day you gave me my skimmer, Ti," Nimisha said.

"You've got a definite gift for design, Nimi, and I won't have it wasted on . . . decoration. Which reminds me: You'll have to think of a color scheme on our way home so your dam won't know what we have been up to."

"I'm sure we could have worked out that problem in just a few more moments," Nimisha went on dismally, shaking her head with disappointment.

"I've no doubt about it," Lord Tionel said, and then turned to Jeska. "And you, young woman, have the good sense to see when enthusiasm needs to be reined in for practical matters. We'd've lost a good forty tonnes of cargo space if we'd kept on with a main tunnel for all conduits."

"Besides being difficult to access," Nimisha said. "What's your favorite color, Ti?"

"Green, of course," he said as they arrived at the dock of his private vehicle.

A complete color scheme, including fabrics, rug, and a well-known furnishings establishment to custom-design sketches, was figured out by the two girls on the short trip home. Nimisha casually left them on the hall table when the Residence Manager opened the door to the girls. The fact that the RM said nothing at all to Lord Tionel, closing the House door almost on his nose, was indicative of the disgrace he was in.

Such a miscalculation in time did not occur again because Lord Tionel installed an automatic cutoff within the Design Room, to save the work and give the girls ample time to reach home in Nimisha's very fast skimmer. So Lady Rezalla had no further opportunity to complain that her birth-father monopolized his daughter.

Having these fascinating and instructive sessions cut short to deceive her mother did not sit well with Nimisha. She knew what she wanted to do with her life, which was far more than most of her peer group did. Especially as she enjoyed none of their so-called diversions whatsoever. She and Jeska kept trying to figure out ways in which to achieve their objective of placating Lady Rezalla sufficiently to really dig into their engineering studies. Circumstance, as it so often does, gave Nimisha the perfect opportunity. And she promptly seized it.

Three weeks after the installation of the alarm that would allow the girls to be home when Lady Rezalla expected them, the breakfast vidcast was full of replays, interviews, and stern statements by high-ranking Acclarkian Peace Guardians concerning the antics of certain young scions who had already received warnings about reckless behavior. The fact that the main culprit was Lord Vestrin Rondymense-Waleska, Lord Tionel's body-heir, was the only reason Lady Rezalla would have continued to view the matter. On a bet to see who could maneuver his skimmer fastest through the rush-hour traffic in a crowded industrial complex, young Vestrin had lost control of his vehicle and had crashed into a public transport, killing nine craftsmen.

"He had no business in that area at that hour," Lady Rezalla said indignantly. "If he must drive at dangerous speeds, let him at least do so at the lake and drown himself instead of killing people. And then to send a minor solicitor to offer the most paltry compensation for the deaths of hardworking and decent folk! Mere craftsmen they may have been, but they were supporting their families and educating their children to be useful citizens, which is more than I can say Vescuya ever did with Vestrin. In fact, they're far more worthy of extreme consideration than that young, heartless lout. *How* such a total disaster of a man can be Lord Tionel's body-heir is beyond me. First Families have obligations, above and beyond the fact that they were the first, and most successful, of the colonists to land on a planet. They endured much to carve out the homes, fields, businesses, space stations, cities, and the amenities of which we are now so proud. That young man needs to be sent where his attitudes can be professionally altered. In fact, he should be made to earn a living as the craftsmen he killed did. He must learn to appreciate what his ancestors endured to give him the advantages he has and doesn't seem at all able to understand and appreciate, much less improve. I shall inform the Residence Manager that Lord Vestrin is no longer received by this House."

"I did so myself, six weeks ago, my mother, when he—" Nimisha stopped, because Lord Vestrin's message had been a blatant threat for her to stop visiting *his* father so often.

"When he what, Nimisha?" Lady Rezalla demanded, tapping her fingers with displeasure.

"When he made improper advances at me, Lady Rezalla," Jeska said, managing a flush. "Lady Nimisha interfered and told the RM Lord Vestrin was not to be admitted to the grounds."

"As indeed he should have. Why was I not told of that affront, Jeska? You are in my employ and I will not have my people subjected to such embarrassments. Even by kin to Lord Tionel." Lady Rezalla turned to Nimisha. "Your sire . . ."

"Is above reproach, my mother, as you certainly know. You have, yourself, remarked on how Lady Vescuya seems to delight in Vestrin's excesses. I know that Lord Tionel does not and will certainly discipline his body-heir over this latest horrific escapade."

"Indeed he will have to," Lady Rezalla said with a sniff. "The Peace Guardians may upon occasion turn a blind eye to an innocent lark by high-spirited young men and women, but they take a different view entirely when deaths are involved. A period in a rehabilitation center is most certainly on the agenda. And community service. Hopefully on a difficult and primitive planet.

"Furthermore, I don't see how Lord Tionel could possibly allow the Ship Yard to be handed over to such a want-wit as that young man. Why, the business would be defunct in half a decade! You know how hard Lord Tionel works and how often the Fleet contracts for him to build their special designs."

"I do, my mother," Nimisha said almost humbly, "which is why I regret, for Lord Tionel's sake, that Vestrin has no interest at all in the Yard." She did not need to add "except for the credit it earns." Lady Rezalla's eyebrow rose sufficiently to have mentally appended that clause. "I have always known how fortunate I am to be your body-heir, my mother, and appreciative of the care you have lavished on my upbringing and education."

"You're a Boynton, after all," Lady Rezalla said at her haughtiest.

"And proud to be, my mother. I would like to utilize my advantages to the fullest extent possible and prove that the privilege I enjoy as a First Family scion is not wasted on stupid pastimes but turned to the best possible effect for my family name and my community."

Even at breakfast, Lady Rezalla was far from slow. She gave her daughter a long, thoughtful look. "I believe we have come round to your fascination with design again, have we not, Nimisha?"

"Yes, my mother."

"And you wish to spend more time at Lord Tionel's Ship Yard?"

"Yes, my mother."

Lady Rezalla poured herself another cup of coffee, added the dollop of cream she liked, stirred it, and took a sip.

"I could have wished you shared my interest in investment and how to recognize the potential of one business over another, but I can scarcely fault you for wishing to achieve . . ." She paused, her lips tight. "As the antithesis of wanton acts born of irresponsibility and lack of purpose."

"Then I may . . . ask Lord Tionel if I may learn more about running the Yard?"

Lady Rezalla had never quite forgotten Lord Tionel's casual remark about leaving Nimisha the Rondymense Yard. It surfaced propitiously.

"Learning how to manage a reputable firm that produces

spaceships is certainly preferable to plowing through public transport vehicles. I shall inquire if Lord Tionel would be willing to instruct you in managerial duties."

Oddly enough the "managerial duties" Lord Tionel graciously
told Lady Rezalla he was willing to teach her body-heir happened
to include "managing" the Designer and helping him complete the
freighter they had started together. That was only the first of the
projects they, and Jeska Mlan, worked on together over the next
few years, during which time Lord Tionel outlined for them a ruth-
less course of academic studies, laboratory experiments, and special use of the smaller Design Room where they could examine and
improve on the myriad components of the modern spaceworthy
craft. Using his influence, he arranged for them to sit the same engineering examinations that would qualify them for full employment in his, or any other, Ship Yard.

As for his reckless body-heir, Lord Tionel sent him to the most
reputable rehabilitation center available, ignoring the pleas of Lady
Vescuya and not informing her in which center her darling son had
been placed. Once the center was satisfied with his moral improvement and an acceptable level of responsibility for his own actions,
he was to spend a year on a struggling colonial planet to learn what
being a First Family scion actually meant. Lord Tionel increased
the compensation to all the families of that fatal crash and took a
quiet, personal interest in the education and promotion of the surviving siblings.

CHAPTER 2

<< ● >>

Five days after Lady Nimisha reached her full majority of eighteen years, her sire was killed in a freak accident at the Rondymense Ship Yard. She and Jeska were in the office, studying Lord Tionel's latest and revolutionary design for a spaceship capable of intergalactic distances; his private design code for this yacht was *gold plate*. Having kept a keen eye on her sire's innovative schemes, Nimisha had already delighted him by making minor, but significant contributions to his special private project.

When the alarm alerted the entire yard to a major emergency, the two young women suited up and joined the search party. A space tug had gone out of control, shearing through the shell of a battle cruiser, propelling structural parts off at speed in all directions. One of them had lanced through Tionel's pinnace as he was returning from a meeting with Admiral Narasharim, head of the Fleet design committee. On such a short, routine journey, he had not been wearing a space suit. Nor had the little ship sufficient shielding to protect its passenger from the steel beam that lanced through the single compartment.

When Nimisha and Jeska learned the cause and the extent of the disaster, Nimisha paused long enough to calculate the trajectory of Lord Tionel's route between the navy yard and his office. Knowing the usual velocity of his trip, the vector of the structural member that had hit his craft, and the approximate point of impact, she calculated the likely course of the pinnace after the collision. Then, after both she and Jeska donned EVA garb, Nimisha commandeered a skiff, speeding to the exact location of the collision. She then followed the calculated path until she overtook the wreckage. They found battered human remains and identified the corpse as Lord Tionel's from his wrist com and what clothing was still attached to his body. Although the Yard personnel as well as the Fleet rescue teams would have given anything to spare the two girls such a ghastly task, they brought his remains in a body bag back to Yard headquarters while other teams were still looking for him. Nimisha and Jeska insisted on accompanying his body back to Acclarke.

When informed first of Lord Tionel's death and then of her daughter's actions, Lady Rezalla fainted for the first time in her life. She had revived by the time Nimisha and Jeska returned from the mortuary. At the sight of the two, Lady Rezalla lost her renowned calm and demanded to know how a gently reared child of the Boynton-Chonderlee family could possibly have undertaken the retrieval.

"He was my birth-sire and he deserved whatever final service I, his blood-kin, could provide. The thought of him, lost in space, spinning further and further away from where he could be most easily recovered, was too painful to bear," Nimisha informed her mother, her face pale and rigid.

Lady Rezalla regarded her body-heir with conflicting emotions, pride and approval vying with—Jeska said later to Nimisha—a tinge of jealousy mixed with anger that Nimisha had endangered herself when there were plenty of others to find . . . him.

"Jeska, pour me a drink, one for yourself and—what will you have, my mother?" Nimisha said, stiffly walking to the nearest chair and collapsing in it with an abruptness that Lady Rezalla would, under other conditions, have criticized as too graceless for a young woman of her upbringing.

"But you went *out* into space," Lady Rezalla said, nodding gratitude as Jeska handed her a strong stimulant.

"In a skiff and in EVA gear."

"In EVA gear?" Lady Rezalla's eyes bulged, her hand went to her heart, and Jeska guided her glass to her lips for a restorative sip.

"We were well instructed, Lady Rezalla," Jeska said, with a worried glance at Nimisha, who was silent with shock. "Part of our managerial training, my lady. In case there should be a major disaster and total evacuation of the premises was required."

"Then what was today's . . . horrid tragedy considered? A minor hiccup in normal procedures?" Lady Rezalla demanded, clearly recovering more quickly than Nimisha was.

"A terrible accident, Lady Rezalla," Jeska said, and she managed to get a handkerchief from a wrist pocket to blot her eyes of tears. "I understand that Admiral Narasharim herself is conducting the inquiry into how the tug was allowed to function without a proper spaceworthy certificate. She will be wishing to call on you, my lady, since neither Lord Vestrin nor Lady Vescuya are presently on Acclarke and someone must—" Jeska's voice broke.

"Take charge. Yes, of course, someone must take charge," Lady Rezalla said, sitting straighter. "We *were* once contracted. We have a mutual child, my body-heir, and I have no doubt she will comport herself in a far more reverent and seemly fashion than that appalling young man who will now succeed him." Lady Rezalla gave a shudder of dismay and repugnance. "Not that he has the talent to emulate his sire." She took another long sip of the brandy. "Nimisha, drink that at once. You're dead white with shock and you must recover your composure immediately. The Boynton in you requires *that*. And at least the worlds will know that one Rondymense scion carries the name with honor and credit."

Nimisha downed the entire glass and then threw it into a corner of the wall.

Lady Rezalla blinked, but firmly pressed her lips together at the pleading look on Jeska's face.

"Yes, the Rondymense name will be honored as fully as I honor yours, my mother," Nimisha said, clinging to the chair as she struggled to rise. "He will never be shamed by his daughter." And she ran from the room, weeping.

"But you're *my* body-heir," Lady Rezalla murmured, confused and a bit indignant. "Go with her, Jeska, and comfort her as best you can," she added, whisking the girl out of the door.

As Jeska turned back before the automatic door slid into place, she saw Lady Rezalla, hands covering her face, shoulders heaving as she, too, wept for Lord Tionel.

He had indeed left the entire Rondymense Ship Yard GmBH with all its assets, designs, and resources to Lady Nimisha Boynton-Rondymense—a bequest that Lord Vestrin Rondymense-Waleska instantly instructed his legal advisors to have reversed. He petitioned to be returned to Acclarke, having endured three years of his exile. His mother petitioned, as well, and had the advantage of being able to return to Acclarke City from the colony where, once she had learned where her son was being incarcerated, she had attempted to supply a few of the elegancies of life for her son. She pursued the claim with all possible vigor. Not that Lord Vestrin had been deprived in any way, for he inherited a considerable estate from his sire: funds so secured that the young heir would be unable to break the trust management and control the sizable principal, but an allowance that would let him maintain a suitable lifestyle.

"He's the vindictive sort," Lady Rezalla said, "which characteristic he must have inherited from his dam's bloodline. Rehabilitation can only do so much—since body-heirs are not permitted by law to undergo the more drastic psychiatric treatments. Her other children display such pettiness from time to time. We've all noticed it." She then dismissed them as beneath her notice.

Lady Rezalla's attorneys were the acknowledged masters of their profession and instantly joined with Lord Tionel's to prove that the bequest was of long standing. In fact, when Lady Rezalla thought back over the years, she placed the transfer of the property to the very week in which Lord Tionel had made his casual remark about leaving his business to his blood-daughter. The Acclarkian courts refused to hear Lord Vestrin's appeal. He had been granted a substantial fortune as befit a body-heir. Since Lord Rondymense's bequest of his Ship Yard went to a blood relative, there was nothing to contend.

Lady Vescuya ranted and raved on about such iniquity to the point where she became a social liability to those who had once professed friendship for her. Certainly no hostess would commit the solecism of inviting both Vescuya and Rezalla to the same function. When a new scandal rocked Acclarke City's First Families, the untimely death of Lord Tionel and its subsequent problems were forgotten.

It wasn't until Admiral Narasharim herself called at the Boynton-Chonderlee House to see Lady Nimisha that Lady Rezalla began to appreciate exactly how much "managerial" instruction Lord Tionel had given his blood-daughter.

While Lady Nimisha was being summoned, Lady Rezalla offered hospitality and tried to discover why an admiral would need to seek out her daughter.

"Lady Nimisha has finished the latest calculations on the femto-second processor and, since I have meetings on the surface myself, I thought to spare her an unnecessary trip to Headquarters."

"The femtosecond processor?" Lady Rezalla asked, trying to sound as if she knew what the admiral was talking about.

"Yes, she's been experimenting with storage fibers and she's

come up with exactly the right composite to handle almost incredible electron transfers. Of course, having the latest Joseph-
son junctions has been of inestimable assistance in solving that
problem."

"Yes, it would, wouldn't it," Lady Rezalla said, smiling graciously.

A brief knock was followed by Nimisha's entrance into the room.

"Here you are, Admiral," and she passed over several of the
tiny round disks that generally held quantities of information Lady
Rezalla thought were quite remarkable. "I do apologize, my mother.
But this is very important," she said.

"We have a little time in hand for you to complete your toilette
before we leave," Lady Rezalla said with only the slightest hint of
reprimand.

The admiral was on her feet, shaking Nimisha's hand and grinning. "I'll see you tomorrow with the test results, shall I?"

"I wouldn't miss it, ma'am," Nimisha said, and guided the admiral to the door, which the RM opened with a deep, respectful bow.
"It won't take me long, my mother," Nimisha said gaily as she shot
up the stairs to her room.

"You must tell me more about these . . . seconds . . ." Lady
Rezalla began when they were settled in Nimisha's skimmer and
on their way to the ballet that was the evening's occasion.

"It's just business, my mother," Nimisha said with a shrug.

"A business that an admiral comes in person to collect is not
just business, Nimisha."

"It is, however, Fleet business, my mother, and I may not
discuss it, even though I know you to be the soul of discretion.
However, I would like to prevail on your financial acumen to
take a look at the Ship Yard records. I may know a nanosecond
from a femtosecond, but achieving trial balances and projections
of what percentage our profits are above last year's is totally beyond me."

"I should be delighted to look them over, my daughter. When had you in mind?"

"Would the day after tomorrow be convenient?"

Lady Rezalla had no real need to consult her delicate wrist pad, but she did. "Quite suitable."

Showing good sense as well as filial respect, Nimisha brought her mother in to her executive office to peruse the Rondymense Ship Yard financial records while she busied herself with minor but necessary executive tasks. Halfway through the inspection, Lady Rezalla closed the file she was studying and sat back in the chair.

"Tionel knew very well what he was doing. And so do you, my dear girl, in spite of that famo-neto-second gibberish you gave me the other day. I shall leave your Fleet discretions and secrets, since you're in them as deeply as dear Ti was. Obviously he trained you to take his place and so you must, restoring the name Rondymense to the honor it deserves."

Neither remarked on the fact that Lord Vestrin had finally returned to Acclarke but was keeping a very low profile, generally taking himself off-planet to hunt with those of his acquaintance who did nothing but divert themselves with whatever foible or folly took their wayward interests.

"I don't believe that I had any idea of exactly the scale of dear Ti's Yard, nor how much construction is currently under way. How can you possibly find time to do little tasks for the Fleet? Much less spend so much time completing that yacht he was enamored of." Lady Rezalla's final tone bordered on the critical despite the good impression the extent of Rondymense's enterprises had given her.

"He trained Jeska Mlan at the same time he trained me."

"He did?" That startled her mother, who hastily reviewed that young woman's behavior but could find not the least trace of unbecoming or pushy manners.

Nimisha laughed. "Ti used to say that Jeska had the ninety-nine percent of perspiration it takes to invent something new and I'd supply the one percent genius that shot us into a new dimension. Actually, we're a very good team. I always have Jeska check my calculations. She's accurate to the exact limits of the data. I might be right in my guesstimate most times, but she makes sure it's substantiated by hard figures."

"Really," Lady Rezalla said faintly, in a mild state of shock.

"Actually, we do more design than administration anyway, since Tionel has always had excellent executives like Jim Marroo, Efram Dottlesheim, and Ferman Miles-Zynker. You met them at the obsequies and I remember you commenting on how impressed you were with their dignity and genuine grief."

"That is true. I was impressed." Lady Rezalla had been, but for reasons other than those quoted by her daughter. She had learned all she could about the men who were—nominally, it now appeared—in charge of her body-heir's inheritance. She would ruthlessly have dismissed any that had not met her high standards, but they all had. Which made dear Ti's dreadful body-heir all the more a tragedy.

"I have no qualms at allowing them to continue in their current responsibilities," Nimisha told her mother, smiling, "doing the bread-and-butter work that supports the icing on the particular piece of cake Ti wanted so to finish. It's mine now, and I'm continuing the work in progress. Some of it, I spin off to the Navy for their experts to try to pick apart. Tionel did that, and I seem to have inherited the same courtesy they extended him. Anyway, he left us copious notes on how to proceed." She gestured around her office to indicate the schematics and plans projected on the wall, all printed out from work down in the Design Room where she spent so much of her time.

"You'd best show me the ship itself while I'm here," her dam said, dismissing the plans that she couldn't read for a virtual shape that she might have more chance of evaluating. "I knew I should have supervised you more closely but . . ." Rezalla's shrug was as elegant as ever. Then she smiled up at her tall daughter. "His genes have done well by you. See that you do well by his legacy."

"I intend to, my mother."

"And, before you get too involved, I suggest that you have your body-heir."

Nimisha thought that suggestion over for a long moment. "Yes, that would be wise, since I intend to test the yacht myself." At her mother's startled gasp, she smiled reassuringly and touched her mother delicately on the forearm. "I'm a very good pilot, you know, but I have a duty to you and the Family. Have you any sire in mind for me?"

"Thank you, m'dear. Lately you have been so limited in your contact with your peers that I wonder that you are interested in men at all . . ."

"Oh, I am, Mother," Nimisha said in such a warm tone that her mother became all the more anxious. But Nimisha did know about Family duty and would never involve herself, even in dalliance, with someone less than totally presentable.

"Only those, I suspect," Lady Rezalla said in a slightly acid tone, "who pretend to be interested in your fascination with parsecs and performance vehicles."

"There are some who have applied to me for recommendations on racing cars, my mother," Nimisha replied, her expression droll. "Over lunches at fashionable eateries and even on weekend parties. I do not live a monastic life."

Lady Rezalla sniffed delicately. "I should hope not!" Nimisha shrugged and her mother went on. "Leave the matter of a suitable sire to me. I shall give you several choices. After all, a body-heir contract is short. And you might even enjoy it."

"Did you enjoy your contract with my sire, my mother?"

Lady Rezalla raised her head, stiffened her back, and regarded her daughter for a long moment. At first, Nimisha wondered if she had broached too personal a matter.

"Yes," Lady Rezalla said, her eyes reflecting sadness, "I did. And he tried to extend it."

"I know," Nimisha said with a moue of regret.

"He was far too committed, even then, to . . . his business." Rezalla rose from the desk to indicate that the subject was closed.

The inspection of the ship—or rather of the skeleton, for the special petralloys that would be the hull plating had yet to be added—was duly conducted, and Lady Rezalla did not affect either specious approval or dismay. She was even allowed into the sacrosanct Design Room. She inhaled sharply when the lights went out, and then exhaled as the Designer displayed the yacht as she would look in finished form.

"Impressive," she said. "I wouldn't have thought dear Ti was so inventive. Much better than his color schemes," she added blandly, leaving the now-bare Design Room.

Lady Rezalla also took note of the respect with which her daughter was treated by all the Rondymense personnel. So the tour ended with Lady Rezalla both pleased and reassured.

As Nimisha conveyed her mother back to the surface of Vega III, she decided that she'd very deftly gotten her mother to take care of screening suitable sires so that she wouldn't have to spend unnecessary time away from the Yard to attend to that family obligation. She had too much scheduled right now to spend time going through bloodlines and gene patterns. Her mother would enjoy the occupation far more than she would. And probably choose a far more suitable alliance. Nimisha's current bedmate would not meet her mother's high social standard, but then, what her mother didn't know wouldn't offend her.

Two weeks later her mother handed her a list of suitable men.

Of the lot, Nimisha decided that Lord Rhidian Farquahar-Hayakawa was the most acceptable to her. She was, of course, acquainted with the man. He was an ardent hunter of alien monsters, charming and handsome, though she deplored his hobby as much as he probably disapproved of her professional involvement. But he was known to be an excellent companion on a hunt, never complaining about the dirt or discomfort, and had often caused her to howl with laughter at his sly and clever jokes. She had never once heard him belittle anyone. He had blue eyes, too, so that feature would be perpetuated. When approached by Nimisha for his service, he was surprised but recovered smoothly.

"You're only eighteen, Nimi," he'd remarked. "Surely you don't need to rush into maternity yet."

"I might as well get it over with so I can concentrate on what interests me. I've the Yard to manage, you know."

"How's that new long-distance yacht of yours coming along? I hear it's going to reduce travel time phenomenally," he said. "Could I make it from Demeathorn to Canopus IV in time to attend both hunting seasons?"

"Only if you learn to handle a spaceship better than you do hunting vehicles," she replied, obliquely reminding him of a near-fatal accident while hunting raptors on Canopus IV.

"Will you do a shakedown cruise with me when the yacht's ready?"

"I need the body-heir contract now, Rhid, but I'll see what I can do when the yacht is ready for trial runs."

"Fair enough," he replied, and then he was willing to discuss the contract for a body-heir. He surprised her by asking for Rondymense Ship Yard stock and added mining concessions from his family holdings as his half of the child's birthright. The agreement was signed, the begetting of an heir was conducted with grace, skill, and such fervor that Nimisha was quite pleased. And just a little disappointed when she became pregnant a scant two months later. Rhidian did not cease his visits, for the contract stipulated a live, healthy child. She didn't object to his company during her pregnancy, since he usually arrived after she had returned from the Ship Yard. He did once mention that he felt she should suspend her operations at the Yard in the last trimester of her pregnancy.

"Why? All I'm doing now is programming the AI's on board and that takes very little physical effort on my part. Still, it's nice of you to be concerned, Rhidian."

"I know you're healthy, and all that, and carrying easily, Nimi. It's just that accidents can—and have . . ." He paused, wondering if he should have obliquely mentioned the tragic circumstance of her sire's death. ". . . happened at the Ship Yard and I should not like to see you miscarry. Of course, if you did, I would naturally honor the contract, which requires the successful birth, not merely the pregnancy," he said, his expression hopeful.

"That's most considerate of you, Rhidian, but I don't foresee any problems, and no one at the Yard lets me overextend myself. I could probably do a lot more than Jeska and my other department heads allow."

Rhidian gave a reluctant shrug. "Well, if Jeska's always with you . . ."

"Always," Nimisha said.

When her daughter was born, Nimisha was overwhelmed with a totally unanticipated rush of maternal devotion that put the half-finished yacht into second place in her life. Lady Rezalla couldn't believe how the birth altered her daughter, nor could Jeska. Fortunately, both approved.

"Having a baby is not at all like designing a spaceship, is it?" Nimisha said, smiling fatuously at the dainty girl that her body had produced.

"I should hope not," Lady Rezalla said sharply, but her expression softened instantly. She, too, was quite besotted with her grandchild.

Lady Astatine was the only relative who retained critical objectivity. "It's well enough," she said. "If it lives and has its health."

Lady Rezalla's suddenly revived hope that Nimisha would dispense with spaceship design and Yard supervision was ruthlessly shattered. Although a registered wet nurse was hired to tend the baby's needs, Nimisha set up an office suite in her domicile, adding vid screens showing the nursery rooms so she could enjoy her daughter's antics whenever she chose. In fact, as Cuiva advanced from crawling to an unsteady walk, only Jeska knew how often Nimisha totally ignored other pressing professional matters.

Lord Rhidian was so beguiled by his firstborn that he continued his visits, even missing an important Trophy Hunt when Cuiva first walked. Although Nimisha had not initially intended to take so much time away from the Yard to supervise her body-heir's nurturing and development, she found time spent with her daughter a source of relaxation from a long day of programming. She was setting up what she knew would be a revolutionary femtosecond control system for the yacht. That such a system also required a whole new generation of central processing units—as well as a staggering cost—meant little to her in her search for perfection.

When the Mark 2 was completed, she did the test runs, her first major absence from her daughter since Cuiva's birth. Rhidian was one of those permitted to come along "for the ride." Jeska was another, along with an "interested" observer from the Fleet Design Department. That had been a compliment to Lord Tionel's good standing with the Department, though Nimisha had the feeling that Commander Modesittin was present more as a goodwill representative. While he asked few but pertinent questions, he had evidently been sufficiently impressed; a more thorough investigation

of the Mark 2's performance resulted in sales of four of this prototype for scout vessels. Nimisha and Jeska had found a way around
the cost of the necessary CPU's, so that the Navy could also *afford*
to buy the Mark 2.

Several of the patents she had registered for improvements in
minor control devices were also purchased in quantity and installed
wherever they would update existing systems. It was obvious that
the Fleet was now as interested in her as a naval designer as they
had been in Lord Tionel. She had several very complimentary interviews with Admiral Levertim Gollanch, who had succeeded to
Admiral Narasharim's position after the older woman's retirement.
There was no harm, Nimisha thought, in cooperating with the Fleet.
She was amused to be invited to a formal dinner by Admiral Gollanch shortly after the interviews.

"More likely to pick my brains than to entertain me," Nimisha remarked to Jeska, who complained when she accepted the
invitation.

When Lady Rezalla heard about it, she considered such interest only right and just and wondered why it had taken them so long
to realize that Lady Nimisha was a fit successor to Lord Tionel.

"They had to be sure of that, my mother," Nimisha said. "They
have, after all, continued to buy Rondymense units. But I designed
some of the systems that Tionel never got around to making."

"So you've informed me," was her dam's droll reply.

So Nimisha attended a very formal dinner at Vega's Fleet headquarters in the Supreme Admiral's quarters. She was the celebrity
of the evening. The other guests, gaudily attired in formal uniforms,
displaying medals for a variety of achievements, ranged from young
to ancient, male and female, and were almost all naval. Two other
civilians had been included and she knew both—naval architects,
each good in his specialty. But, she reminded herself, not as good
as she was.

Well, service to one's Federation was part of the duty of a good Family, but if she had to have a naval officer or other "observer" checking up on her, she would choose with care. After narrowing down the candidates to a short list and conducting a round of private investigations, she made an appointment to see Admiral Gollanch. She'd have Lieutenant Senior Grade Caleb Rustin, she told the admiral, as her Fleet spy.

Gollanch pretended astonishment. "Fleet spy?"

"That is certainly what last week's dinner was all about, wasn't it?" Nimisha responded, sitting totally at her ease in his impressive office. The wood paneling was supposedly resurrected from the wreck of some ancient and honorable oceangoing vessel. The decor was certainly all naval, including the curious instruments by which ancient mariners had been able to deduce their location and make course corrections. "Let us be honest with each other, Admiral."

"You have the forthrightness of your dam."

"I do not. She'd never say anything so direct. My biological father might have."

Gollanch hid a smile behind his hand but his eyes twinkled. "I feel that it is quite likely that we can deal with you as equably as we did with Lord Tionel."

"His understanding was with your predecessor, Admiral Narasharim."

"I can only hope that ours—" He paused to make her a half bow. "—will be as productive."

"Productive in what way? My sire never spoke of his . . . arrangement with Fleet. I knew that there was one, not what it entailed."

"This office has watched your handling of his Yard with interest and respect. I wish to be more fully briefed on your projects in case we may collaborate . . ."

"On my long-distance yacht?" She cocked her head a little to one side.

"The Mark Two vessels have performed well above the most optimistic criteria and yet you have a new design on the gantries."

"There is always room for improvement, Admiral."

"If there is, this department is very interested. I do not intend to interfere in any way with a civilian installation . . ."

"Then that isn't why Rondymense is situated so conveniently at one edge of *your* main facility?"

"Happenstance. The Rondymense Yard predates the Fleet's Vegan base by nearly a hundred years, you know." When she nodded, because she did know, he went on. "It would please me personally, not as admiral in charge of Fleet Design, if you would duly consider recommendations and suggestions from my representative. Since young Rustin is your choice, I shall put him on detached service to the Rondymense Ship Yard."

"He should get a promotion for accepting hazardous duty," she said with a smile. "And another one if our mutual efforts produce results."

"Are you well acquainted with Caleb Rustin?"

"Never met him before the other evening. But he has an impressive record—good engineering aptitude, cleverly displayed when he did that mid-space repair to the comcomplex a meteor sheared off the old *Aegean Sea*. What he jury-rigged that day had been translated into standard equipment to prevent any similar accidents. And he's obviously being monitored for further promotions. At least in the Design division."

Somewhat startled by her knowledge of the lieutenant's record, he covered his surprise with a sly smile. "I'd've lost my bet then," he said.

"Oh?" Nimisha raised both eyebrows in amusement, encouraging an explanation by curving her mouth in a delicate one-sided smile that fascinated the admiral. He was by no means immune to the charismatic charm of the young woman with such speaking gentian-blue eyes.

"Yes," Gollanch said, steepling his fingers and rhythmically bouncing his fingertips together, a reflective habit of his.

"Let me guess," Nimisha said, leaning forward and grinning as shrewdly as he had. "That Marcusi captain."

"How did you arrive at that conclusion?" Gollanch did not yet care to admit how accurate her assessment was.

She leaned back. "He was doing his best—adroitly," she said, raising her hand not to denigrate the captain's performance. "He also seemed exceedingly well informed about my, ah, present design plans."

"Hmmm . . ." Gollanch made a mental note to find out how the captain had been able to access that information. Not even the Fleet had the right to invade a Family's private enterprise without due invitation. "I shall check into that."

"Don't bother. There's nothing I do not intend to share with the Fleet when I have perfected what will improve your ships." She dismissed that problem with a flick of her hand. It was an unusually callused hand for a Family scion, with a wide strong palm, deft fingers, and trimmed nails, unlike the usual elegantly tapered fingers with artificial extensions almost as long again as the finger—a fad that impeded any use of humankind's greatest advantage over most animals. "How can you fault Captain Marcusi for wanting to succeed? He's really very good at it."

"In that case . . ." Gollanch ended the subject with a shrug of his shoulders.

"Good, especially as I made my own"—her delightful grin enlivened fine features that tended, in repose, to be sober, if not aloof—"discreet inquiries, since it was obvious my operation is of interest to the Fleet. So it is very good of you, really, to be so . . . so . . ."

"Accommodating?" Gollanch suggested. On consideration, Rustin was a very good choice, a better match for this woman than Captain Marcusi, who had great ambitions for himself—in which he would probably succeed, bar a bad command decision. Rustin was far more interested in achieving the best results from a project than in making certain everyone knew he had had a hand in it. The lad had good ideas and, as the Lady Nimisha had noted, excellent engineering credentials. Then, without trying to appear rushed, though the admiral had a full day's appointments—a few of them not as pleasant as this one—he smiled at her. "How soon can I send Lieutenant Commander Rustin to Rondymense Ship Yard?"

Nimisha rose. "He's waiting at my skimmer. I promised him a tour of the Yard at dinner the other night. As soon as I could arrange it." She reached her hand across the table and Gollanch shook it with both of his, noticing the workmanlike strength of her grasp. Again that almost gamine grin and the twinkle of her gentian-blue eyes. "He was the only one who didn't hint. He also was the first to ask me to dance and converse on suitable subjects."

"Ah! I will recommend such tactics should similar strategy be needed."

"You are a dear, Admiral," she said, releasing her hand and making her way to the door. There she stopped, considered momentarily, and then gracefully looked back over her shoulder at him. "Lieutenant Commander Rustin may never know *all* I have in mind as design features, but he will be privy to what would improve the performance of the Vegan Fleet vessels."

At such an outrageous remark, Gollanch let out a roar of laughter that brought the officer at the worktop in the anteroom to his feet in surprise. "Such condescension is more than we hoped for, Lady Nimisha Boynton-Rondymense."

"Certainly it's more than you deserve," was her parting shot.

It took Lady Nimisha some twenty minutes to reach her skimmer, where Caleb Rustin was standing, looking bewildered. The long planes of his face were slightly Oriental, often giving him a vexingly unreadable expression. He was regarding his wrist com as if it had extruded fangs and bitten him. When he heard her steps—she was wearing her usual work apparel, including calf-high boots with reinforced toes and soles—he smiled a little hesitantly. His bemusement was still apparent in his light gray eyes, a contrast to the sallow skin and thick black hair. He swallowed.

"Admiral Gollanch's office has just contacted me, Lady Nimisha," he said. And blinked. "I've received a promotion, and I'm not due one yet."

"Ah, but you certainly couldn't be the naval attaché at Rondymense Ship Yard as a mere senior lieutenant," she replied.

"I'm the naval attaché?" There was little inscrutability left in the genuine delight and amazement of his expression.

"Yes, you'll suit me ever so much better than that pushy Captain Marcusi."

"Mar—" Caleb tilted his head and let out a roar similar to the admiral's, though she did not mention the similarity. She noticed the discreet design of his body-heir tattoo, not common in the Navy; she supposed his family had been awarded prize money, possibly in the last pirate attacks. First Families had started the convention of tattooing several hundred years before to prevent the kidnapping of heirs.

"What occasions such mirth?" she asked.

"Because Marcusi fancies himself as adroit, devious, and charismatic."

"He is. Those tactics are useful for a line officer on the fast track to command, but they don't work quite so well on Family."

"May we speak candidly, Lady?" he asked, his expression serious. When she nodded, he went on. "Why me? There were many candidates for you to choose from, some who've had commands and more experience."

"You . . ." she said, pointing her finger at him, "asked me to dance."

Caleb let a small smile pull at his lips while his eyes met hers with equal candor. "That was only because I didn't know what else to do to get you away from the others."

"Ah, but you conversed with me, too."

"What else does one do when one dances?" He seemed surprised.

She chuckled. The ingenuous reply did him no harm at all. A man who had the right priorities, training, and certainly some breeding, though his tattoo was neither complex nor colorful. She gestured toward her skimmer, indicating they could now leave.

"How does a body-heir become a Fleet officer?" she asked.

"When that body-heir's sire is also a Fleet officer," he replied.

As they rounded the little spacecraft, the guard came to immediate attention. He wore the gray and silver of Nimisha's Yard livery. Now he gave a smart salute to the freshly promoted lt. commander, as if he somehow knew Rustin was no longer a mere lieutenant.

"Worrick, this is Lieutenant Commander Caleb Rustin, who has recently been appointed naval attaché to our Yard. He is to be treated with all due courtesies, naval and yard. Secure the hatch for takeoff. We'll just go forward and inform Control of our imminent departure. Thank you."

As she gave the new attaché the promised guided tour of the Rondymense facility, she also put him through some general paces, including a short EVA. There did happen to be a suit that could have been measured for him, since the EVA ready room was equipped with quite a range of sizes in spaceworthy gear.

"Put your name on that one when we come back in," she said when they had returned from the inspection of the Fiver. At the moment the ship was a skeleton of petralloy rings, tapering to the bow and blunt at the stern: her latest attempt to design *the* perfect long-distance spacecraft. He seemed totally at ease, automatically clipping on to safety rings with his suit harness and unclipping as they pushed about the skeleton.

His chuckle came over the helmet com. "This fits me better than my navy issue ever did."

"You should investigate the other perquisites that come with an attaché's position while you're at it."

"Ah, now I wouldn't have thought of that."

"Speak sharply to Admin," she said. "You'll require specialty pay and an extra uniform allowance."

"Should I ask how you know what perks are available to an attaché?"

"I looked them up." She hadn't anticipated a sly sense of humor from him, but it did him no harm. "But you have to sign the authorization."

"True."

She activated the airlock controls, and as the lock rolled back, they reentered the Yard proper. That was the beginning of their stimulating and inclusive association.

Caleb lent his knowledge and naval expertise to Nimisha's often intuitive ideas. He came to appreciate Jeska's precision and practicality. Indeed, he encouraged them to include some of the more radical changes, reveling in their grasp of efficient spaceship design. It was a change for him to work with minds that were not hedged in by bureaucratic shibboleths and antiquated thinking, not to mention Fleet budgetary restrictions. Nimisha had the resources to build a squadron of her versatile long-distance yachts if it so pleased her, and Jeska kept her to what was possible, effortlessly taking over most of the less spectacular management duties.

It was inevitable that Nimisha and Caleb enjoyed some intimacies, the result of long hours of intense, cerebral work that had ended in rather special, to him, interludes. He knew she hadn't taken these incidents seriously: No doubt she dismissed them as the needs of the moment, enjoyed them for that moment, and then forgot them in the face of more pressing concerns as she returned to her overriding desire to perfect an intergalactic spaceship. He had schooled himself to do so as well, fascinated more by her personality and her dedication to design improvement than by her beauty—not that he ever became accustomed to having such a beauty as a companion. With selective breeding and gene control now four centuries in use, no one in her stratum of society could ever be considered ugly; some were simply more beautiful than others. Indeed, beauty was hardly limited to her class, since antenatal gene repair and intelligent nutrition produced handsome folk in every walk of life. Lately, elements of bizarre styles of "beauty" had been introduced, not in the major Families, of course, who were more conservative, but in those lesser Families who delighted to shock. Some of the variants had been spectacular—but artificial in ways that did not quite come off as something the owner would be likely to bequeath to his or her successor.

Lady Rezalla actually approved of Lt. Commander Rustin, despite his rather modest body-heir tattoo, especially after she discovered from Admiral Gollanch that he was due for further promotions in his position as attaché. She could consider a possible admiral appropriate for any long-term association her daughter might make. When not even a "friendly contract" ensued after several weeklong absences with Rustin, Rezalla was almost disappointed. Nimisha did, indeed, know what was due her Family. And to her daughter.

Obviously, Nimisha's passion for naval design far outweighed the need for any legal companionship. The best of all possible worlds, Lady Rezalla thought, for she had long practiced the art of "to have and have not" as far as males were concerned. At least, if Nimisha insisted on such an unusual career, she had chosen one of the most prestigious.

And Lt. Commander Rustin was an acceptable escort, so Lady Rezalla included him on her special guest list, an honor on which he never presumed.

The Mark 3 was built, tested, and put into production over the next three years but, after many severe tests, the perfection Nimisha wanted of it had still not been attained. Candidly Caleb Rustin agreed with her. Jeska, who spent more and more of her time in her managerial capacity, still attended their Design Room sessions and felt that the Mark 3, sleek and compact, could become claustrophobic for the light-year distances it was intended to traverse.

"Why not go back to the ellipsoid shape and keep it pure in that shape?" she suggested. "There's really no need, especially if you plan to have this a surface lander, to have all the bulges and bumps to contain the necessary storage spaces. We've gone a little too far in the opposite direction. Simplicity, especially with the femtosecond AI's now available, might be the way to go." And so Nimisha called up the shape, dragging in the basic units from other successful designs.

Caleb added a new water-purification system that the Fleet had been perfecting, as well as a top-quality catering system, designed to convert pure protein and complex carbohydrate substances into food that not only tasted exactly as the diner wished but provided the necessary nutrients for the maximum efficiency of the human body. Repair units had to operate autonomously should the ship be damaged in any one of the hundreds of scenarios that had to be programmed into the memory banks from those the Fleet generously opened for the project.

Civilians—like Lord Rhidian, who bought the test Mark 3 from her and effusively praised it—found it more than comfortable and certainly fast enough to meet their requirements. The Rondymense

Yard expanded and Jeska became executive director, freeing Nimisha to pursue the elusive ideal with Caleb. The Fleet was attempting to come up with a more economical version, which she and Caleb privately referred to as the Faulty Four, while she refined the satisfactory units of the Mark 3 and started from the beginning to conceive further innovations that would make the Mark 5 nearer to her ideal. She and Caleb spent hours in the Design Room, dragging and drawing, redesigning, reorganizing components, until the day they asked the all-important questions: Would the performance of this design equal Nimisha's optimum? How much would it cost to build? And how long would it take to complete?

"A projection of its performance capability is twelve percent higher than the Mark Four" the Designer replied. "It would take no longer to build than the Four, since much of the same basic design has been refined and can now be utilized. Based on current prices for top-grade materials . . ."

"Have I ever economized on them yet, Designer?"

". . . the cost would take precisely sixty-two percent of the credit currently on deposit."

Caleb whistled.

"I'd've expected a higher cost, considering the complexity of the AI units you've specified and the other refinements on our Mark Four designs," Jeska said, knowing how much Nimisha depended on her opinions. "But I have new contracts just in that will recoup thirty-one percent of that credit within the next two years. Plus the usual maintenance contracts that come in regularly—and I suspect the Zynker-Deltoid Shippers intend to accept our tender for their fleet additions. In short, it's doable," she finished, "without you having to invest much of your own money."

"That's a lot better than I thought," Nimisha said, surprised. "And Lady Rezalla will be pleased that I don't have to touch my capital."

"So, do we build?" Caleb asked, aware he'd been holding his breath.

"We sure do," Nimisha said. "Designer, let's have one more look at those main AI circuits. They have to be in the most shielded part of the hull."

Meanwhile, Cuiva grew from a toddler to a graceful young girl who obediently did ballet training with her grandmother and was every bit as handy with a soldering tool or construction fastener as her mother had been at the same age.

"How many generations is that wretched Yard going to consume?" Lady Rezalla demanded when she found Cuiva about to set off in the space skimmer when she had planned to take the girl to a new anti-grav ballet that had been sold out for weeks. She had had trouble enough obtaining tickets and was exasperated to find her treat preempted. Cuiva might be content enough to keep her grandam company when her mother was busy, but Nimisha had first call on the child's loyalties.

"Tionel's family had it for nine generations, so Cuiva's only the second for us," Nimisha said.

"Which would you—" Lady Rezalla began, bending down to the child.

"Mother!" Nimisha interrupted, so abruptly that Lady Rezalla stared at her body-heir in amazement. Nimisha forced a smile as she dropped into old Terran language that Cuiva ought not yet understand. "Let us *not* descend to competition for her preference. I apologize if I neglected to inform you that I was taking her with me today and for your disappointment. Perhaps you can exchange the tickets."

Lady Rezalla confined her response to a curt nod and, pivoting on one heel, walked stiffly to where her driver awaited her at her skimmer's door.

Nimisha never told her dam that today she, Caleb, and Jeska were taking Cuiva on her first space walk. Nimisha had had a special suit constructed, and Cuiva was going to be able to go over the exterior of the now petralloy-clad Mark 5. Nimisha had promised the child that treat for her scholastic achievements. Cuiva was a better mathematician than Nimisha, Jeska, or Caleb. She was therefore also a better programmer. Nimisha wondered how long she would have to wait until Cuiva was old enough to work on the artificial intelligence programs that would manage the elusive ideal she was herself chasing.

The four of them had a marvelous time and Cuiva showed no problem at all with inner ear dysfunction in the vacuum of space. She obeyed every order explicitly and the naval EVA trainer who attended the sessions remarked that some of his novices did not show as much confidence as the child did.

"We must see that she doesn't become overconfident," Nimisha said.

"Oh, next time she's up, we'll give her a little problem to solve," Caleb suggested. "Nothing to frighten her, Nimi, but certainly something to remind her of the dangers inherent in an EVA."

"Cuiva's sensible," Nimisha said firmly.

"Of course she is," Caleb agreed, wondering if perhaps he had been out of line. But he was as fond of Cuiva as if she'd been his own offspring, and she, in turn, was certainly at ease in his company. "She's your body-heir, and Lord Rhidian is a fine hunter but not a chance-taker like Lord Vestrin is."

Lord Tionel's body-heir had had a shattering accident in a hunt stampede. Body sculpting would be needed, and even with the recent strides in the replication of body organs and bone replacements, he would not be active for a while. Meanwhile he lived in seclusion with his dam, Lady Vescuya, who attempted to amuse him during the process of revision.

"By the way, Nimi," Caleb said, as much to change the subject as to seize an opportunity to remind Nimisha that she'd promised to think the matter over, "have you decided on rejuv?"

Nimisha glanced at him out of the corner of her eye so that he could not see her expression. "Rejuv would not have saved Vestrin when he insisted on being a carpet for a whole herd of Altairian antelopes," she remarked. "But I've made the appointment. One reason why I've spent the day with Cuiva." Then she gave an exaggerated sigh. "All these delays in getting what I want make me think in the long-term."

Caleb laughed. "I don't think it's going to take *that* long for you to get the long-journey yacht you're aiming for. Design's estimate is proving accurate from the work-reviews Jeska keeps filing." He paused and then grinned roguishly. "Of course, I did rejuv long ago."

"You never told me."

"Admiral Gollanch required it. That's where I spent my last leave."

"What? You weren't dancing and dallying with tropical beauties as I so fondly thought?"

Caleb appeared to think. "Well, there was one . . ."

Cuiva approached them just then, waiting like the well-bred youngster she was until there was a pause in adult conversation.

"Yes, Cuiva?" he said, seizing her presence to leave the fuller answer dangling.

"Is ballet fun, Mother?" Cuiva asked.

"Ah, I see your grandmother will keep you from missing me," Nimisha said, giving her daughter a hug and a kiss.

"And," Cuiva went on, clinging shyly to Caleb's hand, "would it be possible for you to take Belac and me out together, too?"

"If Lady Rezalla permits . . ."

Nimisha knew how well Cuiva and Caleb's son got on despite a three-year age difference. She also was aware that one of the reasons Caleb liked his present assignment was the extra time it allowed him to spend with Belac. "I'll make sure of that," she said.

．　　．

Nimisha went for the weeklong rejuv procedure of which Lady
Rezalla approved. She'd been trying to get Nimisha to take it, if
only to protect Cuiva. The ballet was but one of the many activities
she had planned, but it was the one that Cuiva enjoyed the most.
The child was delightfully appreciative and talked quite excitedly
about the various scenes she had particularly enjoyed. All that
week she applied herself to her morning exercises and even reviewed vids from her grandam's extensive ballet library. But the
moment Nimisha returned, she was once again the center of the
child's universe. Cuiva greeted her mother as ecstatically as if she'd
been gone far longer. And Lady Rezalla sighed with regret. It wasn't
as if the little girl hadn't been given all sorts of toys to play with—
from the very feminine to the same scaled-down toolkit her grand-
sire had given Nimisha. Nor had Nimisha influenced the child in
any obvious way, except by her own example of dedication to her
chosen profession.

Therefore, Lady Rezalla was more pleased than concerned
when Nimisha said she was going to solo her new Mark 5 prototype for an extended test run. Her absence meant Cuiva, now a
charming eleven-year-old, would be available to her grandam for
the duration of the six weeks' trial run. All three were satisfied with
that arrangement.

It was a great day for the Rondymense Ship Yard when the Mark 5
prototype was freed from the last gantry umbilical and moored
at the Naval Base station. While the Fiver looked small in the
company of the battle cruisers, even destroyers, she had the sleek-
ness of a stellar racer combined with the toughness of a military
craft.

"Dangerous," Lady Rezalla said, with a delicate shudder. "Why
can't spacecraft be . . . pretty . . . like oceangoing yachts?"

"She is," chorused Nimisha, Caleb, and Cuiva, who was considered old enough to take part in the celebration.

Cuiva never told her grandam just how well she knew the Fiver, inside and out. She did have to try very hard not to hang on to her mother, but she maneuvered to stay close behind Nimisha as the designer did the rounds of the invited guests and accepted official, and personal, congratulations on her achievement.

"Let's not be too optimistic," Nimisha said, dismissing the more ardent comments. "I'll be more sanguine when I've seen the results of the shakedown cruise."

The naval contingent nodded sagely at that remark. Caleb tried hard not to look smug, because he had no doubts himself that the Fiver would pass with flying colors. Then it came time for Nimisha to say farewell to her dam, to Jeska who would capably deal with problems during her absence, and to her beloved Cuiva. Despite the number of people surrounding them, Nimisha raised her body-heir into her arms, hugged her tightly, and kissed her six times before giving her into Lady Rezalla's keeping. She waved to them all until the hatch of the Fiver closed.

A week later, Nimisha brought the Fiver out of warp space at precisely the coordinates she had designated in the Delta quadrant. She was pleased but not surprised. If she'd been a degree off, she would have been upset.

"Run diagnostics on all systems," she told the artificial intelligence that managed ship functions.

"Aye, ma'am," said the tenor voice she had programmed into the AI. Her early years as a test pilot on long and lonely runs had taught her that it was psychologically reassuring to hear another human voice—and the AI, Helm, was the state-of-the-art in that regard, even to making independent queries and initiating standard procedure actions without direct command. She had another AI in the compact infirmary, Doc, and a less broadly programmed one in the galley who responded to "Cater."

She flipped open the safety harness that she had fastened at the sound of the warning bell of reentry and rose in a single graceful movement. "I'll be in the galley."

A needless comment but part of the routine she had established with her AI units. This initial run should shake out the glitches that had escaped the grueling routines to which she subjected each part of a new ship. Responses from the AI's were very much a part of a ship that she wished to produce and sell to both the Federated Sentient Planet Space Authority and private buyers among the wealthy of her acquaintance. Many of them enjoyed flitting about the star system. Many of them preferred to have little, if any, crew and some of them were not competent enough to be permitted to travel alone. Most needed as much backup and assistance as could be crammed into a compact vessel. And a Fleet ship with a single scouting pilot would need the "company," spurious as it was.

The large "day" room was spacious enough to hold large parties in. That would be a boon to those who wished to entertain at their ports of call. It could also be separated into four sections with privacy shields for discreet conferences. The galley was located on the long starboard wall, and the panels on either side of it enclosed additional dispenser units to accommodate an increase in guests. The main airlock was on the port side of the cabin. On either side of the galley facility were the passageways to the six private cabins, far more spacious and well appointed than a naval vessel could permit. A circular staircase on one side gave access to the lower level, which included a well-equipped gymnasium, one of the several hydroponics units, and additional storage space. On the other side, a quick descent pole reached the lower deck, closer to the escape pods. On the main deck, beyond the private cabins, were the main storage units and the larger hydroponics. Through a safety hatch, there was the skiff secured in its own garage, and, through an additional safety hatch, the engineering section and the ship's propulsion system.

The medical unit was directly to the port side of the bridge: compact enough to hold state-of-the-art diagnostic equipment, a life-suspension facility, and an AI programmed to deal with any esoteric disease so far discovered—or any condition a human could be reduced to, including being flattened by the stampede of quadrupeds. The AI medic was a baritone. Nimisha had borrowed his mellifluous voice from Lord Physician Naves, a longtime friend of her dam's. In fact, she'd nearly asked him to sire her heir. Not that she wasn't totally satisfied with Rhidian's performance; his genes had abetted hers in producing beauty, intelligence, and character. She wouldn't have had Rhidian as a long-term partner—hunting bored her and stimulated him—though he had a wry sense of humor that she liked. And he seemed to be rather proud of his biological daughter, evoking Lord Tionel's continued interest in Nimisha. But Rhidian had never understood Nimisha's fascination with space or her propensity to do hands-on work with machinery of all kinds. Which was why Cuiva's early childhood interest in "tinkering" was such a delightful surprise. Obviously the Rondymense genes had dominated.

Nimisha had no intention of pushing the child into her own profession since there were many options for an intelligent, well-trained mind. She was, however, gratified that Cuiva was so happy to play with building blocks and stick-togethers while she was busy at her design screen.

Nimisha's thoughts right now were more on something to fill her empty stomach than on her heir.

"I'll have a mixed fruit juice, a green salad, and Mercassian bread," Nimisha said as she strode across the carpeted deck. A single chair and table emerged from the wall just as the dispenser chimed the arrival of the order. So Nimisha settled immediately to her meal with a pleasant thank-you.

"You're quite welcome. Let me know if you wish anything else," said the dulcet dispenser AI. It spoke in a lilting tone and, while Nimisha didn't need to respond, much less express appreciation, the habit of courtesy had been so ingrained in her that she was unable to break it. Some of her friends found it amusing but then, few of them traveled the distances she did and could appreciate the companionship of other voices, AI or human. And Nimisha had been well drilled by her womb-mother: Courtesy was the Mark of True Nobility and aided the Instillation of Loyalty. And No One of Any True Breeding *assumed* Service.

She grinned, wondering how often she had heard that litany, as she tucked into the salad—crisply green with odd crunchy seasoned bits, just as she liked it. She remembered the day that she had auditioned voices. She'd had half a mind to use her mother's sultry one. But Lady Rezalla would not have considered it in any way a compliment, nor were her mother's highbred tones and elegant diction suitable for any AI on *this* ship.

Nimisha had listened to voices on tri-d, selected those she liked and felt she could bear hearing constantly, and contacted an agency to act for her. The contralto was a young actress, determined to break into big time tri-d, who dutifully read through the material supplied, enunciating culinary words and displaying no curiosity as to the limitation of the audition. She had certainly been grateful for the credit lodged to her account when she finished the day's reading.

The man she had chosen for Helm's voice had been an entirely different matter: He was a well-known compeer, and he had agreed only after haggling with both her and his agent as to price. Once that was finally settled, he had rattled off the required pages of dialogue and vocabulary in a professional manner, but he was curious as to the usage.

"Do I have to be . . . only . . ." and he had leaned toward her, his eyes and manner seductive.

"Dear man, how would I survive listening to your voice thousands of systems away from your presence if we were to indulge . . ." She paused, smiling as she ran a delicate finger down his strongly modeled jawline. ". . . in an intimacy? I know——" And again she paused, this time in compliment. "—your reputation."

When he leaned forward across the worktop that separated them, Nimisha rose from her chair in a graceful whirl toward the door and waved her hand across the control panel. "That'll be all, pet," she said, using her "business" voice, a tone guaranteed to reduce ardor.

With a rueful smile, he tipped her a saucy wave as he exited. "You may be sorry," he murmured. Annoyed, she pressed the fast-close stud of the door controls and just missed his left heel.

Her mother's long-term friend, Lord Physician Naves, had started his medical career as a diagnostician but was now more in demand as a body-sculptor. He had assisted in the massive sculpting necessary to put young Lord Vestrin back together into the handsome figure he had once been before his accident. He had been charmed by her request to use his voice.

"Not that I'm expecting any trouble," she assured Lord Physician Naves, "but when you roll off those unpronounceable diseases and suggest procedures in that gorgeous voice, one is instantly comforted and feels safe."

The older man, who had let his hair go silver—a contrast to his young and vigorous countenance—preened slightly. He was very fond of Lady Rezalla's body-heir and thought her most original to have struck out for herself in a profession of her own: so different from the languorous women and men whom he was called upon to body-sculpt. He smiled and winked at her.

"I've always considered my voice a professional asset. For you, Nimi, I'll be happy to lend my vocal support." Then he went on, repeating a familiar concern of his. "Far too many financiers, bankers, and entrepreneurs in our line. We need some diversity, some other role models for the next generation, or no one will be able to speak in anything except debentures, compound interest, and multiple mergers." He effected a shudder. "There is, after all, only so much you can say about those."

"And infinite queries for you to answer for those of us who think we've contracted something lethal in our travels."

"Precisely." He put both hands on her shoulders, giving her a little shake and sternly eyeing her. "But, of course, I shall be only an emergency feature? You'll be careful?"

"I always am," Nimisha said, having no need to remind him that she had had only very minor scrapes in her career as a test pilot—nothing more than a sprain and bruises. As the saying went, any landing you walk away from is a good one. "Oh, how is Lord Vestrin progressing?"

Lord Naves's expression became very solemn. "That young man feels the world owes him something. Which I assure you it doesn't. His . . . ah . . . reconstruction is almost complete and indeed, there were some improvements he insisted on in the facial reconstruction. Symmetry is just *not* natural. It is, indeed, those minor flaws that give the whole countenance its character. Of course, character is a lack that body sculpting cannot repair. Nor can Lady Vescuya's devotion to her son be considered an asset." He paused, a fleeting look of dismay crossing his handsome and definitely asymmetrical features. "But she has been devoted."

"So he'll be more handsome than ever?"

Lord Naves gave her an odd look. "Illusory, of course," he said, flicking his fingers to dismiss this topic of conversation. "Good luck, my dear," and Lord Naves had given her four tenderly fond embraces. "At least the essence of me will be at your command. I feel much more confident about that."

This shakedown flight was no more than routine, she thought, tearing off a chunk of the Mercassian bread and using it to sop up some of the salad dressing.

One second she was eating, the next, some subtle instinct had her on her feet and running to the bridge, swaying with the erratic motion of a ship gone unstable and yelling "Report!" at the top of her voice.

"Instruments indicate emergence of wormhole—"

"There *isn't* a wormhole in this sector."

"Ship's library confirms wormhole phenomena . . ."

She caught sight of the boiling white pout of disturbance that could be nothing other than a wormhole plugging open the space directly in front of her.

"Helm to starboard! *Hard!*"

If they were lucky, they might just slip under the edge of the yawning maw that seemed to be sucking the ship in. From this angle, the hole looked far larger than it might actually be, for after all it wasn't supposed to exist at these particular coordinates in Delta Quadrant. She'd chosen this area, off main shipping routes, so she could let out the Fiver's engines without running any other vessel down. The seventy meters of her ship were no more than a splinter at its perimeter, yet she might just be able to skim past.

Fighting against the bucking of the deck beneath her feet, she pushed herself into the pilot's chair, fingers flying to program and release a Mayday beacon, propelling it well astern of her ship. With her left arm, she fumbled into the safety harness but had no time to fasten the belt when the ship juddered and inexorably yawed to port, unable to execute the starboard maneuver though she could hear both thrusters and engines roaring to comply. The wormhole had got her and the ship was slipping over its thick lip and down into the brilliant, roiling interior of the tunnel it made. A tunnel to where? She clung to the right armrest, struggling to secure herself in the harness.

"We are in the wormhole, ma'am," said the AI. "What procedures are recommended?"

Nimisha swallowed a totally inappropriate and useless expletive.

"Shut down the drive. Use thrusters to keep us as steady as possible, Helm," she replied, firmly quelling the fright she could not quite suppress. To her immense chagrin, she realized that she had forgotten to program wormhole protocol. Now, in the incredible gullet of the hole, it was too late! Furthermore, she'd never been *in* one. Stable wormholes were relatively uncommon, and no one in their right mind entered one that hadn't been thoroughly probed.

Was the passage through a hole supposed to be this rough? If Helm's reflexes hadn't been femtosecond fast, they'd be mashed against the sides, the hull scored if not penetrated by the protuberances that she saw more as retinal afterimages they passed by so fast. Petralloy was considered the best possible material to clad spacecraft and she had used the most advanced composition for the Fiver, but it *could* be dented and scraped. She could lose the exterior modules and sensors. Was she being sucked into a one-way route to nowhere? Still attempting to fit the harness about her for whatever protection that would afford her, she leaned to port to get her right arm through the straps just as a savage downward plunge brought her forehead against the armrest with sufficient force to render her unconscious.

"Ma'am? Ma'am?" the calm voice of her pilot asked, "your vital signs are showing distress. You should report immediately to the infirmary." When there was no reply, the advice was repeated with an additional query: "Orders are required. No preprogrammed orders conform to the current emergency. Orders are requested. Ma'am?" Then, as the wormhole spat them out into starlit space, Helm added, "Without formal orders, will comply with standard operating procedures."

CHAPTER 3

<<●>>

The pulses from the Mayday beacon were omnidirectional and would connect with any sensor capable of receiving the message, including planetary or lunar satellites or other spaceships.

The first comunit to catch it was on a small intersystem freighter, five light-hours away.

"Hey, cap'n," the sailor on watch yelled to the dozing master of the vessel, "distress call."

"Where?"

When the sailor told him, the captain snorted. "Like we could do anything about it this month."

"It's got a navy tag and one from the Rondymense Ship Yard down Vega way. We gotta at least forward it."

"Rondymense?" The captain struggled to a sitting position. "*And* navy? Label it 'Flash Override.' We can't get there, but we can sure pulse a tight beam to the nearest Naval Base. Look up the co-ordinates and the frequency."

The nearest naval unit, a destroyer on a routine mission, caught another of the pulses and the two warnings reached the Naval Base at Dalonaga.

"Send those coordinates to the plot," the officer of the watch said, wasting no time to get to the transparent three-dimensional sphere that was used during maneuvers. The sphere could be adjusted to any given area of space and display it three-dimensionally. It also pinpointed the present position of every naval unit in that area. Of which there were currently none when the appropriate section appeared on the sector and with it the position of the buoy, a tiny blinking red asterisk.

"The gods wept!" cried the jig. "We had a routine signal about a trial run for a Rondymense yacht out that way. What could have happened? I'll have to bother the captain with this."

"I'd've killed you if you hadn't," was the response as the captain swung onto the bridge, his cheek bearing crease marks from his interrupted sleep. "Crappit! The ID's for that long-distance yacht Vegan Fleet's keen on. Now what the frag could have happened to it? What have we got that's fast enough to get out there and see, Addison?" he asked the duty officer.

"Sir, there's nothing *close* enough, sir," Addison replied, depressed. Then he brightened as he added, "The base at Coyne III has one of the Mark Twos that came out of the Rondymense Yard."

"Send a Flash Override to Coyne III's base commander, requiring him to send the Mark Two with all possible speed to these coordinates." The captain's finger was shaking just a little as he tapped the plot and the winking light. "The Mark Two can be Net Control and do a standard search pattern until we can get more units out there to help. No one's going to hang about when they see who sent that Mayday."

Rubbing his face as if that would assist clearer insight into the emergency, the captain increased the magnification of the targeted zone and began to scratch his skull in perplexity. It was a sparsely occupied area, which is why it was used for testing new ships, and occasionally for naval maneuvers. Could the Rondymense ship have blundered into a missile left over from the last Games? He shook his head at that unlikelihood. If the test ship were an advance on the design of the Mark 2, it would have sensors capable of detecting a missile. After all, the pilot had had time to shoot off a Mayday beacon, so he hadn't landed *on* the missile to set it off. For which mischance the odds would be in gigabytes.

· ·

The Mark 2 from Coyne III was the first to arrive, its captain having had the distinct pleasure of an excuse to redline the engines. It
was joined by half a dozen other vessels, four naval, one commercial, and one luxury yacht that had altered course from a hunting
preserve to answer what might be a much more exciting adventure
for its First Family occupants. All participated in the standard 3-D
search pattern, with the Mark 2, *Swallow,* acting as NETCOS.

The *Swallow,* commanded by a senior lieutenant on his first assignment, had followed all the recommended search procedures,
starting with a long-range scan for a life pod, for debris, for traces
of an ion trail. He did find that. Or, rather, traces of the ship's reentry into normal space.

The emissions were clean enough, what one would expect of a
brand-new ship. But there wasn't so much as a cinder of debris or a
pellet of melted metal to be found. Hailed by the incoming naval
ships, one with an admiral aboard, *Swallow* handed over the NET-
COS to the flagship while he continued on his search pattern. By
now all the ships had moved well beyond the beacon. The one thing
he should have tried to find was any discontinuity in the space
near the beacon, but at that point in time no one had thought to
check for a wormhole.

Fretting during the long sleepless days it took Caleb Rustin to
reach the beacon, even redlining the Mark 4 he "borrowed" from
the Rondymense Ship Yard, he had time to check for reports on
any anomalies, of any kind, reported in that sector of space.

He groaned as the report divulged that eighteen ships had been
reported "last heard from" in this general area. The latest one had
been fifteen standard years previously, an exploration ship, the
Poolbeg, FSPS 9K66E, ten aboard, Captain Panados Querine commanding. The ship and crew had been deemed officially lost in
space seven years ago. The other ships listed as missing ranged
back through the nearly two hundred and fifty years of space history.

No debris of any of the missing ships had ever been found, even at the Moon Base of the notorious Ebevyr Pirates who had terrorized commercial shipping for three decades over a hundred years before. However, many previously "missing" ships, or fragments thereof, including descendants of crews and passengers reduced to slavery by the pirates, were found and accounted for.

When Caleb reported his findings to Admiral Gollanch on his flagship, the admiral immediately set the more powerful search units of his database to sift possibilities.

"Wormhole?" Caleb suggested, wincing.

The admiral looked pensive. "None ever reported at those coordinates, Rustin."

"Possibly why this particular area is one of the more deserted sectors?"

"Having eaten any nearby stars and their planets?" If an admiral chose to be facetious, he could, but Caleb gritted his teeth. It was Nimisha Boynton-Rondymense who was the victim, not some totally unknown unfortunate. "What the astrographer says about wormholes is that they seem to appear in less tenanted space. The few that have been regular occurrences suggest that there are far more of these phenomena than we have documented."

"If Lady Nimisha had seen a wormhole, she'd've included it in the Mayday," Caleb said staunchly.

"*If* she had seen it in time, Commander," the admiral said. "I seem to be arguing against my wishes," he added with a rueful twist to his lips. "I'd like nothing better than to find her . . . and that prototype. Did you redline the Four all the way out there?"

"Yes, sir," Caleb replied without a trace of regret. "Drive and ship performed very well at maximum thrust."

"No problems?"

"I'm preparing a full performance report, sir. You'll have it shortly on a pulsed beam."

"Did well, did it? Then why in name of Holy Icons was Nimisha dissatisfied with the Four?"

"Lady Nimisha . . ." Caleb had to close his eyes a moment, having managed to keep desire under control. By mentioning her name, he was robbed of his calm for a second, but he continued with a firm emphasis on the verb, "*is* a perfectionist, and I must admit that she had already proved to me that the Fiver's drive tested out 12.25 percent more efficient before and after installation."

"Hmmm, really?" The admiral pulled at his lower lip. "Then we shall spare no effort to retrieve the prodigal and her efficient vessel."

"Especially as she made the final adjustments and additions with Hiska's help and not mine," Caleb said ruefully.

By the time Caleb Rustin arrived at the beacon, the *Swallow* and the other vessels that had answered the Mayday were widening their search pattern for debris or any other traces. It was now three days and fifteen hours since the beacon had first begun to pulse. Admiral Gollanch had sent on to Caleb in his faster comsystem science reports on wormhole tracings, but whatever might have been present before the Mark 2 had begun its search pattern had been overlaid by its own ion trail.

The *Swallow's* captain was horrified speechless and then babbled on and on about how he had followed standard search procedures as outlined in regulations and . . . until Caleb had to cut off the sound and look away from the screen. He got his emotions under control and held up one hand to stem the flow from the penitent junior before he flipped back on the sound.

"You did exactly as you should, Fermassy, no fault to you," Caleb said, and had to repeat it several more times until the young captain could be sufficiently reassured.

"What can we do now, Commander? We must do *something*,"

Fermassy insisted. "Lady Nimisha must be found! She's First Family, sir!"

"We are all exceedingly aware of that, Fermassy, I assure you. It is my devout hope that the more sensitive equipment on board Admiral Gollanch's ship may find traces we cannot."

"But both our ships are Rondymense-made, sir!" the young captain exclaimed.

"Which is why we made it here so fast. Ah, and what have we coming in now?" Caleb noticed ships arriving from three directions and welcomed the diversion from Fermassy's self-castigation.

He was not quite as pleased to discover that the luxury yacht that had diverted from its original destination to a hunting preserve was occupied by friends of Lord Vestrin. How the man would enjoy knowing that his half-sister had gone missing in such a dramatic fashion. Caleb sent a pulsed priority message directly to Rondymense Ship Yard and another to Lady Rezalla. Vestrin's dam would like nothing better than to get the Yard back into her hands under a default condition, since the Yard had been left to Nimisha, not to Nimisha and her body-heir.

But Nimisha is not dead, Caleb told himself at the top of his mental voice, denying, denying, denying.

There had been the Fiver's ion trail in normal space, ending some ten thousand kilometers from the beacon. Caleb figured she might well have propelled it as far from the wormhole as possible to be sure it would escape and send its vital Mayday. She was in the most advanced and sophisticated ship in the known galaxy, built of the best materials, all basic ship functions had proved out in the earlier models and no debris was evident. Malfunction was marginally possible. But he denied malfunction. He denied her death. But how could they find a wormhole that had never been seen? How could they even prove that it had been a wormhole that had snatched her out of this part of space?

Despite the most sensitive and sophisticated of instruments, some of which bore Nimisha Boynton-Rondymense's patent registrations, no further trace was found. Machinists and programmers on the admiral's big cruiser made alterations to existing sensors and the original beacon was shortly anchored to a highly specialized satellite. It was programmed to launch a piggyback double probe into whatever wormhole or other spatial anomaly might appear at these coordinates, simultaneously pulsing a broadcast to the nearest drone monitor. When the double probe reached the other end of the wormhole, the piggyback, with the most powerful single thruster in the Fleet's possession, would be immediately released and return with whatever information it could glean in a nanosecond's view of the exit space. Similar units would be constructed and scattered within this relatively unoccupied sector, so that no wormhole could poke its white snout through the fabric of space without instant detection. During the next month, a special station was hauled to the edge of the sector and positioned there, with a Mark 4 on detached assignment, probably the fastest ship that could be scrambled to reach a wormhole.

"We hope," was Admiral Gollanch's remark as he initialed the necessary orders. "I'll make this a three-month duty station, high risk compensation, partnered crews so they'll have something to do while they wait . . ."

"Ma'am? Ma'am?"

"Lady Nimisha? Please answer, Lady Nimisha. Do you wish more to eat?"

"Nimi, get to your feet and get over to the unit. I can't treat you from here."

The sentences, each in a different but recognizable tone from patient repetition to anxiety to command, gradually penetrated Nimi's fogged mind.

She struggled to sit up, rolling her eyes at the pain in her head, trying to remember what had hit her.

"Orders, please, ma'am. I am on standby."

"Standby?" Nimi repeated and forced her eyes open, one hand at her temple so that she felt the dried blood that had congealed there. "Oh." She shed the half of harness she had managed to get on and tried to stand. "Helm, report!"

She made a second and successful attempt to get to her feet and made her way to the medical station. Wove her way, she amended. She'd had quite a crack.

"Doc, how long have I been unconscious?"

"Three hours, twenty minutes, six seconds and—"

"Thank you, Helm," she cut off the hundredths. "I asked the Doc."

"Helm needs to hear your voice, Nimi," the medic said in Lord Naves's soothing baritone. "Now lie down before you fall."

The change in position made her head throb, but the infirmary unit's extensions had snaked out of their niches to clamp on her body for readings.

"Shaken but nothing stirred," the Doc said reassuringly. "We'll just relieve the symptoms and clean up that cut. A spurt of nu-skin will close it neatly."

Nimi grimaced as a swab made her aware of how tender the spot was, but the sudden coolness on her arm from a hypospray meant that the discomfort would soon disappear.

"All systems functioning normally," Helm said. "No damage reported in any section despite the turbulence of the wormhole. The hull has been scraped on both sides but has not lost integrity."

"Wormhole!" Nimisha would have shot upright if she hadn't been entangled with extendables, which were still checking her over.

"Let's just keep our cool," Doc said.

"We were drawn into a wormhole, ma'am, and you were rendered unconscious by the buffeting," was Helm's contribution.

Somehow she got the distinct impression from Helm's voice

that it was her puny human fault that she was vulnerable and he was sorry for her. Hmmm . . . maybe she should reprogram Helm when she got back to the yard. That actor had embroidered on the script with some emotional content that was not to her liking. Damn him.

"What is our position?"

There was a long pause, during which she was given another injection "for shock," the Doc said.

"I'm waiting, Helm."

"Working, ma'am, on establishing our present position with star identification program." Helm was almost a misnomer for the functions handled by that AI: It was not only guidance, but engineering, communications, navigation, defense, and science, as well as commissary for all the supplies on board the Fiver which were not for human consumption. And it ordered those in from the lists supplied by Cater.

Nimi craned her neck to get a glimpse of the main screen.

"You'll have time enough to look at it when you've been cleared by me, Nimi, and have had something to bring your blood sugar up to normal. Cater, prepare a sweetened and restorative drink, high protein, full trace elements."

"Yes, indeed. My pleasure."

Nimisha wondered if she actually heard a note of relief in Cater's voice. The manipulative arms of the infirmary withdrew. "Move slowly now," Doc advised. "No permanent damage, but you gave yourself quite a crack."

"I'll have to see to the armrest design. Pad it better," Nimisha muttered. "Take note please, Helm," she added as she walked slowly toward the dispenser and the cup of steamy liquid awaiting her. Judiciously sampling it, though it was at just the right temperature to be ingested immediately, she thanked Cater and got a fervent "You're very welcome, Lady Nimisha," as she returned to the pilot console.

"It shouldn't take you this long to match spectro-analyses, Helm. What's the problem?"

"I can find no matches, ma'am."

Nimisha blinked. "You're programmed with every single data cube available to the Fleet on every single star system. You mean, that wormhole took us outside the Delta Quadrant?"

"That would be a correct assessment of an inability to identify any of the primaries visible. We are substantially closer to the Magellanic Clouds, so we must be nearer the southern celestial pole. I believe I can identify the constellation Doradus, but it is the only familiar starscape."

Nimisha looked out, not precisely doubting Helm but unwilling to concede that she, and her ship, were lost in space. She knew what configuration of stars she should have seen from the Fiver at the position where the wormhole sucked her in. There were no comfortingly familiar star-patterns visible, but she was still in a populous area, to judge by the multitude of primaries shining all around her.

"Well, if my brains were scrambled, at least yours can't be, Helm."

"No, ma'am."

"What about that double star? Surely it's unusual enough to have turned up somewhere on Fleet explorations?"

"It does not match within the necessary parameters for any double stars on file."

Nimisha eased herself into the pilot's chair and sipped at her beverage. It had a minty flavor and something else, more exotic, but she could feel its restorative rush.

"Int'rusting," she said, matching a tone her mother would use when faced with some unusual situation.

"Shall I log it in?"

"Might as well. Do the whole panorama," Nimisha added with

a sweep of her free arm. "Might be useful sometime. No answer to our Mayday, I suppose?"

"No, ma'am."

At least Helm didn't sound worried. No, the worry was all hers.

"Helm, have we moved from where that wormhole spat us out?"

"No, ma'am. I awaited your orders."

"Yes, of course, since you weren't programmed for the standard operating procedure on exiting wormholes."

"No, ma'am."

For that matter, she didn't know what that would be either, but she could wish he had less need for so many negatives. Had she been conscious, her first action on being spat out would have been to send a probe back through the hole with the present star patterns. However, she hadn't been awake and she couldn't fault Helm for not knowing what action to take in such a situation.

"Then please prepare a new beacon, giving our registration and com-pulse configurations, the spectro-analysis of the stars in our spatial vicinity, and repeat our request for contact with any Fleet or civilian vessel."

"Aye, ma'am."

An affirmative was a nice change.

"Beacon away," Helm said a few moments later.

That was one advantage in having AI units managing the ship. They didn't have to take breaks or eat or go to the head at awkward moments, and they worked with great speed and efficiency. She sighed and drained the cup.

"That did the trick, Cater, Doc."

"I recommend some rest, Nimi, while you're awaiting a response."

"Aren't you the optimist?" she replied with a snort. But the idea of getting horizontal and sleeping was a good one. She'd be able to think better when the headache, as well as the medication that had reduced it, was gone. "You have the conn, Helm."

"I have the conn, ma'am."

She slept her normal six hours and woke refreshed. After a quick shower in water that her purifying system kept fresh enough to allow such a luxury, she dressed and, leaving her quarters, gave Cater orders for her breakfast.

"Good morning, Helm. Any report?"

"Nothing to report, ma'am."

"Good morning, Doc."

"You sound perfectly normal," Doc said cheerfully.

"Thank you. And thank you, Cater, for breakfast."

She asked for music since she liked it in the background when she was thinking hard. Indeed, she had no idea at all of what to do next, apart from waiting beside the beacon, hoping its pulse would alert someone. Her meal finished, she resumed the pilot's chair, staring out at unfamiliar constellations. Why, that band of stars in the grouping to the upper right vaguely resembled Orion's belt, but the rest of the constellation did not match.

"Helm, has your inspection of the immediate vicinity turned up any M-type planets nearby?"

"Three, ma'am." A red light briefly circled the three primaries.

"That many?"

"Yes, ma'am."

"Well, when I find myself twiddling my thumbs, we can always go take a look-see. Might as well." Action was preferable to sitting like—who was it on her tuffet? "I'll give it another three days. That would give time for our initial pulse to reach main shipping lanes."

"Or the curious of this Quadrant," Doc added.

"A search of the records of ships missing in the general vicinity of that wormhole has proved fruitful," Helm suddenly volunteered.

"Oh?"

"Eighteen ships in the two hundred and fifty years of recorded space exploration."

"Oh!" She paused, smiling ironically. "Make that nineteen, Helm, since we've just joined that elite group."

"Yes, ma'am."

"When was the last one reported to Fleet?" She held her breath for his reply.

"Fifteen years ago, Exploratory Vessel FSPS 9K66E, the *Poolbeg*, was reported missing. Her last report came from this general area."

"Fifteen?" Well, she was *not* going to miss Cuiva's Necklacing. Somehow she'd find a way home before *that* auspicious event in her daughter's life three and a half years from now.

Three days later there had been not so much as a peep from the pulse. As it had been sent out in all directions, she was obviously far from any responder, even those discreet Fleet "ears" that Caleb had told her dotted known space. However, that did not mean that there wouldn't *be* a response. Nimisha was not constitutionally patient. She required action. If she'd been traveling to a destination, there would have been other matters to involve her. Hanging motionless in space—even though she programmed a day full of the various activities she had for diversion—exercise in the gymnasium, playing interactive games, and an immense library of tri-d and tapes—was not the same thing as having a destination.

She also spent time with Helm in gathering a file of spectro-analyses of all the primaries in their present starscape. These were inserted into the beacon's data file.

"Helm?" she began firmly after her breakfast on the fourth morning, "How much time does it take a pulse to get from one side of Delta Quadrant to the other?"

"Nine full ship days with the strength of the unit on board."

Slowly she came to the bridge and looked out at the uninformative and strange starscape.

"We shall remain in position then, to allow any searchers time to reach us," she said. "I shall make use of the suspended animation facility, Doc."

"Always ready to comply, Nimi."

"Helm, you will monitor any incoming pulses. You will have Doc revive me instantly if you have received any response. If, however, the wormhole reappears—" She paused, wondering if using that escape from her present position was sensible considering the erratic behavior of unprobed wormholes. "—you will immediately enter it, deploying a second beacon stating the time of this reentry. Doc, if Helm takes us into the wormhole, revive me."

"Is this advisable, Lady Nimisha?" Helm and Doc asked in chorus.

"I can't be more lost than I am now, can I?" she replied. "At least I can leave behind proof that I was here and am still very much alive."

"There are three primaries with habitable planets, Lady Nimisha. Why not investigate the possibility of establishing a planetary base?" Helm suggested.

"A good idea," she said, rubbing her chin thoughtfully as Helm red-circled the three prospects again. "But there is every possibility that the wormhole would return us to our starting point, and that would be the best solution."

"Shall you stay in suspended animation until that time?" Doc asked. "If there is no response to the pulse message?"

"A good point. Who knows when that wretched hole will reappear. All right, let's set a limit of a year to this day for revival *if* neither a message arrives nor the wormhole appears. I don't want to stay away any longer than necessary."

"No, of course not, Nimi," Doc said, his tone approving.

To herself she put the question: Which way would I have to go to get back home? Helm had registered no directional bend in which the wormhole had bridged the space from there to here. Once again she thought how, if she had only been conscious when they reached the end of the wormhole, she could have launched a probe with her current starscape back through the hole before it closed. Though what good that would have done was moot when there were no recognizable primaries at this exit point to guide a rescue party. Eventually, the beacon would guide in a rescue vessel. Eventually!

Helm repeated the orders.

"I am also to be roused if anything . . . extraordinary . . . should occur in our current spatial neighborhood."

"Anything not covered by standard operating procedures, ma'am?"

"You got it, Helm."

Nimisha rose, walking with stiff steps to the infirmary unit. She didn't like this expedient but it was better than waiting around and fretting herself over her inability to *take* action. She'd had several short spells of suspended animation and was none the worse for them. She did dislike not being *present*, but she could trust Helm and Doc to rouse her if anything untoward happened.

"Whenever you're ready, Doc," she began but wasn't sure how much of the sentence in her mind she actually spoke aloud, because the walls around the medical couch rose and snapped shut over her head, the sleep gas already hissing into the enclosed space.

"Lady Nimisha has only been gone five months, Cal," Admiral Gollanch remarked to Commander Rustin, who was pacing up and down in front of the desk. He sighed. "I know it seems a lot longer but you cannot deny that we have done everything possible, impossible, probable, and improbable to locate her. Finishing up the second Fiver would be a good idea. Especially, if putting her through a shake-down cruise will give us any clues as to what happened to

Lady Nimisha's ship. And you tell me that Jeska Mlan, who is the Yard's executive director, agrees. So what's the problem?"

"We can't find the final specs to complete it."

"Hmmm, yes, well, she did warn me that she did not intend to give the Fleet all her secrets. But surely you . . ." and Admiral Gollanch extended his hand invitingly toward Rustin.

"I?" The commander grinned ruefully. "She trusted everyone up to a point. I, perhaps, further than her yard supervisors—equally, I believe, as much as she trusts Jeska Mlan. But she finished some units by herself, in her private machine shop." He paused a moment and amended that statement. "She usually had her special mechanic, Hiska, on hand, but she won't say anything. Not even if there were additional specs that Lady Nimisha kept someplace else."

Gollanch sighed. "She wouldn't have left without storing the final plans somewhere. Would she?"

"I was hoping that she had left them with you, sir."

"With me?" The admiral was surprised enough to jerk a thumb at his chest and cleared his throat. "I'd've said you would be the logical recipient. You seemed to have no trouble working closely together during the Fiver's construction. Surely she confided in you?"

"Up to a point—the point at which we are now stymied in completing the second Mark Five. Oh, we can fly her and she'd be an asset to the fleet as a long-distance scout. She could be sold as a yacht, but she's not yet a replica of the Fiver that Lady Nimisha took out on that run."

"Ah, I see," the admiral remarked, steepling his fingers and bouncing the tips together.

"Sir?"

The admiral gave a droll chuckle. "She did warn me."

"She also wouldn't leave, even on what should have been a routine shakedown cruise, without leaving such vital information in a safe place. She was too precise and careful a designer than not leave a backup."

"I concur. Would she have left them in her residence?"

"I dislike intruding on Lady Rezalla . . ." Rustin said, shaking his head.

"So would I," the admiral replied with much feeling in his voice, "but the concern is not frivolous. And you have been welcomed at the Boynton-Chonderlee House, have you not? Even since Lady Nimisha's disappearance?"

"No problem there . . ." This was true enough, even if he had rarely seen Lady Rezalla. It was Cuiva whose company he sought, taking the girl on outings with Belac, who had similar interests in "designing things." He always made a point of asking the Residence Manager to convey his respects to Lady Rezalla and usually brought some small token for her—a delicate blossom, a rare fruit, or the sweets of which Lady Rezalla was inordinately fond. There was always a brief note of thanks for him at his next visit, handwritten in an unusually bold forward stroke. A penned note was such a treasure that he kept them all, filed in a lacquered box, as examples of a lost art. However, asking could he find a secreted file in the Boynton Family Residence was another matter entirely. "I could ask."

"That is all you can do, Commander," the admiral said with a snort, understanding both the etiquette and the audacious course of action he was asking his subordinate to undertake. *He* wouldn't have dared, but he was not on such terms with the Family as Rustin was. And he very much wanted to commission this prototype for Fleet use—once it had proved itself on trial runs. To have stumbled into a wormhole was a wretched piece of misfortune and not to be considered the fault of the pilot, much less the vessel.

Trying very hard not to show how ill at ease he was, Lt. Commander Caleb Rustin appeared at the door to the Boyntin-Chonderlee House, a baroque creation of outstanding elegance and beauty in the Old Quarter of Acclarke City, at precisely one minute before the appointment received from Lady Rezalla.

It wasn't, however, the Residence Manager (one of the latest Class T AI's) but Lady Cuiva herself who opened the door.

"I heard Grandam say you were coming today," she said, slipping outside.

Caleb smiled down at the girl's anxious expression, and since they were not in a public spot, he gave her a quick hug. That's when he realized that she had both hands clasped behind her back.

"You don't happen to have news about my mother?" she asked so plaintively that Caleb wanted more than ever to have good news for her.

He shook his head, stroking the silky hair that hung loose down her back. Nimi's hair . . . He broke off that thought.

"Jeska says they can't go any further with the Mark Five; you need to find my mother." Her tone was interrogatory as she tilted her head up at him.

He took two steps downward so they were at eye-level. "That's true enough. I'm here to . . ."

Her hands came from behind her back and, with one, she seized his much bigger hand and closed his fingers around what she put in the palm.

"My birth-mother would want you to have these now, then." She stepped back, holding her lips closed, but her eyes watered.

Rustin closed his fingers about the round circles: six of them, a full stack and exactly what he had come about.

"You had them?" he whispered in astonishment.

She nodded and then, with a lift to her chin and in a louder voice, said, "My grandam is expecting you, Commander Rustin. If you will be pleased to enter . . ."

"Mimicking the RM is not done, Lady Cuiva," he said, grinning as he followed her into the impressive foyer with its ancient Terran marble floor in alternating black and white squares. There were fine statues in the many niches, all artfully restored to the condition in which they had left their sculptors' yards. The flowery Acaderillus shrub filled the room with a delicate odor. It was the only indigenous Vegan object in the Residence entrance hall.

Cuiva slipped over to the stationary RM and flicked it back on.

"That's all right, RM," she said. "Commander Rustin is expected. You may conduct him to my grandam." With that and a saucy wink at Caleb, she glided over to the door into her quarters and was gone.

"I will conduct you to Lady Rezalla directly, Commander." The RM turned and started up the left-hand side of the double staircase, also of priceless Terran marble. It moved with the dignity befitting its occupation. Rustin followed, wishing he could have followed Cuiva instead as he slipped the data circles into his tunic pocket.

With his errand accomplished, what excuse could he give Lady Rezalla as the purpose for this visit? And how like Nimisha to have entrusted the data files to her daughter, rather than her mother! Who would have thought it? Well, *he* should have. But one simply didn't go about asking underage children if they just happened to have been entrusted with irreplaceable documents. What to say to Lady Rezalla? She must be thinking he was the bearer of tidings.

He could be! His hand brushed the data disks. He could well be. The Fleet already had permission of Lady Rezalla to take the finished hull out of the Yard. Yes, that was why he was requesting this interview. To inform her that the removal would occur shortly— as soon as he had added to the ship the special adjustments he now had deposited safely in a uniform pocket.

Though Lady Rezalla's quick and piercing glance begged for news of another kind, she did not refer to her missing daughter when Caleb explained the purpose of his visit. He deeply wished he could relieve her fears with some sort of reassurance. No news was still, in its own way, good news.

"And you feel *safe*," she asked, pausing on the word, "taking out the Prototype Five, Commander?"

"It has passed every single test the Fleet can give it, Lady Rezalla," he said quite truthfully. "I have no hesitation at all in putting it through the most grueling maneuvers."

"Except those that would take you down the maw of a wormhole, I trust," she said drolly.

"Indeed, Lady Rezalla. I shall avoid them as I would a black hole."

"Do." And she inclined her head graciously.

As a little present for her courtesy in receiving him, he presented her with the latest "book" of scents—fine sheets of paper, no longer than the palm of his hand, each impregnated with a different aroma—from the parfumeries of the Outer City, famed for their exquisite fragrances.

"How charming," she said with a delighted smile. "You are much too good to me, Commander."

"Nothing can be too good for a lady of your charm and eminence," he replied in words formulaic but delivered sincerely.

She opened the first sheet, inhaling delicately. "Oh, like roses. Terran roses. Attar made from them was supposed to be the most seductive fragrance of all."

She passed the tiny sheet to him and he inhaled obediently without informing her that his nose was woefully inept at distinguishing "pleasant" smells. The funk of recycled air he knew; florals, he did not.

"Elegant. Truly elegant."

"I'd term it dainty, Commander, but then"—she smiled winsomely at him, cocking her head in such a way that he wished she was neither a First Family Lady nor related to the woman he did love—"this scent was contrived for feminine, not masculine, tastes."

"Indeed." He inclined his head, smiling in such a way as to thank her for her discreet flirtatiousness. "I would also like your permission to bring Lady Cuiva to see how we are progressing with her mother's design."

Lady Rezalla gave him a long, almost acid look. Then she made a graceful gesture with her lovely hand. "Forgive me, but I could wish that my granddaughter was not quite so fascinated by her mother's profession." Caleb made a small bow of comprehension. "She has lately insisted that she be tutored in space navigation . . . and doubtless the anomalies that are . . . hazards." Her mouth closed firmly for a moment as she took a deep breath before continuing. "However, the child's loyalty and dedication must be considered. I shall not have it said that I denied her."

"Never, Lady Rezalla," Caleb protested.

The long hand was lifted again, forestalling further reassurances. "You may have heard rumors about the machinations of that young . . . young . . ." A proper term seemed to escape her.

"Scut, milady?"

She gave him a stern look but her eyes twinkled. "That will do until I can think of something more thoroughly derogatory. That scut Vestrin."

"He can't still be pursuing a court action on the grounds that his father made the bequest to Lady Nimisha?"

She nodded, smiling with a wicked and determined gleam in her gentian-blue eyes—so like her daughter's. "As well we were forewarned by you, Commander, for, of course, my body-heir had made a will prior to her departure and, in it, bequeaths all her estate and assets to Lady Cuiva. You will shortly meet Perdimia, who will accompany Lady Cuiva wherever she may go."

"Oh! Yes, I see. Sensible precaution. But surely not even Lord Vestrin would attempt to . . . harm a child. A First Family child wearing such a prestigious tattoo."

"Cuiva is not yet Necklaced in her minor majority, Commander.

I would not put anything past that—no, 'scut' is not appropriate. He may not *be* a bastard"—Lady Rezalla spat the epithet—"but roué he most certainly is. I would put nothing past a creature of so little honor and such great greed. He has laughed . . . *laughed* . . ." she paused again, "at public functions over my body-heir's disappearance." She drew in a deep breath, her nostrils pinched by her wrath.

"You may be sure that I would protect Lady Cuiva with my life," Caleb said, bowing again and feeling almost sick with a combination of anxiety for the child and animosity toward Lord Vestrin.

"I know that, Commander, but you will double whatever precautions you have previously used in any excursions on which she accompanies you." Now she rose, extending her hand in gracious dismissal.

"I shall keep you informed of the progress. You will attend the commissioning?" Caleb asked, hastily adding, "A formality which you, as Owner-Representative, should attend—if you can fit such an engagement in your calendar?"

"I wouldn't miss that for the worlds," she said, again in a droll tone. She always managed to astonish him, despite her adherence to the conventions of Family.

He bowed over her hand and was honored when her fingers pressed his with far more strength than he would have expected from her. But then, Cuiva often mentioned that she took physical exercise every morning with her grandmother. Lord Vestrin would not get past Lady Rezalla if he made an attempt on Cuiva in the older woman's presence.

Rezalla accompanied him to the door, and when it opened for them, she turned to the waiting RM. "Escort the commander to Lady Cuiva's apartment. You may tender your invitation personally. She has missed your company. You may make whatever arrangements for the visit are required."

Caleb said all that was suitable for such gracious condescension and then, pivoting smartly, followed the RM. In the hall, and unobserved, he patted the disks in his pocket. He would have preferred racing back to the Yard to see what they contained, but he was concerned enough about Cuiva to want a word with her—to bawl her out for stepping outside the front door without this new bodyguard. What had she been thinking about?

Although the RM opened the door, a woman quickly inserted herself between Caleb and the room.

"This is Commander Caleb Rustin, Miz Perdimia," the Residence Manager said with just the slightest hint of remonstrance, as if the woman should have known who he was.

She stepped back. She was short in stature but wide in body, as if her legs did not balance her torso in length. Her hazel eyes were keen, and from the way she stood, Caleb had no doubts of alertness, even with the RM presenting him to Cuiva's door. He also noticed, and saw that she caught his swift glance over her person, the knife sheaths in her boot and on her left forearm, and the strap of the one that probably hung down her back as Jeska's had.

"I'd like a word with Lady Cuiva, Miz Perdimia. Lady Rezalla said I should invite her myself."

"Cal?" Cuiva cried, hearing his voice and rushing into the room.

"Lady Cuiva . . . what have we been talking about just this morning?" Perdimia's face was expressionless as she turned to the girl.

Cuiva went from a dead run to a solemn walk between steps. Her face reflected that she did indeed remember what had been said "just this morning."

"Not rushing here and there," she murmured and then brightened as Caleb stepped past the bodyguard and held out his hand to her. She went up on the balls of her feet to rush to him and, sighing, came forward at a sedate pace, but she clung to his hand with both of hers. He could feel her trembling, and when her fingers squeezed, he knew that he wouldn't say anything about their clan-destine meeting on the front steps. Not in front of Perdimia and certainly not after a recent schooling on the same peril.

"Indeed, my young friend," Caleb said, shaking her hands to make her contact his eyes. "How will you ever learn the decorum a Necklaced minor major must have if you don't start practicing . . . right now!" He stared at her to emphasize the final two words and she flushed, but then recovered her ebullience and swung on his arm, nearly pulling him off balance. "I have your grandam's per-mission to show you the Fiver we've been completing." He looked squarely at Perdimia. "I invite you, Miz Perdimia, in your own right as well as in your role as Lady Cuiva's companion."

"Sir, that's real nice of you." Perdimia's face relaxed.

He had a good notion that she quite probably came from a ser-vice family and, like Jeska, had not measured up to the height re-quirement. She had the required background and was making good use of it. More important, she took her job seriously, which reas-sured Caleb in light of what Lady Rezalla had confided to him.

"When? When, Cal, when?" Cuiva said, swinging on his arm. She saw Perdimia's expression. "Oh, Cal doesn't mind, Perdimia. We're old friends," she went on, standing upright again and affect-ing a very mature stance, obviously copied from her grandam. "I used to go out to the Yard all the time with my mother and we even—"

It was Cal's turn to raise eyebrows at her effusiveness.

"Ooops," she said, covering her mouth with her hand and squinching down, grinning wickedly as she knew she should not mention the EVA's her mother had allowed her to do. "His son said I could. He comes with us sometimes, doesn't he, Commander?"

Caleb and Perdimia exchanged glances over Cuiva's head as she went from child to an echo of her grandam in the space of a second. Perdimia gave a shrug and a shake of her head. But she also smiled.

"Imp!" she said affectionately. "When had you in mind, Commander? I check all engagements with Lady Rezalla."

Caleb let his hand pause at the pocket that held the disks—a pause that sharp-eyed Cuiva caught and made her giggle. Then she became adult again and watched as he took out his touchpad and turned it on.

"A week from today? At about this hour? Would that be convenient?"

Perdimia had her touchpad strapped to her right wrist, which confirmed his notion that she was left-handed. "That day is free after the eleventh hour."

"Oh, no, make it earlier, Perdimia," Cuiva said, hanging on to the woman's arm. "I can do a double session of studying the day before or the day after."

The two adults again exchanged looks, and Perdimia yielded.

"Excellent," Caleb said, tapping in the time and date as Perdimia made a note. "I shall speed up the work in train—" Again he paused his hand at the pocket before letting it fall to his side. "—and look forward to the company of you two ladies. I'll collect you, Lady Cuiva, Miz Perdimia, at the appointed hour in the Yard skiff." He bowed to both. "I must return to my duties, if you will be good enough to excuse me now, Lady Cuiva?"

The girl elegantly dismissed him with a wave of her hand as he backed three steps before turning for the door. He heard her giggle and allowed her to hear his chuckle as he closed the door behind him.

He took the skimmer back to the Yard as fast as possible, only just clearing the Old Quarter before he opened the thrusters and poured on the power. He landed at the lock closest to Nimisha's private machine workshop and cycled through it, pausing only to remove his formal tunic in the dressing room. He took the precious disks out of his pocket and jingled them in his hand as he walked himself a leg at a time, into his heavy shop coverall, stumbling a bit as he shrugged it over his shoulders and sealed the fastenings. He strode to Nimisha's desk. Two disks clattered out of his hands in his haste to insert the number one in the slot of the reader. And there it was: the menu of final details that would make all the difference to the incomplete Mark 5 still in its production gantry. The comunit burped authoritatively. He switched on the visual, one hand resting on the little disks that were so bloody important.

"Oh, it's you, Commander," the guard said, swallowing. "For a moment—"

"My apologies, Ferron, I should have checked in."

"That's all right, sir. It's just that—"

"I know. Lady Nimisha preferred to use the private entrance."

"Yes, sir, that's it, sir. And, sir, still no word?"

"Still no word."

"Will you be staying long?"

"Possibly all night, Ferron, so log me in officially. Want to check over some details. We'll be working overtime to finish the Five B from now on."

"Will we, sir? That's good to know, sir." Ferron disconnected.

Caleb let out a sigh of relief. He should have checked in himself, but his little lapse only proved how alert security in the Yard was. Most of the workforce had already gone home now that the Five B was so near completion and three shifts were no longer needed. He made a quick note to have Jeska double-check those on the day shift when Cuiva and her bodyguard visited.

Then he whistled at what was scrolling across the screen.

By all the Lords of Space and Time, she had left the best for last, hadn't she? He skimmed quickly. Some were minor adjustments, mere tunings. Others were guidance chips with subtle differences to the standard ones, if he read them right: just the sort of tinkering that distinguished Rondymense programs from naval. He ran a quick pricing on labor and materials and decided the cost was a fractional increase, if any. And the minor alterations—losing a circuit here, increasing the strength of that one there—made so much sense. He sighed. Some people simply stuck loyally to what worked well enough. What was the old adage? "If it ain't broke, don't fix it"? Well, here was proof that sometimes what isn't broken *should* be fixed.

By morning, when the first shift arrived, he had reviewed all Nimi's little improvements, organized a schedule for their manufacture and insertion, and put out a call for Nimi's favorite mechanic. Hiska would be invaluable in constructing Nimi's improvements. She'd worked with Nimisha on the Fiver, and Caleb hoped she'd assist him now that he was in possession of Nimi's disks. He and Hiska would do the six boards of Nimisha's unique design. He could do them himself but Hiska was the professional and might, now, reveal what else Nimisha had kept up her sleeve. Might, Caleb amended wryly. Hiska was as much a law unto herself as Nimisha was. The two women, from socially opposite spheres, rarely needed to converse as they worked. In fact, one might hand the other a tool without a word spoken. Hiska tended to issue sounds rather than words, though Caleb had heard the mechanic chew out a subordinate in a fashion that would have made a tough petty officer blush with envy. A grunt or a monosyllable was often all she needed with Nimisha, though Nimi would add a please or thank-you as the occasion warranted.

Caleb shook his head, fatigued by the night's concentrations and grieving anew: This particular part of the Ship Yard was more bereft of Nimisha's presence than anywhere else in the Yard, even her executive office.

The door to the outer corridor opened and banged against the wall as Hiska came hurrying in, the lioness ready to protect her lair.

"Good morning, Hiska," he said as if delighted to see her despite the obvious anger that powered her steps as she strode across to the worktop.

Seeing the little stack of info-disks, she came to a total halt. Her eyes met his again, the most urgent question easily read.

"No, no word from Nimi, but Lady Cuiva felt I should have these now." He let the stack slip through his fingers and then straightened them into a neat column. "I don't think any of us want the second Fiver to go out less than her best."

Hiska growled and made the rest of the way to him in a less aggressive manner, her attention focused on the disks. She was a compact little woman with mousy hair cropped to her skull. Her round face had no lines whatsoever—not surprising, since she rarely exhibited emotions of any kind that would encourage wrinkles. Her grunts, snorts, humphs, ohs, and ahs did service for whatever she might be feeling. She had penetrating eyes deep-set under thick brows of the same mousy shade hair. Her hands were oddly much like Nimisha's, square palms with short, clever fingers and incredible strength when she put her body behind her grasp. Nimisha had taken her as her private mechanic years before on the advice of Jim Marroo, then Yard Manager, who had recognized an unusual aptitude in the silent person. There was no question of her dedication to Lady Nimisha and her almost zealous proprietary control of this machine shop.

"If we are to have the best possible chance of finding Lady Nimisha, we need this Fiver in the same condition as the one she went out in. Lady Cuiva gave me the disks yesterday afternoon. I didn't know she had them. I thought Lady Rezalla would have been the custodian," Caleb said bluntly. He was rewarded with as noncommittal a humph as he'd ever heard out of Hiska. "Next week Lady Cuiva's coming up to see how we're getting along. I'd like her to see the ship finished now that we have these." He gestured to the disks. "I'd like you to be especially on your guard,

Hiska, as we have information that suggests Lord Vestrin might be vindictive enough to try to harm Lady Cuiva. You spot any face you don't know, you report it immediately to Security!"

Hiska stared at him, her gaze intensifying with outrage, her eyes going so round that he wondered if they'd pop out of their sockets. Then her jaw muscles tightened and her hands became blunt fists, banging into her thighs. She inhaled deeply and then exhaled so fiercely that Caleb knew no one would get into this workshop or past Hiska to harm Lady Cuiva.

Having settled that problem, he handed across to the mechanic the clipboard with his listing of what needed to be completed.

"If you'd be willing to assist me in translating these specs, Hiska, I'll know there will be no errors in the finished designs."

With more courtesy than she'd ever accorded him before, she took the clipboard from him. She scanned it quickly and gave one emphatic nod. She returned the board to him and went to unlock Nimisha's supply closet. Nimisha would keep on hand supplies of any sort that she might need in her designs. Caleb doubted that there'd be any shortage of exactly what they'd need to make the spare parts or upgrade the boards.

"Need anything at the dispenser?" Caleb called as he went for a stimulant. He'd see how long he could keep up with Hiska before he took a rest. One needed clear eyes and steady hands for some of the delicate assemblies they were about to undertake. If he started to fumble, Hiska would insist on his taking a break.

They'd completed two of the six boards when he broke a delicate connection. Hiska drew her breath in a hiss of concern. Pursing her lips, she reached over and took the tool from his hand, jerking her head at the small office. Her invitation for him to rest needed no elaboration.

"Wake me in two hours," he said.

"Humph," was her answer, and he wondered if she would obey.

She didn't. He was asleep for four hours before she judged him sufficiently rested to continue. And she'd been right. She had completed one more board and several of the finicky alterations on parts she had brought in from the Fiver.

They finished, and installed, all the boards by the time fatigue again overtook Caleb. He slept aboard the ship while Hiska occupied the cot in Nimisha's office when the second shift quit.

CHAPTER 4

"Lady Nimisha?" said a familiar voice as the fog of sleep lifted from her mind. The medical couch was open and not so much as a whiff of the sleep gas remained.

"A full standard year has passed, ma'am," added Helm's tenor voice.

"And no response?"

"No, ma'am."

She felt the coolness of hyposprays penetrating both arms.

"Sit up slowly, Nimi, but I think you'll find you're in excellent shape after that nice long nap," Doc said.

"May I fix you something to eat, Lady Nimisha?" Cater asked.

Nimisha's stomach rumbled.

"Indeed you may," she said, following Doc's advice about movement. She was stiff with disuse. "Helm, plot a course to the nearest of the primaries with an M-type planet. I'm tired of hanging about in space. Let's see what mischief we can get into out there."

"I am programmed to remind you, Lady Nimisha," Helm said, sounding as close to repressive as the AI could get, "that we are constrained to avoid contact with emerging species. It is against FSP policy to interfere with normal evolution when the indigenous population has reached either toolmaking or settled agricultural base level."

"That is, *if* there is an indigenous *and* sapient population," she said with a grin.

"Yes, ma'am," was Helm's not at all contrite response.

Nimisha smiled as she collected the usual post-sleep liquid meal.

"This at least tastes appetizing, Cater. Thanks," she said after the first tentative sip. The gruel for the revived that was offered on naval ships was so bland it was difficult to swallow. That was another of her little improvements for long-distance traveling: savory comestibles.

"And, Helm," she added, "leave an update on that beacon to indicate our new destination."

"Already programmed, ma'am."

She shrugged. She really was almost superfluous.

"Estimated arrival time?" she asked.

"At Interstellar Speed Three, we will reach the heliopause in two days."

"So be it, Helm. We will decelerate and record all data on our way into the third planet. It *is* the third planet, isn't it?"

"Yes, ma'am."

"Standard almost, isn't it?" she murmured.

"Yes, ma'am."

Nimisha made a facial grimace. Oh, well, "yes" was more encouraging than another spate of "no's" from Helm.

She felt the thrum through the deck plates as the Fiver moved forward, gradually increasing speed sufficient to enter IS drive. She watched the stars in the view screen begin to blur, counted down to herself to the translation into the IS speed mode, and braced herself just as the Fiver slid forward. She had become inured to the insertion nausea but was still pleased when it passed as they settled into warp drive.

"Report on insertion and performance, please?" After all, this was still a trial run.

"All systems functioning at normal levels and efficiency."

That was certainly as it should be.

She opened her log and made the necessary entry. Helm would have kept the ship's log updated on a daily basis; she would have to update hers.

The fact that she now had a destination made all the difference to her morale. She felt alive, keen, wondering just what this world would be like. Of course, if there were any signs of civilization, she'd have to veer off. She could almost wish there were a society of some sort to visit. As the first Emissary of Federated Sentient Planets.

Damn. Had she put the universal translator on board? Yes, she must have. She remembered having Hiska install the unit. The woman had given her a shocked and surprised look. But she'd done it.

"Helm, is the universal translator activated?"

"Yes, ma'am. Shall I put it online?"

"No, but I'm glad it's there."

"Yes, ma'am."

"Always prepared for the unexpected, aren't you, Nimi?" Doc commented.

She gave him an ironic laugh. "Except for a wormhole, Doc."

"Well, yes, but you had cleared your course with the Fleet, and they had no records of a phenomenon in that sector, had they?"

"No, they didn't. It's mostly used for their navy maneuvers and testing since it's rather barren of stars and planets."

"Is that so?"

"It is!"

She was certain that there had been intensive searches for her while she had slept. Caleb Rustin, not to mention her mother and Cuiva, would never give up until they either heard the ship's death knell or found her. That was comforting, but she did want to make it back before Cuiva was Necklaced. She looked forward to that day: She'd be able to take her daughter more fully into her confidence and to examine Cuiva's natural aptitudes. No reason for the girl to be one of those gilded—or misshapen for fashion—dilettantes. Useless creatures. Her mother might have been traditional in every aspect of social behavior and a devil for propriety, but she had never been vapid, stupid, or shallow. Boynton women had always been achievers.

The system, which Nimisha whimsically named Primero, adding its coordinates within the present sphere of the galaxy, was so close to "normal" that it was exactly what any exploration team would give all left arms to encounter. There were ten planets, the coldest, outermost few were frozen; then there was another giant, and while there was no asteroid belt between the gas planet and the fourth, the third was in the proper astrophysical position for being close enough to its primary to be habitable. It had three moons, the largest farther out, with two inner ones seeming to chase each other. Must wreak havoc with the tidal system. She decided to call the third planet Erehwon, partly after an old dystopic novel she'd once read and partly because it was "nowhere" backward and that certainly was her present situation. She hovered by the large moon to do the usual basic investigative tests, sending down an exploratory probe and waiting for its reports.

No holes in the ozone layer, the usual mix of atmospheric gases, sufficient seas, and nine continents, three with archipelagoes reaching out like broken fingers to the larger landmasses. Helm, in the AI's science officer capacity, agreed that the planet looked to be eminently habitable.

"Let's orbit and see what else we can discover," Nimisha said, toggling the log to include that order. She'd had the usual space traveler's briefing from FSP about not infecting indigenous sapients with too abrupt a contact with a space-faring race and what to do if—by any remote chance—she met other space-farers. So far the universe seemed very full of sentient species incapable of ever attaining that freedom.

"Shorter day, I see," Nimisha mentioned as they completed one orbit. "And no sign of what we tend to term 'civilization' either."

"No, ma'am," Helm replied. "No artificial satellites. No pulses, no sonar or radar transmissions. Not even radio."

"Let's go in," she said.

The ship continued its inward spiral, quartering the planet's surface as it went. Daylight shone on a land teeming with small and large life-forms, jungles, forests, plains, and mountain ranges of considerable height and depth running like twisted spines suggesting their savage upthrust from basement rock materials. The nightside did not show any fires or the use of fossil fuels. The planet did have ore deposits that would certainly interest developers back in her native portion of the galaxy. That is, if they could establish that there were no sapient inhabitants. Further circling brought her over portions of the continents, Helm assiduously mapping, though Nimisha had turned off that screen. She tried viewing the surface at high magnification to be able to make out details, but it gave her a headache to see surface features speeding by that quickly. So she reduced the magnification and trusted Helm to call her attention to any anomalies. On the fourth lap, Helm spoke.

"Sensors read an unusual metallic mass on the plateau directly ahead."

Nimisha turned up the magnification, but they were too far out to determine what the anomaly was, other than something that perhaps ought not to be there.

"Mark it, Helm. Definitely needs to be seen."

On the seventh lap, another anomaly was discovered.

"Now that's ridiculous. We haven't seen so much as a band of humanoid nomads, but those two metallic blips are not indigenous to *this* planet. I'll bet my Necklace on it."

"Rash of you, dear Nimi," Doc said with an audible ripple in his voice.

"You know me, Doc," she agreed.

"Let's home in on the first anomaly, Helm. I think we've ascertained that this indigenous population is mainly composed of beasts, unlikely to be evolutionarily compromised by our presence."

"There is a third metallic anomaly, ma'am, and I am now reading a fourth."

"We'll have a dekko at those, too."

It was out of the bounds of possibility that *all* eighteen missing ships had landed on Erehwon, though that would have been a logical course of action, given its suitability for humans. This could be rather a fun adventure. Of course, the downside was that if *they* all had been stuck here—since they were still listed as missing—then she might be, too. Well, maybe some marooned male would be passable. Lady Rezalla would be furious when she learned of her daughter making any sort of an improper alliance. But celibate life was not a prospect Nimisha could contemplate with any joy!

As Helm obeyed her instructions and they cruised across the plateau to the first object of interest, the grazers didn't so much as raise their heads from their industrious eating. Great shaggy brown and black creatures, they moved steadily across the grassy savannah, heads swaying back and forth as they ate. She did notice that the young of this species were kept behind a formidable wall of their elders. So there were predators of some sort.

"We are closing, ma'am. Shall I magnify?" Helm asked.

"By all means." She gasped as the sharply defined image filled the screen. "Undeniably a spaceship," she said. "A match on our files?"

"A fair big mouthful for that wormhole to trap," Doc remarked.

Nimisha gave a bark of laughter. "Trap? That's a good description of a wormhole. Well, well. This ship's very old. Maybe we're number twenty, not nineteen. Can you decipher anything of the ship's original ID markings, Helm?"

"Wind, sun, and time have scoured the hull, which was badly damaged."

"In the wormhole?"

"That is a distinct possibility given the turbulence the Fiver experienced. The tube of the hole did not have a regular shape. It was difficult to avoid contact with the walls."

"Which proves the merit of having an AI at the helm, when femtosecond reactions are required," Nimisha said approvingly.

"Perhaps when we are closer, some traces will be legible enough to identify the craft," Helm said, unaffected by either praise or blame.

"An ID might give a clue as the frequency of the wormhole on the FSP side of it," Doc said.

"My very thought, Doc. But it's not very well designed, is it?" she commented, scanning the vessel. "Cumbersome, to say the least."

"No match, ma'am, on available files."

"That old?" asked Doc.

"Not disparaging the files of our Navy, are you, Doc?"

"Even their files do not contain some of the early independent efforts of humankind to probe space for habitable planets."

"That's true enough, Doc," Nimisha agreed, rubbing her chin and trying to figure out what sort of propulsion the ship used with that stern configuration, dented and mangled as it was. She shook her head and gave a sigh.

By now, they were closing with the object, and Helm automatically switched to normal screen.

The ship hadn't been landed with any great skill, for its prow had plowed a long furrow across the plateau to where a high ridge out-thrust from the foothills had finally halted its forward momentum. The furrow was clearly visible from the air, along with the heavy vegetation that had grown up in it. She could distinguish the bleached white skeletons of the giant grazers that had been bowled out of the way of this minor leviathan until it had come to a grinding halt.

"It's been there a long time," she murmured as they closed with the wreck. "How could anyone survive such a crash?"

"The ship was not designed for landing," Helm said. "It is also not equipped with either thrusters or vanes for atmospheric maneuvering."

"Any life signs?" asked Doc.

Nimisha laughed at such optimism. "Hardly, if such dense vegetation has grown up on the avenue it plowed. Probably from the First Diaspora. Imagine being brave enough to go into space in that sort of contraption," she added with some admiration. "Please land, Helm, near the center of the ship. I see some sort of airlock in its side."

She dressed in appropriate skintight protective gear for a first walkabout. As the air had tested pure, she didn't require a breathing apparatus. Pure enough to breathe, but slightly tainted with an unfamiliar smell, she thought as she stepped out of the Fiver and onto the thick grassoid surface covering. Three steps into it, she was glad of the impregnability of her suit, for the "grass" was sawtoothed and managed to leave scratches on the tough material. What digestive equipment those shaggy creatures must have to graze on this, she reflected. She took samples of the obvious varieties growing about her and had to use the vibro blade to sever the blades and stems.

She tripped over the first skeleton, partially hidden in the vegetation and by the remains of its apparel.

"Human skeleton, clad in exceedingly durable clothing," she reported to Helm.

"Bring me a swatch of the material and a bone and I'll do a forensic and carbon-date it," Doc suggested. The longest finger bone was added to her pouch, along with a piece of the material, now so old it tore like paper.

"They must have set up some sort of a camp," she said. There was a clearing of sorts, evidently made by melting the ground into a semi-glaze that defied the grassoid's attempts at succession. There were oddments of metal scattered about, poking up from the dirt that had blown over them. The larger items she unearthed were crushed as if the grazers had put their big clumsy feet on them.

"Analysis suggests this ship was of a design used in the First Diaspora, with chemical fuel engines of the type typical of that period for planetary landing and takeoff," Helm informed her. "I have been able to distinguish sufficient of the faded insignia on the bow to determine that it belonged to a federation known as the United Nations of Earth. We are the twentieth ship to come through the wormhole."

"Thank you for that update on our position, Helm," she said with gentle irony. She had not programmed any humor into Helm, but sometimes he was inadvertently funny. Then she looked at the timeworn spaceship. "Poor guys," she said, shaking her head.

Gaining entrance to the ship was not a problem. A ramp or steps of some kind must originally have been used, but the centuries had allowed a buildup of windblown dirt and debris that reached to the lower lip of the hatch. There were exterior controls where any sensible designer would have put them, and since she was an even more sophisticated designer, it took only moments to open the airlock. She climbed in. The inner lock stood open, and as she neared it, she heard some sort of ventilation system begin to circulate the air inside.

"Not bad," she said. "Some power remains."

"Solar panels have been detected," Helm said.

"Why would they use solar panels if this wasn't a landing type craft?"

"There were many attempts at achieving the optimum use of many power sources—chemical, nuclear fusion, and solar power, both from generator panels and light sails—on early spacecraft,"

Helm said in the pedantic tone he assumed for his "science officer" role.

"Well, they did that right."

Nevertheless, the air was stale and still had an acrid stink that
left a taste at the back of her throat of metals, old foodstuffs, human perspiration, and hydrocarbon hydraulic and lubricant fluids.

"One does have to air the place out every now and then," she
said in her best imitation of her womb-mother.

"Repeat?" Helm asked, mystified.

"Don't bother," Doc said. "I'll explain it to him."

She went forward to where she expected to find the bridge. And
did, though it was dark, since the forward screen had crashed right
into the rock of the hillside and was now shards on the deck. She
used her wrist light and found the appropriate toggle. She pushed it
and faint illumination resulted—enough to see that the bridge was
empty. She hadn't expected to see any bodies. The establishment
of some sort of a base camp indicated there had been crash survivors enough to have suitably interred their dead. The big question was if any had survived long enough to establish a colony.

She tried to access the bridge log, but evidently the small source
of power that circulated the air did not spark the computer systems
into action.

She toured the ship and its cramped crew quarters with bunks
stripped to the metal frames. Lockers had been emptied; dust had
sifted in through the vents over the centuries that the ship had lain
here. The galley, when she entered it, was also tidy, apart from
dust. Again all usable items had been taken. The same could be
said of any other transportable item or equipment that such a vessel would have carried. Well, if one were shipwrecked on an alien
planet, one would certainly use whatever equipment was on hand.
Only where had it—and its porters—gone? Would she find the descendants somewhere else? Had they regressed to a primitive state

in the meantime? Certainly she had seen neither fires nor fossil fuel smoke to indicate any human settlement . . . so far, that is. The climate of the plateau and its position on the continent made it part of a temperate zone. Considering the new growth she had noticed on trees and shrubs, she had landed in this planet's vernal period. Part of the shagginess of the grazers might be due to shedding winter fur.

Time after time, she had to shake her head at the clumsiness of design in the spaceship, the heaviness of the building materials.

"I shouldn't criticize. FSP didn't even have petralloy until two centuries ago," she remarked. "Easy for me to find their design attempts awkward and inefficient. They got this far with what they had. Give them credit."

"Most creditable," Helm agreed.

"Definitely first wave of the Diaspora," Doc said, having finished the analyses.

"Is this ship among the eighteen cited?" Nimisha asked.

"No, ma'am."

She checked all storage areas and found them empty. And dusty. An orderly withdrawal from the ship. But where to? She returned, striding in her own footprints in the dust, wondering if this would add to the mystery of the ship for future explorers. The whimsy made her grin.

She was glad to be outside in the fresher air. She closed the outer air lock to preserve what power remained. She might want to come back and investigate. There were other metallic anomalies to be examined. If there were actually four ships already marooned on this planet, had the groups joined forces? But if they had joined up, why had they not made use of even such basic requirements as fire, for heating, cooking, and lighting? And built shelters of some description? Or used caves? A rudimentary necessity, or at least a comfort. She had fireplaces in rooms that were heated by cheap and nonpolluting substances. She'd even had one at the Yard in her private office for those late night sessions with her subordinates. And tête-a-têtes with Caleb. Oh, dear, better not think of him, she thought in dismay.

She prowled around the rusting ship and found the little graveyard, sited in the churned up soil of the landing, above and to one side of the ship's resting place. Nine metal shafts were etched with the names of the dead: three women and six men. So it had been a mixed crew. The dates were four hundred years ago.

How many generations would that be? Nimisha wondered. If there had been any.

"What was the last registered disappearance that might have been a wormhole eating a ship, Helm?"

"Say again, ma'am?"

Helm liked his commands and queries crisp and uncluttered by personal opinion.

"What is the date the last ship disappeared?"

"Sixteen years ago, ma'am."

Well, that was much better than four hundred years, she thought, firmly banishing the sinking feeling of utter despair. She'd already slept away one of that sum.

"Is there any significant interval between disappearances?"

There was a definite pause as Helm worked on the answer. "A regular pattern cannot be established by the disappearances of ships."

"That could be accounted for," Doc put in, "by the fact that the disappearances themselves took time to be registered."

Even sixteen years—and then the problem of catching the wormhole as it opened at this end. But she'd miss so much of Cuiva . . . her darling daughter . . . She gave herself an admonitory shake.

"I've seen all I need to here," she told her ship. "I'm coming back aboard. Helm, please lay in a course for the second anomaly. We'll fly at a low enough altitude to see if we can spot any abandoned settlement these people may have built."

The second blip proved to be the *Poolbeg* FSPS 9K66E. It had landed circumspectly near a small stream. It, too, showed that it had had a rough passage through the wormhole, with gashes that in one place had damaged the hull integrity.

"She'd have had ten as crew, from the type she is," Nimisha said. "Any word on her?"

"She is listed as lost in space, ma'am, sixteen years ago."

"We know that. What other information have we on the *Poolbeg*? Can you get a response from the ship?"

"I have already been calling and received no answer. I am accessing the comunit. Shall I display the result?"

"Just the last entry now, please, Helm."

On her screen was the entry, dated fourteen standard years before.

This is Lieutenant Commander Jonagren Svangel, acting captain of the Poolbeg. *As we have sustained damage to our drive and cannot make the repairs required, we have voted to leave the ship to explore our immediate surroundings in the shuttle. We hope to make a base camp in the foothills . . .* a map was inserted, showing the projected goal *. . . and live off the land. Our botanist says there are enough nontoxic edibles to supply us with a fair diet and we have plenty of additives to supplement what we can gather or hunt. Some of the indigenous animals are ferocious, but they can be avoided. We will try to get back and update this log at regular intervals.*

"And didn't, poor wretches," Nimisha murmured.

"Shall I spool back, ma'am?"

"No, but copy to our files and for the material we're storing in the beacon."

"Did you intend a physical examination of the ship or its environs?" Helm asked.

"Yes, and break out sidearms for me. I want something that's powerful enough to stop 'ferocious indigenous animals' in their tracks. Obviously the captain of the *Poolbeg* met with a disaster," Nimisha said.

"How do you construe that?" Doc asked.

"Because an acting captain is making the entry," Nimisha said curtly, on her way to the airlock where she donned the heaviest of her coveralls and attached the repeller harness. "Besides which I can see two graves from here. They were down to eight crew when they left the *Poolbeg*." She slid the stunner on to its belt hook and completed her exit apparel with a full-face helmet that had a neck protector. She wouldn't be able to turn her head as easily, but the protection might prove a wise precaution.

She paused briefly by the grave sites, pointing the recorder at the markers. Then she stood at attention for a moment, hand on her heart to salute the Service dead. They had died on the same day, two weeks before Svangel's final log entry. She wondered where the others had met their ends, since no one had returned to the *Poolbeg* to make updates. She detoured slightly to get a sample of the water. The shallow stream burbled down a rocky channel. Winter runoff, if this were the spring of Erehwon's year? The water was cold and clear in the sample tube.

The *Poolbeg* had been left as shipshape and neat as the older vessel. It had not been stripped of quite as many of its fittings, nor had all the supplies been taken with the marooned. Sixteen years would reduce the supplies the Fiver carried to crumbs. And the *Poolbeg* was new enough that whatever it had dispensed by way of comestibles could be used by the Fiver's catering unit. However, she could come back when she needed more, if she couldn't find local substitutes.

In fact, since they hadn't taken the small captain's gig, she decided she'd use that for an aerial reconnaissance of their proposed base campsite. And so she informed Helm.

"It's got full power. Why waste mine when this is available?" she said in an unarguable reply to Helm's polite but negative response to her idea.

"I'll run basic checks on it, but initial readings indicate all systems are go. It's *designed*, you know," she added with some heat, "to remain in full working order for years, considering the distances exploratory ships have to go. I know the model. It's still in service and I've flown one. It is also supplied with missiles, which my skiff isn't." Another oversight on her part: that she hadn't thought to load her skiff's weaponry for the shakedown cruise. Then she added a final rebuttal. "Besides, if there *are* survivors, they'd recognize it and that would establish my bona fides."

On her way, she spotted examples of what anyone would call "ferocious animals." They were the size of trees, and even if someone had stunned one—as the dead captain may have—sheer momentum would have kept them moving forward. The largest one was close to ten meters from ground to undulating shoulder, or what she thought was a shoulder, since the creature did not have definite sections that could be easily labeled "legs" or "body" or "head" or "tail." It was a lump that moved by contracting and expanding its muscular frame along the ground. Nimisha wondered if it was as agile on uneven surfaces as it was on the more or less level one it was now traversing. The front part seemed to swoop down into the grassoid, raising to give her the sight of the appendages of some smaller creature disappearing from view. She didn't see a mouth, as such, or eyes, when the giant creatures raised up their front ends to investigate the gig. She increased her altitude to well above their full length. That they were aware of her presence could not be denied.

She had patched the gig's comunit into the Fiver's to allow Helm to make a record of her progress.

"Is there any chance that that life-form can spring from the ground?" Helm asked.

"I'm at one hundred meters. I doubt it. But I won't risk the possibility. This *is* a very alien world. They definitely know I'm above them. Whoops!"

Several wet and slimy looking ropelike objects were hurled at her from the two largest of those raised up from the ground. Neither made contact with the gig.

"Tongues?" Nimisha asked, more of herself than expecting an answer.

"There is nothing remotely similar to this life-form recorded in the *Xenobiological Encyclopedia*," Helm said "Rule out 'tongues,' since they have now detached from their primary source."

The thick strings fell back to sear the grassoid where they had fallen. Steam rose.

"*Whatever you do,*" Helm suddenly said, tone urgent, "do not shoot at them!"

"Not that I was going to, but do tell me why?" Nimisha asked.

"On reviewing the tapes, I have ascertained that the captain tried to use a projectile weapon and the segment that he hit dispersed into fragments. He was covered by the substance, which is extremely toxic, and died before anyone could assist him. Lieutenant Senior Grade Barbra Weleda tried to resuscitate him and the toxic . . . material . . . transferred itself to her body. According to the report, there wasn't much left of either to be buried in the graves you honored."

"I see," Nimisha said after swallowing against nausea. "I wonder that any of the crew has survived if this is the sort of welcoming committee they met." She flipped on the toggle for the sensors, setting one to find metals and another to locate the polymers used when the *Poolbeg* was built. "We'll just see. I'm following their proposed route. They would have been wary of these . . . slime slugs."

"An earlier entry by the acting captain indicates that they used the shuttle to make an aerial reconnaissance of considerable depth before they departed to establish a base," Helm said.

"They hadn't run out of intelligence, just good luck," she said as she aimed the gig at a narrow gap in the foothills. She left behind the feeding territory of the slime slugs for a winding hilly pass that was strewn with boulders and such debris that slugs could not have writhed through. "Seismic activity?" she asked Helm.

"It does not appear to be a very old world, and seismic activity has been noted in the archipelagoes. That debris, however, is more consistent with land or mudslides."

"Yes, I think I would agree," she said, looking from one of the steep sides to the other and judging the deposits on the floor of the pass. "No vegetation to attract the hungry. Or bind soil with its root systems." And the rocky path kept those slugs from getting through.

She came out of the pass—there were thirteen bends in all—into hilly country, the valleys dotted with many lakes as far as she could see in either direction.

"Definitely glacial formations," Helm said, echoing her own thoughts.

"I agree. Rather pretty," she said and then saw more of the big buffalo types grazing. There were other species as well, smaller, and each kept their distance from the other as they ate.

"Overfly one of the lakes, would you please, ma'am? I'd like a reading on any aquatic life."

"I should get a sample of the water, too. I'd love to take a full bath," Nimisha said. "The stream by the *Poolbeg* isn't deep enough."

"*When* I have checked the denizens of the desired bathing place," Helm said sternly.

"Of course, Helm."

So she hovered over the nearest of the lakes, a brilliant blue reflecting the clear skies above, and sent down a sample tube. She could perceive flowing figures in the water. While the explored galaxy had provided many, many different forms on land, water dwellers seemed to follow basic designs: the bottom feeders, the middle swimmers, and the upper-level insect catchers.

"Bottoms out at thirty meters, along a crest. The shallows support reed and water grasses," Nimisha said. "I'm testing the water." The results followed on her words. "Well, definitely drinkable, with only trace minerals and nothing toxic. I shan't, however, go fishing quite yet."

"Nor bathing," Helm added repressively.

"That's right."

"*Alert!*" Helm's voice reverberated through the speakers in the cabin.

"Whatever for?"

"To your port and high up, a flying object of considerable size."

Nimisha swung the bow of the gig accordingly. "Considerable size," she agreed drily; indeed, it was probably larger than the gig. She reached the toggle to arm the forward missiles.

"It has seen you and is diving," Helm warned. "I am too far away to be of assistance."

"Good thing I took the *Poolbeg*'s gig then, isn't it?" she said, gaining altitude and setting her sensors to magnify the oncoming menace. " 'Ods blood!" she exclaimed, an archaic epithet that one of her more effete acquaintances had resurrected and used for many occasions. "It's twice my size."

"More than twice, ma'am. My advice is to fire now."

"It's better to wait until I can see the whites of its eyes. If it has any."

The gig answered her touch on its control plates with more height and speed. The distance closed between predator and intended victim—she didn't think anything with a head that crammed with teeth and already salivating at the thought of a tasty morsel half its size had friendly intentions. She bracketed her target and sent off two clusters of missiles: one at the blunt skull of the massive avian, and a second to take off one wing. Its body was long and narrow and not a good target yet. If she missed killing it, she had a chance to veer off and come up under to get the belly—if that should happen to be its vulnerable spot.

The first cluster took off the head; the second sheared the left wing, and pieces of the creature rained down to the ground, some of the carcass landing partially in one of the larger lakes. She definitely deserved her rating as crack marksperson, she mused. As she passed over it, the corpse was slightly twitching. She swung around for a second, closer look.

"Zounds!" she exclaimed, swallowing.

"That is phenomenal," Doc remarked, evidently accessing her screens.

"I'm beginning to think that the *Poolbeg's* crew might have succumbed, too, if this is what they had to contend with," she said ruefully as she watched the amazing amount and variety of scavengers that swarmed over the dead flier. They oozed out of the lake and from holes in the hillside; using many varying kinds of propulsion from feet to flippers to a smaller variety of the slime slug mobility, they began to feed. "Recording, Helm? We'll need to register as many types as possible. All of them carnivorous."

"Omnivorous might be the more exact classification," Doc remarked.

She turned away from the gorging, rippling mass beneath her and aimed for the foothills.

"If you don't hurry, you'll be late for the party," she said as she saw still more creatures gathering to partake of the feast. Did Erehwon give life to anything that wasn't dangerous? What would have happened to her if she had taken a swim in the first of the tempting blue lakes? She shuddered. She would get enough water from the stream by the *Poolbeg* to bathe in safety in the Fiver.

. .

It was sunset on Erehwon when she reached the point indicated on the map as the *Poolbeg*'s base.

They had chosen well: high up on an isolated plateau, backed against a precipice down which fell a graceful cataract, so they'd had fresh water in easy reach. They had even started to build dwellings out of rock. There was no sign of the larger shuttle they'd used to transport themselves. No sign of discarded equipment either. She landed the gig as close as she could to the half-finished dwellings. No, correction: The shelters had been finished. The roofs had collapsed inward. Could the avian she had just dispatched, or more of its kind, have dive-bombed the houses? She found no corpses, but she did find pots and eating utensils in one, messed up with the debris of the roof. She found scatterings of other possessions and a graveyard containing five larger and six smaller graves. She could see where markers had been hammered in, but no inscriptions remained. As she stood in the evening wind, watching Erehwon's sun go down, she rather thought that winter winds could have blown away anything short of a stone slab. Had the winds blown in the roofs? Had the camp been untenable in the winter season? They would have had the weapons to defend themselves against aerial dive-bombers. Or had such forays continued until their weapons had been emptied? Where had they gone?

"It is respectfully recommended that you return to the Fiver, ma'am," Helm said after a longish pause.

"I think you're absolutely right. I'll be with you shortly."

And she was, dead tired, and quite ready to eat seconds of the delicious meal Cater prepared for her.

"May I respectfully request that further aerial reconnaissance be done by the Fiver? The bow is equipped with asteroid defense missiles," Helm said the next morning as she entered the bridge in full protective gear.

"A good notion. I can follow in the gig. It's already been exceedingly useful so far, and I don't think it will fit on the Fiver even if I were to remove the skiff."

The small skiff, suitable for either planetary use or short hops to a space station or between ships, would have to be abandoned in order to shoehorn the gig into the garage space. She didn't wish to lose any equipment even if the skiff was unarmed and possibly too frail to withstand an attack by the aerial menaces Erehwon had spawned.

"I recommend a high-altitude search, ma'am."

"I concur," she said. "Patch it into the gig." She hoisted the supplies she had collected—food, water, and some heavier weapons—and exited the Fiver to the gig.

At three thousand meters, they leveled off and retraced her flight to the ruined base camp. She paused briefly at the lake, magnifying the site where the avian had fallen. There wasn't a shred left to show her kill. This was a hungry world, as well as omnivorous. When they reached the base camp, they hovered to take aerial records of the deserted buildings.

"If I were being attacked from under and over, I'd go somewhere no one could reach me," she said. "Let's continue to the mountain range. There may be caves that are suitable."

Humankind started off in caves, and they were still useful natural refuges on many worlds. Especially when colonists were starting off with only elementary tools with which to create new homes and societies. She had no idea what sort of equipment an exploratory vessel carried as standard supplies. They crossed another high plateau to the rough-toothed crags of the mountain range.

"Metallic object to starboard, ma'am," Helm told her as they traversed another deep valley. This one was covered with vegetation that resembled the Terran-type forests planted on Vega III, varietals that had adapted to slightly different soils. A robust river followed the course of least resistance toward a distant sea, foaming over rapids and flowing into pools that did not tempt her to bathe in them—just yet.

The shuttle was visible on the ground. And suddenly a flare lanced into the sky.

"Someone's alive," Nimisha said with a tremendous feeling of relief.

"Three . . . no, four humans, one young," Helm confirmed.

"I think that river meadow will accommodate both of us," Nimisha said. "I'll go in first and explain why I've purloined their gig."

"I doubt they'll mind," Doc said. "I'll want to check them over as soon as possible. This world breeds a lot of peculiar things."

"It does indeed," Nimisha heartily agreed. As she swung down and circled to land, she saw that the roof of the shuttle was scarred and dented. She wondered which denizens had been able to leave combat marks on a petralloy hull.

Two men, one of them with the child in his arms, and one woman came racing to the edge of the meadow, shielding their eyes from the glare of the sun. They wore uniforms and coverings of what must be local fur hides. The temperature outside registered as twelve degrees Celsius . . . cool. The woman wore a long tunic of the most beautiful gray-blue fur. The child was dressed in leather with a fur coat.

"Ma'am, are we glad to see you!" cried the man who reached her first. The other was encumbered with the child and the woman had a noticeable limp. All three were grinning from ear to ear. The child burrowed its head into the man's neck, suddenly shy in the presence of an unknown person.

"Jonagren Svangel, ma'am," said the man in the lead, reaching out his hand to grasp hers. "Lieutenant Commander and acting captain of the *Poolbeg*."

"Well done, Commander . . ." she started to say and then saw the ineffable sadness in his face. She was filled with an unexpected desire to see that sadness dispelled.

"There're only the three of us left—and Tim, of course," he said as the others arrived. "This is jig Casper Ontell and Ensign Syrona Lester-Pitt."

They shook hands amid a babble of greetings until Jonagren held up his hand. "You're not the rescue party, are you?" he said, his tanned and weather-beaten face losing the exultation of being found.

"No, in fact, I'm trapped, too," she said. "I'm Nimisha Boynton-Rondymense. I was doing a shakedown cruise on my ship, there, when it was captured by that damned wormhole. Come, the Fiver's landing and I'm sure you'd like a change from whatever rations you might have left."

"We've been pretty much living off what we could find," Casper said, spreading an arm in the direction of the meadow, river, and forest behind them. "Not everything is toxic." He grimaced.

"Just most," Syrona said shyly.

"I've a medical unit, Syrona," Nimisha said, leading the way to where the Fiver had touched down as delicately as a fashionable lady not wishing to sully her footwear on soil.

"How many in your crew? Were you able to launch a beacon back through the wormhole?" Jonagren asked eagerly.

"As I said, I was doing a trial run on my ship . . ."

All three adults stopped as they took in the sleek lines of the Fiver and her scratched hull.

"No, I didn't escape entirely without some damage," she said, seeing them focus on the scrapes. "But nothing that breached hull integrity."

"You were lucky," Jonagren said ruefully.

"I've no other crew aboard. I use AI's for Helm, Doc, and Cater," Nimisha went on and wondered at Jonagren's intense look of disappointment. She noticed that it was Casper, still holding the child, who took Syrona's arm to assist her up the ramp.

"Permission to come aboard," Jonagren said at the hatch in the traditional request. His eyes glinted with just a hint of humor. A very likable man, was this Jonagren Svangel, Nimisha decided.

"Permission most certainly granted," Helm said, startling all four newcomers.

"Oh!" There was a very professional gleam in Jonagren's eye.

"Any business for me?" Doc asked.

"May I offer you refreshment?" was Cater's query.

"Syrona, would you like to go first?" Nimisha offered, gesturing toward the medical unit.

"No, Timmy first," she said anxiously. "I've been so worried he's not getting a balanced-enough diet."

Timmy had other ideas, screaming with fright at being placed on the strange surface. An extendible snuck up behind him and administered a mild sedative and, when he had calmed down, he permitted himself to be laid supine on the couch. His eyelids drooped and his frantic breathing eased.

Once the boy was settled, Nimisha gestured for the men to go to the dispenser while she asked Syrona what she'd like to drink.

"Oh, anything with caffeine and restoratives in it," Syrona said, a tired smile on her face. "Timmy doesn't sleep well, and I'm pregnant again."

A deep sadness in her eyes suggested to Nimisha that she had lost more than she had birthed. That would account for some of the small graves at the ruined base camp. When Nimisha brought Syrona's drink to the medical unit, Timmy looked to be fast asleep, his head angled to one side, hands lax and open at his sides while his mother watched. Syrona drank absently as she observed the visible reports the medical unit was processing.

"He's a bit underweight, Ensign Lester-Pitt," Doc said at his most reassuring. "A course of vitamins and trace minerals this planet doesn't seem to provide will fix up the deficits. You, ma'am, are far more in need of my assistance."

"How do you know my name?" Syrona asked in surprise.

"The AI's are patched into my system," Nimisha said, touching the comunit on her belt.

"Oh!"

A quiet beep indicated the end of Timmy's medical.

"I'll show you where you can put him," Nimisha said. Syrona stood to pick up the boy.

"I'll do that," Casper said, rising from the table and wiping his mouth with one hand. "You let the doc see to you, Syrie."

Nimisha led the way to the accommodations, and Casper whistled with soft appreciation at the amenities.

"I did design it with long-distance travel in mind," she said.

"*You* designed it, Lady Nimisha?"

"Let's dispense with titles, Casper," she said in mock-sternness. "We're all the same rank—castaway." She reached over the built-in worktop and flipped on the toggle that would allow them to hear Timmy should he wake. His father deposited him on the bunk and covered him tenderly with the thermal blanket, his fingers rubbing the soft, light fabric.

"He's the only one to survive," Casper said once they had gained the passageway. "Syrie's pregnant again."

"Well, Doc will doubtless report it."

"She keeps losing them. So did Jesse and Peri. They . . . died. We couldn't stop the bleeding."

"What happened to the rest of the crew? The ship records indicated eight of you left."

Casper made a bleak sound. "Encounters with the unfriendly natives."

"Are there any other kind?" Nimisha stopped and he nearly ran into her.

"Creatures. Nothing with any true sentience that we've found if, by 'sentience,' you mean capable of rationalization and learning.

We had to give up exploring," he said. His eyes went immediately to the medical unit, but it was now covered and the mist obscured Syrona's form.

"I'm doing a full diagnostic on her," Doc said in a low voice. "She is pregnant. With proper additives and rest, she has every chance of bearing a live child. The leg bone can be repaired, of course. And I'm doing some other minor repairs while she's under anesthesia. Nothing too bizarre, although I'll know more when the lab reports are done. I estimate she'll be with me for another two hours. Then I'll tend to you two."

"Chatty type, isn't he?" Jonagren commented with a grin. He had several plates of food before him, obviously favorites, and was talking with his mouth full.

"Old family medical man," Nimisha said after ordering a meal from Cater and bringing it back to the table to join the two men. "His bedside manner is marvelous, and his voice is reassuring all by itself."

Casper, with an apologetic nod to her, went back for more food.

"We're probably all just anemic and full of intestinal parasites," Jonagren said. "Not much of a challenge to a high-class medic."

"I live to serve," Doc remarked.

Jonagren looked at Nimisha in surprise.

"Helm and Doc are programmed for independent conversation. Cater prefers to stuff you."

"Glad to let her," Casper and Jonagren replied in chorus, grinning at each other.

"Do not be too greedy, gentlemen. Your stomachs are unaccustomed to very rich foods," Doc said.

"They aren't going viand-wild," Nimisha said, noting that the men had chosen high protein and complex carbohydrates as well as salad greens.

"I asked my stomach what it wanted," Jonagren said, showing

an unexpected touch of whimsy, "not my taste buds. We've done pretty well, thanks to the bio unit in the shuttle, and no one got poisoned . . ." His face went bleak.

"Don't blame yourself, Commander," Doc said. "From what we've already seen of the denizens of this planet, you did well enough to bring the four of you through the last sixteen years."

"He did, Lady Nimisha," Casper said firmly. "The first duty of an officer on a hostile planet is to survive."

Jonagren gave him a queer look.

"Well, it was as much up to . . . them . . . as it was to you . . . to see that they did," Casper said, obviously referring to an ongoing argument. "You couldn't be everywhere every minute." He turned to Nimisha. "We lost three crew people when the avians attacked us early one morning our first winter at the base camp. We'd rigged a scanner to warn us, but they came in swarms. Those of us who could made it to the shuttle. The roofs caving in got Morissa's baby and shattered her rib cage. Pluny was poisoned by some crawlie when he was fishing. Raez got trapped by a zonker."

"A zonker?"

"One of the nastier pieces of work this planet evolved," Jonagren said, pushing back his plate and wiping his mouth. "Sneaky thing, has lairs in the forest in some of what we took to calling Zonk trees. It also lies along branches and tries to snag unwary creatures. Powerful thing for all it's not very large. But it makes up for its size with its craftiness. Once what it uses for arms traps something, the kindest thing to do is kill it. We got out of there as fast as we could . . ." He shrugged, his face falling once again in sad lines that were graven on his face.

Sixteen years he'd been here, Nimisha thought, and estimated that he couldn't have been much more than thirty when they'd been marooned. He didn't look mid-forties when he stopped thinking guilty or sad. Fleet exploratory teams were given longev treatments, as well as implants. The women must have removed their implants in order to perpetuate their numbers on this wretched planet. Brave of them, actually, Nimisha thought.

"Now that you've eaten, would you gentlemen care to freshen up? I even have new clothing, if you'd like a change."

"Too right," Casper said with a wide grin, plucking a fold of his almost-threadbare garment away from his body. "We used up all we had in stock and are experimenting with leather pants." He scrubbed his head, looking rueful. "Some hides just don't tan."

"Some hides I wouldn't wear if I had to go naked," Jonagren added as Casper eagerly rose.

"There are empty cabins down both companionways. Take your pick," Nimisha said.

"I really should formulate a report, Nimisha," Jonagren said, looking over at the bridge.

"It's kept this long, Captain," she said, touching his hand, "and you'll feel better after a cleanup."

She was too polite to say that they badly needed cleaning-up; once in the warmth of the Fiver, a ripe odor had begun to emanate from their persons.

"We *need* to be clean," Casper said, pausing at the corridor. "We stink! Sorry, ma'am."

"Just dial your size from the cabin clothing dispenser," she said. Casper hesitated, looking over his shoulder at the cabin where he had deposited his son. "I'll listen for him."

"Thank you, ma'am."

As soon as both had left and she'd heard the cabin doors slide shut, she programmed the air refresher for a rapid recirculation. The pong was rather obvious, mixed with noxious smells that made her nose itch.

"Nothing dangerous in the smells," Doc said.

"How's Syrona doing?"

"She's tougher than she looks. But she's badly undernourished. Nothing that can't be fixed. Like the left tibia." Doc sounded professionally smug. "Three months pregnant with a female child. Good genes. Did some judicious tinkering to restore the pH factor and administered a rich IV."

Half an hour later, Helm announced that both men appeared to be resting in their cabins.

"Resting?" Nimisha asked. Jonagren had wanted to start his report, not take a nap, as soon as he had bathed and dressed.

"A little something I asked Cater to add to the last helpings they had," Doc said. "They need the rest more than they need to report or be reminded of those crewmates who died."

"I'll just take a turn round their camp."

"That's inadvisable, ma'am," Helm said instantly. "You heard the list of the dangerous creatures, some of which you might not recognize. I would await the escort of one of the survivors."

"Then let's test the river water and do other tasks that don't put me in any danger whatever," Nimisha said somewhat acidly, although she knew Helm's remark was sensible. Crawlies and zonkers and murderous avians and slime-throwing slugs. "I promised to listen for Timmy, too."

Using the scanners, she was able to get a look at their campsite. It was well laid out. She could see spy-eyes in the trees at the edge of the meadow. There was a newly seeded garden plot; the shimmering that surrounded it suggested they'd used a repeller field to keep it from being invaded. They probably had dug the garden out first, laying the repeller field under as well as around and over the garden. She noticed the solar panels mounted to provide power for the shuttle. She also saw the ladder leading to a cave in the cliff side. A hoist had been rigged at one side, to bring up supplies. She saw piping that indicated they must have running water in both the cave and the shuttle. They had done well with what they had. They had probably turned off such unessential power users as their comunit so that they hadn't heard the Fiver's initial call broadcast. Only sensible since they had given up hope of any rescue. Though they'd been quick enough with a flare when they'd heard the incoming aircraft.

"Helm, did you access data profiles from the *Poolbeg* on these three survivors?"

"Yes, ma'am," and the small data screen on the pilot's control panel lit up.

Lt. Commander Jonagren Svangel, the current captain, was forty-four years old. Right now he was lean and obviously fit. His face had acquired lines from sixteen years of stressful responsibility, not usually seen when longevity treatments keep a face youthful looking. While nowhere near the masculine beauty of Lord Rhidian, or Caleb Rustin's more rugged looks, he was definitely attractive. He had exhibited a ready sense of humor. His records said that he had joined Exploratory after two exemplary tours on the cruisers and a commendation for his quick response during an onboard accident that might have left more dead without his leadership. He had study credits for biology and xenobiology, and had passed in the top percentile the survival courses required by the Exploratory Arm of the Fleet. He came from a Fleet family whose members invariably reached captain's rank during their careers.

Lieutenant Junior Grade Casper Ontell was forty-six, also a career naval man from the Bodem system. This was his second tour of duty with Exploratory. He, too, had taken study credits for botany and chemistry, and had done very well in the required survival courses.

Ensign Syrona Lester-Pitt, now thirty-six, was from Demeathorn Blue City and, before she had joined the Fleet, had major Kill credits of some of the worst predators that hunting planet produced. She had been communications officer, and had taken advanced medic courses.

"Wonder if she knows anything about the coelura," Nimisha murmured. One of Lady Rezalla's few unfulfilled desires was to own a coelura spin. She and hundreds of other First Family women! The ultimate in a natural fabric that molded itself to its owner's body and could alter shape, color, and form at its wearer's discretion. Coelura spins were severely limited by the Cavernii, who had developed a way to keep the gullible avians from being spun to death with demands for their "weavings." At one time, the coelura had been close to extinction. The little avians, far more compliant than anything on Erehwon, were limited now to two spins a year, one for profit, and one to make a nest for their offspring. Their numbers were increasing, but a coelura spin was costly and the waiting list for available spins very, very long.

Nimisha whiled away the time her guests were asleep by inserting into the record what they had told her about the deaths of crew members. She'd learn about the occupants of the smaller graves later. That Svangel still keenly felt that he ought to have been able to protect his crew did him no disservice. Survival courses were useful, but none of them could catalog all the disasters that could befall a team on an alien planet, especially a team that had no escape. FSP Navy exploration issued parameters to their teams, indicating what "normal" hazards could be overcome on a suitable M-world. If the team found more dangers than a well-equipped colony could deal with, they could indicate that the planet wasn't worth the effort. This would be one she thought she'd put on that list. Unless, of course, all these ferocious types were limited to this continent. That didn't seem likely. She wondered if the team had had time to investigate the other landmasses. Certainly they had early realized that they were stuck in this quadrant and chances of rescue were slim.

While the *Poolbeg* would never take off from Erehwon, now that there was the Fiver, the other two habitable planets could be explored to see if one was less dangerous.

There were also two more metallic anomalies to be investigated here. Maybe the cycle of the wormhole was shorter than fifteen years. Maybe some other unwary ship, not yet considered missing, had also been spat out in this sector. That might give a larger genetic pool to the survivors. Nimisha felt her spine twitch. With Syrona already producing children, obviously they had considered procreation one method of surviving—even if this generation was never rescued. For herself, she hadn't anticipated having more offspring . . . Oh, dear, dear Cuiva . . . there would never be another as wonderful as her anywhere in the galaxy!

CHAPTER 5

The two men woke almost simultaneously and appeared, dressed in new clothing and obviously refreshed. As soon as she had heard the faint sounds of activity in their cabins, Nimisha asked Cater to produce a snack for them. Cater, having seen what their appetites were like, produced several platters of sandwiches, bowls of fruit, pitchers of juice, and a thermal carafe of coffee.

"We ran out of coffee too soon," Casper said, inhaling deeply, a broad smile on his face when he saw the carafe and smelled the brew. "Timmy's still sacked out. His color's better, too."

"I would have expected that," Doc replied though Casper hadn't addressed the medical unit directly. The man looked surprised by the spontaneous answer. "Syrona is progressing nicely but, since she's in here, I took the advantage of doing a little more repair. Analysis only confirmed what was obviously lacking in diet and you'll find her much improved when I log her out, Casper."

"Yes, well, thanks, Doc," Casper said with a nervous grin.

"You'll get used to them," Nimisha said with a little laugh. "I forgot their participation might be a surprise to you. Join me. I was just about to have a snack."

Casper cocked an eye at her. "If that's what you call a snack, I'd hate to have to plow through a feast."

"Oh, I'm sure you'd manage fine."

Jonagren had lost some of the more obvious signs of tension with the rest and shower. He really could use a bit more weight on his bones, thought Nimisha. Maybe his face would fill out, too, taking away some of those rawboned planes. Abruptly she decided that no, she liked his face the way it was—full of character. Some of the lines around his mouth and eyes were laugh lines. The ship suit was the right length for his body, but he looked gaunt in the standard sizing.

"What a relief not to have to forage for a meal," he said, rubbing his hands together before he settled at the table. He also commented on the coffee. "That's the best treat of all," he said and poured a cup for himself before Nimisha could. He held it up to his nose and inhaled the wonderful aroma.

He had a nice smile, which echoed in his eyes as he made contact with hers over the rim of his cup. He took a long pull and allowed himself a sigh of deep satisfaction before reaching for the nearest sandwich.

"Lettuce?" he exclaimed in amazement.

"We have some in the lower deck hydro-garden," she said. "I'll have to plant more, since I wasn't expecting company."

"There are edible greens here, but it's not the season for the best ones yet," Casper said, reaching for his second sandwich and licking his lips of the crumbs left over from the first.

"Did you by any chance explore the other two M-type planets in this area?" Nimisha asked.

With their mouths full, both men shook their heads.

"Not with . . . the damage . . . we sustained reaming our way through that wormhole," Jonagren said, managing to speak through his food. He looked down at the sandwich he held as if remembering it wasn't the best of good manners to talk while chewing.

"Go ahead," Nimisha said. "I don't mind if you talk around it."

"We couldn't fix it short of a Fleet facility," Jonagren said. "And the exterior nodes were sheared off. Pluny tried to jury-rig some sort of receptor, but we'd been knocked about a good deal in the passage. That's why we didn't even get off a beacon when we were dragged in. Might have saved you a few problems if there'd been one."

"On the other hand, I wouldn't be here now, would I? It's usually the Navy that rescues us civilians, isn't it, not the other way round." She smiled at the two men, focusing her eyes longer on Jonagren, wanting in some way to let him know that his burden was now being shared.

"While it certainly is a treat to see a fresh face—and a beautiful one," Jonagren said, unexpectedly dealing her a compliment as easily as Rhidian could, "*with* a fine ship to give us more mobility in any future plans, we would just as soon not have wished anyone else to be stuck here with us."

Nimisha was delighted to hear him sounding more cheerful. Good food, rest, and "a fresh face" seemed to have improved his morale considerably. "Did you notice the other three metallic anomalies?"

"Yes, we were able to get a good look at that ancient heap on our fly-by. By then we realized our first landing of the *Poolbeg* would be her last stop. Pluny jury-rigged exterior comunits. Captain Querine hoped we might salvage something from one of the other two and the plan was to use the shuttle to have a look." He sighed and once again the lines of stress were prominent in his expressive face. "Plans change."

"So you don't know if those ships had any survivors?"

"We saw them on our way in and detected nothing," Casper said. "Not that that means anything. They could have holed up somewhere away from the ferocious stuff."

"Well, I've those two sites next on my list. So you couldn't have gone on to the other two M-types even had you wanted to?"

Both men shook their heads, Jonagren evidently regretting it more than Casper did.

"Well, then, we've things to do and plans to make," she said, trying not to sound too fatuous. "I did manage to get a beacon out, hopefully well beyond the reach of the wormhole. I have placed another at the point we came into this space. It's a standard omni-directional FTL model. How long the pulses will take to reach a destination, or even make contact, is debatable. I've been updating the beacon this side. It'll be stripped once contact *is* made, so you might want to send a report for it to pass on. You're no longer missing."

"But *you*," Jonagren put in with unexpected whimsy, "are."

"You did say that you were designing this as a long-range vessel," Casper began.

"Not quite *this* long-range," Nimisha replied with a grin.

"The Rondymense Ship Yard has done a lot with the Fleet designers," Casper continued, warming to his theme, "so is it possible they'd be *very* keen to recover this one?" He looked around him, enviously. "It's stars above anything Exploratory has ever offered scouts."

Nimisha nodded, pleased at his perspicacity. Jonagren's eyes were sparkling again.

"They shall leave no turn unstoned," she said, "to find it."

"That—and your appearance, ma'am—are the best news we've had in almost two decades!"

"The only news we've had," Casper added.

The two men had worked their way through most of the sandwiches while she had consumed one.

"I'll just get more coffee," she said, rising, just as they all heard a wail of fright, muted by a partially closed door.

"It's all right, Timmy. I'm coming," Casper called. In his haste, he knocked over his chair, then hesitated, unsure whether to pick it up or get to the boy to comfort him.

Jonagren gestured for him to go and picked up the chair.

"There have been several babies who didn't survive?" she asked Jonagren in a low voice.

He shook his head. "Miscarriages, two stillborn, for Jesse. Peri's girl lived only a week. None of us has the expertise to do an autopsy—even if we'd wanted to—and we weren't able to get back to the ship. A fever took their first when he was ten months old, and weird allergies and an accident took the other surviving toddlers even though we guarded them night and day. Timmy's nearly a miracle for us. Maybe we should have started having kids earlier, when we were all healthier. I don't know." He gave a shrug.

"Cater, please prepare something appetizing for a—" Nimisha paused, looking at Jonagren to supply Timmy's age.

"Six-year-old," Doc said, as if he had been waiting for a chance to get a word in. "Preferably high protein and complex carbohydrates made to look like his favorite food?" Now Doc waited for Jonagren to speak.

The commander grinned as he shook his head slowly from side to side. "He'll eat anything that doesn't eat him first. I'd say that's why he's still alive: an iron digestive system."

"Oh, it'll be so nice to cater for a child," Cater replied with a lilt in her voice. A plate appeared on the dispenser with a glass of white liquid. "Is he familiar with milk?"

"Excellent food for a growing child," Doc said. "Good idea, Cater."

"Thank you, sir," Cater replied demurely.

"Does she lower her eyes and blush, too?" Jonagren asked in a muted tone.

"Sure sounds like it," Nimisha said. She collected the food just as Casper entered, leading the boy by the hand.

Timmy looked much refreshed and subtly healthier. He saw the glass and pointed.

"You have milk?" His eyes were wide in his tanned face. "Syrie, Casper, and Jon keep telling me about it, but I've never had any but hers when I was a baby."

He took a sip and tasted it going down, making his swallow audible to the adults watching. Then a big smile crossed his face and there was a definite resemblance to Jonagren, not Casper. So, Nimisha wondered who was Syrona pregnant by this time? Casper seemed so attentive and loving that she'd originally assumed that Casper and Syrona were partnered. Well, they had said there had been other children: doubtless they had done what they could to provide a larger gene pool, even if disaster, fever, and miscarriages had ruined their attempt.

"That's good!" Timmy exclaimed, not quite catching the entire milk mustache on his upper lip.

"Try the sandwich, Tim," Jonagren said. "The kind of bread we haven't been able to make here." He turned to Nimisha. "We got a wild yeast and we did find a wheat-type grain cereal and ground it to flour consistency. But the bread had a tough texture. Hard to chew."

"The crackers turned out well," Casper said, winking at Jonagren before he turned to Nimisha with mischief in his face. "He likes cooking."

"And damned lucky I knew how," Jonagren said with a sharp nod of his head.

"You all had survival training," Nimisha said, quite aware of the fact that she had only a modicum.

"Yes, but Jon turned out to have a gift for making"—Casper wrinkled his nose—"what edibles we tested safe taste pretty good."

"The trick was tenderizing the flesh—"

"He'd beat it for hours."

"—and then use the herb-types we found to take away its natural taste."

Jonagren leaned back in his chair, extending his legs and assuming a very relaxed pose. That he and Casper were able to joke about the shifts they had been reduced to was admirable in both men. She hoped that Syrona would prove as compatible. When she had a chance again, she'd see if Helm couldn't access their psych profiles and see just what she should watch for and avoid. So often in long-term forced relationships little petty matters assumed an importance out of proportion.

"How's that sandwich, Tim?" Nimisha asked into the easy pause that followed that exchange.

"Best thing I've ever eaten," he said with a charm all his own. "May I have another when I've finished this one?"

"You certainly may, or you can ask Cater to prepare—" Nimisha paused, realizing that Timmy had little experience with "normal" foods. "—a burger," she finished hastily. "I used to adore them when I was your age."

"On a bun, please, with what d'you call it . . . the red sauce . . ." Casper said, waving one hand as if to drag the lost word out of the air.

"Ketchup," said Cater, who could respond to any catering question.

"What is it?" Timmy was slightly dubious.

"High protein and tender enough to chew with no problem," Jonagren replied.

"I'd like to try it, please," Timmy said, popping the last of the sandwich into his mouth.

This time Casper collected the plate and the aroma of charcoal-broiled meat wafted through the room.

"I wouldn't mind one of those myself," Jonagren said, and Nimisha realized that all the sandwiches had been eaten. "Medium rare." There was such an expression of wistful anticipation on his face that Nimisha suspected all the indigenous meat had been well done or destroyed to sear parasites out of the flesh. That much she remembered from her survival lessons: You cooked any unknown meat very well or abstained.

"I could manage a small one myself," Casper said. "Rare, please, Cater!"

Nimisha chuckled behind her hand as they hastily strode to collect their latest orders. There were looks of total satisfaction as they began to consume the burgers.

"More ketchup, please, Cater?" Casper began, but when he started to rise, Nimisha signaled him to remain seated and collected the tube from the dispenser.

They said nothing as they ate, just as hungrily as if they hadn't cleared away a dozen sandwiches between them.

"It is good," Timmy said, licking his lips and his fingers as he finished his portion. "Thank you, ma'am," he added with a little bow in her direction and then one in Cater's.

"We didn't want him growing up a barbarian," Casper said in a low voice for Nimisha's ears only.

"He's charming," Nimisha said. "I know. I've met many who are not as well mannered as Tim is."

The boy sat back, rubbing his stomach, and suddenly looked around. "Is Syrie still asleep?"

"Syrie's in the medical unit," Nimisha said quickly. "Her leg's being straightened."

"Oh, she'll be so happy," Timmy said. "Jon did the best he could." He shot a grateful glance at the captain.

"I ought to have waited until she was conscious, but we were low on any analgesics by that time," Jonagren said, his tone bleak, "and we decided it was kinder to try to set the leg while she was out. I'm a much better cook than medic."

"The leg is now straight, sir," Doc said. "You didn't do a half bad job for a novice. I would surmise that the bones slipped slightly before you could splint it. You'd no regen gel left?"

"No, we didn't." The animation that Jonagren had shown, joking with Casper and eating, abruptly disappeared.

"Let me take you on a tour of the ship," Nimisha said, breaking the awkward silence. "It's more spacious than you'd imagine."

"Private cabins, even," Casper said admiringly.

"I wasn't constrained by fleet regulations, Casper," Nimisha said, leading them past the admired accommodations.

"How many can she sleep?" Jonagren asked.

"Six singles, but sleeping platforms extend to double size," she said, feeling an unexpected rush of blood to her face. Fortunately she was leading and hoped no one noticed. "Two washrooms but, as you saw, each cabin has a separate head unit."

"A real toilet, Casper said," Timmy said in a chirp. "Not like the head on the shuttle—but we can't use that anymore."

She showed them the various storage units and then the upper deck hydroponics garden that featured the usual broadleaf plants that were essential to a space-going vessel's air health.

"Some of these are Terran varieties," Jonagren said, and named pumpkin, squash, and the ti plant. "Do I see carrot tops?"

"You do. Good for eyesight," Nimisha said.

"And gravelot from Vega, if I don't miss my guess," Jonagren said, fingering the furry silvery leaf of the plant. "That's hardy enough to last even when air temp's down to near freezing. Saved many a crew from carbon-dioxide poisoning."

"That's why it's included," Nimisha said. "We've a second hydro unit on the lower deck."

They spent more time, as she had expected looking around in engineering, asking all kinds of questions that showed their own expertise and Fleet experience.

"I've manuals for every aspect of the Fiver if you'd like to see them."

"I certainly would," Jonagren said, rising from a crouch by the drive console, his knees cracking.

"You need more oil in your diet," Doc said, surprising them.

"Does he listen in to everything?"

"Everything that happens to be even vaguely medical," Nimisha said. "I can shut him off if you like."

"What? And risk annoying the medic?" Casper made his eyes wide with dismay at the mere thought, while Jonagren dismissed the idea with quick gestures of both hands.

"If you knew how good it is to hear different voices . . ." he said. "This is some sweet ship, ma'am."

"Nimisha," she corrected him.

Jonagren nodded acceptance. "You're quite a designer, but you called it the Fiver, so it's not your first?"

"No, the first four have gone into production, smaller than this, as personal transport yachts for the First Families who need or want the prestige of possessing their own spaceships or as transports for corporate executives. But useful as experiments. And with some utility for the Fleet. The fourth was . . . nearly what I wanted, but I didn't have the space I decided is optimum for its purpose."

"So, just what differences did you incorporate in this prototype?" Jonagren asked.

"Let's get back to the main cabin. I've wide screens there and I'd be more than happy to show you."

Casper just chuckled as he took Timmy's hand to lead him forward.

Nimisha was still explaining the rationale behind some of the improvements when the chime sounded and the medic unit released Syrona.

Casper was beside her in an instant, wrapping her in a sheet, helping her sit up, reassuring her. Her appearance had also been enormously improved by Doc's ministrations. Jonagren smiled, cocking his head in appreciation, but as she watched Casper help Syrona dress, it became obvious to Nimisha that he was definitely Syrona's mate, not Jonagren.

"D'you want a bath? There's a real tub, Syrie," Casper began.

Sitting up, Syrona immediately looked for Timmy, relaxing with relief when she saw him. "May I get out now, Doc?"

"Of course," Doc said with grave condescension. "You'll find that leg is working properly. You might experience a twinge or two while the muscles learn to stay where I've put them, but you can walk soundly."

She took a few trial steps and the relief and joy brought tears to her eyes. She tried to stem them, biting her lip.

Nimisha went to her, pushing a dithering Casper out of the way, and embraced the woman. "Now, now, it's all right. Crying's good therapy, you know. The bravest men and women know its healing power."

Syrona Lester-Pitt indulged herself in that luxury, allowing Nimisha to lead her to the nearest couch and settling them both so Syrona could weep in more comfort.

"Tea?" Casper exclaimed, swiveling his body toward Cater.

"Milk or lemon, sir?" Cater asked.

"Lemon?" Syrona managed to gulp in surprise through her tears.

"Lemon, I'd say," Nimisha told Cater and had to deal with a new outburst of tears from Syrona. She glared up at the two men, both of whom seemed perplexed, and Timmy, who looked worried. Nimisha smiled reassurance at him over Syrona's head and continued to pat and hug the woman.

"With extra sugar," Doc added.

When Casper brought this to Syrona she reached eagerly for the cup. Nimisha tactfully balanced the cup in the shaky hands that Syrona lifted to her mouth. She managed one sip, then wept a few more tears, sniffled, and rubbed at a runny nose. Jonagren took a napkin from the table and passed it over to her. Nimisha held the cup while Syrona blew her nose and wiped her eyes. Then Syrona took back her cup and gave everyone a watery smile.

"Even a cup of tea," she said in an unsteady voice. "You don't know what this means." She held the cup up as if voicing some inner toast.

"I think I do," Nimisha said gently. "Would you like something to eat, too?" she asked when the cup had been drained. Timmy had nestled in close to Syrona on the other side while the two men had pulled chairs closer, offering moral support and sympathy by their proximity.

"I ate a burger, Syrie," Timmy said, grinning impishly. "And drank milk!"

"Milk?" Syrona swallowed. Sniffing again, she was about to use the make-do handkerchief when she stopped. "I can smell burger. Oh, my word!" And she closed her eyes, hands tight against her lips to prevent another outburst of tears.

"I would prescribe food," Doc said.

"How do you like your burger?" Nimisha asked.

"Medium rare," Syrona said as if this was almost too wonderful to be believed.

"Medium rare, coming up," Cater said. "And did you wish ketchup on it, ma'am?"

"Ketchup?" Syrona's eyes shot wide in amazement. Shaking her head and laughing weakly, she commented, "Why am I surprised that this ship would have such a sauce? Even Fleet units do. But it's been so long . . ."

"Too long," Casper said, retrieving the burger, smothered with ketchup. "Some foods simply cannot fade from continuous use. The burger is universally a favorite. Yours, ma'am." With plate balanced on one hand, he made a bow to bring it to Syrona's hands.

They watched her as she tried not to bolt the food. After three quick bites, she slowed down, smiling hesitantly around.

"Good, isn't it?" Timmy asked, nodding his head to give her a clue to the necessary response.

"Nimisha's given us a tour of the ship while you were otherwise occupied," Jonagren said, relaxing again. "She's the chief designer at Rondymense Ship Yard. We're on the Fiver, and if it took no damage after its trip through that fragging wormhole, then it's definitely better designed than the old *Poolbeg* was."

"Wait'll you see the cabins, Syrie. Your own head and a bathtub like you told me about, and soft covers that aren't fur," Timmy rattled on. "And all kinds of growing things that don't try to attach to you and—and—"

"Easy, lad," Casper said, laughing.

"If that burger will stay your hunger," Nimisha said, for the food had disappeared quickly in spite of the small bites Syrona had taken, "perhaps a bath and clean clothes will restore you completely."

"A bath sounds like heaven."

"I cleaned you up quite well," Doc said, sounding miffed.

"Yes, of course, sir," Syrona replied and then stopped, realizing that it was an AI she was talking to.

"Doc tends to be cheeky," Nimisha said by way of explanation and apology.

"I'd love a bath, with hot water, and proper cleansing gel and—" Syrona paused. "Any fragrant oils on board?"

Nimisha chuckled. "I have a respectable inventory. You've only to look at the dispenser menu and dial the one, or ones, you want."

Syrona stood, and both men leaped forward to offer a hand each to their crewmate.

"I can get up myself now," she said in an almost haughty tone and proved it. A teary smile crossed her face and she firmly held back more tears. "And that's a *real* pleasure. Thank you so much, Doc," she added, turning toward the medical unit.

"My pleasure, I assure you."

"This way, Ensign Lester-Pitt," Nimisha said, formally gesturing the way for Syrona. "The com equipment is standard for reportage, Captain," she told Svangel, nodding her head in the direction of the bridge. "And Casper, I think we also have tape entertainment suitable for Tim. Just check with the library."

"Great! We didn't have much on the shuttle unit, mainly manuals."

"I can read," Timmy said, puffing out his chest.

Nimisha was following Syrona's proud gait—nearly a strut—to the living accommodations. She knew the library included some younger child entertainment tapes, because Cuiva had mentioned old favorites she wouldn't mind seeing again when she was traveling with her mother. No one saw the pang that thought gave Nimisha.

She stayed with Syrona at the ensign's request.

"It's so good to see another woman," Syrona said apologetically. "It's not that Casper and Jon haven't been solicitous and reassuring. They've been wonderful . . . but—" She paused with a wry smile. "—there's something about having a member of your own sex around. And I'm sorry to have wept all over you . . ."

"You have nothing to apologize for, Syrona," Nimisha said, assuming a mock scowl. "Now what had you in mind for fragrance?"

"Sandalwood," Syrona said, stripping off a uniform that was thin to transparent in places. "And lots of bath foam . . ."

The water was pouring into the deep tub that would accommodate any size human body. There was a shelf to sit on in its circle. The steam rose, carrying with it the aroma of sandalwood. Syrona inhaled deeply and took the two steps up to insert herself down

into the hot bath. She, too, was terribly thin, her pregnancy apparent as an abdominal bulge between gaunt pelvic bones. Her skin
was now free of the scrapes, bruises, and dry patches she'd arrived
with. The injured leg, still slightly pink from the medic unit's ministrations, showed a straight line of tibia.

"Oh, this is heavenly."

"Your sandalwood soap, ma'am, and a sponge. A Lytherian
sponge—they're softest."

"Expensive, too," Syrona remarked as she dipped the delicate
bath accessory into the water. "Oh, I've dreamed of this!"

The water was deep enough for her to be buoyant and, sitting
on the ledge, she fitted her head into the appropriate concavity in
the wall of the bath, her eyes closed, steam rising gently in aromatic waves. Nimisha sat on the slip bench, quite pleased with the
effect the amenities of the Fiver was having on this survivor.

With her eyes closed, hot water bringing more color to her face,
Syrona had the bone structure that would make her—once she
was in better condition—a very attractive woman. Her dark hair
began to curl about her face. It had been cut rather raggedly to just
below the ears. Nimisha studied the resting face and saw the character in it, the lines made by the last years of struggle, perseverance,
and repeated disappointments. She wondered how many children
Syrona had had, and lost.

"Timmy's Jon's son," Syrona said without opening her eyes.
"The boy Casper and I had together died of a fever. I miscarried
twice, and then they made me wait until they could build me up."
She gave a snort. "I don't think the indigenous diet was good for
any of us even if it was edible. We ran out of the supplements we
took from the *Poolbeg*'s supplies. No vitamins, too few trace minerals; I think that's why we had so many spontaneous abortions. But
we hadn't thought of increasing the population while we had *them*.
Casper insisted that we'd be found before we had to start a

colony." Her eyebrows quirked in amusement. "That man's the eternal optimist," she added, her lips curling a trifle in a fond and loving smile. "Jon's more of a realist so the two balance each other." She opened one eye, clear now and a pretty light green. "Jon's a good man," she said firmly.

"I've already decided that," Nimisha remarked with a chuckle.

"It's been harder on him when he knows how much Casper and I care for each other."

"I should imagine so," Nimisha replied casually. "While you were still being treated, I caught up on the basic facts of the expedition's history. There are two other habitable planets within a reasonable distance."

Syrona's eyes flew open and she regarded Nimisha solemnly. "You're First Family. None of us are, though my older sister is body-heir to my mother. But Jon's family is longtime Fleet and he's . . . he's very good," she finished in a rush. "Don't—don't—" Syrona flushed deeply and closed her lips tightly.

"I have no intention of denying him human rights, but," Nimisha said with a little smile, "I think we both need to get to know each other a *little* better."

"Oh, fraggit, Lady Nimisha," Syrona said, squeezing her eyes closed with embarrassment. "I didn't mean it to come out that way. Sounds like I'm pimping for Jon."

Nimisha burst out laughing. "Is that how Fleet works out these partnerships for long-term voyages? A spokesperson to sound out the chosen?"

Syrona opened her eyes and regarded Nimisha squarely. "Well, it generally works out. Of course, there's usually more choice available. But sometimes a crew member has to settle for what's left over. Not that *I* would consider Jonagren a leftover."

"That's encouraging."

"It's just that Casper and I have been mates a much longer time. Peri was Jon's." A look of intense sorrow crossed Syrona's face and she closed her eyes against painful memories. "She's been dead a long time now."

Her voice cracked a bit—partly the remembered loss and partly fatigue.

"I think you ought to rest by yourself, Syrona," Nimisha said gently, touching her arm as it lay on the tub side. "Until the water cools. Good to soak and let the sandalwood soothe you."

"I didn't offend you, did I, Lady Nimisha?"

"Nimisha, please, Syrona. We're equals on this planet. And all First Families!" she said as she slid the door closed behind her. To her relief, she heard Syrona chuckling.

Nimisha paused a moment before rejoining the others. Syrona hadn't wasted any time at all in setting out the interrelationships of survivors, possibly because she felt that was her duty in smoothing the trio into a quartet. Well, Nimisha found Jonagren Svangel not only attractive enough but also an interesting human being— certainly one she would find acceptable and deserving the comfort of "human rights," as she had so drolly put it. But she was not about to rush matters. If nothing else, the situation was slightly awkward for them both. She was civilian, as well as First Family, and he was Fleet and leader of his group. She'd have to figure out how to set him more at ease. What with all that she had had to do prior to leaving on the shakedown cruise, she hadn't had a chance for an intimate interlude with Caleb. Intercourse was still one of the most effective therapies for the relief of stress. No doubt why it was part of the Human Equation, rather than required solely for procreative purposes.

At breakfast the next morning, they started to make plans.

"I'd very much like to have a look at the other two anomalies, Nimisha," Jon said politely.

She heard Fleet in his tone and grinned back.

"That would be my first order of today," she replied, looking at

Casper and Syrona for agreement. Both nodded first in Jon's direction. "I don't have room on the Fiver for the *Poolbeg*'s gig," she said.

"I think it might just be possible to fit—without your skiff," Jon said thoughtfully. "As you pointed out last night at dinner, the skiff has no defense capability, but the gig does. We might need that when we investigate the other two planets. There seems to be sufficient fuel on board the Fiver to make both journeys feasible and still get back here."

"We can store the skiff in the cave," Casper said. "Plenty of space there. Does it have repellers?"

"Yes, but why would it need them in the cave?" Nimisha asked, puzzled. They had been *living* in the cave, hadn't they?

"Well," Casper replied, scratching his head and grinning wryly, "as long as we make noise, nothing comes to investigate us, but I wouldn't want to leave the gig silent and unprotected."

"Oh," Nimisha said softly, still puzzled.

Syrona caught her eye and grinned. "It's mostly the mess they leave behind," she explained. "The acid residue could damage even petralloy. Shame to mess a new skiff exterior if it can be protected."

"I'm agreeable," Nimisha said. "Are you sure it will fit?"

"Casper and I did a bit of measuring, and it will," Jon said, "but this *is* your ship, Nimisha."

"And one that I hoped to sell to Fleet for long-distance exploration. So let's test all its capabilities."

Jon's eyes echoed his smile. Were they gray or blue? Nimisha still wasn't sure. They were large and well set in his head and, now that he was definitely relaxing, filled more often with a droll sense of humor.

"Do you have anything else you want to bring on board?" she asked. The two men had gone out in the last light of the spring evening and she'd watched them climb up the ladder. They'd taken two loads from the cave, which they'd stored in the shuttle before returning to the Fiver. Casper had brought in some handcarved toys and a stuffed creature that was obviously Timmy's comforter. It was made of animal fur, stuffed with some sort of plant fiber, and wore a small Fleet uniform, complete with ensign bars. Timmy had greeted it with a loud cry of delight, and immediately sat down to tell it all about the new ship it was on.

"No," Jon said, shaking his head, then grinned in apology for his bluntness. "We stored whatever could be useful in the shuttle last evening."

"All right, then, Helm, let's open the hatch and see about switching my skiff with the gig," Nimisha said. "I'll take it up to the cave. I'm curious to see where you've . . . survived."

"It has served its purpose," Jon said.

"And may again," Nimisha remarked.

Jon beckoned to Casper. "Let's do it, then."

She followed them back and watched for a moment as they used the anti-grav handles to move crates and make the necessary room for the skiff.

"Don't worry. We won't scrape the shining new walls," Jon said, noticing her dubious expression.

"If it'll fly, Jon'll fly it," Casper said. "Been with him when he squeaked through some very tight asteroid belts."

Jon shook his head. "But not the wormhole."

"Even Helm, and he can respond in femtoseconds, had trouble keeping the Fiver from careening into the walls," Nimisha reassured him. "Anyway, that bedamned hole didn't even have a constant diameter."

"Hmmm," was Jon's rejoinder.

She had to admit, when they had adjusted the supplies in the garage area, that the skiff might indeed fit, though tightly. She got into it and, after making sure the men had stepped back, eased the little craft out and then up to the cave.

The entrance was partially obscured by drooping vines from

which a flutter of tiny insectoids departed as the top of the skiff brushed them loose. Rather like colored snowflakes and not much larger. Surely they weren't the acid-droppers. Then she turned on the skiff's lights for a good look at the cavesite.

They certainly had done their best to make it a home. Hewn wooden partitions closed off spaces for privacy on either side of the wide entrance. She could see that they had also built a rock wall across the rear of the cave. The amenities included roughly built couches, chairs, tables, a fireplace, and a cooking area. Shelves had been built and there were lighting fixtures on the walls, powered by the solar panels she had seen outside. There was even a rug, woven of rags all space-blue and gray. A bookcase, now empty, had obviously held reading materials.

When she heard the gig engine thrum softly, she slid down the lift rope to the ground and ran to see Jonagren Svangel's performance. He lined up the gig with the open hatch and, with a precise exhibition of his skill as a pilot, backed the vehicle inside the Fiver. He left just enough space on one side to permit him to disembark, but there wasn't more than finger's width between the gig and the wall of the cargo hatch on the other.

"Well done," Nimisha said, applauding when he emerged. He was grinning in almost boyish delight at his success.

He jumped down to the ground beside her, an I-told-you-so look in his eyes.

"Indeed you did," Nimisha said. "You're good enough that I'll even let you take the Fiver to our first destination."

Jon laughed, cupping her elbow and walking her to the main entrance. "Considering Helm would automatically correct any errors I might make, I accept the offer."

They entered the spacecraft laughing.

"Helm, Captain Svangel is herewith authorized to fly the Fiver, and you are to insert that order in today's log."

"Log so reads, ma'am," Helm replied. "If you will respond for a voice record, Captain?"

"This is Captain Jonagren Svangel, Helm, accepting the authorization of Lady Nimisha Boynton-Rondymense to act as additional pilot of the Fiver. Will that suffice, Helm?"

"Yes, Captain."

Nimisha winked at the now-authorized pilot.

"Set us a course, Helm, to the nearest of the two anomalies you discovered on this—" Jon turned to Nimisha. "We never bothered to give this planet a name."

"I've called it Erehwon," Nimisha said.

"Nowhere?" Jon said after a blink of surprise and a bark of laughter. Casper and Syrona joined in the laughter.

"Well, it is the back of nowhere, isn't it?" Nimisha said.

"All too true," Jon said ironically. "Helm, set us a course to the nearest of the two anomalies on Erehwon."

"Casper, Syrie, Timmy, join us," Nimisha said.

There was a manner of intense satisfaction about Jonagren Svangel as he took the pilot's chair and waited while it adjusted to his longer frame. "More comforts than at home," he said.

"Course laid in, sir," Helm said. "Maximum fuel conservation."

"Accepted. Let's go," Jon said, leaning to one side on the armrest.

As the Fiver lifted away from the meadow and the place they had lived for so long, Nimisha noticed that only Syrona glanced down. Timmy seemed to be fascinated by the altitude and the speed with which the ground dropped away as the Fiver angled her nose skyward. Once she had reached the programmed altitude, the engines throttled back and were almost silent, minute use of the thrusters keeping her on course.

"It's not a bad-looking planet," Nimisha remarked.

"In the safety of high altitude," Jon replied. "Lovely ship. Smooth as a baby's . . . ah, cheek."

Nimisha grinned at the quick substitution, obviously made in deference to her social standing. She caught the turn of head from both Syrie and Casper but she ignored them. They maintained this altitude for nearly an hour before the Fiver smoothly tilted forward and began her descent. They were passing over one of the oceans between the continental masses.

"What about life-forms, Helm?" Jon asked.

"Those are being observed and catalogued, sir." One of the auxiliary screens lit up.

Timmy drew back, wide-eyed at the size of the aquatic leviathans pictured on the screen.

"Well, I did see little butterfly things in the foliage at the cave," Nimisha remarked, "so not everything on the planet is oversized."

"Chichim—he was our geologist—thought this planet was possibly in a late Pleistocene epoch. He was hoping to find fossils before . . ." Casper's voice trailed off. "I mean, the size and variety of life-forms does compare to that period in Earth's history. And there is evidence of at least one ice age. We got"—he turned to Nimisha—"too busy surviving to do much real exploration."

"We managed botanical research and what biological specimens didn't want to eat us," Syrona added, somewhat defensively.

"We did an in-depth survey of our immediate area, which was relatively free from the largest carnivores and grazers," Jon said firmly, "as well as a complete sampling of riverine life-forms."

"A lot were very poisonous," Syrona put in.

"Good thing I didn't get a bath in that lake," Nimisha said.

"Ooh, you're right about that," Syrona said feelingly. "Jon got Peri out before something with tentacles tried to drag her under the surface and we hadn't even known it was there."

"Not quite a cetapod," Jon said, "but similar, from what we saw. Very strong. Peri had marks on her leg for weeks."

"The surface feeders were small enough to be fished, and there were nine types that we could safely eat," Casper added. "Two are very tasty grilled."

"I like burgers better," Timmy said, turning on his mother's lap to look up appealingly at her face. "Can—may I have a burger for lunch, Syrie?"

"I believe that can be arranged," Syrona said with a straight face, but her eyes danced. A second long rest had given more sparkle to her, and she had managed to trim her hair with sharper scissors. It curled like a cap about her head. Though her face looked smoother, there hadn't been time to fill out the hollows in her cheeks or completely eradicate the dark circles under her eyes.

The Fiver was over land again, the topographical features discerned even at their present height.

"Much the same geologically," Casper remarked. "Though that's some desert area with not so much as a shrub or ground cover to show the presence of water."

They were angling across the desert when they encountered deep canyons and, in their depths, the sparkle of water a long way down. Gradually that terrain gave way to more of the grasslands, and they could see the black clusters of the grazers moving steadily across it.

"Well, maybe over that mountain range we'll find something new," Casper said, ever the optimist.

"Our objective is seven kilometers directly forward," Helm said. He brought that image up and magnified it.

"That's new," Jon observed drily. "Not one of ours."

"Not by a long shot," Nimisha agreed. The metallic mass was strangely formed, with rounded semicircles on its uppermost surface and what looked like atmospheric fins buried in the dirt. "It seems to have had a sharp prow."

"Until it met the hard rock," Jon added. "Broke its nose."

"It does look sort of like a bird, doesn't it, with the fins legs and those blobs on the top a series of eyes," Syrona said. "Is it a green metal or is that paint?"

"It's badly scraped, whatever," Casper remarked. "If it came through the wormhole, it took more damage than we did."

"Alien. It looks very alien to me," Nimisha said.

"Helm, land the Fiver half a klick from the vehicle," Jon said. "We'll take a closer but safer look from the gig." He caught Nimisha's eyes, looking slightly apologetic for assuming command so automatically until she gave him a wave of approval. "Force of habit."

"I enjoy being a passenger . . . now and then," she replied evenly. And she did when she was certain, as she was with Jonagren Svangel, that the pilot was at least as competent as she knew she was.

She rose to go change into her protective suit, then turned back to Syrona. "Come along in the gig."

"Thank you but I'd just as soon stay here and have . . . a burger," Syrona said in an equable tone. "Timmy, did you still want one, too?"

"Sure do" was the enthusiastic reply and the boy danced ahead of his mother into the main cabin.

Nimisha had changed and found two spare suits for the men when she felt the slight bump as the keel of the Fiver settled to the ground.

"Here, you'll need these," she said, encountering the men on their way from the bridge. The smell of burger was tempting.

"Thanks. Our gear's long gone," Casper said, but, after taking the suit from Nimisha, he edged toward the dispenser. "But I wouldn't mind a burger for the trip."

"Come on then," Nimisha said, giving Jon his suit.

"I'll meet you at the gig," he said, pulling his protective gear on over what he was already wearing. "Order me one, too, Casper. Medium rare and no ketchup."

They were both finishing the last bites of their burgers as they joined her in the gig. Casper licked his fingers clean.

Jon sat in the pilot's seat that Nimisha had tactfully left for him.

"Letting me do all the work today, huh?" he said, snapping on the harness and switching on the engines.

"You got her in, you get her out," Nimisha said blandly.

"Aye, aye, sir."

"I'm a ma'am—I'm civilian."

"Yes, sir," was Jon's bantering reply.

Any lightheartedness vanished at the sight of the wrecked ship's obviously alien design. Circling the wreck showed the deep scores in its hull. One whole side of the aftersection had been pulled open. What looked like a small gig had been jammed against the largest hole. That may have been more luck than planning, but the obstacle would have kept smaller objects, like bodies, from being sucked into space.

"Hope they got their crew out," Casper said, shaking his head at the damage.

"I'd guess that that was cargo space and they lost whatever they were carrying," Jon said. "If that is the stern of this vehicle."

"I'd hazard the guess that they didn't back into their current position," Nimisha said with a droll grin at Jon.

"You're right about that. How could such a crazy shape be spaceworthy?" he remarked, shaking his head.

"Maybe it was never meant to land. Only they had to, with that great rent in their stern," she said.

Jon kept the gig hovering above the wreck so they could estimate the size of the alien vehicle. It was bigger than the *Poolbeg* and nearly as large as the ancient Diaspora wreck. The prow of the ship had been knocked sideways by the force of its landing, so the pointed shape resembled a bird looking over its shoulder.

"It's been here a while," Casper said, pointing to the vegetation growing from dirt on the top of it. "Hold it, Jon, there's some sort of design or glyphs on the side."

"I've been taping, Cas," the captain said. "Might be oxygen breathers, or why would they pick the M-type?"

"No choice," Nimisha suggested, having looked for some evidence of escape from the vessel. "And no tracks leading from it."

"It's been down a long time," Jon said. "Shall we have a look inside?"

"Why not?"

Nimisha was glad that was decided so effortlessly. There was no way she was going to relinquish the chance to see the inside of an alien spaceship.

They got in through one of the gaps in the hull toward the stern of the ship, which was again birdlike, resembling a fantail, bulging slightly on the end to accommodate a solid parabola of odd tubes.

"Funny sort of propulsion units," Jon said.

"No radiation readings, or Helm would have mentioned it," Nimisha said, switching on her wrist light and swinging the beam around the aperture.

Athletically, Jon Svangel hiked himself into the opening, then reached down to give Nimisha a helping hand. Casper was beside them in another moment.

"I'd say the aliens are smaller than we are," Jon remarked, crouching as he made his way forward. They all had to bend to clear the passageway.

"Much smaller," Casper said, banging his head on a mass of piping. A piece detached itself and dropped with a thud to the deck. A whiff of something acrid floated in the air for a moment before dissipating in the light breeze blowing through the wreck.

They were glad to enter an area where they could stand upright: the central round ball of the ship, which was obviously a command area.

"I feel like a giant," Nimisha remarked, looking at the small, almost child-size, seats and consoles. The worktops were filled with boards of rocker switches, dial knobs, and toggles, surrounding what had to be display screens, and there were large screens on one wall: shattered or crazed, but their original function was still obvious. She twiddled and switched and pulled and nothing happened. "I didn't expect any reactions," she murmured.

Jon and Casper were prowling about, looking at broken equipment on the perimeter of the chamber, peering into cabinets that had cracked doors or facades. They could not access the sharp prow where the bridge must have been situated; the passage to it was crushed against the stones of the hillside.

Nimisha noticed the pole and the hole in the deck and called their attention to it. As the size of the opening would not accommodate any of their adult bodies, they could only shine light down it.

"Access to crew quarters, I'd say," was Casper's comment.

"If we could rig enough lights so he wouldn't be scared, Timmy would fit," Jon said.

Casper was shaking his head.

"Not when I've mobiles we can send," Nimisha said. "Helm can control them. There's no need to ask a six-year-old to go down a hole in the floor."

Jon regarded her for a moment, then nodded. "Agreed. I have to reframe my thinking to include available resources I haven't had access to for years." Then he added, "Do your mobiles have additional lighting?"

Nimisha shook her head. "Self-contained units."

"What other surprises has the Fiver?" he asked in a wry tone.

"I like to keep something back from you Fleet types," she said.

"Why didn't you send them first, to scout the place?"

"Because I like to do my own reconnoitering. Get a feeling for the craft and who or what might have been on it."

"Whoever, they're a long time—"

"There is a party of unknown bipeds approaching from the hills, ma'am," Helm announced suddenly. "They appear to be armed with a variety of primitive weapons."

Nimisha unclipped her beltcom. "Can you patch through this hull?"

He could and she held up the unit so they all could see the furtive approach of the small bipeds.

"Further orders, ma'am?"

"We don't know that they are aggressive," Nimisha said.

"Aggression can come in many sizes," Jonagren remarked succinctly and he crouched to return through the low passage to their point of entry.

"The foremost question in my mind," she said, following him, with Casper behind her, "is are they descendants of the original owners?"

"Great minds," Jon said.

"I do have a translator on board the Fiver," Nimisha added. "Helm, can you pick up any sounds?"

"They are not making sounds," was Helm's reply.

"They are then attempting to creep up on us undetected," Nimisha said, amused. "What do we do?"

"Go out and act friendly, of course," Jon said.

"So they tell me," Nimisha said, regarding the weapons that were being brought toward them in the possession of small people who might dislike visitors on board their ship. If this was their ship. But who else's would it be? Unless, for some unknown reason, sentient—possibly even sapient—bipeds were limited to this continent of the nine land masses on Erehwon.

"I wonder how long they have survived here," Casper said as they reached the fracture through which they had entered.

"They are on the hill above you and the ship hides you from their view," Helm said.

"Thanks," Nimisha murmured, turning to the captain. "What do we do?"

"Walk out where they can see us, hands open, palms up."

"Let's hope that's *their* indication of peaceful intent, too," Nimisha replied. "Helm, on guard!" She switched on her suit's repeller, knowing that it had been designed to protect her against a variety of more sophisticated weapons than those being carried toward them. Jon and Casper did so, too.

"Forward and to your left," Helm said. "You're not yet visible, but they've sent two on ahead. You may meet them. You will. Now."

And they did. Nimisha was never sure exactly what happened, the encounter was over so quickly. Projectiles of some sort came flying at them from the two midget bipeds that reacted faster than any of the humans did. But Helm was faster and his stun beam caught them. The weapons were deflected by the individual repeller shields and fell uselessly to the ground.

"The others are retreating," Helm said.

Nimisha leaned down to pick up the impotent darts.

"Be careful!" Jon said, holding out his arm to prevent her. "The tip could be poisoned."

Casper had sprinted to the two supine figures. "Hope Helm didn't give them too much stun."

"We're lucky he could," Jon said. "At least we know they have some sort of nervous system that can be affected by stunners."

"I adjusted the beam to a strength sufficient to stop creatures of that size and weight," Helm said, and Nimisha thought the AI did not appreciate this aspersion to his common sense. "I had projectiles on targets, as well."

"Well, the translation device is on the Fiver. Let's take them to it," Nimisha said as she and Jon joined Casper by the limp bodies.

Jon knelt down and touched the fur-covered throat of the one nearest him.

"A pulse of some sort. Maybe Doc can figure out what they're composed of besides fur." He rubbed his fingers together. "Nice feel to it. Wonder how warm it is."

The two bipeds wore not much more than their weapon belts. Their sex—if they were of different sexes—was not obvious.

Casper bent and picked one up. "Heavier than you'd think," he remarked.

Jon took the second. Nimisha, craning to regard the head drooping over his arm, wondered at the blank oval face devoid of recognizable orifices.

Aliens! A spurt of triumph raced through her. Nimisha Boynton-Rondymense had met aliens! Sapient aliens, able to make and use tools, and who had once been space-farers. All kinds of questions tumbled about in her head: How long had they been marooned? Had they seen other humans to know that they should be wary of them? Had they regressed to a primitive existence? What stories would they tell about their landing here? Did they know where their home system was?

Then she realized that Jon and Casper were carrying on a conversation dealing with such queries and grinned.

"Helm, let's get back to the Fiver as quickly as possible."

"Advisable, ma'am, as there are now a multitude of these creatures advancing in a menacing fashion toward the gig."

"Lifting," Nimisha said, having seen the van of a small army appearing on the hilltop. She slipped into the pilot's seat as the two men were gently depositing the aliens on the deck.

They were up and out of range just as the army charged down the nearside of the hill, making loud hooting noises.

"So they do have voices," Nimisha said, turning the gig. "The Fiver's not that far away and they can really move," she added, making rapid forward progress.

"Let us then remove ourselves from danger while we treat these two," Jon said. "We could meet the Fiver back at the ocean. I doubt they can follow us that far."

"Do you doubt my ability to park the gig in Fiver?" Nimisha asked, amused.

"Never," Jon replied, and Casper gave a snort of laughter. "But why waste time landing?"

"Point." And so Nimisha suggested a rendezvous to Helm. She had a chance to see how gracefully Fiver lifted from the surface and sighed happily . . . even if no one in her quadrant might ever see it again. Idly she wondered if Caleb Rustin might not have gone on to finish the Mark 5 that had been skeletal when she left on the shakedown cruise. Would Cuiva realize that Caleb should be given the disks she had entrusted to her for safekeeping?

She landed the gig on the beach close to the Fiver. The aliens had not roused from their stun during the short run. Jon and Casper reassured her that they were still breathing and seemed to have a pulse in their short necks. As no facial orifices were visible, they weren't able to judge what optical or aural arrangements existed in the oval "head." Each hand had three digits, one opposing.

"If they can launch darts, they've tool capacities," Casper said, subtly pleased. "Sapient. How marvelous!"

"The feet are more flippers than feet, with vestigial toes . . . of a sort," Jon said, having gently felt down the four limbs of the one he was examining. "They don't smell bad, either."

"No, they don't, but with all that fur, how do they perspire?"

Jon picked up one limb, inspecting the sole. "Callused and bare of fur. Well, fur would've rubbed off on rough surfaces if there had been any, wouldn't it?"

"Let's see what Doc's diagnostics can tell us about them," Nimisha said.

"That's sensible," Jon said, kneeling to pick up the alien he had been examining. He stepped out of the gig and the alien bounced out of his arms, sprawling on all fours before it started across the beach in a dash. "Hold yours down, Cas," Jon cried.

Nimisha, who had been following Jon, started off after the fugitive. She had always been fast on her feet, and with legs twice the length of the alien's, she was able to catch up with it. Tackling seemed the logical way to halt its progress. It squealed at the sudden impact in the sand and tried to wriggle away.

"I won't hurt you," she cried, trying in this awkward position to radiate goodwill and positive feelings. It took Jon's assistance to subdue the creature. It might be small, but it was strong and writhed so violently that the two humans were afraid of hurting it. A dark band of what seemed to be one long eye centered in the upper third of its face sparkled with angry determination to free itself.

Casper had wisely put a wrap about the feet of the other alien. He was halfway to the Fiver with his still limp captive in his arms. As Nimisha and Jon carried theirs, it hooted in a desperate tone to the other and writhed in their arms, an action that required them to hold it more tightly than they wanted to.

"Really, we are not going to hurt you," Nimisha repeated in as reassuring tone as she could manage. "I hope its flesh doesn't bruise, or Doc will have my guts for garters."

"Your what for what?" Jon asked, startled.

"I've a friend . . . oh, do stay still, dear . . . who collects archaic words and phrases. That's one of them. He's also got some marvelous . . . 'Ods blood!" she exclaimed, as their burden writhed violently. "Like that—expressions from bygone days."

"'Od's blood?" Jon repeated.

"He didn't know what it means. Ah, here we are and not above time . . . another phrase Pheltim collected."

The two now had their captive inside the Fiver and Nimisha palmed the hatch shut.

"Bring the other one in here, too," Doc called. "They'll both fit in the unit. Once I've figured out what I can use to sedate them."

Casper's alien, lying in the medic unit, was still unconscious. Seeing the disposition of its colleague, the one Nimisha and Jon were holding made frantic efforts to escape.

"Oh, it's my size!" Timmy cried. He had been eating—a burger, to judge by the bun still clutched in his hand as he moved to get a closer look at the creature. "Are you hungry?" he asked solicitously, his face on a level with the alien's as he graciously broke off a bit and held it out.

The creature, whose optics seemed to be placed in a narrow band across the front of its "face," ceased struggling for a long minute. What Nimisha now took to be some sort of air intake had slitted open and was fluttering rapidly.

Encouraged, Timmy held the piece closer. A wild sniff, and the alien redoubled its effort to free itself.

"I've got enough from this one to be able to choose sedation. Put yours in before it damages itself struggling like that," Doc said. "Oxygen breathers."

"It might be vegetarian, Tim," Nimisha said, "but that was thoughtful of you."

Nimisha and Jon deposited the creature beside its fellow and Doc closed the canopy, which then misted with gas. The little alien used its small fists on the plastic, but its efforts diminished as the sedative took effect and it collapsed in a heap.

"Not the best way to make friends, I might add," Doc remarked.

"They weren't of a mind to be friendly," Nimisha said.

"You can look at the darts," Jon said, putting the two in a specimen drawer in the medical unit.

"There was an army of them about to overwhelm us."

"Yes, we saw," Syrona said. "Tim was a bit concerned for you. Even if they are closer to his size than yours."

"There were a lot of them," the boy said, eyes wide, and looked at the bite he had offered the alien. Then he popped it in his mouth. "I'm glad I'm not veggit."

"Let us know when you've found anything interesting, Doc," Nimisha said. Then, ruffling Tim's hair, she added, "That burger smells good. Think I'll have one. All that exercise gave me quite an appetite."

Jon and Casper followed her to Cater's dispenser and gave their orders, as well.

"Red blood," Doc said just as Jon was about to bite into his rare burger.

Nimisha smothered a laugh at Jon's expression. Almost defiantly, he closed his teeth on the bun. She leaned closer to him. "It isn't real meat anyway, even if that's the way it masquerades and tastes. It's got much more protein than mere flesh would have."

"We should have reassured the alien on that score," Jon said, flicking one eyebrow up rakishly.

"If these are the descendants of those in that bird ship," Syrona began, "they've done very well to survive on this hostile planet, the size they are." With that the others heartily concurred. "I heard their hoots and asked Helm to see if the translator could make something of them."

"Purely noise, to frighten an enemy and express aggression," Helm said. "Their vocal equipment goes off the scale into higher frequencies, so you didn't get the full effect."

"We tried shouting at the slugs and the bison-types. Had absolutely no effect on them," Casper said, sounding droll.

"Neither did our weapons," Jon added, equally droll.

"My, my," Doc said in surprise. "Well, the PanSpermia clique will be glad to know that they may have had it right all along."

"What are you talking about, Doc?" Nimisha asked.

"Surely you remember the two camps of thought about what aliens will look like when, and or if, we ever met any?" Doc asked.

"I do," Jon said, looking at Casper, who nodded.

Doc went on, obviously enjoying a lecturing mode. "Biologists have always been divided on the subject of whether or not we will ever find humanoid bipedal life-forms such as ourselves. As we know, it took astrographers long enough to admit that there just could be far more M-type planets with a proper atmospheric mix and carbon-based than earlier stargazers suspected. However, on the subject of what life-forms could emerge from the same sort of primordial stew, biologists remain in violent disagreement. One group insists that the percentage against encountering humanoids like yourselves is too high. The sentient, or perhaps I should say, sapient life-forms on other planets will be very alien. The aerial monsters that attacked your settlement, Captain Svangel, might be considered sentient, since they purposefully kept attacking you. But sapience indicates wisdom. And the avians showed little of that. However, back to the point, one group of biologists insisted that humanoid life-forms couldn't happen.

"The other, equally vocal and determined group, the Pan-Spermians, who postulated that once Life originates anywhere, that accident or design could cause that basic pattern to spread out through a galaxy. An excellent example of this is the evidence of life found in a meteorite that originated on Mars. And later confirmed in the initial Mars probes and landings."

Jon grinned at Nimisha, who smiled, remembering history lessons of humankind's earliest explorations of its own solar system before the First Diaspora.

"Am I boring you?" Doc asked.

"No, no, please continue, Doc," Nimisha said courteously.

The Doc cleared its throat in a very human fashion. "Many eminent biologists were willing to recognize that a hardy life-form, like some bacteria, might be able to survive such a journey through space—"

"Arrhenius' theory," Nimisha interrupted, cocking her finger at Jon, who grinned.

Doc went on as if there had been no interruption. ". . . Lasting decades, hundreds or thousands of years, and thus plant the seeds for biologically compatible life on another similarly hospitable world. If they check out, that theory is validated."

"Oh." Nimisha smirked with anticipation.

"The very fact that the stunner disabled them," Doc continued, "indicates that they have a central nervous system that can be stunned. They also have a hemoglobin blood similar to ours." Then he chuckled. "I have been busy during my peroration," he added. "Let's add to a nervous system an amazing circulatory arrangement and a heart-type pump and the bellows they use for lungs. Neatly packaged between their shoulder blades. Which adds more proof of being a humanoid type. Ah, one difference! They can withdraw their genitals into their bodies for safekeeping. A wise precaution, but there may be more than two sexes. I'd need to check other specimens. One does have a prod withdrawn in its body, but it also has an egg sac. A blood filter, a waste compartment for liquid and solids. There are some odd fissures in the hind end that probably open for evacuation. Muscle tissue, strong skeletal frame, articulated joints, but we saw them at work, didn't we? Definitely humanoid. I'm just getting to the brain but . . . hmmm." Doc broke off. "That's odd . . ."

"What?"

"Different structure, though I can discern divisions that might be comparable to human lobes. Very dense brain matter. Just how high on the scale their intelligence is will have to be estimated by their reaction to other stimuli. I'm willing to call them not only sentient but sapient."

"Aggressive, too," Casper remarked, "so they have a territorial imperative. However, except for their size, we haven't established if these little folk are the descendants of those on that ship."

"Why else were they determined to protect it and drive us away?" Nimisha asked.

"I'll tell you one thing—I don't think they are indigenous to this planet," Doc said. "They have residual accretions of minerals in their muscles and systems that they haven't been able to either use or evacuate. Once the organ is full up, I suspect it causes them a lot of problems, up to and including early demise."

"Are they capable of speech?"

"They've demonstrated that they can make sounds. Whether these sounds form a consistent language we have yet to see. Certainly they have tongues, so they can vary the sounds they make. They also have teeth . . . omnivorous variety. Not as many as humans, but the type of dental equipment suggests they can be omnivorous."

"We didn't do them any harm restraining them, did we?" Nimisha asked.

"Flesh is dense, dark in color. I cannot detect any contusions on their extremities. Remarkably tough creatures. It would take a lot to pierce their hides or break their bones. Possibly why they survived the crash of their space vehicle so well."

"Good point," Nimisha said with a laugh. "I don't think many humans would have survived that crash."

"Or that these did," Jon added, gesturing to the limp bodies in the medical unit.

"I've done what I can. They no longer have intestinal parasites, and I was able to laser the accretions out of their organs. Could be some sort of gall bladder. But they didn't need that foreign matter filling it up."

"When will they wake?" Syrona asked.

"And what do we do with them when they do?" Nimisha asked.

"Feed them?" Casper's expression was amused.

"Any ideas on what they eat, Doc?" Nimisha asked. "Meat certainly turned that one off."

"Stomach contents have been analyzed and they have recently eaten grain products and a protein I cannot identify with what few biological entities of this planet this ship has been asked to examine. I can see no reason why what is nutritious for us may not be equally edible for them, given that we may have descended from the same type of primordial pond scum."

"The burger was protein, not scum," Syrona said.

"But not in a recognizable form or with a familiar smell," Doc replied.

"You've been living here longer. And you made bread," Nimisha said, turning to Jon. "That's grain. Fish is protein—did we scan enough of the area around the wreck to know if there is a body of water in the vicinity that would supply fish?"

"I can provide fish for them, and greens," Cater replied. "Helm sent me an update of what you have been eating, Captain."

"Thanks, Helm. As efficient and forethoughtful as ever," Nimisha murmured.

"Only doing my job, ma'am," was Helm's response. They all chuckled.

"We'll take fish—cooked, I think," Nimisha said, looking at the three for confirmation. "And greens, plus some sort of bread, coarse grained, but a finer quality than what Jon made." She shot him a teasing glance. "And water in clear glass."

The requested items were available within minutes.

"They're waking up," Doc advised them.

"Let's move the table closer to the med unit so they can see the food. You don't generally offer edibles to an enemy," Jon said.

"We hope," Nimisha said as she took one end of the table

nearest her to help Jon move it. Casper and Syrona, with Timmy's help, set the food on the table. "Tim, you're small. Stand in front and offer them food. Take a piece of each and show them you're willing to eat it."

"Sure, only I wish it was burger instead of fish," Timmy said, promptly taking his position.

"If we are seated," Nimisha went on, "we may not look as threatening."

"You took the course, too?" Jon asked her, pulling chairs to form a row well behind the set table.

"No, it just seems sensible," she replied, and he nodded approval.

"I'm opening up," Doc said.

"Talk to them as soon as they start moving, Timmy," Jon said. "It doesn't matter what you say."

"But what *will* I say?" Timmy asked, anxiously turning to his mother.

"Tell them who you are, who we are, that we didn't mean to scare them, and are they hungry?"

"When do I eat?"

"Drink first and offer it to them," Doc said. "They'll likely be thirsty after what I've done to them."

Everyone watched as the alien creatures began to stir.

The more violent captive of the two roused first. They could tell by the sudden tautness in its body.

"Hi, I'm Timmy. I'll bet you're thirsty," the boy said, pausing to take a drink of water before offering the glass.

The alien hissed, but its now-open black optical slits were obviously focused on the glass as it watched Timmy drink. If it drew back from his extended hand, the action was more in an automatic defense.

"Move slowly, Timmy," Syrona said. "Maybe place the glass beside it in the unit?"

Timmy did so, taking the three steps slowly, glass still in his outstretched hand. Some of the water slopped in his hurry to put it down and the alien backed away, crowding into its fellow, who was just beginning to stir.

"Try it. Good clean water," Timmy said, taking the second glass and again drinking from it. "And we got good food. You can have what you want to eat." He picked up one of the bread slices and moved to place it beside the glass.

"Eat a bite, Timmy," Jon murmured softly.

"Oh, yeah, I forgot." His next words were muffled around the slice as he bit into it before placing it beside the glass. "See? I'm eating it. And drinking the water, too. Try it. Won't hurt you. Please?"

The alien sniffed at the wet spill that had become drops on the nonabsorbent covering of the medical unit. It put one of its two fingers on a drop and watched it run away from the touch. It sniffed the glass and then, slowly rising to a seated position, lifted the glass in both hands and took a tentative sip. Its fellow had now roused and was watching, turning its head just enough to take in what was happening.

Having had a quick sip, the first one made a short soft sound to its companion, who also pulled itself up into a sitting position and reached for the offered glass. It took one sip and then another before handing the glass back.

"Would that mean Ay is dominant over Bee?" Syrona asked.

"Ay was awake before Bee," Nimisha said, smothering a chuckle.

"Give Bee its own glass, and the greens, Timmy," Jon said. "Eat some before you put them down where they can reach them."

Timmy, obviously enjoying his role, did so, taking a bite of the green leaf with exaggerated eagerness before adding it to the offerings. He got a second piece of bread, breaking off a piece and eating that before giving the slice to Bee.

Ay took the bread and sniffed it, licked it, and bit into it, chewing quickly and then nibbling more enthusiastically. Bee took the leaf, sniffed, licked and then crumbled the whole thing into its mouth, swallowing almost instantly.

"You're supposed to chew your food, not swallow it whole," Timmy said, frowning.

"They caught that facial change fast, didn't they?" Nimisha said as both aliens stopped eating, their bodies tense.

"Smile, Tim," Jon said.

"I didn't scare them, did I?"

"I don't think so. They're eating again."

"They must be starved," Timmy said. His offerings were all gone and the water drained from the glasses. "What do I do now? Fill the glasses?"

"Hold out your hand and then gesture to the table, showing them they can leave the medic unit," Jon said. "Smile."

"They're not smiling back," Timmy said, but he was urgently pantomiming what he wanted them to do.

There was a low-voiced exchange of sounds before Ay pushed itself forward and slid off the unit, landing lightly on its feet with knees bent, ready to move.

"No, it's all right, come along. It's much easier for you to take what you want," Timmy said with expansive and explanatory gestures.

"He's good at this," Nimisha said in a low voice to Syrona.

"We used to do play acting at nights or during long storms," Casper said. "Passed time, and it was amazing how much dialogue we could remember from plays we'd seen a long time ago."

"In bits and pieces," Jon added, also keeping his voice low.

Slowly, and with Timmy encouraging them every step, the aliens made their way to the table, clutching their glasses against their squarish torsos. Timmy pointed at the glasses, patted the table, and picked up the pitcher.

"You put 'em down and I'll pour. We might spill otherwise. Ever used a pitcher before? Yes, that's right, put the glass down, Ay. You're Ay, and you're Bee. I'm Tee." And Timmy started to giggle at his wit. Both aliens reacted, taking two quick backward steps before they realized Timmy's unusual noise was not harmful. "I'm pouring, I'm pouring you water," he said, hastily putting action to words. Then he stepped back and glanced over at the adults watching him. "I'm sorry. I shouldn't've laughed like that, should I?"

As the aliens were far more needful of water than concerned about his odd noises, they were quick to take possession of and drain both glasses quickly. They replaced the glasses on the table and turned meaningfully toward him.

"I get the message," he said, cutting off another giggle as he refilled. "What about some more of this nice bread?" he asked, passing the plate from one to the other.

As daintily as if they were at a proper tea in Lady Rezalla's salon, they used one finger and the opposing thumb to lift a slice from the plate.

"We got some fish, too," Timmy said. Then regarded his mother. "I can eat it with my fingers this time?" When she nodded, he pinched a portion of the cooked white flesh and, tipping his head, dropped the morsel down his throat.

Ay and Bee watched, their jaws dropping slightly open. Their eyes glittered. Then they relaxed and continued eating bread. Ay approached the fish, and its sniffing was quite audible, the vents of the vertical slit visibly fluttering. So quick was its pincer-like motion that the piece of fish was in its mouth before the humans caught the transfer. Then it turned slightly toward Bee and pointed to the fish. They both set about snatching pieces, alternating bites of fish, bread, and greens until they cleared all that had been set out for them.

"You were hungry and thirsty, weren't you?" Timmy said.

Syrona covered her mouth, her eyes twinkling with amusement.

"You've said that a time or two, I guess," Nimisha commented to Syrona.

"A time or two."

Having fed themselves, Ay and Bee now regarded Timmy. The observers could see that they were no longer as tense as they had been. They were, she thought, seeing the almost imperceptible movements of their head, and the flick of their digits, assessing their current surroundings and the inhabitants.

"Now what do we do?" Timmy asked the adults, raising his hands, palms upward in query.

Immediately the aliens assumed a similar position.

"Good question, Timmy. Why don't you sit down on the floor and see what happens?" Jon suggested quietly.

The aliens' heads moved slightly, indicating they knew where the voice came from.

"So." Timmy crossed his legs and sat down.

The aliens leaned slightly forward and turned to each other; Ay made a sound and Bee lifted one shoulder, but both settled down cross-legged, too.

"Their knees are funny," Timmy said, but he kept his expression bland.

"Now, Tim, point to yourself and say your name."

"Timmy or Tee?"

"I told you that boy's a born comedian," Casper murmured.

"He's the best one at charades, certainly," Syrona replied in the same careful tone.

"Timmy! Tee!" said the boy and then, without a cue from Jon, he pointed to Ay and cocked his head, eyebrows set at an inquiring level. When there was no immediate response, he leaned toward them, cupping a hand behind his ear.

"They don't seem to have ears, Timmy. That gesture may not be understood."

"Tee! Timmy," he repeated, pointing to himself and then at each of the aliens in turn.

Ay said a sound.

Bee said a sound.

Timmy shook his head.

"Any ideas, Helm?" Nimisha asked softly.

"A liquid noise, neither vowel nor diphthong," Helm replied. "I have not heard sufficient of their sounds to replicate them."

"Tee. Timmy!"

"TTT," Ay said, stuttering out the consonant but unable to complete the "ee" sound.

"Hey, that's great!" Timmy said, clapping his hands. This startled the two, who reared back away from him. "Ooops!" he said in dismay, hunching his shoulders and clapping fingers to his mouth.

"Oooo!" repeated both aliens at once, turning to each other as if both pleased with his word and their repetition.

"Try more vowels, Timmy."

"Vowels?" Timmy turned for an explanation.

"A, e, i, o, u," his mother replied.

"Ay is what we named him."

"AAAA," Ay echoed politely.

"Bee?" Timmy said, pointing to Bee.

"EEEE," Bee said.

"We're going to have to change their names," Timmy suggested.

"Try 'I' . . ."

The vowels were easier for the aliens to manage and they went through the five.

"Open your mouth enough, Timmy," Jon suggested, "so they can see how you make the Tee sound."

Timmy did so, grimacing and showing his teeth, his lips peeled back as far as possible. The boy kept on, and the aliens seemed to be trying to enunciate what they heard.

"I have turned to a wider frequency band, ma'am," Helm said in a quiet voice. "Human aural equipment is not adequate to hear all the sounds they do make. I have tracked their voices up to fifty kilohertz, far beyond what humans are capable of, and nearly the limit of my receptors. Also, there are some glottal stops, fricatives, and labials that do not register properly. In their own voices, they are approximating the sounds Tim makes."

At just that point, Timmy threw both arms up in the air in total frustration and exasperation. "I give up. Can't we do something else?" he asked, turning toward the adults.

"Yes, why don't you show them around the ship, Tim?" Nimisha suggested.

"Great!" Timmy leaped so quickly to his feet that the aliens, surprised, slid backward from him with great agility and speed. "Aw, sorry. I keep forgetting. It's all right. Get up—" He made appropriate gestures. "—and I'll show you the ship."

"Ooo uuu t eep," Ay said, peeling its lips back in an effort to emulate Tim's exaggerated pronunciation.

"Let's give that alien a high score for trying," Jon said in a whimsical tone.

"Helm," Nimisha said in a low voice, speaking over her shoulder toward the bridge, "keep on recording at the necessary frequencies and see if they speak to each other while Timmy's showing them around."

Timmy was leading the way now, chatting all the time. The aliens were a good head taller than he was. They walked with a very smooth gait though they were slightly knock-kneed.

"So what do we do now?" Syrona asked when the trio was out of earshot. "We've doctored, watered, and fed them and—"

"I'd say we take them back where we got them," Jon said,

looking at Nimisha, who nodded agreement as did Casper and Syrona. "Showing good faith . . ."

"As well as giving Helm time to parse their language," Nimisha
added. She peered out the front screen. "We've enough daylight
left, I think, to bring them back before any of the nocturnal predators you told me about emerge from their lairs."

"Let's see if we can arrange another meeting with them in . . .
say, two days' time?" Jon went on, checking with each of the others.

"Sounds good to me."

"Tim'll need the break," Syrona said, but she was obviously delighted at her son's performance. "I didn't think he'd be able to do
so well."

"He did a great job," Casper said.

"Still is," Jon added, for Timmy's voice could be plainly heard.
"He hasn't had much chance to . . . socialize. Only barely remem-
bers the others."

Nimisha thought of the society into which her daughter had
been reared, with all its restrictions and traditions. "I don't think
Tim has suffered any neglect you could have avoided. I'm a parent,
too, you know."

Syrona blinked. "No, I didn't realize."

Nimisha laughed. "The subject never came up. Cuiva should
be just over twelve now. My mother has her in keeping—" She
stopped speaking for a moment, gave a little sniff, and went on.
"We'll have to get Timmy to do the pantomiming."

"Is there a chance the aliens will think he's in charge?" Syrona
asked, startling herself at the notion.

"Not when they both see us handling the gig on its return, with
Timmy safely belted in a passenger seat," Jon said with a grin.

Being escorted with Timmy to the gig after they had toured the
Fiver did not surprise Ay and Bee. They did not resist when they

were belted into seats just as they had seen Tim do. On the other hand, their ship awed Tim when he saw it.

"Looks like a gigantic bird—nicer than the ones that dive-bomb you, though. Ah, its head got broke."

Jon had explained to Timmy what he wanted to communicate to the aliens. Timmy did a good job, pointing to the setting sun in the west and then to the east, making a circle with his hands and passing it twice around the sky. Ay nodded, with Bee as quick in comprehension.

"Two days. We meet. Here. Your people . . ." Tim swung his finger to indicate the adults.

That caused Ay and Bee to communicate with each other with oo's and uu's and other unheard noises. Then they both nodded.

Bee took a half step forward, bending at its midsection, and raising a glass to its lips with one hand, and then miming food in the other that it chewed lustily.

"I getcha," Timmy said, clapping his hands. Again the reflex action of the two aliens was to recoil from the noise. "Does it hurt their ears or something?" he asked Jon.

"Could be. They hear in a different range than we do."

"Oh." It took a moment for Timmy to digest that information. "Like the whistlers?"

"Like them." Jon nodded. "He's referring to a flier we've encountered, not as large as some, but when it dives it emits a whistle. Only if you hear it, it's homing in on you and you'd better find cover fast. We think the noise is used to paralyze some of the indigenous creatures." He turned to the aliens and mimed drinking and eating.

Neither Ay nor Bee moved as the others went back to the gig.

"You better move back," Timmy said, leaning out of the hatch and flipping his hands at them.

"I'll take off vertically, Tim," Jon said from the pilot's seat. "Don't worry."

Timmy watched the two figures, who braced themselves against the slight wind of uplift, as long as he could on the rearview screen. Then he took a seat and very shortly was fast asleep.

"Hard day's work when you're only six," Casper said with great pride and affection.

CHAPTER 6

There were two malicious attempts to injure Lady Cuiva, so clumsy that Lady Rezalla was outraged: How could anyone think a message bomb or a poisoned plant sent to her granddaughter would reach its intended victim?

The Residence Manager had, in any case, been programmed to investigate any package or hand-delivered formal invitation sent to the House. The RM detected the dangerous message immediately and disarmed it. The RM then informed Lady Rezalla, the Acclarkian Peace Guardians, and Commander Caleb Rustin of the incident.

The message folder was similar to any of hundreds manufactured on the planet; when opened, it was set to detonate an explosive.

"For a younger child," the APG said, examining the now-impotent device, "it would have caused serious injuries. Your granddaughter would have sustained only minimal damage."

"*That*," Lady Rezalla said scornfully, "is not much comfort. I want the perpetrators caught and punished to the full extent of the law."

"Dear lady," the APG said ruefully shaking his head. He had been chosen for this assignment because he knew First Family protocol and how to deal with indignant members of that society. "We shall certainly do our best to arrest the perpetrators. But, in fact, this," and he jiggled the disarmed message envelope, "was useless as well as stupidly contrived since, obviously, your granddaughter's age and size were ignored. I do, however, respectfully suggest that this House go on an alert status against subsequent invasions of its privacy and/or the causing of injury or distress to its residents. I shall instruct the patrols that they should keep an especial watch on your House, Lady Rezalla."

She repeated her first demand in an even more disapproving manner, which he took with the grace for which he was noted.

"Be assured, Lady Rezalla, that my department does not treat this matter lightly. The Peace Guardians consider the protection of members of Acclarke's illustrious First Families the most important aspect of their many duties. May I comment on your wisdom in employing Perdimia Ejallos as Lady Cuiva's constant companion."

Lady Rezalla regarded him with an expression of displeased surprise.

"Oh, yes, Lady Rezalla, we have already investigated the young woman's background and family. She will guard her charge with her life."

"That's what she's been employed to do."

Commander Rustin's response was to rig about the House the most sensitive alarm system the Vegan Fleet possessed. He got permission to install a repeller shield in the ground vehicle that was generally used by Lady Rezalla, Cuiva, and Perdimia for their social activities and other excursions. He presented both Lady Cuiva and Perdimia with a top-secret personal alarm. His presentation was as offhand as he could manage, considering the necessity for keeping Cuiva ignorant of the malicious message.

"Cuiva, I've a little gift for you today," he said, displaying the golden band in its velvet case.

"A Coskanito?" Lady Cuiva exclaimed, noticing the name discreetly printed in gold on the cover. "Oh!" she cried, examining the delicate bracelet within.

Coskanito was not only the maker of the special body-heir Neck-

laces for the First Families but also of elegant adornments with unusual, hidden facets. This bracelet, which fastened snugly around
the wrist, immediately detected any increase in pulse, consonant
with its wearer's alarm or excitement. Perdimia recognized what it
was instantly but connived with the commander to exclaim over
its charm so that Cuiva would not realize she was wearing a personal alarm. Contained in the circuitry was a homing device, so that
Cuiva's location could be traced anywhere on Vega III.

When the commander later, and privately, gave Perdimia a silver bracelet from the same maker, she was both pleased and even
more concerned.

"You don't think . . ."

"That Lord Vestrin will try again? I certainly do, Perdimia,"
Caleb said. "He's known to be a vindictive sort."

"I'd look to his dam more than him, sir," Perdimia said, her expression angry.

"Vescuya?" he asked. Perdimia nodded. "That's a point. Especially since it is Lord Vestrin who has seen Cuiva whereas I doubt
his dam has."

He took that suggestion more seriously when the second attempt was made: An exotic flowering plant was sent by an "unknown admirer" after Lady Cuiva's appearance—well guarded—at
the ballet. The leaves of the plant had been coated with a contact
poison, and the blooms had been treated with a dust that would
have badly affected the lungs of anyone sniffing the fragrant blossom. The RM had detected the poison and reported it.

"Poison is generally a woman's choice," Lady Rezalla remarked,
circling the dangerous plant on the table where it had been set until the AGP could arrive.

"Would Lady Vescuya . . ." Commander Rustin said. He had
been close enough to answer the RM's emergency pulse in moments. He had not mentioned to anyone that he had, in fact, taken

new quarters in a nearby building where a naval security unit had been set up for permanent surveillance of the Boynton-Chonderlee Compound.

"Lady Vescuya most certainly would," Lady Rezalla said scathingly. "A worm of a woman. Can't figure out why dear Ti ever consorted with her, except she had quite a talent for attracting the opposite sex. Cultivated it into an art. Can't stand any member of her own sex. Nor we her, for that matter. That would explain why the letter bomb was so ineffective. She never bothered to check how old Nimisha's body-heir is! Stupid woman! Ineffectual! I've always suspected that she isn't full-blooded First Family. There are certain standards that all of *us*,"—she placed her hand gracefully on her chest—"keep no matter what the provocation."

"Provocation?" the commander repeated.

She looked down her elegant nose at him despite his superior height. "I have been tempted occasionally, Commander, when events have seriously tried my patience. I consider it my duty, however, to adhere to the strictures and disciplines of my lineage. Make no doubt of that!"

"I do not, Lady Rezalla, I fervently assure you." He bowed low in apology for any unintentional affront to her dignity.

Cuiva never knew of the existence of this dangerous gift. The AGP, now attached as additional protection for the Boynton-Chonderlee Compound, took the plant away for forensic analysis. The RM had of course taped the delivery; the tape showed a man wearing the livery of a well-known courier agency. When the agency representatives were shown the tape, they said the person was not employed by them and was illegally using their livery. They opened their personnel files to prove their point. They were horrified and promised to do all possible to protect the Boynton-Farquahar body-heir. The other courier firms were put on alert, just in case their agency was misused for a similar errand.

The day after the plant's delivery, a third untoward event occurred in the space adjacent to the Rondymense Ship Yard. An old freighter hulk, ostensibly bound for the supply dock, suddenly started its engines, its trajectory inexorably making for the gantry around the Fiver B; a trajectory that could not be random, since the gantry was nowhere close to the main supply station. When there was no response to the Navy's first hail and warning to sheer off, the naval yard defensive batteries blasted its engines and it was intercepted by a high-speed tug before it reached the Fiver's vicinity. The tug deployed a strong netting material around the hulk and gently braked it to a stop. When it was boarded, after very careful remote scrutiny, it was found that it had been carrying considerable explosive material, surrounded by scrap metal to make it a giant shrapnel shell. The experts deduced from the installation of the explosive and the detonating device—which was set to explode on a sudden deceleration, such as might be caused by contact at high relative velocity with another object—that had it come any closer to the Ship Yard it could have easily caused significant damage, not so much from the explosion itself as from the fragments propelled from the point of detonation by the explosives.

"To my mind, that is just a further example of their ineffectuality," Caleb told the admiral when they discussed the matter with the Fleet Security staff.

"*Their?*" the admiral repeated. "Is this a gang? I thought you said you were certain that the Rondymense body-heir was behind the attempts on the child."

"I do, but I think his womb-mother is as deeply involved."

The admiral stared angrily at the commander. "First Families are supposed to be above such antics. Especially someone with an FF tattoo. If they have aggressions, they can dissipate them on the hunting preserves set up for that purpose. But to attack humans! And a child at that. Revolting!"

Caleb Rustin and the others in the room murmured agreement.

"Proof of such aggression will have to be without the shadow of a doubt, you know," the admiral said sternly.

"If they are as stupid as these three attempts indicate," Caleb remarked, "they are likely to give themselves away in an irretrievable fashion."

He looked over to the Security chief, who was there to report on the investigations of how, or why, a derelict freighter had been in that vicinity and illegally packed with explosives. Lt. Commander Barney Bellpage stood and flashed images on the main screen of the admiral's ready room.

"We've traced the freighter, which was bought from the scrapyard for far more than it was worth by an unknown using untraceable pay-bearer credit chits," he reported. The subject freighter was seen hanging amid the remnants that infested the area. "The freighter was towed, part of the purchase fee, to coordinates and left there. Beyond any surveillance drones, naturally."

"Naturally," the admiral said drily and waved at the commander to continue.

"With so many private and public fields available to the perpetrators, we are slowly sifting through arrivals and departures, and the APG is tracing the supplier of the explosive material. Unfortunately it is a readily available commercial product for construction contractors. We are also checking the construction firms to see if any quantities of explosives in their inventories have suddenly disappeared.

"Unfortunately, that takes time," the commander went on sourly, "but we should have some leads shortly. The APG is also tracing unusual deposits in credit accounts of some of the less respectable traders in such substances. They are quite upset about the attempts to harm a body-heir, and one not even of her minor majority. As they are well aware of the penalties for being accessories to such a heinous crime, they are assisting our efforts. They suggest, most respectfully, that the explosives might have originated off-planet."

Looks were exchanged among those in the office: they all knew that both Lady Vescuya and Lord Vestrin had been off-planet for some time.

"No matter, we merely extend the search," the admiral said, bringing one fist down on the table to emphasize his resolution. He turned toward Caleb Rustin. "How soon will Five B be ready for space? The safest place for that child is on her and out of this system."

Caleb was speechless for a moment. That solution to Cuiva's safety had never occurred to him. She was far too young to be an asset to a search party, even if its object was finding her mother. Certainly accompanying the search would remove her from harm's way. Could Lady Rezalla be persuaded to such a course? She doted on her granddaughter.

"APG is aware of our suspicions as to the source of these attempts," he began.

The admiral snorted. "And can do nothing without absolute, airtight proof that a First Family scion would dare harm the body-heir of another. It's unheard of. Totally out of character for any First Family!" His sarcasm mirrored his disgust with the notion that First Families, merely by virtue of their social status, were totally free of greed, dishonor, and underhanded activities.

"Lady Rezalla believes that Lord Vestrin's dam is behind the attempts," Caleb said, "not Lord Vestrin. Though the freighter stratagem is more in keeping with his personality than the message bomb or the poisoned plant."

"Lord Vestrin's logged off-planet with a hunting party," Bellpage said with a weary sigh.

"Are you absolutely sure of that?" Caleb asked.

Bellpage sat up straight and stared at Caleb. "Yes, I see your point. If the admiral will excuse me, I'll check further. We have a patrol unit near his destination planet. I'll insist on vid proof of his presence."

The admiral waved him off on that errand.

"Lady Vescuya remains in Acclarke," Caleb said. "But her activities are being closely monitored." He grinned. "She's a very busy lady."

"See if you can persuade Lady Rezalla to allow Lady Cuiva to go off-planet. She *will* be safer," the admiral said. "The three-month shakedown cruise would not be too arduous for a girl her age and her safety would be assured."

To give Lady Rezalla credit, she considered the notion only briefly before agreeing.

"I'd even considered putting her into suspension to keep her safe," Lady Rezalla said, but she dismissed that option with a flick of her long white fingers, delicately tipped in a pink that matched her flowing attire. "And keep her safe we must! She is, unfortunately, too young yet to have a body-heir to whom she can assign her possessions."

The very notion of that shocked Caleb. He did happen to know that Cuiva had started menstruation, but the very thought of the twelve-year-old child having a body-heir merely to preserve her assets unto the next generation was nothing short of brutal.

"I will *not* allow that man, nor his dam, to succeed, or profit by their machinations," Lady Rezalla said in the harshest voice he had ever heard her use. Her tone made him straighten to full attention. "The ship can carry a crew of six, if I correctly remember such details from Nimisha's rattling on about its unique specifications."

"More if necessary, milady, though not in as elegant a manner."

"Manner be damned if my grandchild's life is at risk. Perdimia, of course, will accompany her. Jeska will have to stay and run the yard, since she does that well, according to my reports."

"She does," Caleb admitted. His mind was already leaping forward to the tasks of altering the luxury cabins to accommodate more crew and choosing a crew of utterly trustworthy credentials and skills.

"I shall check with my legal staff and see how to compose a Will that will secure my granddaughter's assets, and those of her mother. I will inform you within the hour of the results, Commander. Keep yourself available to my call."

"I shall, my lady."

He bowed himself out of her chamber. Outside, he let off a whoosh of surprise. That had been incredibly easy.

"The shakedown cruise lasts three months, which is a start," he murmured to himself as he left the House. "And that gives time to find any evidence there might be that Vestrin and Vescuya are behind the attempts. If we're lucky. After that? We haven't even any idea of which direction to search in!"

There had been no reports of any activity from the monitors on guard in the section of space where Nimisha had expected to reenter normal space: both Caleb and the admiral had known the details of her flight plan for that test-run. No one still knew if, indeed, that wormhole had been the cause of the disappearance. Nor had anyone come forward with any other explanation for why nineteen ships had gone missing in that area. He would rather they had a destination in mind. Even the maw of the wormhole.

Frustratingly, it took three more weeks to test Five B with the augmented and refined elements that had been on Nimisha's disks. Hiska noticeably lost weight and apparently would keep going until she fell asleep at her workstation. Lord Vestrin definitely was part of the hunting party, and discreet inquiry revealed that he had been seen boarding his friend's space yacht at Vega III Port. However, that did not keep him from having hired someone to act as his agent. GoP were doing their own hunting. So was the Fleet. Lady

Vescuya was being closely watched. Lady Rezalla, who was well liked and respected by her contemporaries, subtly queried them about the woman's associates and social activities. Lady Vescuya's methods might be amateurish and clumsy, but no one could find a link between her and either the message bomb or the plant.

On the advice of the APG as well as Caleb, Cuiva was housebound and a rumor was circulated that she was suffering from some malady. Lord Naves, in fact, was to be seen hurrying to the House several times a day. Emergency medical equipment was delivered and specialists arrived and departed. If Lady Vescuya had a spy watching, she might be fooled into thinking the poisoned plant was responsible for such activity. Lady Rezalla curtailed her social visits and canceled several engagements for herself and Lady Cuiva.

Two further inept attempts to damage Fiver B were foiled before any damage could occur. The first one was a robotic device, its reservoir charged with an acid that could destroy almost any metal. The second was an unmanned personnel gig, similar to those used by the Yard for short hops between construction sites. When it responded to an identity request, the answer was not only wrong but also delivered in the flat tone of a bad recording.

"The most sophisticated of the tries," Caleb said when the gig was tractor-beamed into space and its explosive package disarmed. Of course, whoever had sent it could not have known of the increased security at the Yard, or that all the access codes for traffic to and from Rondymense had been changed.

"Their information was fortunately out-of-date," Bellpage said. "We now have off-planet suspects that we are investigating."

"The sooner that ship is out of here, the better. And Lady Cuiva on it," the admiral said.

"Lady Cuiva must first be seen alive and well," Lady Rezalla put in. She had accompanied Caleb Rustin to Fleet Headquarters. "Completely recovered from a mystifying childhood fever. Her legal position as body-heir is unassailable. Nor, I am assured by our so-licitors, can it be contested." She gave a smug smile. "Even so, Commander, I expect you to find my daughter before she can be legally assumed to be . . . dead." Lady Rezalla's expression chal-lenged the commander.

"My intention, I assure you, Lady Rezalla," Caleb replied firmly.

"Have you chosen a crew for the Five B?"

The admiral cleared his throat and offered the pad with its crew profiles to her. He and the commander had spent hours matching psych profiles and duties to provide the best personnel mix for the three-month test run.

"Lady Cuiva will be accompanied by Perdimia, of course," Caleb said. "Lieutenant Commander Kendra Oscony is not only a communications expert but has advanced credentials as a mathe-matician and will continue your granddaughter's education in that field." Lady Rezalla bowed her head in acknowledgment. "Ensign Mareena Kawamura has special training in biology and botany and will instruct in those areas. Chief Engineer Ian Hadley has an intimate knowledge of the Fiver's propulsion and Interstellar Drive, as well as a keen interest in astronomy."

"Astronomy limited to the stars of this quadrant, though," Lady Rezalla remarked.

"All too true, my lady, but he would be ecstatic to chart new ones and quite capable of assessing whatever spatial anomalies we encounter. His wife, Lieutenant Junior Grade Cherry Absin-Hadley, is our semantics expert and xenobiologist."

Lady Rezalla raised her eyebrows in surprise.

"One never knows, my lady," the admiral murmured.

"Nazim Ford-Coattes is the second pilot, having been a test pi-lot on the Fiver with Nimisha and one of her trusted employees," Caleb went on. "Gaitama Rezinda is on board as our joat—a jack of all trades. She is also a Rondymense employee of long standing.

She is by way of being an unarmed defense specialist, as well, and can instruct Cuiva in that skill and keep the rest of the crew physically fit. Lord Naves himself gave our medical unit private tuition. Should we have a direction for a positive search, the catering unit has been augmented to make use of available natural materials that can be converted to human nutritional requirements."

"Well," Lady Rezalla said approvingly, "your crew seems exemplary in the range of their qualifications, abilities, and backgrounds, even to representatives of good, solid Minor Families. The Hadleys are unexceptional and so are the Ford-Coattes. Clever of you, Commander, to realize that Cuiva's education must continue uninterrupted. Among the impedimenta I brought today—"

"Which has already been stowed in Cuiva's cabin aboard Five B," Caleb said.

"Excellent. You will find the carton containing disks and learning tapes for those courses I wish Cuiva to study over the next three months. These will be in addition to what the crew can teach her. Perdimia will supervise strict lesson hours. My granddaughter will be kept busy and out of your way."

"Lady Cuiva will never be in our way, Lady Rezalla." When Caleb saw a scowl beginning to form on her aristocratic features, he hastily added, "Nor will her position in society, despite her youth, be forgotten."

"Gratifying indeed." Lady Rezalla rose and extended her hand to the admiral, who had leaped to his feet. "We shall see you at the commissioning, then, when Lady Cuiva will formally launch the Five B."

"Until tomorrow then," the admiral said, bowing over her hand.

"Oh, I have . . . issued an invitation to Lady Vescuya." Lady Rezalla's smile was subtly vindictive. "She shall see . . . Cuiva return with me to Acclarke."

"That is all arranged, then," Caleb said. The APG had found a look-alike child to take Cuiva's place.

"Rather a nice child, too," Lady Rezalla said without condescension. "She is to accompany me to an undisclosed location for
an extended holiday."

"And," the admiral added, "reappear with you whenever Lady
Cuiva must be seen."

"The surveillance will continue, you know," Caleb said.

"Of course," Lady Rezalla replied. "I have no more intention of
risking that child than my own granddaughter. Less, if the truth be
told, since I have her on trust from her parents. Not that the child
will not profit from being in the household of a First Family, you
realize."

She had turned so that she did not see the amused glances that
the admiral and the commander exchanged.

"Actually," Gollanch said, when she was gone, "Lady Rezalla's
solicitors—although I am told most discreetly that they hold a
watching brief on the matter—are most alarmed. There is a way in
which Lord Vestrin could have Rondymense Ship Yard returned to
his control."

"There is?" Caleb was shocked. "How? Why?"

Gollanch waved one hand irritably. "Damned complicated body-
heir laws. If both Lady Nimisha and her daughter can be proven
dead before the daughter reaches her minor majority, the bequest
is returned to the main Rondymense estate. Lord Tionel made no
other provision. Oh, don't worry. With Lady Cuiva safely on the
shakedown cruise, the APG feels certain he can prove Lady Vescuya's duplicity. Or find Lord Vestrin's accomplices in the matter of
the mechanical attempts. Hiska, that odd mechanic of Lady Nimisha's, has given the APG some information on five former employees of the Yard who were dismissed for theft. She told Jim Marroo,
who has informed the APG, and he agrees that there could be ill-
feeling. The men have apparently served their penal sentences and
have been seen near the Yard by more faithful workers. The stolen
items were valuable, and they are of a temperament to take revenge

if they had the chance. However, we're on to them now." The admiral smiled with considerable malicious satisfaction. "We have only to keep Lady Cuiva safe for the duration of the shakedown cruise and the whole matter may be resolved."

"I devoutly hope so," Caleb said, nervous enough to finger the crease of his dress uniform.

The next day was a great occasion with many important government and Fleet representatives, along with the cream of Acclarke's Society, coming to watch the Spacing of the Five B. Although most of Vega III knew that Lady Nimisha Boynton-Rondymense had disappeared and that this second Mark 5 was to search for her, the actual commissioning ceremony did not reflect this. Lady Cuiva duly activated the traditional bottle of champagne—an excellent vintage had been chosen from the Vegan vineyards—which was sent at speed against the prow of Five B and satisfactorily broke, leaving globules of the wine and shards of glass to do a gavotte in space until a patrol could surreptitiously corral them. Lady Cuiva declared, in a firm alto voice neither affectedly adult nor obviously childish, that the Mark 5 B was duly commissioned. The gantry fell away and the tugs pushed her gently, her riding lamps blinking, to her new mooring out of sight of the audience in the spectators' gallery. A naval band played a spirited tune and Lady Cuiva passed among the various senior members of the construction crew—pausing to embrace Hiska—before being shepherded by her grandmother into the private office. She reappeared shortly to accept refreshments. If she was quiet and seemed almost overcome by the crowd, such modesty was expected of a child her age. Lady Rezalla kept her close by, which was also proper. No one saw anything odd in the fact that Hiska seemed to shadow Cuiva's moves, scowling if anyone came near to the child.

Once the champagne reception got under way, no one was in a

position to notice the Five B slip its mooring and continue to drift away from the Yard; nor could they see the substitute hull, complete to the ID, slide into the vacated space. When the guests finally made their way to the lighters that would take them back to Acclarke City, they only saw what they expected to see—a Mark 5 prototype serenely moored, riding lights lit and blinking.

CHAPTER 7

Jon and Casper rigged a camouflaged remote device at the meeting place that Ay and Bee had been shown.

"That way we can go check out the fourth wreck," Jon said, brushing sand from his hands with the satisfaction of a job well done, "and still keep an eye on developments here. You don't know what it's like to have facilities and parts again," he added to Nimisha, rolling his eyes expressively.

"From what I saw in your cave-site, you did pretty well at improvising out of available resources," Nimisha replied.

"Needs must when the devil drives," Jon said with a wry grin and a shrug. "There was so much more we could have, should have, taken from the *Poolbeg*, but we didn't dare try a long journey back after the rocks those damned avians dropped stove in the starboard vents."

"Had you noticed them on the way to the plateau?"

"Noticed, yes," Jon replied.

"Certainly didn't think they were smart. Or organized enough to take offensive action," Casper put in.

"I think they got mad at us for gunning down those we did," Syrona said, shaking her head.

"They were organized?" Nimisha asked, incredulous.

Jon gave a harsh laugh. "Near as makes no never mind, Nimisha. Some came as a group, others whenever they found a rock big enough to do damage."

"Fascinating. Could we call it tool-using?"

Syrona gave a little laugh. "If you stretched the point a long way." She held out her arms as far as they would go. "They sure wouldn't be my choice of *sapient* beings." She gave a shudder.

"Ay and Bee are nice," Tim said softly, his eyes wide from listening to the adult conversation. "I didn't like the bombers."

"The one I met certainly wasn't friendly," Nimisha agreed, also shuddering at the danger she had survived.

In the false dawn, with the garage lights on so that Jon could check his position, he reversed the gig into the Fiver. Then, as the sky began to brighten with Primero's sun, they set off for the fourth wreck. Helm suggested a triangular approach, to avoid any sighting by the small aliens.

They reached their destination by midday and knew from the cargo pods and other bits strewn across the rocky landscape that no one in the old freighter could have survived the landing. Its cargo, protected by the heavy-duty plastic in which it had been shipped, was another matter. Only a few pods had broken open on impact with the ground and lay scattered about in small heaps, but the main line of pods led directly to the wreck. Helm had only to follow the debris to its source.

"That's an oldie," Jon remarked when magnification showed them the smashed freighter's ID. "Good hundred and fifty years old. Probably was sent out at the time of the Second Diaspora."

"If it was carrying colony supplies, we might find a lot of useful equipment," Casper said, rubbing his hands together in hopeful anticipation.

"Will it be good after so long?" Syrona asked.

"Should be," Jon said, "unless the contractors were dishonest. Those may be old cargo pods, but they were vacuum-sealed to load. The Navy still uses that model because it is durable and sturdy."

They reached the wreck, its forward section broken off from the stern by the force of its landing. But then, as Casper remarked sadly, the freighter had never been intended as a landing craft. Supplies would have been lightered down to the surface.

"Commander," Helm said, "if you can plug in a portable power source, I can access the ship's computer system and discover, from the pod markings, the contents from the manifest."

"Excellent idea, Helm," Jon said, grinning. "That would save a lot of guesswork."

"Scanning indicates that some of the inner cargo holds withstood the force of the impact, though opening the hatches may pose some problems," Helm added, sounding as surprised as it was possible for an AI to sound.

"We're in luck," Casper said brightly.

"We hope," was Jon's reply.

Syrona bit her lip not to laugh but Nimisha had no similar need to be tactful.

"You really are a team, aren't you?" she said, chuckling at the two men. "The optimist and the pessimist."

"It's worked so far," Jon remarked unabashed.

Getting to the main computer with an independent power source was not a problem. The bridge area had split wide open, and while the explorers had to remove vegetation—carefully, since Syrona identified some of the growths as highly toxic—they were able to reach the main data console. They cleared off the accumulation of dirt and debris and found the units were intact. Once powered up, leads attached, Helm went right to the manifest and started scrolling the items.

"Prefab parts, farm tools, hand tools, extra power packs—"

"That is, if the recharger survived," Jon said.

"Oh, you!" Syrona said with disgust.

"Well, it would be our luck that it was packed in one of the cases that broke open," he said with a grin and a shrug.

"No, Captain," Helm interrupted. "Manifest lists two pods of recharger units still intact on board." He paused the scrolling list at the appropriate entry.

"So there, too," Nimisha couldn't help but put in, grinning.

"Hey, disassembled ground vehicles," Casper said, crowing with delight and pointing at the entry.

"Helm, pause at that entry," Jon said, leaning his hands on the console and peering at the screen. "Won't do us any good if they're open vehicles . . . Ah, no, good choice. Closed vehicles and some with light repellers." He looked pleased, but then his expression changed abruptly. "I don't suppose there's fuel gel aboard in any quantity."

"I will scan ahead, Commander." The speed with which it did rendered other items unreadable. Then the screen stopped to display fuel gel supplies. "Fuel gel is listed as part of the contents of several holds, two of which are still intact. Some of the strewn pods probably contain that item."

"Satisfied?" Nimisha asked.

"It's a start," he said.

"The question now is whether or not you're enough of a mechanic to assemble one," Nimisha said, folding her arms across her chest.

"If I'm not, I'm sure you are, Lady Nimisha, if you built a ship that could survive the wormhole with so little damage," Jon replied, giving her a bow.

"That was not I. That was Helm's piloting."

"Thank you, ma'am. Shall I continue to scan the manifests?"

"Yes, please," Syrona said. "For seeds, medical supplies, food essentials." She turned to the men. "My turn, I think, since you are so happy to find your particular hobbies."

"Hobbies?" Jon exclaimed.

"Well, she has a point, Jon. We need everything . . ." Casper swung his arms out in an expansive gesture.

"So you don't think we should investigate the other two M-type planets?" Nimisha asked, having listened long enough to their enthusiasms for the riches of the ship's cargo.

"Ah . . ." Jon looked over his shoulder at her in surprise, with a slightly guilty expression. "Yes, well." He paused again, flushing a little with chagrin. "I think we've all been so concentrated on surviving on this planet that the notion we're no longer stuck here hasn't quite seeped in." He raised his hands apologetically.

"We can do both," Casper said, ever the intermediary. "Establish a better base here and then go exploring. Or vice versa," he added quickly.

"And there're the aliens now, too," Syrona put in, slightly hesitant as she made eye contact with Nimisha. "It is up to you to say, Lady Nimisha. You are captain of the Fiver."

"That's not at issue," Nimisha said. "And I do understand your excitement over all this . . . wealth. It must be secured before we go haring off to any other world." Then her eye was caught by an unusual item on the list that was still scrolling down the screen. "Windmills? Helm, do we know where this ship was bound for, when it was diverted?"

"Vega, ma'am, possibly for Acclarke City on Vega III when it was first founded. Records confirm the loss of this vessel at an unknown location—"

"And there are prairies and deep water tables on Vega III," Nimisha said, nodding.

"Windmills are good for more than pumping water out of the ground," Jon said, intent on the lists still rolling past. "We could establish a much better living standard with all this."

"For the little people, too?" asked Timmy, who had been sitting in the captain's chair and undoubtedly pretending he was the master of the freighter.

The adults exchanged glances.

"If they are willing, yes, Tim," Jon said. "There's more than enough here to share."

"They may not want our help," Syrona said gently. "But we will offer, won't we?"

The other three nodded.

"They might even be better scroungers than we are," Casper said, grinning.

Jon looked out of the split hull to the wide-open space beyond the ship's final resting place. "They may even have found the wreck and not figured out how to open the pods."

Casper looked around him. "Or someone may have survived. I've noticed a significant absence."

"I'm just as glad there are no skeletons," Syrona murmured.

"Considering what I've met of the local life-forms," Nimisha said, "with this section wide open, the scavengers would have removed any edible debris."

"Shall we see what else is to be seen in the wreck?" Jon asked Casper.

"Why don't Tim, Syrona, and I do a survey of the pods outside. See what's worth securing," Nimisha suggested. Though she sided with Casper in optimism, there was no sense in wasting valuable resources. She tried not to think that she might not be rescued. The others had accepted the fact. Would she have to?

"Excellent notion," Jon said. Casper and Syrona nodded in agreement, so the two groups went about their chosen tasks.

"Helm," Nimisha said into her wrist com, "track the men. We'll be in plain sight, but Jon and Casper will not."

"I can keep watch over more than two groups, ma'am."

"Concentrate on them," Nimisha said firmly as she and Syrona, aiding Tim over the longer steps, made their way to the ground. "Lemme have a look round, Syrie," she said, holding up her hand to mother and son. "There don't seem to be any tracks, but then, the wreck's been here for centuries. Local interest would have waned."

"I'll do that, Nimisha," Syrona said, "since I'm more familiar than you with the tracks of the indigenous species." She grinned and, giving Timmy a little shove, added, "You help Nimisha, dear."

Nimisha held out her hand and suggested that they examine the cluster of pods a few meters from the ship.

"What're in these, Helm?" she asked when they got to the first weathered and intact unit. First she had to scrape off the mud and ingrained dirt from the stenciled coding.

"Clothing," was Helm's prompt response.

"Keep a running account, please, Helm," Nimisha said. Next it was Timmy who found the markings on a pod of blankets.

By the time Syrona had rejoined them, without having found any suspicious tracks, Nimisha and Tim had found that fiber tents occupied a third, then more clothing and blankets, and bolts of fabric. The next few were marked "Miscellaneous," but Helm's probing determined that some of the miscellany was metallic.

"Scissors? Needles? Pins?" Syrona exclaimed, her eyes widening with pleasure. "I got to be a pretty good furrier, you know, when we found bone that wouldn't splinter. Casper kept experimenting because he was sure he'd find one that would make a good needle."

Nimisha grinned, thinking that optimism brings its own success.

They walked on, checking the strewn pods. Some had burst open, with little left in them but blown dust and debris: the contents had either deteriorated open to the weather or been removed.

Syrona examined the closing mechanism on an unopened crate. "Well, I suppose the little folk might have figured out how to open them—if they had enough strength in their digits."

"Digits, Syrie?" Timmy asked confused. "Digits are numbers."

"Digit is another word for finger," Syrona said.

"Confusing. You always said numbers for numbers, not digits."

"True, but digit is a synonym. Don't worry, I'll teach you about them soon, Tim," his mother said.

"Oh." He frowned. "I'm getting hungry, Syrie. Do we have to look at all of 'em?" He made an expansive gesture toward the long line leading several kilometers beyond them.

"I'm feeling a little empty, myself," Nimisha said. "Let's go back and see what the men have found, and we'll all have a snack on the Fiver."

Timmy brightened and skipped ahead of them on their return.

"It's so . . . so reassuring to know there are supplies on hand," Syrona said, running her fingers across the sides of the pods they passed as they retraced their steps.

"Oh, we'll be rescued before we need to tap into any of this," Nimisha said, cocksure.

Syrona gave her an odd glance. "You're counting on it?"

Nimisha regarded her frankly. "I," she said, placing a self-deprecating hand on her chest, "am not that important, but the Fiver is. Vegan Fleet and Rondymense Ship Yard will spare no effort to locate it, and me. And now you."

Syrona let out a sigh. "There is no record of that wormhole at those coordinates, Nimisha. Don't get your hopes up no matter how valuable that ship is. We're a very long way from Vega, or Altair, or any of the other settled areas of space."

"That's all too true, Syrona, especially as that wormhole makes such sporadic entries," Nimisha agreed, gesturing toward the wrecked freighter. "However, while you were marooned here, there've been many technological advances. I'll bet anything that Vegan Fleet and the FSP Navy will set up the very latest equipment at the Mayday beacon I managed to get off. They'll find us."

Syrona did not comment and they walked on in silence and were almost to the wreck, where Timmy was squatting and looking up through holes in the hull.

"I didn't mean to upset you, Nimisha," Syrona said at last.

"I'm not upset, Syrona, but it doesn't hurt to have two optimists in this expedition, does it? I've a particular reason to need to be back at Vega in another—" She counted. "—eighteen months."

"Your daughter's Necklacing?" Syrona asked.

"That's it."

"Even at the best speed your Fiver can do, you might be late."

"You're as bad as Jon," Nimisha said, keeping rancor and exasperation out of her voice. She told herself firmly that Syrona had suffered a lot in sixteen years: She had been forced to be a realist.

The two men came swinging down, feet first, from the larger of the holes Timmy had been looking up at.

"There's a lot salvageable aboard her," Casper said cheerfully. "And with what Helm says is available in prefab units, both on the ship and spread out across the landscape, we could each have our own private quarters."

"That's what you think," Syrona said with some asperity.

"Yes, ma'am," Casper said, pretending to avoid a blow.

"When," Jon said, pausing for emphasis, "we have found the best possible spot to set up a more permanent colony." He grinned at Nimisha, and she realized she must not have concealed her dismay at that abrupt remark. "I include the other two unexplored worlds, which we definitely should investigate now that we can," he said with a placatory bow in her direction. "At least we have plenty of stores to start off with."

"I hesitate to mention this," Casper said with a rueful smile, "but I'm . . . hungry."

"Me, too, Cas, me, too," Timmy exclaimed, grabbing Casper's hand and swinging himself about. Syrona nodded agreement.

"Unanimous?" Jon asked, looking at Nimisha.

"No question of that," she said and led the way back to the Fiver.

. .

When Timmy was engaged in eating and watching a vid, the two men told the women what they had discovered in the rest of the ship.

"I don't think there were any survivors, not with the damage to the bridge area. Below, we found skeletons—practically every bone in their bodies had been broken," Jon said soberly. "Helm augmented our findings by his sensor readings. The log data he's accessed so far indicated that they'd dumped fuel in the hope of surviving a crash landing. Maybe one or two did. Crew complement was eighteen on a vessel this size. We found twelve skeletons. We figure the other six would have been on duty on the bridge. Nothing could have got into the crew quarters. The doors were still shut. In fact, we had trouble prying them open."

"Helm reports accessing their names and home ports," Casper said. "Their families will benefit."

"*If* we can get a report back," Jon said with a diffident shrug.

Nimisha waited a moment, controlling her irritation. Out of the corner of her eye she saw Syrona give Casper an anxious look.

"You really are a pessimist, aren't you, Captain?" It took Nimisha all her self-control not to color that remark with her true feelings.

"I've had to be . . . ma'am."

"Hey, you two, there aren't enough of us to be at each other's throats," Casper said, a placatory smile on his face.

Jon laughed and waved toward Casper. "The eternal optimist."

"I came, didn't I?" Nimisha said. She smiled all around the table. "The point is, we can *improve* our situations now, can't we? We can make a serious attempt at cultivating another alien species. We can investigate the other two M-type worlds. I'd rather one that didn't have as many predators if we want to be safe until . . . help . . . comes!" She stressed those words. "Because help *will* come." She glared at Jon and then at Syrona. "I am proof."

"Of what?"

"Oh . . ." Nimisha's patience was strained. "Proof that our technology is capable of finding us, no matter how far away our home worlds are."

"You, you mean," Syrona said almost angrily.

"I've heard enough of this," Doc said in a stern voice. "You do not need to wrangle with each other. You're all you have. So hear this, loud and clear. The euphoria of discovery has dissipated and you're all experiencing a quite logical swing toward depression. There is no need for acrimony. My programming tends for me to side with you optimists, but then I am aware, as an extensively programmed Artificial Intelligence, how far our technology has progressed from state-of-the-art as you would have known it, Captain Svangel. Message pulse sending is now highly refined, and a pulsed message *will* reach some listening ear, if it hasn't already. I highly recommend that you finish your meals and get a good night's rest. You'll need it tomorrow for clear thinking in dealing with the small people. Understand?"

"My apologies," Jon said formally, and bowed to Nimisha.

"Mine as well," Syrona said meekly.

"None are needed," Nimisha said and rose. "Helm, has the remote shown any activity at tomorrow's meeting site?"

"There has been peripheral movement in the area, but no alien was visible, nor were there sounds that could be recorded and added into the base for semantical analysis."

"Maybe they're just not curious," Casper said, getting to his feet. "C'mon, Tim, we're all having an early night to be rested for tomorrow's meeting."

"Can I finish watching this adventure? It's exciting."

"A soothing nightcap might be advisable," Doc said charmingly. "Cater, do provide us with an appropriate beverage."

"My pleasure. What may I serve you, Lady Nimisha? A tea perhaps?"

Whatever it was, herbal and tasty, had undoubtedly been laced with a mild sedative, Nimisha decided the next morning when Helm's chimes roused her. She had slept like the proverbial log.

Helm announced that there were significant movements at the proposed site, so everyone climbed into the gig after Jon carefully exited the Fiver's garage. They had patched in both Doc and Helm to the gig and, through that control board, to their wrist units, which would be recording the proceedings. Nimisha fixed a comunit to Tim's belt, rather than wrapped about his much smaller wrist. Jon suggested an earring, so that Tim could receive advice from his mentors during the interview; a small receiver was found and planted behind his right ear. He strutted about, pleased with his equipment.

"A reception committee," Nimisha murmured when the gig, coming in at an angle over the obscuring bluff, showed them the throng that had gathered.

"They've set us a table, too," Timmy cried excitedly, pointing.

When the adults saw the rest of the carefully set scene, they exchanged amused glances. There were four stools set well back from the table, just as they had been positioned to allow Timmy to make the initial contact on the Fiver. There were little piles of what were obviously samples of edibles on pottery plates, as well as cups and several pottery jugs.

"Nice design on the pottery. Looks painted on with fine brush-work," Jon murmured. "Glazed, too."

"The best china for the visitors?" Nimisha replied.

"No diagnostic unit though," Syrona remarked with a sigh of relief.

"They are showing a nice degree of intelligence by reproducing our first encounter as well as they have," Jon said.

"All right, Tim, you're our resident ambassador," Casper said. "You go first."

"*Me?*" Tim went all wide-eyed and nervous.

"They've set everything up for you, honey," Syrona said encouragingly, giving him a little shove toward the gig's open hatch.

"They have no weapons with them," Helm said, his low reassurance making Tim square his shoulders and advance. "Based on Doc's medical reports, they are at ease and waiting. No elevation of pulse or heartbeat."

"We're right behind you, cadet ensign," Jon said.

"So long as you *are*." Tim muttered, but he took the step forward. Then he paused and gulped as he reached ground level and began to appreciate just how many were assembled up the hill beyond the meeting place. "There's an awful lot of them, isn't there? What do I say? What do I do?" Apprehension made his voice quiver.

"Walk up to the table, Tim," Jon said. "We'll prompt you. Put your left hand behind your back if you want suggestions. I suggest that you point to yourself and say your own name. Then ask for Ay and Bee. Let's see if they remember the names we gave them."

"Shouldn't one of us go with him?" Syrona asked anxiously.

"Tim's a brave lad," Nimisha said, assessing the rows and rows of quiet gray aliens seated in their odd cross-legged position. "He'll do the ambassador very well indeed." She made certain her voice was loud enough to reach Timmy's ears as he advanced. He must have heard her, for he suddenly stood a little straighter.

Four aliens rose and came forward to the table, bowing to Tim, and then bowing again to the larger humans and gesturing to the seating provided. Timmy bowed back.

Obediently the adults sat down, though the stools were more suited to smaller rear ends than theirs.

"Notice the much darker coats of two of them," Nimisha said softly. "Would that indicate age?"

Jon shrugged. "We should have painted Ay and Bee on the two while we had them. They all look exactly alike."

"They won't when we get used to them," Casper said. "I think they mean to get used to us."

Nimisha firmly hoped so. That would be a plus for the *Poolbeg* crew, and for herself and the achievements of the Fiver. She tried to settle on her stool, but it was too unstable on the soft ground for her to really relax or even put her full weight on it.

"Tim," the boy said, pointing to himself. "Ay? Bee? Oh, hey, they know who they are!" As two of the four aliens took an additional step forward, he turned about to grin at the adults.

Ay bowed again and said quite plainly, pointing to itself, "Ay."

"BbbbbEEEE," the second one managed to get out, having a lot of trouble with "b," which sounded more like "bubbubb," as it stepped forward. It took a plate carefully in both three-fingered hands and held it out to Tim. Then it took one of the unevenly chopped pieces and popped it into its mouth, chewing vigorously and making a thing of swallowing.

"I don't know what it is," Tim asked plaintively, eyeing the dish with anxiety.

"Doc says the offered food will not harm you but he can't guarantee the taste, Tim," Helm said softly, using the earring amplifier.

Tim reached hesitantly, but he took the food, sniffed it as the aliens had done, licked it. "Not so bad." He popped the morsel into his mouth. "Chewy," he added. "Like the nuts we found, Syrie."

He smiled, then rubbed his stomach and licked his lips. The two who stood beyond Ay and Bee recoiled slightly.

"Whaddid I do wrong?" Tim asked anxiously.

"I don't think you did anything wrong," Jon said quietly. "Take another piece and don't make faces."

"I thought it'd help if I showed 'em I liked it," Tim replied, but he took another morsel, chewed it, and swallowed. Ay offered him a pottery cup with water in it. Then Bee picked up another cup, took a careful sip, and handed it to Tim. He sniffed at it, since that seemed to be acceptable behavior. "Some sort of sweet-smelling stuff, like the fruit you picked last year, Cas."

"Doc says neither will harm you, Tim," Helm said through the earring.

"Hey, the juice is good," Timmy said after the first sip, and drained the cup. Bee was quick to refill it, and Ay presented a different plate of small brown balls that Nimisha thought might have been cooked. Ay ate a ball before offering the plate to Tim.

"Doc says it's a meat product and harmless," Helm informed him.

Tim popped a ball into his mouth, closed his mouth, and then reacted in distress, opening his mouth wide, fanning it.

"Harmless?" Tim drained the fruit juice with a sigh of relief. "Hot stuff—not hot to touch, hot to eat. Wooof!"

His antics seemed to amuse not only Ay, Bee, and the other nearer aliens, but all those observing. Muted hoots and ooos rippled through the audience.

Bee said something liquid in sound to Ay, who changed plates to some green sprouts.

"I know what these are," Timmy said and crammed a handful into his mouth, nodding enthusiastically. Another ripple of hoots circulated the audience.

Ay picked up another plate and, after showing it to Tim, waved its free hand in front of its mouth and put the plate to one side.

"Thanks, Ay. That was hot all the way down," Tim said. "I wouldn't mind some more of the first stuff," he said, and picked up two more morsels from the plate. This appeared to please the audience.

"Is it possible to get samples of all they have offered?" Helm asked.

"Tim, why don't you load some of the food on the greens plate and bring it back to us," Jon suggested.

"Shouldn't I ask first?"

"Make gestures," Jon said and Tim went through an elaborate pantomime, of filling a plate, taking it to the adults, and bowing as he pretended to serve it.

Ay and Bee turned to the other two, sound rising and falling in the ensuing conversation.

Ay made the selection itself and indicated that it would like to do the serving. Timmy shrugged and gestured for him to proceed.

Bee produced more cups and filled them with the fruit juice. It used the largest plate to convey the cups to the adults, following after Ay.

"It is tasty," Nimisha said.

"Tim's right about having had it," Syrona said, "but it's not in season right now. So where did they get it from?"

"Curiouser and curiouser," Nimisha said.

"Weapons, pottery, food preservation technique," Casper said, grinning. "And smart."

"Now, if we can only figure out how to exchange—" Jon stopped as the two very gray aliens came forward, bowing not quite as deeply as Ay and Bee did.

Jon rose carefully and bowed at the same angle. Casper, Syrona, and Nimisha followed his example.

Ay and Bee stepped back, out of the way, as if they had done their part in introducing one species to the other. Two others came out of the crowd, carrying stools similar to the ones provided for the humans. When the legs of these were firmly pushed into the ground, the dark grays gestured for the humans to sit. Jon indicated that they should be seated first. They motioned for the humans to sit.

Jon held up his fingers. "One, two, three." He mimed that they should all be seated at once. "Sit." He matched action to the work.

The darkest gray personage hissed as it sat, turning its head slightly to its companion and making some liquid comment. The other nodded.

"Ex and Wye?" Nimisha said out of the corner of her mouth, leaning toward Jon.

Ex touched one digit to its chest and "ooool" was the sound that came out.

"Ex equals Ooool?"

Ool nodded vigorously and the mouth slit opened. The other gray clearly said, "Ooook," pointing to itself. Then it indicated Ool and repeated that sound.

"Help, Helm," Jon murmured.

"The true sound goes beyond human hearing, Commander. Repeat the sounds you do hear as closely as you can," was Helm's advice.

"Ool, ooooool?" Jon pointed to Ool. Then struggled with "Ooook."

The two grays titled their heads from one side to another, regarding each other with black bands of eye slits wide.

"They're too polite to laugh," Syrona murmured. "But they have a sibilant . . . let me try my name. Sy-ron-ah."

"Ssssooo ah," was Ool's attempt and it struggled with that much.

"Tim?" Tim offered, pointing to himself.

"Immmmm." For some reason this sound was repeated not only by Ool and Ook, but by Ay, Bee, and then the audience.

"Pay dirt," Casper remarked in a low tone.

Ool and Ook exchanged several remarks.

"If they could be kept talking," Helm said quietly, "more sounds could be registered and there would be a better chance of isolating words within the sounds."

"What do you call this?" Jon said, holding up the cup and pointing to it.

Ool and Ook once again exchanged glances. Ool said a quick combination of vowels.

Jon pointed into the cup. Ook replied with another set of sounds. And the audience repeated these. Then the aliens began to chant the sounds that had already been made, starting with the names of the two grays, Syrona's name, Tim, and the word for cup and for the juice. The name, "Immm" caused what must be alien laughter whenever it was repeated.

"Let's everyone sing along," Nimisha said softly, struggling to keep from laughing aloud. "Cup," she said in a louder voice, holding it up. Pointing inside, she said, "Fruit juice."

The audience came in right on cue, and that was how the rest of the morning went: each species getting a chance to point and name things in its own language while the other struggled to replicate the sounds. Occasional ululations rippled through the audience, but the overall reaction seemed to be one of enjoyment.

"Makes me think of the sounds from old Terran Africa," Syrona remarked at one point when a warble had been musically extended.

Then Jon raised his arms for silence, a gesture understood by the aliens. He pointed to all the humans and said very clearly, "Hu—manz." He put his thumb on his chest "Hu—man."

"Ooooh—maaaa—zuh!" Ool said carefully.

Jon repeated the word, aspirating the "h." "Yu-man-z."

"Yu-ma-z," was as close as Ool, Ook, Ay, Bee, and the crowd got. But Jon clasped both hands above his head in approbation. He gracefully turned his hand to Ool and Ook, then circled his fingers toward Ay, Bee, and the audience.

Ool gave a quick bob of its head. "Ssss-imm," was the carefully enunciated reply, with Ool opening its mouth wide and showing the regular row of tiny pointed teeth before the lips closed on the "m" sound.

"Maybe that's why they laughed at my name," Tim said. "It's something like a word of theirs after all. Ssss-immm," he said, enunciating with lips and sound.

The hooting was widespread, and many repeated Jon's gesture of clasping their hands above their head.

"Helm, are they saying shim or ssssh-im?" Casper asked.

"On the decibel recorder it is two separate sounds. Sh'im is closest," Helm replied after a nanosecond's deliberation.

"Sh'im," Jon said, pointing to them. His thumb in his direction. "Oo-man."

"I am picking up private conversations in the audience," Helm said. "I am recording. They are relaxed and enjoying this."

"Best show in town," Casper said, rolling his eyes with amusement.

They kept on pointing at and naming things, from the dirt and stones underfoot to the shrubbery, the stools, the ruins of the old ship, the sky, sun, and moons until the sun was high in the sky.

At last Syrona admitted to a splitting headache, which allowed Nimisha to say she, too, had one. Tim had been quiet for some time, but sat quietly on his stool, watching the Sh'im leaders.

"Have you enough to work on now, Helm?" Jon asked as both Sh'im and Humans seemed to take a pause.

"Yes, Captain."

"Good, then let's wind up this session and thank our hosts." He rose, bowed to Ool and Ook, and gestured to the gig. Then he pantomimed the sun going down and raised one finger.

Ool bobbed his head and held up his two fingers. Then turned his head from side to side.

"Now does that mean a bob is no and a shake is yes?" Syrona asked.

"That would be my interpretation," Helm said.

So Jon lifted two fingers and shook his head and bowed again.

Ool, Ook, Ay, and Bee rose and bowed. So did all the Sh'im in the audience, and with that the two groups separated.

"I don't know when I've been more exhausted," Nimisha said as they returned to the gig.

"That's normal enough when trying to reach a rapport with new . . . ah . . . aliens," Jon said. "I'm whacked."

"Thank goodness," Syrona muttered, but she gave Jon a quick grin to take away the sting of her comment.

"And Tim's our star," Jon said, putting his arms across the boy's shoulders and then catching him as the boy stumbled. "Our tired star. I think he rates as many burgers and as much ice cream as he can eat."

"If he doesn't fall asleep first," Casper said.

"You have been followed," Helm said softly. "They do not carry arms."

"Don't turn around," Jon said quickly, twisting Tim who was about to do just that. "They would be curious about our transport."

"Ay and Bee'd've told 'em," Tim said tiredly, plodding along.

"I think seeing's believing," Syrona remarked, reaching out her hand to help him.

"Shouldn't we at least wave goodbye?" Nimisha asked, keenly aware of being under surveillance.

"A bow would be safer and equally appropriate," Jon replied.

They had reached the gig now and, when Jon murmured "about-face," they did so as well as any drill team, bowing at the line of Sh'im who crowded the crest of the hill, some creeping up to peek through the shrubs. The hisses, hoots, and other sounds which could only have been made by Sh'im vocal equipment carried on the still midday air. Once again bows were exchanged. Then the Humans entered the gig and the hatch slid shut.

"That's hard work," Casper said, wiping sweat from his forehead. "Cater, something cool and tart, please. Tim, what do you fancy?"

"Anything cool," Tim said, flouncing down in the nearest chair. "I never thought talking could be such hard work," he added.

"Cater, please increase the cool and tart order by . . . all of us?" Nimisha looked round at Jon and Syrona, who nodded.

"My pleasure. This is a combination of tart fruity flavors, unsweetened," Cater said in her lovely alto voice. "It should be refreshing to the entire body."

"I agree, Tim," Nimisha said, taking two glasses from the dispenser counter and bringing one to him.

"Using a different section of the brain," Jon said. "Not one that ordinarily gets much exercise. But I think we did well." He lifted his glass in a toast.

"I have acquired a great deal of phonetic information which I will now analyze. Your next session in two days' time will be much easier. Hand units can be adapted to synthesize their words in tones they can hear and reduce theirs to ones you will understand." Helm paused. "Verbs would be very useful."

"Some languages on old Earth didn't have the verb 'to be'," Syrona commented after a thoughtful sip of her drink.

" 'Cogito, ergo sum,' " Jon said, laughing.

Nimisha regarded him with surprise.

"Latin can be very useful," he added, and his eyes twinkled at her with humor.

"You continue to surprise me, Captain," she said, raising her empty glass in a toast.

"More?" Jon asked, reaching for the pitcher.

"Yes, please."

"You continue to surprise me, Lady Nimisha. I thought First Families were above normal courtesies."

Nimisha blinked. "Not if you were raised by *my* mother."

"Orders please, ma'am?"

"Oh, yes, Helm, we'll be returning to the Fiver shortly." She gestured to the controls. "You or me?"

Jon grinned. "Shall we give Casper a turn? He needs the practice."

"Which means," Casper said, rising and putting his glass down, "that your headache is worse than mine. Well, I don't mind if I do." He seated himself at the control panel and checked the screens to be sure there were no Sh'im lurking close enough. Just in case, he lifted vertically, very slowly.

As the gig rose above the obscuring hill, they could all see the Sh'im on their way back across the broad plain where the bird ship had carved its final path.

"Do we wait for a formal invitation to see where they live?" Nimisha asked.

"I have the feeling that that would be appropriate. I would suggest we bring the Fiver and perhaps rig an exterior screen so a vid can give them the usual out-of-this-world briefing," Jon said.

"Hmmm. That could be very interesting," Nimisha mused.

The invitation to visit the Sh'im settlement was issued halfway through a very productive session at the original site. The visual aids, carefully prepared by the Federated Sentient Planets Exploratory team for showing to sapients, was avidly watched— three times, in fact, after Ool and Ook asked with many bows and gestures. The tape included space views of Earth and its moon, diagrams of Sol system, the two sexes that inhabited it, and the many animals that still roamed the Wildlife Preserves. The first moon landing and the subsequent installation and the space station were included, and then the first great colony generation ship that was launched to Alpha Centauri binary system. Mathematical equations were included, since this had always been considered the best way to bridge a semantic gap. While the humans watched for signs of especial interest in the reruns of the tape, they saw none.

Many small comments were made and recorded by Helm during

the replays. When the third showing finished, Tim, Jon, and Casper began to acquire action verbs by demonstration. Vocabulary increased in a quantum jump as both species could now repeat what they learned in their own way and get across meanings.

By afternoon, the Sh'im were able to indicate that they were indeed descendants of those who survived the crash. They had remained near the wreck, hoping to be rescued. The cliffs not far from the wreck were riddled with habitable caves. The survivors had explored these when such equipment as they had was still operational.

"If we're figuring their notion of a year correctly," Nimisha said, "that was not quite a hundred of our years ago."

"Yes, but we can't establish if they are from this general spatial area or if they got caught by the wormhole," Jon said. "Helm, have you anything we can screen that looks like a wormhole?"

"Yes, Captain," was the prompt response. "I recorded the one we came through."

"Oh, well done, Helm," Casper said. "We bounced around so much that we couldn't get any sort of an accurate record."

"I suspect it's only because of you, Helm, and your response time that we weren't badly damaged," Nimisha said.

"That is why an AI Helm is superior to the fastest human reaction times," Helm said.

Jon leaned toward Nimisha and whispered, "Do I detect a bit of condescension in that reply?" Then he nearly fell off the stool when it responded to his change of position by tilting.

Nimisha smothered a laugh. "Helm is only stating a fact," she replied, recovering her composure.

The humans also learned that the Sh'im had two sexes, and that the darker the coat the older the being. They did not have long life spans, thirty years being an average. The female tended to have multiple births—two and three, produced every year for ten years.

The male also tended the young, who matured quickly and could help in providing food for the latest arrivals by the time the next group were born. An increasing population appeared to be the main reason why the Sh'im had been searching for a suitable planet: to relieve overcrowding on their home worlds. They had three, but the humans could not grasp if these were M-type planets in separate systems or three planets in the same one.

"Three M-type planets would be most unusual in the same system," Jon said.

"Unless they've terraformed or Sh'immied others in their home system," Nimisha said. "If they could fly in that crazy bird, they might have been technologically superior in other ways."

The Sh'im had power from windmills, laboriously constructed out of local woods, which is why there had been no metal echo on the Fiver's screens. Over the hill and at the original town site, the windmills were busy spinning in the good breeze. The Sh'im had four towns, since they were prolific even with the number of predators on Erehwon. That was why the two-day interval was needed: to allow the leaders of the other townships to arrive, go home and report, and return for the next session. They had a form of chemoluminescent lighting in their caves. They had blown glass artifacts, some in brilliant colors. They were able to draw water from artesian wells, and they had power to smelt and manufacture metal implements. They hunted in large groups for protection and to transport meat back to their homes. They dried and stored the meat in the large pottery containers they produced from local clay and fired in kilns. There were a few metal containers from the shipwreck, but these were rarely used, more treasured as objects to venerate. They had looms and collected fur from the huge grazers to weave into rugs for their homes and for use at night in the coldest part of the year. Otherwise they did not use clothing or footwear. They had written glyphs, and the young were taught basic lessons. In each cliff site an elder kept meticulous records of births, deaths, achievements, and a general history.

"We shan't be breaking any FSP laws, then," Jon said with a sigh of relief, "if we help them upgrade to a higher technology."

"How much higher do they need to go?" Nimisha asked.

"Well, a repeller screen would keep them from the periodic attacks of the avians," Jon said. "If Helm has sufficient parts to make them."

"I do," Helm replied, and Nimisha frowned.

"Why not?" Jon asked. "They've already shown us more edible vegetables and burrowing creatures than we were able to find. They've had a more balanced diet than we managed."

"The terrain here is different," Nimisha said.

"Not that much," Jon said.

"It's not that I object to offering what the Fiver has," Nimisha began, not really sure how to present her real objection.

"I'd say it's more the time it'll take us to do installations, isn't it?" Jon said, glancing sideways at her, one eyebrow raised.

"You come right to the point, don't you?"

"I don't see why not," was his quick reply. He touched her arm lightly. "I do want to see what the other planets are like. Those orders remain whether or not we have the *Poolbeg*. In the light of what we now know, one of them might be Sh'im, and we can return them to their own civilization. Or tell their planetary leaders where they are."

"They wanted to found a new colony. Basically, they have," she said, almost resenting how well he read her body language.

"If their ship had landed intact, they'd've had more essential tools and equipment, as well as bodies, to found an efficient colony."

"I don't see what prevents us from giving them stuff from the freighter," Casper said.

"Do we know they haven't found it?" Jon asked. "They indicated that they've done some considerable exploring."

"I think they would have mentioned it," Syrona said. "Though that would have been a long way for their shorter legs to go. Most of the open pods we saw had been damaged in the drop. We didn't see any intact ones that had been opened manually."

"Good point," Jon said. "More to cement good relations with them."

"We are being candid?" Nimisha asked.

"As they have had space drive, even if none of those now alive ever flew a ship, I feel we should be as honest as possible," Jon said. "I rather like them."

"I do, too," Nimisha began and then realized she had no reservations. Being open and forthright saved all the trouble of remembering what they should or should not say; or what useful technology they could give the Sh'im to improve on what they had already achieved. "Of course, we'd have to modify equipment for three-fingered hands."

Jon grinned, and if he could read her body language, she could read his. He was relieved that she was willing to be open.

"They will need tools that give them a different leverage than we'd need," Casper said thoughtfully. "Their body center of mass is at a different height above the ground, which requires a different lever length, and their smaller handspan means they would need smaller spans for tools."

"Look, Nimisha," Syrona said, "I know you're anxious to investigate the other planets, so why don't you and Jon go do that while Casper, Tim, and I stay here to help the Sh'im. Tim's had so much fun with the young Sh'im . . . and I'd really like to stay here." She glanced down at her hands, which were nervously pulling at the seams of her coverall.

Instantly Casper put a sympathetic arm about her shoulders. "Pregnant and all, I'd say that might be wiser, love." He looked up at Jon and Nimisha, not exactly pleading but obviously siding with his mate. "And for Tim's sake, too."

"I beg your pardon, Syrona," Jon said, executing an apologetic bow. "An excellent proposal, since priorities are pulling us in two directions. Two birds with one stone . . ."

"Where's a stone here big enough to get one of those murderous avians, much less two?" Syrona asked, giving a nervous little laugh, but she was clearly relieved by the reception of her suggestion.

"We'll stock the gig from Cater's supplies so Tim won't go without burgers," Nimisha said, chuckling.

"I think he's taking to what the Sh'im eat all the time," Syrona said with another laugh, not quite as nervous. "Those nutty morsels, not the hot stuff."

"So let's take a group of Sh'im in the Fiver to the freighter wreck, shall we?" Jon proposed. "See what they can use from the pods. The Fiver can bring back quite a bit. When there's enough here, we can go exploring."

He glanced at Nimisha with a look of approval for the versatility of the ship. She waved a hand, accepting the idea. An exploratory voyage with him would certainly allow her to get to know him better. She liked him, but with Syrona and Casper so intent on their making a partnership, she felt herself resisting. She had the notion that he was resisting the pairing as well, which both put her in charity with him and made her wonder why he didn't attempt to forward an interest. Maybe he resented being catapulted into an intimacy even though she knew she was feeling the strains of celibacy, possibly more than he was. Perverse of her, she knew.

Then more immediate concerns diverted her from such rumination.

Ool and Ook were surprised to see Helm's tape of the freighter and the pods. And delighted when they understood that these supplies would be available to them. Even their most adventurous scout parties had been unable to traverse the mountain range that lay between the two wrecks. Nimisha had had Helm make maps of Erehwon from space, a Mercator projection, a Goode's Homolosine, and a Lambert Azimuthal equal area for detailed views of smaller areas, plus modified cylindrical and conic projections for the hemispheres. Helm could also, on request, put up on any screen the 3-D spherical globe. She had him print up an Azimuthal for the area in which the freighter had come down, complete with topography.

The freighter had come down on the eastern edge of this continent, and to the south of the Sh'im, the formidable mountain range separating the two portions. Three very dark-furred Sh'im were fascinated by the maps, poring over them. They hooted loudly and with great appreciation when Helm screened the 3-D of Erehwon and they could watch it turning. Nimisha had him do the same for Vega III and old Earth. In their turn, they responded by unrolling carefully preserved star charts, printed on a flimsy material that Casper suggested was the Sh'im plastic analog. The colors were as bright as when they had first been printed; the designations of the various stars provided no clue to any of the humans or Helm as to their current galactic position. The Sh'im had colonized three different star systems, one quite far from the home world, which proved they had been space-faring for a significant period of time. None were apparently near Erehwon, so the Sh'im were probably just as lost and distant from their original star system as the humans were. Neither species took encouragement from that fact.

Ool and Ook quickly picked a group to go with the humans. Syrona chose to stay behind, as she was feeling oddly queasy. Doc ran a check on the fetus and found nothing untoward. For good measure, he administered a spray of broad multivitamin and trace minerals. He recommended some peace and quiet, with her feet up, and she was as glad to have the gig to herself while the others went on the Fiver. Tim was essential in any team working with the Sh'im.

"Good thing they're on the small side," Casper remarked as the furry bodies of the Sh'im took up most of the floor space in the main cabin of the spaceship.

"Warn them we're taking off," Jon told Tim, who was sitting with their guests.

"He hoots as to the manner born," Casper said with due pride as Tim relayed the message.

"Not that they'll feel much movement," Nimisha said at the controls. She and Jon had arrived at a tacit arrangement: They took turns piloting the Fiver. She felt that was only fair. Jon was not only acting captain of his own group, but also a very deft pilot. She could not object to his taking turns and it allowed her to watch someone else obviously enjoying the command of the Fiver. "Take her up in a vertical lift, Helm."

"Yes, ma'am."

"Any reason you didn't use Fleet usage?" Jon asked idly.

"This Fiver is a civilian ship," she said with a grin. "The Fleet will program its own Helms, if they decide to use AIs."

"The Fiver survived the wormhole a lot better than the *Poolbeg* or the others," he commented, jerking a thumb at the broken bird-ship in the rear screen. "If that's what an AI can do, I'm for it."

"Thank you, Captain," Helm said.

"You're welcome, Helm. That was one superior job of pilot-ing to come through that wormhole with only a few scrapes." He shook his head, apparently recalling the battering the *Poolbeg* had taken.

"Can we please see where we're going, Nimisha?" Tim asked, leaning into the bridge area.

"Helm, if you would be so good," Nimisha said.

"Of course, Lady Nimisha." In the next instant there were star-tled hoots of the Sh'im and a rustling and moving about that made Jon look around the partition.

He was grinning broadly, but signaled a thumbs-up to reassure her about their passengers.

Later on, Tim had them line up at Cater's dispenser worktop and gave orders for food and drink. Cater had accepted samples of the Sh'im edibles and was able to re-create them. Tim had a burger and served Jon and Casper. Nimisha had a cheese pasta dish and a salad, since they now had access to the fresh produce from the Sh'im gardens. The broad green leaf was neither spinach nor let-tuce but had a definite and pleasant taste, more like fennel.

Even at cruising speed, it took several hours to make the trip. However, as it was the vernal season, they would have six hours of daylight in which to conduct their work.

The humans had arbitrarily decided which pods they'd open first: tools, blankets, some of the prefab building, the disassembled vehicles, and the repeller shields. If, for instance, the older Sh'im allowed those to be mounted on the cliff, the danger of stone-dropping avians would no longer terrorize them and the town could expand out of the crowded caves. The gardens could be extended and more edible leaves and roots provided, especially as they could put the repellers to work underground as well as over it. Further afield, the Sh'im gathered wild grains in season where it grew natu-rally. Although the harvesting was fraught with the peril of avian attacks, the Sh'im managed to keep casualties low. To protect their towns, they had devised a powerful catapult—similar in structure to the ancient crossbows. They were evidently good marksmen. While the humans had not seen the device in action, both Jon and Casper allowed that it would be as effective as the gig's missiles. They were of two minds about installing a missile system on the cliffs. Nimi-sha had suggested that as long as the Sh'im had an effective defense, they should reserve their more advanced technology for the time being.

Then they were fast approaching the wrecked freighter, and Timmy was excitedly telling the passengers—in broken Sh'im—about the marvelous things they would soon see.

"Where shall I land, Lady Nimisha?" Helm asked.

Nimisha looked at Jon and Casper. "Near the biggest clump of pods. I think that constitutes a fair selection of what's available."

"Won't they want to see the freighter?" Casper asked.

"They'd find it awkward climbing into it, I think," Nimisha said. "Unless you have ladders available."

"Point," Jon said, "but I think we should take a couple of dark-furs on a tour to show good faith."

"It's not as if they could fly it away, is it?" Casper added.

"All too true," Nimisha remarked wryly.

"I can't remember if we closed the hatches on those skeletons," Jon said, frowning. "We should have."

"If there's time, I'll grab body bags and cover them up," Casper said. "Leave it to me. We can hold a proper burial ceremony next time we're back. I suspect we'll be making additional trips. I know we'd have the gig while you're gone, but Syrona wants a house, a proper house," he said with a long-suffering sigh for the vagaries of his pregnant partner. "I think I do, too, complete with a fireplace for the cold winter nights Ay was talking about. Have you ever felt how thick the fur on him is?"

Nimisha nodded, for she'd had occasion to touch some of weavers when they showed her their looms and what they were currently working on. It was a craft that had always fascinated her. She might try her hand at it when they got back from their exploration of the other two M-type planets.

Though none of them discussed the subject, once Helm had regretfully admitted that none of the primaries listed on the Sh'im star charts matched anything in his data files, they were individually coming to terms with the fact that, quite possibly, they might spend their lifetimes on Erehwon. That is, if one of the other planets was not gentler in its climate and indigenous species. Not that she was eager to leave the Sh'im and Erehwon. There were only four of them and not a sufficient gene pool. She'd have to have children by Casper, as Syrona had had one by Jon. Or more.

"They exude a sort of lemony smell, don't they?" she observed, bringing herself ruthlessly back to the moment.

Helm set the Fiver down so gently there wasn't so much as a bump.

"Well done, Helm," she said and touched the control to open the two hatches.

The exodus was remarkably like a stampede as the Sh'im leaped daringly from the open hatch down the human-adult-sized steps to the ground. Jon, Casper, and Nimisha followed as Sh'im swarmed about the pods, hooting and ooing and dancing with excitement.

"Tools, I think," Casper said, consulting the printout in his hand and going to the nearest pod on his list. "Jon, the next one has tools, too. Nimisha, you open the third one. Jon, go to the fourth on the left. It's listed as prefab units. I'll join you as soon as I open up."

Though the Sh'im were small, they had unusual strength for their body size. They were also good observers and they needed only to be shown what to touch on the digital locks—each commodity had its own series of four numbers—and managed to undo the tight clasp.

"One way to teach them our numbers," Jon said, pleased with their quickness.

Rather than requiring the Sh'im to scramble up and into high pods, Jon and Casper tipped those containers still upright to their sides for easier access. Soon enough, all the pods in that first strewing were open and the contents examined—even the farm tools that had been designed to be drawn by some four-legged draft animal.

Neither Jon nor Casper—and certainly not Nimisha, who'd been
city bred—could explain exactly what the more complicated equipment was used for, though they did recognize a plow.

"I can see juvenile shaggies from those grazers on the other
continent being taught to pull one of these," Nimisha said, laughing at such a whimsy.

"They have tried to domesticate them," Casper surprised them
by saying. "But so far they've only found the ones the herd rejects,
the weak or lame. So long as you feed them, they're amenable to
being kept enclosed. The trouble is they grow up and break out of
any enclosure the Sh'im have been able to construct."

"There are other, smaller, grazers," Nimisha said. She remembered seeing them eating apart from the bigger creatures.

Casper grinned. "They've tried. Fast as the Sh'im are, those
deer types are faster. We weren't able to hunt them, much less catch
any. First hint of danger and they're off . . . at incredible speeds.
Like the springbok types from old Earth."

"Didn't the Altair III colony domesticate their deer types?"

"Finally," Jon said with a grin.

The Sh'im also spent a great deal of time trying to figure out
the use of some of the tools, talking among themselves and turning the equipment this way and that. Then Jon found a pod full of
disassembled wagon elements. He showed the Sh'im the instruction booklet with its illustration of the finished product and they
went into a frenzy of excitement. One group was trying to push
and shove the pod toward the Fiver in their eagerness to take possession of its contents. Others were wildly running up and down
the line of pods trying to find a similarly marked one. Jon and
Casper managed to convey, with Tim acting as pantomimist, that
as many as the Sh'im wanted would be transported. In this first
trip, they should take back samples of everything that looked to be
useful.

"I had an easier time of it with my girls," Nimisha said. She and her group happened to find blankets, clothing, pots, pans, and domestic items. They had run back to see what was causing so much hooting and ululation. "The wooden wheels with the metal rims they're using now are pretty good, considering the materials to hand, but these low-pressure balloon tires will revolutionize travel. Good thing they were reinforced with that plastic fiber."

Jon grinned. "Whoever stocked this vessel thought ahead to cope with unknown and undoubtedly rough terrain."

What the Sh'im considered essential to take back with them was more than could be accommodated in the Fiver. There were plaintive ululations from the Sh'im as they pared down the stack of treasures to fit the available space. That was when one of the dark-coats was pinned down under one of the crates, ooooling piteously. Instantly, Sh'im and humans went to its aid, but it was obvious from the way its foot hung, it had been hurt.

"I can't do anything with it there, you know," Doc said tersely.

Ay and Bee came forward and purposefully led the way for the dark-coat to Doc's facility, patting the injured Sh'im and volubly reassuring the others who crowded about anxiously.

They got Illi, for that's what Tim understood its name to be, safely on the couch. Though it was wide-eyed with apprehension, a whiff of some gas near its face had it reposing in happy comfort while Doc made his examination.

"More of a bad bruise, with some ligaments torn," Doc said. Tim did one of his mimed explanations, which was passed back through the ship to those waiting for a response. "Its joints are bulging with mineral deposits, and it's got the worst case of accretions I've seen so far. But then it's older. I'll just remove them while I regen and nu-skin the graze. He'll return in far better shape than he came."

That was when Tim suggested they accommodate the passengers in the sleeping cabins, a move that opened up more space in the main room. They also used the gymnasium space on the lower deck.

"Helm, are we overloading?" Jon asked as he settled in the pilot's seat for the return voyage.

"No, Commander. The Fiver is capable of lifting considerable tonnage without stressing the engines," Helm said.

Jon, his eyes sparkling with suppressed laughter, grinned at Nimisha, seated in the next chair over. She grinned back rather smugly.

"I'm really looking forward to seeing how she flies on IS drive," he said.

His words were delivered in a level, thoughtful tone, but she got a hint of his eagerness to put the Fiver to that test.

"How many trips will we have to make, Captain, to provide the Sh'im with enough to keep them happy before we go?" she asked.

"Not how many trips, Lady Nimisha, but how few we can get away with," he replied, some impatience coloring his voice.

They made six trips, to equip all four towns with repeller screens, enough wagons and the fuel to run them, and farming and domestic equipment. Only one pod of blankets and fabric was brought, since not much was needed with spring in the air. With many willing hands, Casper and Syrona had a fine two-bedroomed prefab house in four days, with running water from their own well and a septic tank for waste products. They had a shower and a bath in a small but adequate bathroom. The Sh'im produced basic furniture items, like beds, chairs, chests, and tables that craftsfolk had made, working late into the night, in gratitude for the help the communities had received from the humans.

At Doc's suggestion, another, longer trip was undertaken, to bring the *Poolbeg*'s diagnostic unit to the main Sh'im town.

"As I mentioned in my analysis of Ay and Bee, they had residual accretions of minerals in their systems. These are present in varying quantities in all those Sh'im I have treated for broken bones and cuts. I have automatically removed the accretions as a preventative treatment. We do not wish to upset our little allies, but I would like to use every opportunity possible to remove those accretions from all the Sh'im, especially the dark-coats, like Illi, who was all but crippled by the deposits. Those are not at all beneficial."

"D'you know how many thousands there are of them?" Nimisha asked.

"Perhaps when they are completely confident of our goodwill toward them, a proper program can be initiated. In the meantime, I will remove the material whenever I can. I will program the *Poolbeg* unit to that effect."

"You're the doc," Jon said.

"It's a very good idea," Syrona said, Casper nodding agreement.

While the *Poolbeg*'s diagnostic was not an AI unit, Doc updated its memory with information on the Sh'im anatomy and biology, as well as the physical profiles of the humans, especially Syrona. He programmed in automatic checkups for Tim who was showing substantial physical improvement from the nutritional program Doc had initiated. Additional supplies and a maintenance check had the unit in perfect working condition. Syrona was reassured by its availability, more for Tim's sake than her own.

Then Syrona came up with an excellent notion. She was, after all, a communications expert. So a satellite pulse beam was constructed, to be put into position by the Fiver when it reached the proper orbit for the satellite, on its exploratory trip to the other M-planets. That way, the Fiver could keep in contact with Erehwon. They found sufficient units to make a powerful enough comsat, with solar panel wings to keep it operating for several generations, if necessary. Nimisha was impressed with Syrona's professional abilities, seeing her in a new light. Syrona was also improving in health and vitality from the better nutrition she was receiving.

"If you've no objection, Syrona," Nimisha said when they were reviewing the comsat's design, "I've some bits and pieces of newer communications technology that I made Fleet give me." She grinned, tacitly admitting that she had acquired the "bits and pieces" by devious means.

When Syrona saw the specifications for the new solar panel wings, she couldn't wait to install the upgrades to her design. Nimisha realized then just how much of the equipment in the cave had probably been designed by Syrona, though the two men had done the construction.

Once Nimisha and Jon were certain that Casper, Syrona, and Tim would be housed and safe—their home had its own solar-powered repeller screen—they decided they could leave. The Sh'im were sociable by temperament and used any occasion for celebration: The housewarming, even if the Sh'im didn't know the custom, was an excellent excuse for a party.

"They could be at this for days," Jon said quietly to Nimisha as they watched the Sh'im doing a very energetic and athletic form of dance that even Tim could not imitate, though he was willing to try.

"I don't know about you, but I avoid leave-takings whenever possible," Nimisha commented.

"Good thing Syrona and Casper have moved their things out of the Fiver, then, isn't it?" he asked, making eye contact with her.

"Indeed." She rose. They happened to be sitting well beyond the bonfire that was warming the chill spring night air for the spectators.

He got to his feet and, putting a hand under her elbow, guided her away.

"I did warn Casper we might just leave now they're settled," he said after they were well away.

"I'll hope we can return before Syrona delivers. I promised her I'd be there for her," Nimisha said.

"If that ship of yours is as fast on IS drive as you say, we will."
Jon's voice rippled with amused challenge.

"Oh, she can move," Nimisha assured him.

And the Fiver did, with Helm managing one of the quiet vertical
lifts that he was so good at. He achieved a higher altitude than was
generally required before he cut in the main engines and kept them
on minimal power until they were out of range of the acute Sh'im
hearing. Then, at Nimisha's command, the nose of the Fiver tilted
up, toward the unnamed stars, pierced the atmospheric envelope,
and increased speed to a safe system maximum.

Nimisha felt elation grip her as the Fiver was once more in
space and doing what she had been designed to do. She was about
to admit that in the Fiver she had reached the perfection she had
been seeking so long.

Then Helm announced they had achieved the altitude for the
release of the comsat.

"Let it go, Helm," Jon said.

To herself, Nimisha added, "And let it receive news of home."

Jon touched her arm. "Let's get some rest, shall we?"

"Helm, you have the conn," Nimisha ordered.

"Yes, ma'am," Helm replied.

Jon and Nimisha walked across the main cabin, but when
she opened the door to her compartment, he once again touched
her arm.

"If I'm not rushing matters . . ." he began, cocking his head a
little in tacit appeal, a shy, or rather nervous, smile tilting his mouth
up on one side.

Since Nimisha had experienced a sudden rush of sensuality at
his first touch, this second physical contact only emphasized what
she had been denying: that she was very much attracted to him.

"No, I don't think you are," she agreed and took his hand. "We
could shower together and save time," she added.

His chuckle was deep and charged with eagerness. As she shed her one-piece coverall, he turned on the water and, with remarkable speed, was also naked by the time she stepped into the stall. The touch of his skin on hers was quite the most wonderful sensation, and matters progressed with great pleasure from then on.

In fact, Nimisha reflected when she heard the gentle chime from Helm and awoke to find herself curled against Jon's long body, he was quite possibly the best lover she had ever had. Of course, the prolonged celibacy that both had endured produced an intense hunger that had done much to increase their ultimate mutual satisfaction. Several times. She decided that morning to have Doc remove her implant. Tim should learn how to deal with human children and, if she chose to have a male this time, he could be a mate for the girl child that Syrona was carrying. With a proper medical unit to monitor pregnancies, she was not averse to increasing the human population.

"Jon . . ." She caressed his shoulder, running her hand down to his chest to the strong pectoral muscles, then tweaked him. Hushed awakenings were one of the minor pleasures of having a good lover. Indeed, as the Fiver sped toward the heliopause, they left the cabin, and the bed, only to eat, bathe, and do cursory checks of their progress.

"I heard Helm," he murmured and slowly turned toward her, capturing her hand and kissing the palm. "I just didn't want to move."

"How long to heliopause, Helm?" Nimisha asked.

"Thirty-five minutes, ma'am."

"That's time enough to spare," Jon said, and rolled over onto her.

Dressed and ready for the translation into IS drive, Jon grinned as he gestured for Nimisha to take the pilot's chair. She grinned back and took it. She'd have been quite willing for him to do the honors but liked it in him that he gave her preference.

The actual translation was accomplished effortlessly, with Helm increasing Interstellar Drive toward the nearest system with an M-type planet.

"The journey to the programmed destination will take four days, seven hours, and twenty minutes to reach the heliopause, ma'am," Helm announced. "All systems are functioning at recommended levels."

"Thank you, Helm. You have the conn," she said, rising. "I don't know about you, Jon, but I'm starving."

"Burgers?" Jon asked, his expression merry.

"No," she said firmly as he stepped aside for her to precede him to the main chamber. "Cater, I'd like a proper big breakfast, please."

"Double that, Cater," Jon said, following her and placing an arm about her waist the moment they had cleared the partition. "I'm rather tactile, Nimisha. Do you mind?"

She shook her head, grinning up at him, and looping her arm around his waist.

They ate, dawdling over the meal and talking about nothing in particular, until Jon, taking a deep breath, asked a question that Nimisha knew had been on his mind for some time.

"Could I possibly see the specs for the Fiver, Nimisha? I'd under-stand," he added hastily, raising one hand, "if you were reluct—"

"Helm, bring up my special design disks on the cabin screen," she said, leaning back, pleased by his interest in her work.

"Thanks, Nimisha." His eyes were warm with love as he gave her hand a special squeeze. She returned the pressure.

"Fleet will have the specs by now, anyway," she said.

"They will?" He was surprised by that.

"I assume so. I had a second hull nearly finished when I took this one out on what was to be a short testing run . . ." She gave an ironic chuckle. He pressed her hand again. "I gave—" She paused, suddenly overcome with a longing for the daughter she might never see again. "I gave Cuiva the final design disks. She'll know when to give them to Caleb Rustin. And I hope she has. If they're to find us, they'll need a second Fiver."

Jon sat up straighter, his eyebrows lifting. "Caleb Rustin . . . tall guy, blue eyes, attached to Vegan Fleet?"

"You know him?"

"I was jig on the ship he was first assigned to. Good man." He gave her a long thoughtful look.

"He was my Fleet spy." She never talked about previous alliances and did not intend to now, so she deliberately deflected the possibility of that question.

"Your what?" Jon's voice reflected conflicting emotions: anger, surprise, and indignation.

"Well, you can hardly blame Vegan Fleet Headquarters for wanting to keep their eyes on my designs, can you?" When he shook his head, his eyes flickering with questions, she went on. "I did get a chance to choose my—" She chuckled. "—naval attaché. He was the best choice I could have made, though I'm not sure who was more surprised, he or Admiral Gollanch. He had some very good notions, and had seen naval action against that annoying band of freebooters over in the Beta system. I'm not averse to using other people's ideas when they're as good as some Caleb came up with. Actually, I'm more of a tinkerer than an innovator."

"Considering the performance of this ship. Lady Nimisha, I question that description." He gave a snort of denial.

"No, really, that's the truth. You know how Fleet economies constrict real advances," she said. "I'm under no such restraints, so I can tinker and refine a system until I've achieved the optimum possible performance no matter what it costs. Of course, I do keep an eye on the best way to achieve what I want at a suitable price.

The designs have to be feasible if I'm to make a profit from the yachts."

"You have to know *how* and *when* to tinker."

" 'If it ain't broke, don't fix it?' " she quoted, grinning.

As the designs shown on the screen were getting to the more interesting alterations she had made, he was torn between looking at her and them.

"Well, I see you've worked on the missile recoil problem." He gave her a quick admiring glance. "The solution is so simple, I'm surprised it was overlooked."

"I don't think it was, Jon. But it required a new design of buffer that was expensive until my Yard found a substitute material that could be imported from Altair rather than Earth. Transportation expense is often an inhibiting factor, as you know."

"All too true," he admitted and they continued to discuss her "tinkering," which he called "inspirational" or "inventive" until she was almost uncomfortable with such unstinting praise.

"You know," he began, taking his eyes away from the data on the screen, "I've known many career Fleet women, but I've never before met one so . . . possessed by the design factors. Oh, I've heard them complain about the inadequacies of this or that system—"

"Males do, too," she reminded him.

"Of course we do, but we don't often know how to rectify the problem. This Fiver of yours is a total beaut inside and out." He shook his head, partially in envy, partially in approbation. "Hey, Lady Nimisha Boynton-Rondymense can blush!" He stroked her hot cheek. Then turned her chin so he could kiss her mouth.

Of one mind, they rose and adjourned to her cabin.

"The AI's have no access here, do they?" he asked as he closed the door behind him.

"Only comunit. And I shut it down for out-going until I address it."

"That's good!"

And very shortly, Nimisha was intensely glad that there was no contact with the other intelligences aboard the Fiver.

Late that night, while Jon was soundly asleep—she was grateful that he was a quiet sleeper—she crept out and to the medical unit.

"Doc, please remove my implant," she said softly, settling herself on the couch.

"Local?" he asked, responding in as low a tone.

"Yes."

"You do know what you're doing?"

"Yes. I do. And now's the time to do it."

"For what it's worth, I agree with you."

"Thank you."

"Thought you might need a vote of confidence. You're a very healthy young woman, Nimisha, and should carry and deliver a fine healthy baby with no more trouble than you had with Cuiva. Especially since you will have me to keep you in tiptop form. I took the liberty of checking Captain Svangel's gene patterns when I did his physical—" When she made an inarticulate sound of surprised protest at his initiative, Doc chuckled in his best Lord Naves imitation. "Only routine at the time, of course, but vital information to have on hand on an alien and basically unknown planet. I found no genetic incompatibilities between you." While he was talking, he had deadened the spot on her leg that contained the implant. She felt nothing even when he sprayed on the new skin. "There. That's done. If my reading of your menstrual cycle is accurate, you are likely to be fertile in the next two days. Good timing, Nimisha. That's all. Except check in with me each morning while we're on our run to the new M-type."

Nimisha slipped out of the unit and thanking Doc, made her way back to her cabin and into the head, the faint noise of flushing rousing Jon from sleep and to renewed activity. She was not averse to satisfying him, and herself.

•   •

Helm called them to the bridge just after they felt the translation into system drive.

"Unidentified object drifting off the port bow, Lady Nimisha."

"Magnify," she said as she and Jon slipped into the seats and automatically netted in.

"I don't think that mess poses any problems," Jon said, regarding the twisted, battered flotsam.

"It was once a spaceship," Nimisha said.

"It had no luck coming through the wormhole. And I think that's what happened to it."

They got close enough to circle the wreck, but it was too battered and compacted to give them any idea of its original shape. No markings of any kind remained. Helm did an analysis of the metallic composition, but that was unexceptional enough, containing no unusual alloys that might have given them some clues as to its origin.

Jon asked for a spatial map of the area and, after some figuring, decided that the vector of its current velocity did not point to the same spot where the Fiver and the *Poolbeg* had exited from the wormhole.

"How could that be? Are your figures correct?" Nimisha asked, astonished.

"Check 'em yourself." Jon handed the pad over to her, grinning. "I could hope that there is an error. If there isn't, then there may be more than one wormhole exit in this area of space."

Nimisha regarded her calculations with dismay and slowly handed back his pad. "I don't like to think of *more* wormholes emptying who knows what in on top of us."

"That one's going to do us no harm," he said consolingly, and had Helm record its presence and their disturbing calculations. "Where'll it end up, Helm?"

"Plotting its current trajectory, it will probably be attracted by the gravity of the fifth planet and impact on that surface," Helm said.

Jon saluted the wreck. "I wonder how many other vessels met a similar end in this part of the galaxy."

"Unknown, Commander," Helm replied.

"A rhetorical comment." Jon grinned at Nimisha.

They continued inward, examining the other planets of the system, none of which would sustain humanoid life.

The M-type planet had three moons, one with a thin atmosphere but obviously dispersing, for what plant life was still supported was starving for oxygen. They continued on to the planet. Its atmosphere did not check out as eminently suitable, in its present geological age. Even as they made their first orbit, they could see that the active volcanoes in its mountain ranges spewed forth black dust and pyroclastic materials, as if celebrating the arrival of the observers. Though life-forms, small and large, were scanned, there seemed to be more aquatic types than land surface dwellers. A smart option with such volatile landmasses. The vegetation managed to cling where it could and was lush enough but all too primitive to be useful, even as basic stuff for a catering unit to turn into edible substances. What oases of habitable areas there were without nearby volcanic action were few and far between.

"Maybe in a few millennia, all that volcanic activity will calm down," Nimisha said, not entirely disappointed since she already was quietly nurturing the good news Doc had given her early that morning. Even Rhidian had not succeeded in his first attempt to impregnate her for her body-heir. She would tell Jon later. She wished to savor the news herself for a while.

"Who knows when they'd grow volcanoes, too," Jon said.

"Let's come back in a few centuries and see if it's calmed down."

"You've had rejuv?" Jon asked.

"Of course, though I resisted when it was first mentioned. Have you?"

He nodded. "There were moments a while back when I bitterly resented having to deal with longevity."

"Not now?" she asked in a teasing voice. She had discovered that she could tease him about almost anything without him taking offense. Caleb had so often backed off when she spoke whimsically or sarcastically that she had controlled her habit. Caleb had been far too aware of his anomalous situation as attaché and determined not to "presume."

Jon glanced at her, his expression tender, and he stroked her bare arm. "None at all."

His genuine spontaneous responses were another point in his favor. Rhidian had always been on his dignity, even in bed with her, as befitted a First Family scion—polite, courteous, and appropriately concerned for her enjoyment, delivering his query as a necessary ritual. Jon never needed to inquire; he knew! Caleb had been . . . well, a nice lover, but . . . unimaginative. With Jon, she could be as spontaneous and inventive as he, which added a zest to their love-making. She had also discovered, in the moments when they conversed—and they seemed to have a lot to talk about on many subjects—that Jonagren Svangel came from an old and property-owning family in the Scandinavian peninsula. It probably accounted for his innate self-confidence with none of the posing that a colonial First Family male would display. Lady Rezalla—if she ever saw her mother again—could find no fault with his lineage. He could be as stern as command required him, or open and frank in discussing anything that they had so far considered. Sometimes he was even so outrageous that he could surprise her out of long-held notions that his observations made her reexamine.

With considerable time to fill in the journey, they had watched new tapes as well as the old favorites she had. First he had wanted to update his understanding of naval technical advances and the general history of their worlds during the time he had been marooned. He was apolitical, as most naval officers found it expedient to be, but he had definite ideas about individual rights and other domestic issues on Earth, and opinions about some of the colonial worlds' issues. He always called them "colonial," which amused her. Though the adjective was essentially accurate, any one from the "colonies" would have risen up in indignation at its use. Certainly Lady Rezalla would have been outraged, as would Rhidian. She wondered about Caleb's reaction, since he was Vegan by birth, but they had never discussed the subject. Jon had such a nice way of teasing her about her "colonial" status that she humored him. She could warn him about her mother . . . later, when the need arose. She could hope that it would, but she was becoming more and more resigned to the improbability.

Resignation to the loss—no, absence, she told herself firmly— of her daughter, Cuiva, was another matter entirely. The thought of a new baby did not reduce the longing for her firstborn, but it was comforting.

She had checked with Doc each morning during the fertile period, and he ascertained that ovulation had taken place. Shortly thereafter he confirmed that an egg had been fertilized.

Despite her good health, she started feeling queasy before they reached the heliopause of the second M-planet system. In such close companionship, Jon noticed her distaste for breakfast, as well as for any pungent food smells, and jumped to the right conclusion.

"Pardon me for being personal, Nimi, but could you possibly be experiencing morning sickness?" Jon asked.

"I did offer you a remedy, Nimi," Doc said, sounding miffed.

"You *wanted* to be pregnant by me!" Jon gave a whoop and a holler and swung her about the cabin in his arms. "And you never even warned me you'd taken out your implant."

"My option, you know," she replied. "And I wanted to surprise you."

"You've sure done that." Then he was pushing her toward the medical unit, his expression altered to one of deep concern.

"No need to worry, Jon, dear. Doc says our genes are eminently compatible."

He hauled her back in his arms again to kiss her thoroughly, a spontaneous reaction that she found far more satisfying than Rhidian's fatuous expression when she had informed him of Cuiva's conception. In fact, Jon kept on hugging her, doing a sort of two-step dance of success all around the main cabin until she had to stop him since the motion was making her nauseous.

"I'll settle that for you, Nimisha," Doc said when Jon contritely stopped the whirling, "if you'll deign to visit my couch."

Jon immediately escorted her there and held her arm out while an extendable hypospray permeated the skin with an anti-nausea drug.

By the time they reached the third possible M-type system, she was well over that stage. This world, with two moons, was more hospitable in climate and terrain than Secondo's. On one moon, when they did an exploratory orbit, they saw a crater, its center showing a metallic signature. Helm took them in low enough to record the anomaly, and the analysis provided them with the resting place of yet another of the eighteen missing spaceships. To establish its identity, they would send the analysis back to Navy Headquarters on Earth—when they finally made contact again—and see if a match could be found in their data banks. Its metallic signature was definitely similar to FSP materials.

"The other wrecks could still be traveling onward," Jon remarked. "We may never find them."

"I think it's amazing we've located any of them, considering the odds."

"True. I'm just overwhelmingly glad you found . . . me." His eyes sparkled.

"Later; we'd best do what we came for . . . for a while, at least."

To their astonishment, they found evidence from space of some sort of discernible ruins at the confluence of two rivers that meandered through the flat plains of one of the smaller continents.

Once Helm had checked the immediate vicinity for possible dangers, they kitted themselves out for on-site exploration. They found a rusted shuttle of such an awkward design that Nimisha wondered that it had landed at all, its exterior eroded by time and weather.

"Acid rain?" Nimisha guessed, putting her gloved hand on some of the pitting.

"Perhaps. They do seem to have built some sort of a settlement," he said.

"And a cemetery," she said, noticing eight stone markers. Time and weather had obliterated the shallow carvings of names and dates.

"I'd guess some element of the First Diaspora," Jon said, squatting down and running an index finger across the indistinct legend. He rose and, silently, they walked over to what was left of stone walls. They stepped over them into a compound with the ruins of several small dwellings. Splinters of wood, protected by insertion in the stones, proved that the unknown builders had acquired wood from some other place, since there was none on the broad plains.

"They didn't go in much for mixed crews at first, did they?" she asked.

Jon shook his head, digging his toe into the dirt clogging the remains of a hearth. When the metal tip of his boot hit something, he used a trowel to uncover the corroded remains of a pan.

"The deceased had no survivors," she murmured, unconsciously stroking her still-flat abdomen.

"Life-forms are approaching cautiously through the vegetation," Helm said. "Some are large enough to be dangerous."

"Let's not take unnecessary risks right now," Jon said, taking her arm.

They ran back to the Fiver and were safely within it when the creatures could be seen on the main screen.

"Carnivorous, to judge by the shape of their muzzles and protruding fangs," Helm reported. "And large enough to suggest the reason the compound was walled."

"Well, let's see what else this planet offers prospective settlers," Jon said, shedding the protective gear.

"Thirsty work," Nimisha said, ordering beverages for both of them from Cater while Helm lifted.

Careful quartering of the planet showed no further remains of interest.

"And it's boring, geologically speaking," was Nimisha's complaint. "Normal plains, old mountains, wide rivers, three oceans, and a dozen seas."

"Some rather unnice indigenous specimens, six-legged, too," Jon said. "More extendibles to capture us and teeth to eat us with. Also, there doesn't really seem to be much in the way of easily obtainable metal and mineral resources. Deep pit mining would be necessary, and we will need metals when the freighter's cargo is used up. As it will, the way the Sh'im proliferate." He gave her hair an affectionate ruffling, which she liked, though she hadn't expected to. "While we will try our best, I don't think humans are given to litters as the Sh'im are."

"Well, it's a good place to have to fall back on. Or give the Sh'im in a few generations. Though this primary's a lot brighter than Erehwon's."

"Oh, you'd noticed that about their eyesight, too," Jon remarked.

"I didn't. Doc did," Nimisha said. "The Sh'im optical equipment is not happy with bright sunlight. Their home-world sun must be much dimmer. Maybe the real impetus for them to colonize is that their sun's old and dying."

"At first I considered it possible that they habitually required a midday rest," Doc said. He had had his own reports to make of the two planets they had investigated, but he granted them the courtesy of silence unless they asked him a direct question. "Then I noticed that their eye slits become narrower as the Erehwon sun nears zenith. Their eye slits are wider at night, and I don't think it has that much to do with their night vision, which is better than that of you humans. I've compared their optical equipment with that of other minor species available on data file. I suspect that you're right, Nimisha. They originate on a world with a dimmer sun, an older world."

"Would tinted lenses help, Doc?" Nimisha asked.

"I would suggest it, though the problem seems to affect the younger ones more than the darker-coated elders. Perhaps the pigment alters with age, and their sensitivity to harsh sunlight is reduced."

"Put wraparound sunglasses on your list of things to do," Jon said.

"I have," Doc replied blithely. "May I suggest that since the necessary investigations are complete for this planet, we return forthwith, posthaste, and immediately to Erehwon? You have promised to assist Syrona in the birth and she might just deliver early. I neglected to request a connection between my diagnostic and the *Poolbeg's* unit."

So Helm plotted the most direct return flight to Erehwon, and when Nimisha told him to come as close to redlining the drive as possible now that the engines were well broken in, they made it back at a record speed. She spent a lot more time sleeping, which Doc reminded her was a normal part of the first trimester.

She did try to access the beacon at the wormhole exit.

"Not that I expected anything," she murmured when there

were no messages. "Not as far away as presumably we are from home."

"We live on hope, you know," Jon said gently.

"It's almost two years since I pulsed the Maydays from this side," Nimisha said.

"We know we're far away from our homes, love." He stroked her hand. "Too soon."

"Or the damned beacon's malfunctioning."

Jon gave her a mock-surprised look. "A Rondymense unit malfunctioning? I find that hard to believe."

His teasing reassured her. She knew that the beacon had been functioning. Wasn't it receiving the updates Helm sent?

"Report on all systems, please, Helm," Jon asked, as he was the day's pilot.

"All systems are in perfect working order. All diagnostics are in the optimum range," Helm reported. "I have taken the liberty of forwarding a message through the comsat, giving our ETA," he added.

"Well done, Helm," Jon said, smiling over at Nimisha. "We can expect a welcoming committee!"

Nimisha considered this for such a long moment that Jon raised his eyebrows in query.

"I haven't missed them. I should have."

He leaned over and kissed her. "Thank you," he said, his eyes glowing.

"No, I thank you, Captain Svangel," she said softly. "I've never had a . . . a more restful voyage." She grinned.

"The voyage is not yet over." He held his hand out.

"Helm, you have the conn," she said, rising and following him back to their cabin.

"You will want to see the improvements," Helm said, interrupting the afterglow of their activities.

"Improvements?" Jon said, dutifully donning his coverall while Nimisha was still struggling to sit upright on the bed.

"Yes, Captain. Truly impressive."

The two humans made eye contact. It was rare for Helm to comment. Nimisha hurriedly pulled on a clean coverall and joined Jon in the pilot area.

"Now *that* is worth seeing," she said. "Helm, are you taping this? They'll surely want to see the aerial view. Impressive! They *have* been busy!"

Where there had been but the one prefab L-shaped building, there was now an avenue of twelve residences, all slightly different, as the prefab units had been designed to allow variations. These were neatly fenced with space for small gardens that did not entirely feature edible plants. There were more flowers in the largest unit that housed Syrona, Casper, and Tim.

The most surprising building was the large triple-span barn with a corral to the right of it: a corral in which they could see four-legged animals that had to be the smaller deer that the Sh'im had not been quick enough to capture. She'd want to hear how Casper had turned cowboy in the gig. Since it was early morning Erehwon time, they also saw farm units and wagons on definite tracks that wheeled vehicles had packed down.

"They've tripled the amount of cultivated fields," Jon said. "The repeller shields have made a big difference."

"And look at the prefab sheds by the cliffs!" Nimisha added. "Does every family have a ground unit now?"

"Have they completely emptied the freighter? Look at all the empty pods." Jon pointed as the Fiver swung around the bend of the cliff, and they could see the entire Sh'im town, not just the peripheral buildings. "Seem to be using some for rain barrels . . ."

"And tree houses," Nimisha added with a whoop of laughter.

"I hope some were saved for storage purposes," Jon said.

"Casper's the optimist. He'd've put some aside for a bountiful harvest with all those fields under cultivation."

Their arrival had been seen, and the powered vehicles were making for what had obviously become a landing site. The gig was parked by a large prefab hangar. There was sufficient room for the Fiver to set down.

"They've collected the skiff, too," Nimisha said, spotting the vehicle inside the garage as Helm did a neat vertical landing. "Well done, Helm. Not so much as a bump."

"Of course not, ma'am," was the imperturbable response. "All running systems inactive. Performance data will be stored for analysis by fourteen hundred planetary time."

"Very good, Helm," Jon said. "I'd like a report on any necessary service, maintenance, or resupply required."

"That will be available at the same time, Captain."

Someone banged on the hatch that was still space-locked. The two humans grinned at each other just as Helm released the hatch. "Apologies tendered."

"None required," Nimisha said and, taking Jon's hand, they went to meet their friends.

Tim was first, brown as a nut, followed more sedately by his parents. Syrona waddled, she was so near the end of her pregnancy. She looked as healthy as her son and obviously relieved to see Nimisha. When the two women had embraced, while Timmy and a beaming Casper greeted Jon more circumspectly, Syrona held Nimisha off.

"You're pregnant," she said, accusingly.

"Well, what else had we to do with the time between planets?" Nimisha said. "But how could you tell? I don't show yet."

"Yes, you do," Casper said, grinning. "You're glowing."

"I am?" Nimisha turned in astonishment to Jon and then back to Syrona.

"Indeed you are," Syrona said and then kissed her cheek, squeezing her hands to indicate how very happy she was for Nimisha.

Then the Sh'im, who had tactfully allowed the humans to greet each other, moved forward. Ool and Ook wanted to know if their search had been successful, so Jon told them there would be a showing of tapes of the planets that evening when they could rig the exterior screen to allow all to see.

CHAPTER 8

In order to cloak their exit from Vegan space, Five B slipped into the middle of a large convoy of drone-pulling freighters.

"It's not exactly the kind of exit I'd prefer to make," Caleb remarked to Lt. Commander Kendra Oscony, his executive officer, seated beside him in the bridge compartment.

She grinned. "Ignominious for a ship of this caliber," she said, her glance sliding around the control panel. She had had some simulated training on a mock-up at Fleet Headquarters. But even the best virtual simulations never equaled the reality. "She is some beauty. When can we slip the dogs?"

"As soon as we've cleared the comsats," he said, almost as eager as she to be free of their cover vessels. "We don't want our markings too visible."

"We've only got an interim marking, RX-25. The admiral isn't being overcautious, is he?" she asked.

"If he isn't, I am," he said firmly. "Lady Cuiva's safety is as important as the task of finding her mother."

She cleared her throat at that subtle rebuke. He took the edge off it by giving her a grin. "I sure never thought to be this lucky," she said.

"Nor I," Caleb admitted, trying to make friends with his executive officer. He knew the XO by reputation, although he would never tell her that it was her fine mathematical abilities that had decided her selection for this shakedown cruise.

"She's a nice child, too."

"She is," Caleb agreed.

"Coming up to the last comsat, Captain," said Helm, and Kendra shook her head.

Caleb grinned more broadly. He was accustomed to the AI trio on a Fiver, having helped program and install the original units. It would take the naval segment of this crew time to adjust to having independent AI's as integral entities. The Chief Engineer, Ian Hadley, had been over all the design specs; he had spent hours with Hiska, who had actually talked volubly about the refinements that Lady Nimisha had made to drive components. Gaitama Rezinda had received intense briefing by Hiska on how to deal with any adjustments that might be required during this shakedown cruise. The young Rondymense Yard employee had been a bit goggle-eyed over the responsibility, but there was no question that she was capable of handling the job if Hiska had approved her. Caleb had given Hiska the choice of being the shakedown cruise jack-of-all-trades, or joat, as such mechanics were called. She had declined on the grounds that Lady Nimisha had given her the responsibility of attending to her quarters, workspace, and office, and not even to find her patron would she abandon that position of trust. Which, Admiral Gollanch remarked, was very well, since the woman had personality problems that could have proved awkward even on the test run.

"In that case, Helm, proceed to maximum Insystem speed," Caleb said.

"Aye, Captain."

Caleb wasn't certain that Nimisha would approve of him programming naval parlance into this AI, but with six naval personnel on board, it would simplify matters.

"Time to heliopause?"

"At maximum speed, eighty-two hours, thirty minutes, ten seconds and—"

"Thank you, Helm."

"Aye, sir."

Kendra smothered a laugh.

"You have the conn, XO," Caleb said, releasing the safety net and rising.

"Aye, sir." She slipped over to the seat he had vacated.

With an AI Helm, it was not actually necessary to maintain a watch schedule, but naval tradition required it.

In the main cabin, he found Lady Cuiva and Perdimia having a snack.

"All settled in?" he asked.

"Yes, Captain," the two replied in chorus. Perdimia grinned and nudged Cuiva with her elbow.

"May I join you?"

"But, of course," Cuiva said, inclining her head in an imitation of her grandam.

Caleb ordered on his way to Cater's dispenser and received the caffeine drink and the sandwich he'd requested, all neatly and appetizingly arranged on the naval crockery supplied to the unit.

"How long will it take us to reach . . . that place?" Cuiva asked.

"As soon as we're past heliopause, we'll translate into Interstellar Drive. Then it'll be a week on IS before we return to normal space and begin the testing."

"Just as my mother was going to do?"

"Just as I am sure your mother did do," Caleb said.

"Everyone's very nice," Cuiva added after a moment's silence.

"We had no trouble picking a crew when they heard the Five B was going out to be tested," Caleb said.

"Even Hiska was pleased," Cuiva said before taking the last bite of her snack.

"How could you tell?" Caleb was startled into asking.

"Oh," and Cuiva waved an airy hand just like Lady Rezalla would, "Hiska talks to me."

"You're one of the privileged few."

"But she talks to you, too, Caleb," Cuiva replied, blinking, and that was the first time she had not hesitated about using his first name. He was making progress.

"On business matters only."

"She said you're very good," Cuiva remarked.

Perdimia shot a surprised glance at Rustin, who had to chuckle at such a confidence.

"I'd never have known had you not told me," Caleb said.

"Oh?" Cuiva's eyebrows shot up and now she resembled her mother more.

"I think," Perdimia interrupted gently, "that it's time we said good night, Lady Cuiva. It's been a very long and exciting day."

Cuiva obediently slid out of the chair. "Thank you, Caleb, for allowing me along on this trip."

So, Caleb thought, she prefers not to refer to the real reason she's on board. That was fine by him. No reason to upset the child needlessly.

"I know your mother meant to take you out on the Fiver when she returned from the shakedown cruise," he said, rising in deference to her rank. "Since I could appoint the crew, I asked for you to ride along with us."

"We will find my mother, won't we, Caleb?" Cuiva asked, her heart in her expressive blue eyes.

"Indeed we will, Lady Cuiva."

Cuiva's eyes were suddenly filled with tears and she took a deep breath. "If I may call you Caleb on board the Five B, you may certainly address me as Cuiva, Captain."

With that, she pivoted on her heel and walked briskly toward her cabin.

"She'll be fine," Perdimia murmured before following her charge.

"And safe," Caleb said to himself. He finished his meal and then went to his own cabin, to finish stowing his gear.

They were three hours away from the heliopause when Helm announced receipt of an encrypted message from Admiral Gollanch.

"We're to meet a courier at these coordinates," Caleb said after decoding the message. He was puzzled as well as annoyed. They were to heave to and await the courier's arrival. He tapped the numbers into Helm.

"You don't suppose there's been news from—" Kendra broke off.

He had the same thought: there'd been contact with Nimisha. His chest was filled with a sudden surge of some conflicting emotions. He wanted above all else to have Nimisha safe and sound, but he also, almost equally, wanted the chance to test the Five B. If by any chance it was a fault in the ship that had caused her disappearance, rather than the wormhole, he wanted to *know*.

Both Caleb and Kendra were right. The courier had a copy of the pulsed message that had been intercepted by a small interstellar freighter on the outskirts of explored space. It contained a message from Nimisha giving all the information her Helm had been able to collect as to her location—a location so far away that it was estimated that the Five B, traveling at maximum IS speed, would take four years to reach it. Fleet and Navy had verified the pulse beam as genuine. If the pulse had taken nearly sixteen months to reach this side of the galaxy, would Nimisha still be alive? Caleb firmly edited that thought out of his mind.

"Has a message been sent back, confirming receipt?" he asked. Even if the return pulse took another sixteen months to get back, it would reassure Nimisha that rescue was on its way.

"Yes, Commander," the courier said with a grin. "Like right then, saying you'd been ordered to those coordinates. I heard the CO say that updates will be sent to her on a regular basis." Then he handed over to Caleb the disk containing the new orders.

"I've got additional supplies for you on board, Commander," he added. "Admiral Gollanch's respects. You'll be away longer than you're provisioned for. And these." "These" were two packages: the sealed one had a note in Lady Rezalla's angular hand tucked under the gold cord of the distinctive Coskanito wrapping. The second, larger one obviously contained gowns, and Caleb lifted the cover high enough to see folds of white and gentian-blue.

Caleb had little doubt that the Coskanito box contained Lady Cuiva's necklace and he slipped it under his arm. The dress box he carefully put to one side while he gave orders for those on the Five B to help the courier crew unload the supplies. Well, the ceremony would be a few years late, that's all, but he devoutly hoped that it would be Nimisha who conducted that important ceremony for her daughter somewhere and sometime.

Admiral Gollanch's new orders to Captain Rustin were for him to proceed at maximum speed on IS drive to reach the beacon that Nimisha had had the good sense to release.

Handing the disk to Nazim, who was in the pilot's chair, Caleb told him to give Helm the data. He took the packages and went to find Cuiva. She was dutifully doing lessons in the cabin she shared with Perdimia. Cuiva gasped when she saw the dress box.

"I've very good news, Cuiva," Caleb said, gesturing for Perdimia to remain where she was. He sat on the edge of the bed. "Your mother's been found. Or rather, she's sent out a broad pulse that has finally been received. We're going to make all haste to the coordinates, but I have to add that she's very, very far away from where we are now."

Cuiva struggled not to break into tears; it was to Caleb, rather than to Perdimia, to whom she turned for comforting.

"Don't hold back the tears, Cuiva, dear," Caleb said. "You've been brave a long while, and there's just me and Perdimia here and we'll never tell."

She didn't sob long, despite her intense relief at the news. She was very shortly in control, drying her eyes on the handkerchief Caleb produced. Then he handed over the Coskanito box, which she clutched to her chest.

"A pulse message sent by your mother from way the south side of the galaxy was picked up at the edge of explored space by an interstellar vessel and relayed to Fleet Headquarters. The message has been verified as originating from equipment only she had available. My orders are now to proceed at all speed to that point."

Cuiva sniffled as she rocked slightly, the box in her arms. "So that's why my grandam has sent this. So my mother herself can Necklace me in—" She looked at the ceiling, reckoning the time to her fourteenth birthday. "—one year, and eight months."

Caleb cleared his throat and looked anxiously at Perdimia for assistance.

"It'll be longer than that to get where your mother is, Cuiva, luv," he said as kindly as he could.

"But Mother has to put on my Necklace!" Cuiva exclaimed, sitting upright in her anguish.

"And so she shall, but it's going to take us roughly four years to reach that part of the galaxy, judging by the length of time it took the pulse to reach occupied space."

"Four . . . years?" Cuiva's voice squeaked in surprise. "But I'll be too old to be Necklaced."

"No, no," Perdimia started to say.

"My mother *has* to do it—"

She burst into tears again and Caleb took her in his lap this time to comfort her, stroking silken hair that had the feel of her mother's under his fingers. Hastily, he transferred his hands to her slender shoulders and back.

"Now, now, honey." He rocked her soothingly.

"There's cold sleep, Cuiva," Perdimia said, gently smoothing Cuiva's rumpled hair from her flushed and tearful face. "If Captain

Rustin and Doc agree, you can go to sleep the day before you'd be fourteen and wake when we find your mother. Then she can properly Necklace you."

That solution seemed to ease the tears, and Cuiva sat up on Caleb's lap, still hugging the jewelry box.

"But you'll all be older . . . and so will Mother, if it's going to take *that* long to get there."

"But you," Caleb said, pushing one finger gently on the tip of her nose, as he would no longer dare to do to a son who was already in the Academy "will be just fourteen. Which seems to be the important issue we have to resolve."

"What about my grandam?" Cuiva sniffed, and then remembered her handkerchief and blew fiercely into it before wiping her cheeks. "She'll miss the ceremony, and so will my cousins and uncles and aunts."

"You'd really miss them?" Caleb asked teasingly.

"Not great-grandam Lady Astatine," Cuiva admitted candidly. "And some of my cousins definitely. But there's the celebration . . ."

"Nothing that Cater can't match, if not exceed," Caleb said. "I feel she's quite capable of spreading the most impressive minor majority feast ever presented this very select company. Wherever we have to hold that all-important ceremony," he added quickly.

While she considered that offer, Cuiva gradually eased her grip until the box settled to her lap. Now she handed it to Caleb.

"I think you'd better put this safely away then. Until we find Mother."

"You could go to sleep now, if you wanted to," Caleb suggested, but he heard Perdimia's mutter of dissent just as Cuiva shook her head.

"No, I've lessons to learn," Cuiva said firmly. "I want to know as much as I can from Commander Oscony, Chief Hadley, and Mareena. Then Mother will know I haven't wasted travel time or the pains you took to be sure I had good instructors while I'm away from Acclarke. I'll go to sleep"—she straightened her shoulders in a brave gesture—"the day before my fourteenth birthday." She turned to Perdimia. "That's the correct way to handle this problem, isn't it, Perdi?"

"It is certainly one solution," Perdimia said. "Perhaps Captain Rustin or Kendra or even Gaitama can think of another one. It's good to examine all available options."

"Well spoken, Perdimia," Caleb said, rising from the bed, the Necklace case in one hand. "We'll see what alternatives we can come up with."

"Thank you very much, Caleb," Cuiva said, suddenly adult again. "When will we be making the translation?"

"We're three hours from heliopause right now."

"But the Five B will have to get up to speed first before translation," Cuiva said.

"Correct. Did you want to stay awake for that?"

"It's uncomfortable, isn't it?" she asked, affecting unconcern.

"I'm accustomed to it, but if you'd rather be asleep, you won't notice it at all."

"I am rather tired," Cuiva admitted.

Perdimia was on her feet. "Then perhaps I'll just fix your bath, dear, and get you settled. You can read until you're sleepy . . ."

"That's an excellent idea," Cuiva said, still adult. "I do have that tape Chief Hadley recommended as an introduction to astronomy."

"Good night then, Cuiva, and sleep well. I'll put this—" Caleb lifted the hand holding the Coskanito box. "—in my security drawer."

"Thank you, Caleb."

And with that he left. He did exactly as he promised her. He did, however, open the jewelry case to have a preview of that magnificently crafted jeweled Necklace that would match the tattoo on Cuiva's neck. To his surprise, Nimisha's was also tucked in the box. It did not quite match her daughter's, but that was as it should be. He sighed. When they found Nimisha, she'd be able to wear her own Necklace as she placed the new one on her daughter's neck. This journey would certainly prove the Five B as a long-voyage vessel. He wondered if some instinct had prompted him in his careful selection of the crew for what had initially been just a shakedown cruise. Their endurance and patience would be vigorously tested in four years on a vessel this size.

And since this was going to be a much longer voyage, maybe he should give Cuiva the option to do a Junior Officer Qualification. It would give her another incentive for two years of lessons. Not a bad idea to make her a Practical Factor. He rather thought Nimisha would approve.

Syrona, with Nimisha and Casper in attendance and Doc supervising, was delivered of a fine healthy daughter.

"Helm, spread the word outside," Nimisha ordered.

"Oh, she's lovely," Syrona exclaimed when Nimisha put her daughter in her arms. "Just look at all that hair, and the eyelashes. Why she's marvelous! So much bigger than Tim was, and listen to her wail! She's much more robust than he was."

"You had me watching over you most of the pregnancy, Syrona," Doc said at his smuggest. "All the extra nutrition and the good catering you received makes the difference."

"When I think of how weak Tim was . . ." Tears formed in Syrona's eyes, trickling down her cheeks. "Oh!" she exclaimed, startled, as the afterbirth came out in a rush.

"That's all right now," Doc said, and a receptacle appeared in which Nimisha could deposit the placenta. "And a little something to encourage your milk."

"I didn't have much with Tim," Syrona said apologetically.

"You will this time," Doc promised. "And if you don't, Cater has substitutes that I know will do almost as well. Put the child on that platform, Nimisha, so I can record the vital statistics."

Nimisha did so. "Can I wash her now?" she asked almost testily. She knew the Sh'im females were waiting eagerly to see the new human baby. They were going to be surprised to be shown just one child since they had multiple births. Of course, the baby—Hope was the name Syrona had chosen for her—was much larger than Sh'im young at birth. Maybe that would help balance matters. Once she had finished with the gentle sponge bath she carefully wrapped the baby in the soft blanket Syrona had knitted, made from finely combed fur of the big shaggies.

Then Nimisha handed the neatly packaged little new bundle of life to its father.

"Go show her off, Casper," she said. And that's what he did, his face nearly cracked with his joyous smile as he displayed his daughter. Sh'im were oohing and ululing softly—whether it was out of courtesy for the newborn or because there was only one offspring to be shown Nimisha didn't care. None of Syrona's fears for this child had materialized, thanks to Doc attending her so early in the pregnancy and counteracting the effects of poor nutrition.

"She's so big," Casper was saying, showing her to Jon and Tim, and then to Ool, Ook, Ay, and Bee, who had crowded in close since they were, in effect, the oldest friends of the humans.

"She's not white," was Tim's critical assessment.

"She's certainly not as red as you were at birth," Jon said, ruffling the boy's hair.

"You mean, that's a natural color for a baby?"

"You've seen the Sh'im young," Jon went on, "and frankly she's an improvement on those gray slugs."

"Ssssh," Tim said fiercely. "They'd be offended."

Jon laughed, and glanced up at Nimisha, still in the hatch. "Can we see Syrona while Casper does the honors?"

Nimisha beckoned them in, and Tim squeezed up the stairs ahead of Jon and rushed to the entrance of the main cabin, where he suddenly slowed and tiptoed to the medical couch.

"Mom?"

"I'm all right, Tim. Come on over," Syrona said, holding out her arms to him and smiling.

He was in her arms in two running steps, crying and hugging her. "I thought it'd never come."

"You mean, Hope, love?" Syrona said gently. "Why she didn't take long at all."

"She took hours, Mom!" The words were nearly a wail.

Nimisha glanced at Jon, who held back from congratulating the new mother.

"I don't think he's ever called her that—unless he was sick," Jon remarked softly. He put an arm around Nimisha's shoulders and hugged her against him, kissing her cheek. "Cater, I think it's champagne time," he said in a louder voice. "And I think Tim ought to try a sip of it, since he's now the oldest in his family."

Nimisha was always amazed at Jon's attitude toward his biological son. He never exhibited any paternal feelings toward the boy, yet he was as careful of him as Casper was and was just as proud of Tim's ability to cope with their new life among the Sh'im. Tim certainly could speak their language with far more fluency than any of the adults. Either he had more acute hearing—which Doc agreed was true—or he intuitively placed the sounds he couldn't hear in the context of the sentences. He still had to use the voice box, though, since his vocal cords could not approximate all the sounds Sh'im words used.

Jon was handing Nimisha a proper champagne flute—one drink wouldn't hurt, Doc assured her—from the tray he carried. She walked with him over to the couch, where he gave a glass to Syrona and one to Tim. A fifth remained on the tray that he set down on a nearby table.

"That is, if Casper ever comes back from showing Hope off."

"No fear of that," Nimisha said drily. "A few hungry howls and he'll come back as fast as he can."

"Will she howl much?" Tim asked. But he was more interested in the bubbles rising up in the glass. When the adults raised their glasses in a toast, he followed suit.

"To the healthy Hope we've just received," Jon said.

"To Hope!" Tim's voice was as triumphant as the others. "I don't like it," he added, running his tongue over his teeth as he firmly set the glass down on the tray.

"It is an acquired taste," Jon remarked.

"And this is a special occasion," Nimisha added.

"For which I am infinitely grateful," Syrona said with a sigh, lying back against the pillows and closing her eyes.

"You all right, Syrie?" Tim asked.

They all heard a faint wail. Tim frowned. "Hope," he said with a note of complaint in his voice.

The sound was coming closer and then Casper was rushing into the Fiver, baby cuddled close against him.

"She's hungry, dear," Syrona said, reaching out for her daughter and deftly putting her to her breast.

Jon tactfully led Tim to a table, half-pushing him into a chair. "So, what was the Sh'im reaction, Casper?"

"I think they didn't expect her to be so big," Casper said. "Oh, champagne? Thanks."

"You can have mine, too, Cas," Tim offered.

"I will. They were surprised that there was only one, but we'd figured they would be, since they have multiple births."

"Humans are capable of them," Doc remarked.

"It is much easier to have one at a time," Syrona said firmly.

"Then why do you have two breasts?" Doc demanded.

"Symmetry," Nimisha replied, grinning at Jon.

"A point," Doc said, "but a woman could very easily suckle two children at once."

"If she had nothing else to do," Syrona said, her tone a little tart. "You can talk all you want, Doc, but you will never have babies. And, were I you, though I am indeed grateful for such an easy birth of a healthy child, I'd shut up about how many babies a woman should have at one time."

"I stand corrected," Doc said, sounding unusually meek.

"Thank you," Syrona said. She smoothed the fuzz on her daughter's round little head.

"I may not like champagne, but is there something else I could have because I'm a brother?" Tim asked wistfully.

"Cater, what have you that could convince our Tim that this is a celebration?" Jon asked.

"I believe I have just the thing," Cater said.

"Wow!" was Tim's response when he saw the three-layer cake, iced in white with lavish pink decorations adorning it. He brought it, along with plates and cutlery, back to the table, and displayed it to the men first. "It's got 'Happy Birth Day, Hope' written on it, Syrie!"

"You'd better be sure to leave me a piece, you ravenous lot. I'll have quite an appetite when I finish feeding this daughter of mine."

Traveling on IS drive as the Five B was, they could not receive additional pulsed messages.

The amenities on board did, indeed, prove felicitous. Unlike the accommodations on ordinary naval vessels, each cabin was so well built that no exterior sounds penetrated to disturb the occupant. This meant more privacy, a valuable commodity on an extended trip. Fortunately, though, the psych profiles had been accurate: There were no unpleasant altercations. Each specialist held classes that included more than Cuiva and allowed her the opportunity to interact with other people in the learning process. She had the sort of temperament that responded well to competition and discussion, a facet of education not available during her private tutoring. Caleb's idea of making her a JO, and giving her projects to be signed off on to prove she knew the material, was received with delight by Cuiva and nods of approval by the rest of the crew. She very much wanted to learn as much practical material as she could, to show her mother her achievements. The competition, friendly as it was, still inspired her to achieve at the highest possible level despite her being the youngest of the students.

She had received very good basic training: If she wasn't at the top of the class, she was rarely lower in the scale than second. She was most interested in astronomy and stellar navigation. She soon mastered everything Chief Hadley had to offer, so they both resorted to the educational tapes provided by the extensive ship's library.

"Some of these are just theories," Hadley warned her. "Can't take them as fact yet. Too da—" He cleared his throat and altered his phrasing. "Too bad we can't stop and examine some of the systems we're passing, so you could see examples."

"But we'll come out in a totally unknown sector of the galaxy," Cuiva said, her eyes gleaming with anticipation, "and we'll be the very first to catalog ever so many new primaries and systems."

"Must admit I'm looking forward to that opportunity myself, young lady," Hadley said. "Now, let's do some exercises. We've missed Gaitama's general lesson watching that tape."

The main cabin was often sectioned off, to allow for multiple activities to be scheduled. Plays were rehearsed privately and then performed on the lower deck in the gymnasium. Perdimia had a little pipe that she taught Cuiva how to play. Gaitama had brought along a lap harp that she had made; Caleb had taught himself guitar, and Cherry had studied violin. All on board could sing, and so they included musicals in the evening entertainment. Cuiva was enchanted with so many things to do and new skills to learn. If she privately mentioned to Perdimia that Lady Rezalla might be shocked at all she was being taught—including some of Gaitama's unusual skills— she was overjoyed at the chance to learn what regular people did. The long journey continued.

"Twins!" Nimisha's shriek of dismay echoed through the Fiver and brought Jon out of their cabin, where he had gone while Doc did his monthly examination.

"I thought you were expanding more than is normal," Doc remarked in a deceptively casual tone.

"*Thought?*" Nimisha did not diminish her tone. "You've known for the past seven months, if not immediately after you told me I'd conceived, that I was having twins. In fact, I suspect that you may well have done something to ensure the egg split so that I would!"

"Nimisha. Really!" Doc's indignation sounded honest enough.

"I don't trust you, Doc."

"Is it true, Doc?" Jon asked, hurrying to the diagnostic couch. Delight and concern warred with each other in his expression as he helped the bulging Nimisha to sit up. She was bulky enough to need assistance, and that annoyed her even more. She had not been nearly as large with Cuiva.

"It is true that Nimisha is carrying twins. I thought I was hearing a mere echo of the heartbeat, but I now perceive that there are undeniably two. Some of my equipment is basic, you know, and

amniocentesis and other more esoteric requirements in a maternity
unit were not deemed required."

"Since you did a lot more than listen to fetal heartbeats in
those tests you've been regularly subjecting me to, you've *known!*"
Nimisha's eyes were flashing and her mouth was set in an angry
line. "And I don't trust you not to have interfered. You had the
chance."

Jon, looking abashed, scratched his head before he met her
irate gaze.

"It might not be Doc's fault, luv. There are twins in almost every
generation in my family. In fact, I'm one. I have a twin sister."

"You never mentioned her."

"It's not a fact that Fleet needed to record."

"Is it in your sister's file?" Nimisha demanded.

"She went into law," he said, still chagrined.

"Why, I'm no better than the Sh'im."

"I'd say you were not quite as good as the Sh'im, my dear,"
Doc remarked at his driest, "since the majority of their multiple
births are triplets."

"That is small consolation." Her tone was acid as she slipped
off the couch and waddled toward Cater, requesting a snack. She
turned back for one more angry shot at the AI. "No wonder I eat
more than Tim does." She whirled on Jon as she heard him trying
to smother a laugh. "You watch out, Captain!" She waggled a finger at him.

"Whatever is wrong with having twins, dear heart?" Jon queried,
striding ahead of her to collect the ordered snack and bring it back
to the table. His agility only emphasized her own uncomfortable
condition.

"*How* am I going to cope?" She turned around in her chair and
shook a fist at the med unit. "And if you remind me that I have two
breasts, I'll—I'll—reprogram you!"

"Not until after I've assisted your delivery," Doc said, totally unrepentant.

Nimisha snorted but was far too peckish to bother to reply as she picked up the leg of poultry she had ordered along with the vegetable salad and the baked potato that was served with other indigenous roots to which she had taken a particular liking.

She concentrated on eating as an excuse not to look at Jon, but he could outwait her petulance. He sat with folded arms, tipping his chair on its back legs, to wait until her temper improved. She finished her meal without a single word, but Jon, quite familiar now with his lover's moods, knew that she had regained a normal perspective.

"What are they, Doc? Boys? Girls?" Jon asked.

"Boy and girl. So if Nimisha will deign to accept the fact that I did not interfere in any way except to ensure the healthy development of both fetuses, I will feel less threatened."

"Well," Nimisha began, though Jon could see she was not quite convinced of Doc's innocence, "you could have warned me earlier. You've known a long time, Doc. I'm sure of that."

"Yes, I've known, but considering your speech when Hope was born, I kept my counsel. There was always the chance that one twin would dominate and absorb the other, or it would spontaneously abort."

Nimisha clutched at her belly in unconscious rejection of those possibilities. Then she allowed a penitent smile to spread across her face.

"Boy and girl, huh? Then we'll be able to use both names, won't we, Jon?"

He leaned across the table and kissed her with the tenderness that he had displayed toward her throughout her pregnancy. She stroked his cheek and allowed the kiss to continue.

"The Sh'im females will approve," she said when they parted.

"There's that," Jon blithely agreed.

. .

Nimisha went into labor with both Jon and Syrona assisting Doc. As the medic had predicted, she had less trouble delivering the twins than she had had with Cuiva.

"But then, you've kept fit and you're a multipara," Doc said. "Second delivery," he explained.

The Sh'im were overjoyed to see that the humans could follow what they considered the best way to increase population. If Nimisha had worried about how to feed twins, she found herself overwhelmed with offers of assistance. The Sh'im suckled their offspring until teeth appeared, after which they chewed food into pulp and fed it to their young. But many continued to lactate. Since Nimisha was unable to feed the lusty twins for more than six weeks, Cater supplied formula milk, increasing its strength as the babies grew. There was always someone quite willing to feed Perria and Sven their bottles. Jon proved as devoted and affectionate a father to them as she could have wished: far superior to Rhidian, or any other man of her acquaintance.

Nimisha was as glad to be freed up from heavy maternity duties as there was so much to be done: organizing improvements in all the Sh'im settlements, teaching those who were now past producing young and wished to take on new duties, and using her own engineering skills to develop useful tools. Often she thought fondly of Lord Tionel and the "toys" he had given her to assemble and disassemble. Those designs and that experience were proving to be incredibly useful now. The one disappointment, the anxiety that nagged at the back of her mind when she was falling asleep at night, was *when* would they hear news from home? The beacon seemed to absorb the updates Helm sent, but he reported no incoming pulses.

When Syrona had twins, Nimisha's suspicions about Doc's interference, however well intentioned, surfaced. Though there were no multiple births in either of Syrona's and Casper's families, Doc insisted that he had not interfered. Good food, proper rest, perhaps some unknown factor in the planet itself had caused Syrona's ovaries to release two eggs at once. Even the small grazers, called boks in deference to the old-Earth-type antelope they resembled, were having multiple births.

"Could have something to do with the fact they feel safe," Casper suggested. He was far from upset to know that Syrona was carrying mixed twins. "A general fertility increase for all of us."

Nimisha refused to be convinced. It was all too true to say that everyone felt safe now in the six Sh'im towns; their allies rarely had fewer than three births at a time, and more accommodations had to be raised. With repeller shields to protect settlements, they no longer needed to seek caves for shelter from the avian denizens.

In order to reduce that danger, the four adult humans led a large band of well-armed Sh'im, transported in the three air vehicles available, for a concerted attack on the mountain mews where the avians bred their young.

The nests, with as many as twenty eggs, were destroyed, along with as many of the female defenders as possible. At Doc's suggestion, they also left out poisoned substances, reluctantly prepared by Cater to simulate what the avians preferred to eat. The poison that Doc concocted, having examined the flesh of an avian before scavengers could devour it, would inhibit the formation of healthy yolks in the eggs.

"We may succeed in reducing the population on this continent in the next decade or so," Doc remarked.

"You're fixated on eggs, Doc," Nimisha said slyly.

"Not at all, m'dear Nimisha," was his airy reply, "but it does get to the heart of the problem."

When the resources of the freighter were exhausted, the hu-

mans turned to the primitive mining that the Sh'im had already begun, and Nimisha focused her design talents on designing better
mine hoists, drills, tracks, and carts.

"Rather primitive . . ." she said, dubiously reviewing the
sketches.

"I'm no mining engineer," Jon replied, "but I don't see why
those wouldn't work. You based them on data from the library."

"I just wish there were an easier, less physical way of achieving
the same results," she said. "It's bloody hard work, even if we have
been able to locate the main lodes without having to do a lot of exploratory prospecting."

"The Sh'im won't mind," Syrona said.

"They'd be delighted to have work for some of the maturing
younglings," Casper said.

"They don't pay attention to lessons. Ay says we've made life
too easy for them," Tim put in, disgusted. He was usually included
in planning sessions since he often contributed good ideas, being
closer in so many ways to the Sh'im. He, Ay, and Bee formed quite
a triumvirate. "Used to be that as soon as they had all their teeth,
they were sent out to hunt, gather wood, and search for tuber
plants."

"Well, I've designed the mining equipment for three-fingered
usage," Nimisha said, tapping the drawings.

"What'll *I* use then?" Tim asked, affronted.

"You don't need to mine," Syrona said.

"I gotta show 'em all that I can do everything they can, and
better. Then they can't figure out ways to show me up," Tim said
with a malicious grin.

The others all laughed.

"We had noticed that little trick, Tim," Jon said approvingly.

The inauguration of the Fiver-Sh'im Mining Company involved
Nimisha as chief engineer so completely that she failed to notice
any indications that she was beginning a third pregnancy.

"Nimi, pet," Jon began one morning as they started the day by indulging in the most pleasurable of activities, "you can't be putting on weight *just* here . . ." He spread his wide hand across her abdomen. "And, unless I'm mistaken, you seem to be a trifle touchy here—" He touched her left breast.

"Oh, shaggit," she murmured, feeling her belly and wincing as she prodded her breasts. "I *am* pregnant. Not," she added hurriedly, kissing him, "that I mind. The twins are old enough."

"Have you seen Doc?"

"No, I haven't," she replied quickly and then grinned. "And it's too late for him to fiddle me again."

Jon turned a chuckle into an amused snort before he gathered her close against him. Then, with one finger, he traced the tattoo on her neck. "I never thought I'd father Vegan First Family progeny . . ."

"Let me remind you that *we* are the First Families of Erehwon, and that's an achievement reserved to two families alone! Not many planets can boast that kind of hierarchy. Or do I mean hegemony?"

"Oligarchy?" Jon put in.

"Aristocracy . . . of some sort or another."

"Whatever," Jon said, and then he turned serious, smoothing her long hair back from her face. "Get Doc to check you over. You've been working pretty hard in the mines. And you're to stay out of them from now on, hear me?"

"Oh, come on, Jon," she said, a bit annoyed. "It's not as if we've had any problems, not with being able to seal the shafts the way we have."

He pulled her back when she started to rise. "No, I'm serious, Nimisha. You take enough chances as it is. Please don't take unnecessary risks."

"And I haven't."

"We all have," he said in a very serious tone. "We all know we have, but there's even more at stake for you now." Once again he placed his hand on her abdomen.

"We can't ask the Sh'im to do what we won't. Tim's notion on that score is very accurate," she protested.

"Even the Sh'im females know when to stop working, lover mine."

Nimisha looked down at a stomach no longer flat, feeling here and there as if trying to estimate what was going on inside. "I can't be that far along. I've been feeling so energetic. Last time it was all I could do to get out of bed some mornings."

"It's your third—" He inhaled sharply, for any reference to her first daughter tended to sadden her.

"My third, yes. And Cuiva will be fourteen in three days. My dam will put on her Necklace—" Nimisha bit her lip, tears forming in her eyes. "—and pronounce that she has reached her minor majority so she can take her rightful place in society. Won't my dam just love that!"

"Oh, my love . . ." Jon held her tenderly against him, wishing there were some way to relieve her anguish.

"We can't be at the *end* of the universe, can we, that we've heard nothing?" she asked piteously.

"I devoutly hope not," Jon said firmly, doing his best to comfort her.

"I *designed* that beacon. It's eating our messages, so the receiver's working."

"I do feel more confidence in anything you've designed, love," Jon said with a twinkle in his eye. "Now if it had been Fleet issue, I could entertain doubts."

She sniffed, rubbed tears from her cheeks, and gave him an overbright smile. "I'm silly. There's not a damned thing I can do about it. Nor you, but you're sweet to worry over it." She kissed him, pushed him away, and decisively swung her legs over the side of the bed.

•   •

She didn't immediately check with Doc. Jon had to remind her twice. When she did, Doc sounded peevish.

"I honestly didn't know," Nimisha said, imbuing her tone with innocent surprise. "Jon noticed my belly protruding more than it should the other morning . . ."

"Other morning?" Doc repeatedly sarcastically.

"Two mornings ago, all right? I had to supervise the drilling of that new shaft in the iron mine."

"Had to?"

"Had to," she said, getting angry.

"You're fine; fetal health and development is normal." She felt a spray penetrate her left buttock. "That's concentrated full-spectrum vitamins and minerals. I'll send Cater the information for dietary additives. You may follow your troglodyte imperatives until even you can't fit in those holes you're digging."

Unaccustomed to such curtness from Doc, Nimisha made haste to leave the Fiver and indulge in the "troglodyte" activities on her schedule. All too soon she discovered a sudden claustrophobia, and because Ers and Uv were now well able to supervise the underground work, she let them.

Other Sh'im, aided by Helm, were printing out the Sh'im history found on board the Bird Ship, as well as translating Sh'im glyphs into English. Helm was also translating a short history of humankind into Sh'im for Ool, Ook, and any others who might be interested. The older Sh'im, unable to work as long or hard as they had in their younger days, found that reading passed the time enjoyably. They repeated the information in storyteller sessions in the evenings, amusing the youngest Sh'im.

At Nimisha's suggestion, Helm had glossed over human pre-space history and emphasized the space exploration and colonizing as more palatable to a species that had never indulged in wars and massacres. Then she accessed some of the ancient tales Nurse had read to her, and she made time every evening to read to Perria and Sven, who loved nothing better than a chance to curl up with Mimi, as they called her, and be read to.

"We'll miss you, you know, Cuiva," Caleb said, his remark echoed by everyone else gathered the day before Cuiva's fourteenth birthday.

"I don't believe I'll be aware of time passing," she said with a charming smile that reminded him of neither her mother nor her grandam. It was completely Cuivish, a development of the last year as she picked up womanly traits from the other five women on board the Five B.

She had learned everything she could from the specialists and signed off on every area open to a Junior Officer. She had then delved into independent and rather esoteric studies, almost exhausting the formidable resources of the onboard library. She had written two operettas that she had directed and performed in—scripting eminently suitable parts for crew and the three AI's, though Cater was the weakest of the cast and generally managed only the easiest of lines, similar to her programmed responses as Cater. Cuiva had composed music that Cherry, the most accomplished of the musicians on board, had genuinely acclaimed as close to brilliant.

"My grandam would definitely not have approved," Cuiva had said with one of her wry grins. "First Families do not perform for payment."

"Who's getting paid?" Kendra had demanded. She was usually cast as the heroine, since she had a light but well-placed soprano; as Caleb was usually the baritone hero, she had no objections whatever. Their onstage romantic parts had led to offstage intimacies.

But despite all these activities with companions who had become a surrogate family, Cuiva did not waver from her intention to sleep until her mother could Necklace her on her fourteenth birthday.

Gaitama, swearing all the time at losing her good friend, had constructed a special cabinet to be secured in the gig, which had been programmed to exit the garage and return to base if the ship had to be abandoned for any reason. Caleb had insisted on that precaution, and Cuiva had accepted it. At last, she thanked them all for what she had learned from them, kissed them all, and then laid herself down in the medical unit. With all her friends watching, Doc initiated the suspension.

The entire crew felt her absence in the first weeks, and Perdimia became quite depressed.

"I should have gone to sleep, too," the bodyguard said. "That would be in keeping with my contract with Lady Rezalla."

"You're watching over her all the time as it is," Caleb said, knowing how often Perdimia slipped out of the main cabins and into the garage to be sure the life signs on Cuiva's sleep capsule were functioning properly. He was somewhat at a loss to find her occupation, until Doc suggested that Perdimia study nursing with him. It was always a useful profession, and she had sufficient time to qualify in the two and a half years remaining of their trip.

"But I'll be Lady Cuiva's companion when she wakes," Perdimia said in a weak argument.

"And certainly she'll need special attention in the first week after she's roused," Doc responded. "And if Lady Nimisha has, as we suspect, gone into suspended animation until she is rescued, your new nursing skills will be an important factor in her complete recovery."

Perdimia was persuaded, and once agreeable, she applied herself with the same sort of single-minded dedication that her charge had shown. If she spent her free time reviewing the tapes made of Cuiva's performances and recitals, that was her option. She wasn't the only one who did so.

And the Five B continued on her course for yet another long year.

CHAPTER 9

"This is my ninth tour here," Lt. Commander Globan Escorias said as he reported to Captain Nesta Meterios, the current commander of the scout ship *Acclarke*, one of the Mark 4's. The officer he was replacing had boarded the courier ship with such avid relief on her face that he had grinned back at her on his way off the FSP supply ship. This had brought human and equipment replacements and consumables for both the *Acclarke* and the space station known as "Wormhunter." In fact, in his first tour, he'd coined the name "wormbusters" for the astronomers constantly scanning the area for any sign of their quarry. It was the hope that *he* would be aboard the *Acclarke Four* when the wormhole reappeared—and the extra pay—that kept luring him back.

"And just what does that imply, XO?" the commander asked sourly.

"Nothing really, sir," Escorias replied quickly. Maybe there was another reason for relief on the former XO's face as she left the *Acclarke*. "Only that I am already fully aware of the duties, parameters, and operating procedures relative of the *Acclarke* as your executive officer. Unless, of course," he added quickly as he saw her expression darken at his glib response, "there have been significant alterations with you as captain."

He closed his eyes briefly, wincing because that hadn't come out any better than his first cheerful remark.

Captain Nesta Meterios sighed, her face patient. "I wish I could tell you there were. There hasn't been so much as a—"

Red lights came on and the siren wailed a full alert.

"Helm?" the captain demanded. This was not the fully programmed independent AI that Escorias knew had been designed for the Fivers, but its reaction time was still faster than a human's.

"Sir, sensors indicate an unstable rippling effect in the area bordering sectors five and six."

"Alert the station. I spoke too soon," she said, gesturing for him to follow her out of her ready room and down the short passageway to the bridge. "XO, General Quarters," she yelled, inserting herself into the pilot's chair and gesturing for Globan to net into the second seat. "On the view screen, Helm." Then, under her breath, "If those supplies aren't secured . . ."

Board lights blinked into green readiness to indicate that all crew were reporting in at their battle stations, though out of the corner of his eye, Globan saw one crew member wearing only a towel tucked about his waist.

"Net in, prepare for emergency breakaway," the captain ordered.

It was obvious to Globan Escorias by the console that Helm had already anticipated a precipitous departure. The VSS *Acclarke* was always on standby, and Globan automatically took in the comforting gauge that registered full power available. What he couldn't easily explain was *why* the wormhole was so damned close to the station and the *Acclarke*, which were supposed to be several hundred thousand kilometers from the coordinates where Lady Nimisha's ship was lost.

"XO, find out the status of the wormbusters. Someone's going to insist on finishing some experiment, and they're closer than we are to that damned ripple."

Globan saw that the ripple was now a discernible wave, with light like combers breaking through in places.

"Spatial disturbance is growing," Helm said dispassionately.

"Fraggit," said the captain. "Tell the wormies to get into their escape pods. *Now!* Drop whatever they're doing and get into their pods!" Her voice began to rise from contralto to a frightened soprano pitch.

Globan felt his heart pounding with excitement. To be here when it happened had been the ambition of everyone who had served the long, tedious hours on the Nimisha watch, as the Fleet officially called it.

"Helm," he said, following the standard procedure he'd never thought he'd have to originate, "dispatch a pulse back to Coyne III, with these coordinates for the wormhole."

Meterios shot him a furious glance and then recovered herself as she realized he was fulfilling his duties and initiating an operating procedure in which he had previously been well drilled.

"Aye, sir. Pulse dispatched," Helm responded.

"Probe ready for launch," Meterios said.

"Probe activated and ready, sir," Helm responded.

"XO, are those wormies getting to their pods?" Meterios asked.

"We're not supposed to be so close to it," was the annoyed response to Meterios's query. "We're supposed to be far enough away for observation."

"Observe the phenomena from your escape pod, Dr. Qualta," Globan said, recognizing the voice of the senior astronomer on the Wormhunter.

"Helm," Meterios said, "get as close as you can to the station and forward of it."

Globan was not at all sure he liked being a sacrificial offering to anything. He also doubted by what means the captain thought to protect the much more vulnerable space station.

Dr. Qualta had left the comunit open and he could hear noises, metal and other clackings. "Move it, Dr. Qualta," he said into his comunit, knowing the propensity of the older woman to procrastinate. "Don't haul anything in with you," he added, rating a startled glance from Meterios.

"Oh yassssus," the captain cried, her voice rising to a near squeak.

Globan gulped, wishing he could get that much out of his mouth as first a whiteness appeared in black space where none had been. It widened slowly, approximating a grinning tooth-less maw. That's what those who had seen wormholes called it: a maw.

"Hold steady, Helm," Meterios said, trying to keep her voice even.

"Probe's launched," Helm said. They could already see the flare of its rockets as it streamed across the all-too-short distance between the *Acclarke* and the widening lipless smile of the wormhole.

"Full reverse, Helm," Meterios said.

"Full reverse already engaged, sir," was Helm's calm reply.

"Then why are we moving forward, Helm?"

"The engines are fully engaged, Captain," Helm said. "The wormhole is powerful."

"Gods above," some crewman said, "look what's happening to the station!"

Meterios abruptly signaled Globan to look while she tried her best to increase the resistance of the *Acclarke* to the superior force drawing it steadily into the wormhole.

"The station's breaking up, Captain."

"Launch, you worm-watchers, *launch*!" Meterios screamed.

"The order has been given," Helm said even as Globan reached for the intercom. "This unit is operating on emergency override, Captain."

The captain nodded, accepting the fact that an AI's reflexes and preprogrammed procedures had taken over control of the ship.

She and Globan watched as the individual pods shot out of the now-twisting structure of the space station, its interlocked units breaking up into shards and flying debris. Several of the pods even seemed to be making headway from the disaster area. Then they, like the heavier *Acclarke*, were inexorably drawn toward the phenomenon. Globan realized he was grasping the armrests and leaning as far back in the safety net as he could, being pushed even further into the padding by the increased velocity with which the ship was being pulled in.

"*Net in, net in!*" the captain yelled. "If they aren't netted in, they'll be pulp," she murmured and groaned, unable to close her eyes as they entered the maw. "Helm, can you establish the position of the piggyback?"

"It is operational, sir, and some distance ahead of us."

"I hope the shagging thing works," Globan muttered. He had so hoped for some action on this duty. Well, he was getting far more then he had ever expected. The Fiver had been missing for over five years now. In fact, the rescue mission aboard the Five B ought to be nearing its destination, half a galaxy away—a distance they were about to take by shortcut. At least he hoped they would end up where Lady Nimisha and the Fiver had. Of course, there was absolutely no assurance that they would. They could well be number twenty on the Missing Ship list.

This wasn't an easy ride. Even with the refined devices incorporated into the *Acclarke*, as well as the faster response time of an AI helmsman, they were still bounced and dropped and dribbled along a corridor that seemed to contract and expand in no regular pattern. Now and then Globan could see the riding lights of the poor wormbusters in the pods; the behavior of light in the wormhole was as capricious as the diameter of its gullet. Just so long as it had no stomach, Globan thought. Except for the flashing of prongs and spears of rock or unknown debris, the *Acclarke* was traveling too fast for either occupant of the bridge to discern any details of the innards of the wormhole. The pods were being bounced back and forth like so many balls. He didn't think even the most efficient netting could save lives. What a hideous way to die!

The gravitational pressure eased far more abruptly than it had begun. Globan realized that he was dizzy from holding his breath, and then they were flung forward again at such a high velocity that he thought his skin would peel off his bones.

"Return probe just passed us, sir," Helm's dispassionate voice reported.

Globan managed to turn his head enough so he could see Nesta Meterios's pressure-flattened face. She didn't appear as comforted as he was that the probe device was working. Unless, of course, the entrance maw closed before it could exit. Its engine was the most powerful Rondymense had ever constructed, driving a slender package at IS drive speeds. But would it be powerful and fast enough to exit on the right side, leaving a view that could be identified by other searchers?

As abruptly as they had been swallowed, they were spat out into black space. The wormhole pouted once more, as if it hadn't liked the taste of them at all, and closed up. There was no sign whatever that that particular portion of space had ever been breached.

"A standard beacon, two points starboard, Captain," Helm reported in its unemotional baritone, "has been identified as similar to the type used by Lady Nimisha's Fiver. It is still pulsing a Mayday and has data to be downloaded."

"Download by all means, Helm," Captain Meterios said in a breathy voice, but she was back down in the contralto register. "Damage report? Crew?"

Each station reported; some of the six voices sounded shaky.

"Prepare to retrieve the station's pods," she said in such a bleak voice that Globan knew she shared his doubts that they'd find any survivors. "Helm, engage retrieval pattern."

"How many should there be?" Globan asked, releasing his safety net while scanning their immediate vicinity for the blinking lights that an inhabited escape pod should be emitting.

"Twelve," the captain replied, licking pale lips in a shock-white face.

He wondered how he looked and then realized that his mouth was dry as dust. He had no idea how long that incredible journey had taken.

He released his harness. "I'll check casualties."

"Do," Meterios said. "Helm, easy as you go to the first pod on the starboard. It's nearest."

"Aye, sir."

Globan entered the day room—which also held the medical facility—just as the man in the towel led in a yeowoman with a broken arm and face scratches.

"You're not in uniform," Globan said, taking charge of the injured yeowoman and jerking his head toward the crew quarters. He pretended not to hear the muttered response. "When you are, bring the captain a mug of stim."

"I'll do that, sir," another man said, holding a rag to his forehead. "That was the Chief Engineer," he added in an undertone.

"The least he could do is tattoo his rank on his arm," Globan remarked with a wry smile as he helped the yeowoman into the sick bay. "Let me see that first," he added.

"Nu-skin'll take care of it, sir," the man said, pointing to the appropriate cabinet on the wall.

Globan knew enough about lacerations to confirm the self-diagnosis just as the medical rating arrived to take care of the broken arm. There were several other minor cuts and certainly bruises, but they were all attended to before Globan joined the medic, Parappan, at the main hatch to receive the escape pods. Before Helm had eased the *Acclurke* near enough to gently grapple the first one, Globan sorted out the crew he had had no time to be introduced to. The Chief Engineer was Evard Hinvic; Ace Parappan, the medic; the gunnery officer, Brad Karpla; the yeowoman was Tezza Ashke; Luthen Drayus was the com jig; and the yeoman was Fez Amin, who doubled as captain's steward.

It took hours to locate and retrieve eleven pods. Globan decided not to think about what had happened to the one that had not been debouched on this side of the wormhole.

Five passengers had died because they had not securely netted themselves into the shock-absorbent couch provided. The other six were injured, one critically; she was instantly placed in the medical unit, while Globan, Brad Karpla, and the Chief Engineer tried to make the others as comfortable as possible.

The captain appeared, speaking to each of the survivors, none of whom could quite believe that they were still alive.

"I have good news," Nesta Meterios said. "The beacon is packed with updates from Lady Nimisha. She has found human survivors of the *Poolbeg* and another ship." She acknowledged the weak smiles at her attempt to lighten the atmosphere.

That news shocked others out of self-absorption and depression. "In fact, they have a thriving community on one of the M-type planets," she continued. "Three were discovered in her initial survey of this sector of space."

"Then Lady Nimisha is still alive?"

The captain gave a real smile. "Alive, well, and, with the survivors of the *Poolbeg*, colonizing Erehwon. Last update is three weeks ago."

"Erehwon?" the chief exclaimed, looking up from spraying nu-skin on the multiple abrasions of the civilian communications expert from the space station.

"That's 'nowhere' backward," Globan said.

"Appropriate, I'd say," the captain remarked in her dry voice.

"Yes, I guess it is if you don't know where you are."

"Wasn't that a story from pre-space travel times?" the civilian asked, trying to distract himself from his discomfort. No one seemed to know.

"Then the Five B hasn't arrived yet?" the chief asked.

The captain shook her head. "It isn't due for several more months. We took the shortcut. Helm, did the probe safely clear the wormhole?"

"Unable to confirm, Captain. However, judging by the speed at which it was traveling and the duration of our time within the phenomenon, there is a good chance that it exited before closure."

"But you're not sure?"

"No, sir. That cannot be ascertained, despite factoring in the variables of the wormhole itself and choosing the best possible conclusion. Since the wormhole did not exhibit any stable size or exert a constant rate of speed while we were within the phenomenon, we cannot be sure the return probe was able, or in time, to exit. However, the possibility is significantly favorable that its size allowed it passage where a large object would have been retained."

Globan blinked, trying to assimilate that spurt of almost contradictory phrases. He thought the captain was experiencing a similar difficulty.

"If it did, it did," Nesta Meterios said finally, raising her hands in fatalistic acceptance of the circumstances. "Damage report, Helm?"

"The hull came in contact with the sides of the wormhole on nine separate occasions but sustained no significant damage. All systems are in working order."

"If you have stripped the coordinates of this M-type planet Lady Nimisha has discovered . . ."

"I have, sir."

"Then let us proceed to that world. Doc, what is Dr. Qualta's condition?"

"Serious, sir, with broken ribs and internal bleeding that has now been stemmed. The doctor will require monitoring. Unless there is another patient requiring diagnostic evaluation, it would be best to retain Dr. Qualta in this unit."

The captain looked from the medic, who was closing a scalp wound with nu-skin and regen gel on one of the wormhunters, to the chief, who was dealing with a station technician's skinned legs and arms, to the other patients who were either making use of the couches in the lounge or eating.

With a nod of her head, Nesta made it plain to Globan that she wanted a private word with him. He followed her back to the bridge.

"One thing bothers me, XO," she said. "There are messages on the beacon that Lady Nimisha ought to have been able to strip, reassuring her about the Five B's rescue mission and other matters." Meterios's expression did not conceal her grave concern. "I had Helm scan the beacon, and he discovered small holes that might be meteor damage and could have affected any relays to her on this planet she's found."

Globan nodded, trying to radiate calm reassurance. To him, the captain appeared still somewhat dazed by their wormhole ride and the extent of the injuries to the Wormhunter's personnel. He hoped she'd been given a proper stimulant. Well, that's why there was always an XO, even on a ship as relatively small as the *Acclarke*.

"Which reminds me, XO, did you bring any disks for me? We never got to that part of our introductory meeting."

She sounded a bit more like a captain then. Globan had forgotten the packet completely. He felt for it in his uniform pocket and handed the disks over.

"Mostly mail," she said, opening it and shuffling through the various disks. "Always welcome. Perhaps more so now than ever before. Ah, and some updates for the library. D'you think," she went on more slowly, her brown eyes clouded, "that the supply ship made it out of danger?"

Globan relaxed a bit and grinned. "She was burning her way homeward before I reached your office, sir."

"Yes, I should imagine she was. I hope they made it." She stood, hands lightly clasped behind her back, regarding the sprinkling of stars visible. "This seems almost as empty an area as the one we left."

"I wasn't aware that wormholes also ingested planets or moons or suns, sir."

She shrugged.

"I do know, sir, that Fleet Headquarters has sent a warning to all naval units to avoid the . . . area we just left to prevent any further inexplicable disappearances."

"Too late for us, of course, but high time. I wonder how long it took them to make such an obvious order." She glanced over at him. "Forget I said that."

"Said what, Captain?"

She awarded him a smile. "This will not be your normal tour of duty, Escorias."

"No, sir, it won't."

"Perhaps you'll wish to settle in."

"Jon!" Nimisha cried as Helm delivered the news that had been pulsed in from the *Acclarke*.

He came racing to the bridge, his eyes wide with apprehension.

"No, it's not me," she exclaimed. She was far bulkier this time and suspected twins again, no matter if Doc kept on saying, "Fetal development is progressing with no problems." She was in her last three weeks of pregnancy and wanted nothing more earnestly than to be delivered.

"Report, Helm," she said, trying to get comfortable in a pilot's chair that had not been designed to accommodate her present mass.

"A ship identified as the VSS *Acclarke* is in IS drive heading in this direction."

"No message?" Nimisha was both annoyed and surprised.

"I have dispatched a welcome," Helm said, "but there has been no acknowledgment. Possibly their exterior comunits have been damaged in the passage through the wormhole—if that was their mode of entry into this section of space."

"They couldn't know we've even got a comsat, dear," Jon said, pressing her shoulder with a consoling hand. "It won't take them long."

"If you tell me to be patient one more time, Jonagren . . ."

"I wouldn't dream of it. Nor dare." And with a second quick squeeze of his hand, he backed off. "I'll tell the others. At last, rescue."

"We don't know that," she said, pushing herself to her feet with difficulty and arching her aching back as she followed him into the main cabin. "I'd say if they accessed the wormhole exit buoy, they got sucked in, too. VSS *Acclarke*? I don't remember a ship of that designation at Fleet Headquarters."

"We've been gone a long while," Jon reminded her on their way to the hatch.

"Still," she said, pausing to grip the back of a chair, "if it came through the wormhole and was able to access the buoy's information and head here, it might well be one of *my* ships."

Jon paused in the act of taking the first step down, eyebrows raised in surprise.

"Only an AI Helm could make it safely through the wormhole, you know," she said with understandable pride.

"Thank you, ma'am."

"You saved us, Helm, no question of it."

"I'll spread the good news," Jon said and disappeared.

"Oh, save me," Nimisha murmured, perching on the arm of the chair, panting from her recent exertions: she who had been able to run kilometers for the sheer joy of the exercise. She was overwhelmingly grateful to the groups of Sh'im who minded the rambunctious human children, Hope as well as three-year-old Perria and Sven. She was going to have Doc replace her implant. This was her last pregnancy. Period. End of her maternal increasing! She had intended to have at least a girl by Casper for Tim's sake, since they had to spread the gene pool as wide as they could. Well, they might have had to . . . But how could they have counted on being rescued after so long? When there hadn't been a single pulse beamed back to her beacon? It wasn't as if she didn't adore the twins, mischievous demons that they were. But much as she loved them, they could not ease that aching need for her far-distant firstborn body-heir. Surely by now the pulse had reached a listening comsat *somewhere* in the civilized galaxy! And surely this new arrival might have news: some message from her grown-up daughter. Her dam would surely have put the Necklace on Cuiva, wouldn't she?

"Don't be so vapid, Nimisha Boynton," she chided herself.

"You are far from vapid, Nimisha Boynton-Rondymense," Doc said. "Helm says the ship should arrive within two or three days. It would certainly have accumulated some news in the six years since our arrival here. If I do not misread Commander Rustin's ingenuity, any ship set to watch for the reappearance of that wormhole will bear personal messages for you. Most certainly one or more from your daughter, and many from your dam, Lady Rezalla."

"Mother will certainly have something to say about my absence," Nimisha said drily.

"Possibly the official mail might include a means of rescue from this outpost of civilization."

"Outpost of . . ." Despite herself, Nimisha chuckled, though even that activity was difficult with so much mass in front of her. "We are, aren't we?"

"Indeed, my dear Nimisha, you and the Sh'im have civilized this continent." There was the slightest emphasis on "this."

"Now what's at the back of your devious mind, Doc?"

"With the complement of a ship's crew, expansion may be feasible," he said, highly pleased.

"I'll tell you this, loud and clear, Doctor Lord Naves, from the moment I deliver my current little package, I am *out*—" She paused for emphasis. "—of the maternity business."

"Which I would strongly advise, my dear Nimisha," Doc said, with a ripple that she could not quite translate.

"What's behind that advice, Doc?" she asked suspiciously.

"The conservation of your energies for other tasks eminently suited to your particular training and expertise," he replied, in that oh-so-bland voice he could assume. "As I have heard you remark, you, Jon, Casper, and Syrona constitute the First Families of Erehwon. I cannot see any group usurping that position."

She heard excited voices then, the higher pitched ones of her twins, as well as Timmy's alto warnings. The six other humans on Erehwon piled into the Fiver's main chamber. Syrie had evidently left her young twins, boy and girl, with their Sh'im caregiver. The adults all had questions, and their babble made Nimisha hold up her hands for silence.

"I know no more than Jon's told you. Helm says they're on their way. He's sent a message, but it has not been acknowledged. But in two or three days they'll make it here. They are heading directly here, so clearly they downloaded our data."

"Oh, shroo-oom," Syrona exclaimed, using a Sh'im sound meaning excited anticipation. "News, people, new faces. Rescue?" Her expression flickered through hope, distress, and delight, and ended up in uncertainty.

"There wouldn't be boys my age on a naval ship, would there?" Tim asked plaintively.

"We don't know that it *is* a naval ship, Tim, so you may retain your number one status," Casper said, circling the boy's wide young shoulders with an affectionate arm. "Grab Hope before she spills whatever she's ordering from Cater," he added, pointing to his three-year-old daughter who had just marched up to Cater and politely requested a drink.

"You are allowed a fruit juice at this time of day," Cater said, following programmed orders on the care and feeding of human young.

"Can I get you anything, Nim?" Tim asked solicitously.

Jon had taken Perria and Sven off to clean their hands and faces, which managed to attract far more dirt than Sh'im younglings ever collected.

"A drink. I think I was on my way for a drink before I stopped," Nimisha said wearily.

Syrona gave her a surreptitious glance, trying not to be too obvious in her check on her very pregnant friend. Nimisha gave her a reassuring flick of her hand.

"The arm of this chair is the right height, that's all, Syrie. I did move as fast as I could when Helm reported receiving a message. At long, long last!"

She accepted her drink from Tim, thanked him, and gratefully sipped it. She could neither drink nor eat much at one time anymore, so small, frequent snacks had become her habit.

"Backache?" Syrie asked, and without waiting for an answer, started to rub exactly where she could give Nimisha the most relief. Nimisha had done the same when Syrona had been pregnant with Calum and Camilla.

Jon returned with his children, who tugged him toward Cater.

"I'll see them served and seated," Tim said, immediately taking charge.

"He's so good with them," Syrie said proudly. "I wonder, though, are we presuming on his good nature too much?"

"I don't think so," Jon said. "The Sh'im take over once they're outside and he goes off with the younglings. He's only just back from their latest foray."

"Maybe there'll be a way to get him back to Acclarke and a peer group," Nimisha said.

"He does fine here," Casper said, "Doesn't he, Syrie?"

Syrona put both hands gently on Nimisha's arms and pressed gently. "Even if we could get back, I don't think we'd want to." She paused and craned around to look at Nimisha's face. "You would, of course, for Cuiva's sake."

Nimisha didn't trust her voice to answer, nodding instead. Cuiva had gradually assumed far more importance than anything she could achieve at the Ship Yard. The Fiver had proved itself and, if the ship on its way to them was one of her design and had survived its wormhole transit as well as the Fiver had, she had proved her design and could . . . do something else, more challenging. If only Cuiva . . .

A pain shot through her and she gasped.

"Uh-oh," Syrona said. "Doc . . ."

"Bring her over here."

Jon was beside her in an instant, helping Syrona lift her to her feet. He half-bent to pick her up, but she stopped him. "Walking's useful," she said, and then gasped as a second, far sharper pain caught. "Maybe not this time."

He grunted as he settled her in his arms and made a joke of groaning at her weight, depositing her quickly within the diagnostic unit as extendibles moved to preprogrammed positions.

Casper and Tim were herding the children out again, leaving Jon and Syrona to cope with the delivery.

"We've got this down to a fine arrrrrrt—" Nimisha's gasp cut off her attempt at humor and Syrona was pulling the voluminous smock up over the swollen abdomen even as the couch adjusted itself for the task ahead.

"This is going very fast, Nimi," Doc said. She felt the cool of the hypospray, and then a third unbelievably intense contraction was cut off.

"What happened?" she cried, alarmed.

"You won't feel a thing now," Doc assured her at his most persuasive.

She exhaled a relieved sigh and leaned back against the pillows now propping her into a more comfortable position. Jon took her left hand in his and, with the other, dabbed at her face with a cool cloth.

"Thanks, love."

She couldn't feel but she could see the action of the uterine muscles, and she adjusted her breathing accordingly. At Doc's urging, Syrona pushed down on Nimisha's abdomen and, with a startled cry, kept the emerging baby from a headfirst collision with the foot of the couch.

"A boy," Syrona said.

"But I can't have had one so soon," Nimisha exclaimed, noticing no appreciable diminution in the size of her belly.

"Take it, Jon," Doc said quickly.

"I'm having more twins?" Nimisha demanded, furious.

"No," Doc said calmly. "Triplets."

Nimisha was speechless, which was just as well, because both Jon and Syrona were too busy handling three babies and the afterbirths. Syrona, holding the first son, rushed to the open hatch and called Casper back.

"Doc?" Jon said in a tone of outrage that gratified Nimisha.

"Yes, yes, I knew, but as you also know, Nimisha didn't come near me during the first trimester. This is all your, or her, doing. Or maybe there's something in Erehwon's soil that is increasing human fertility. I don't know, but I swear upon my Hippocratic oath—"

"You're an AI, you never swore one," Nimisha roused enough to protest weakly.

"Lord Naves did," Doc replied so caustically that Nimisha realized he had not tampered with this pregnancy, though how he could have, she couldn't guess. "I'm replacing your implant right now," he added.

"Saves me insisting," Jon said firmly.

Nimisha groaned. Holding the girl he had taken while Casper coped with the third, another boy, he strode to the head of the couch and kissed her tenderly.

"I don't mind having so many children from you, Nimisha Boynton, but I don't like you so distressed."

"She's perfectly healthy, Jon," Doc said. "I wish I knew what to look for to isolate the factor of so many multiple births in you two women. The good aspect is how far up this will raise you in the esteem of the Sh'im."

"There is that." Despite herself, Nimisha started to laugh almost uncontrollably and was immensely grateful for the analgesic that prevented her abdominal muscles from hurting at the abuse of laughter.

"No, she's not hysterical," Doc said when the others looked concerned. "At least she sees the funny side of this."

"I'm not sure I do," Jon said almost savagely.

The need to placate him sobered Nimisha and she pulled his face closer to her, stroking his cheek and then parting the wrapper of the child he held so she could see the face of her latest daughter.

"She looks like Cuiva did," she said, blurting it out, and then she was crying as uncontrollably as she had been laughing.

"I'll handle this one," was the last thing she heard Doc say as a friendly oblivion overtook her.

She woke in her own bed, Jon dozing in the chair, his head propped on one hand. She was sore, but at least she could see her toes again, and she breathed such a sigh of relief that Jon woke with a start.

"How are you?" he asked, dropping to his knees beside the bed, clasping her hand and then smoothing her hair back from her face.

"I feel a little sore, and a great deal foolish for that emotional show."

He smiled. "Shock is what I'd call it. Does the girl really resemble Cuiva?"

"As she was at birth," Nimisha said, trying not to let the sadness she felt color her words. Then she looked around. "Where are the babies? Are they all right? I never even looked at them."

"They're fine, Uk, Eloo, and Lal are minding them in the spare cabin. They've been bathed, fed, and are sleeping."

"You look so tired, love," she said, fingering his silvering hair back over his right ear.

"I am," he admitted. "Doc did replace your implant. Five children are more than enough. More than enough."

"I haven't really minded, Jon, but having them one at a time in the normal fashion would have been much easier."

He gave a tired chuckle. She patted the other side of the bed, which he normally slept in. "If the babies are in Sh'im keeping, you need your sleep."

He slid in from the foot of the bed so he wouldn't rock her, but when he measured his length beside her, she snuggled against him, grasping his left hand in hers and pillowing her head on his upper arm. He was asleep almost as soon as she dropped off again.

CHAPTER 10

Nimisha did not join the welcoming committee when the *Acclarke* landed on the field. In the days since the news of their emergence and contact with the beacon, she had been slow to recover from the birth of the triplets. Neither Doc nor Jon had to appeal to her common sense to remain resting in the Fiver.

She was alerted by Helm when the *Acclarke* was on Insystem drive and he could initiate contact at her command. Which she did almost immediately, unable to wait until anyone else could join her, so eager was she to speak to those on the *Acclarke*.

"Lady Nimisha Boynton?" the astounded captain asked, staring at her with disbelieving eyes.

"Boynton, yes, indeed, Captain . . . ?"

"Nesta Meterios," the other woman said quickly. "And most gratified to see you alive and so well."

Nimisha managed a brief smile. "Not half as pleased as we are to know you've survived that bloody wormhole." Then she had to ask. "By any remote chance, is my daughter, Cuiva, on board, Captain Meterios?"

"No, my lady," and Meterios sounded shocked at the very idea. "The *Acclarke* is a *navy* vessel. But I do have good news in that regard, Lady Nimisha. A pulse giving the location of your beacon was received four years ago, and the Five B, with Captain Caleb Rustin, your daughter and her companion, and six other handpicked crew set off by Interstellar Drive to rescue you."

"Oh, Cuiva," Nimisha sighed, her throat closing and her heart pounding at the very thought of seeing her daughter again.

"Lady Nimisha?" Captain Meterios asked anxiously. "Are you all right?"

"I am overjoyed to the point of being speechless, Captain. Have you any idea of their ETA?"

"They can't be but a few months away now, my lady. The *Acclarke*, however, is carrying mail packets that have accrued on board in case the wormhole opened. Which it obviously has, since that is how we got here. You are living on the Fiver? The planet is dangerous?"

The captain could see no more than the pilot area, so Nimisha grinned.

"I'm on watch, Captain, but not at all alone on this planet." She had one ear listening for the babies who, for once, were all asleep at the same time. "In my initial survey of this world, I discovered four other crashed ships. Two groups survived. The most recent, the FSPS *Poolbeg*, has four survivors—" She named them. "And the other group has been here even longer, and we owe much to them for their survival skills."

"How fortunate for you."

"Indeed, Captain, especially since the second group are aliens." Nimisha managed not to laugh at the stunned surprise on the captain's face. She heard a male voice excitedly asking for more details.

"That was Lieutenant Commander Globan Escorias, my XO, Lady Nimisha." The captain's voice had an edge that suggested she did not appreciate the interruption. But the screen widened to include the dark-visaged officer, bouncing about in the seat beside her in his urgency to know more.

"Aliens, Lady Nimisha?" he asked. "Sentient aliens? Humanoid?"

"They are not merely sentient, but we consider them sapient, too." Noting the dismay on the captain's face, she added quickly, "From a space-faring, colonizing species, so we have not compromised their evolution. They are our friends and valued allies," she said as firmly as she could.

"Yes, yes, of course," the XO put in hastily. "Sapient aliens. This will astound the civilized worlds."

"Erehwon may now be included in that number, Commander."

"Oh, yes, decidedly, yes, of course it would. My congratulations, Lady Nimisha."

"And our thanks for your design," Captain Meterios said, firmly taking over the contact. "The *Acclarke* is the model Four, my lady, from your Ship Yard, with some alterations and upgrades for naval use. Truly, without an independent AI Helm we would not have survived the journey through that appalling wormhole."

"No, you would not. The *Poolbeg* and the other three ships, who had no such AI reflexes, were badly damaged by their passage."

"We were also able to rescue the survivors of the space station," the captain said.

"Space station?" Nimisha repeated, confused.

"A space station, the Wormhunter," Meterios explained with a vacuous smile, "was set up to monitor such phenomena and located ten thousand kilometers from your Mayday marker, Lady Nimisha"—Nimisha grimaced at this constant use of her title; she had become far too accustomed to Erehwon informality, although Lady Rezalla would not approve—"safe enough, we thought, but the wormhole opened just in front of it. I ordered them into escape pods and to net up tightly."

"No space station exists that could survive a trip through that wormhole," Nimisha said, shaking her head.

"Exactly, Lady Nimisha. It broke up very quickly by the force exerted on it and went through as a twisted mass. It and the escape pods were drawn in well ahead of the *Acclarke*. Powerful as the engines are, my lady, we were unable to reverse out of danger."

"I thought you were supposed to enter the wormhole and find me," Nimisha said.

"Yes, but we would have preferred to enter on *our* terms, my lady," the captain said crisply.

"Yes, of course. How many pods were there?" Nimisha asked.

"Twelve, but only eleven exited. Those who had fastened the netting securely came through in much better shape. Some did not respond quickly enough to the order to abandon the station. They tried to bring things with them." The captain evidently expected instant obedience. Dangerous as it had been to stop and collect equipment or personal effects, scientists operated on different standards. "That's why the group's leader, Dr. Qualta, was so badly injured. She is now recovering satisfactorily."

"Another one of my units, no doubt," Doc said rather smugly at that point.

Jon with Casper close behind him arrived at that moment, so Nimisha introduced the two *Poolbeg* officers.

"Captain Meterios has informed me that Caleb Rustin is bringing Cuiva on the Five B, the long way round," Nimisha said, clinging to Jon's hand. He pressed back, giving her a quick encouraging smile.

"Your arrival is eagerly anticipated, Captain," Jon said. "Helm, have you given the *Acclarke* our exact coordinates?"

"Yes, it has," Captain Meterios replied so smartly that Nimisha wondered if the woman disliked using AI units. "We shall touch down in approximately eight hours and twenty minutes, Lady Nimisha, Captain Svangel."

"Be prepared to celebrate, Captain," Jon said warningly. "Our allies, the Sh'im, enjoy every opportunity to do so, and this is certainly a special event. My compliments, Captain Meterios, to you and your crew."

Nimisha nodded once again in farewell; what little energy she had was depleted by the exchange and the knowledge that Cuiva was on her way here. Then a thought struck her forcibly.

"Oh, shaggit, whatever is Cuiva going to say about having *five* siblings?" she exclaimed.

"She's your daughter, Nimi. She'll handle it just fine," Jon said, beaming.

"Oh dear heart, there won't be any news for you and Syrie and Casper."

He hugged her. "That's a very small concern, believe me. Career naval personnel learn to think of their shipmates as all the family they need. And I believe that's true enough. Even though we were very close as children, I don't think I saw my twin sister but once after I graduated from the Academy. She was killed in a high-speed rail accident on the Cross-Orient express." He gave a sigh and a little shake of his head. "A long time ago, love."

"What's happened?" Syrona cried from the open hatch, hurrying in with Tim, who was leading Hope by the hand.

Jon recited the tale as he acquired a restorative from Cater and brought it to an exhausted Nimisha.

"Your daughter is on her way?" Syrona cried, slipping into the seat on the other side of Nimisha. "Doc, does Nimi need some help?"

"For once I think the only problem with her is intense joy and relief," Doc replied. "If she would deign to lie upon the couch, I'll check her over."

"I'll be all right, really, I will," Nimisha said, waving her hand in an aimless fashion and then starting on the warm drink Jon had brought her.

He took the cup and hauled her to her feet. "One can have a bit too much joy all at once, you know, and I'd rather the incoming didn't see you looking quite so pale, as if you'd seen a ghost."

"Which I have, in a way," Nimisha said, and even as Jon swung her feet up on the medical couch, she started to weep quietly.

Jon smiled and leaned down to kiss her cheek. "It's all right, love. It's all right."

She didn't even protest when she felt several hyposprays penetrate her arms.

"Bed rest for you, Nimi," Doc said at his gentlest. "Syrona, who's available to manage the babies?"

"I'll go see," Syrona said, but she paused by the medical unit on her way out the door and kissed Nimisha's cheek. "I am so happy for you, Nimi."

"I'm rather happy for myself, really, in spite of my tears. Tim, where are Perria and Sven right now?"

Tim chuckled. "Getting dirty, Nimi. Don't worry about them. You listen to Doc."

"He sounds so grown-up," Nimisha murmured to Jon.

"You wouldn't think so if you heard him with the Sh'im younglings," Jon said with a disparaging snort. He slipped his arms under her body and carried her to their cabin, despite her protests. "He's the ringleader of most of the trouble the pack gets into."

"I guess I won't worry about them," she said, sniffing back her tears, but they seemed to keep coming despite her best attempts to cease sniveling.

Jon threw back the top fur, lovingly created by Sh'im female hands, and settled her on the bed, tucking it around her flaccid body. Then, he sat down beside her, taking her hands in his and caressing them, speaking in soft, soothing tones.

"I know you don't like to admit to any weakness, dear Lady

Nimisha Boynton-Rondymense," he said, grinning at his sudden formality, "but I know how very much you've missed your firstborn and body-heir. You wouldn't realize how often you speak her name in your sleep. I could almost be jealous," he teased, stroking her hair back from her tear-flushed face.

"Doc gave me something . . ." she said, her voice thick and her enunciation beginning to slur.

"I hope so. You need the rest."

She tried to grab his hand, because she had to say something to him before she lost consciousness.

"My apologies to the . . ."

She thought she heard him chuckle as her eyes inexorably closed and everything went dark.

Jon was quietly moving about their cabin when she roused from the induced sleep. She lay there, eyes barely open, watching him dry his tanned, muscular body. It was very early in the morning, or late at night, so she suspected he had just returned from the welcome party.

"What are they like?" she asked, her voice thick with sleep.

"Awake, are you?" He leaned over the bed and kissed her. His grin was devilish, and he quirked one eyebrow up high so that she knew she would get a candid rundown. "The children are all taken care of, luv, so don't fret over them." He chuckled. "A bit of a surprise for our visitors. Or, I should be more specific, the naval ones. Captain Meterios was shocked out of her skivvies, and I doubt I shall ever restore myself to her good opinion, even after Syrona had a go at her." He cleared his throat. "We neglected to mention Syrona's rank, and I think I'll predate a field promotion to lieutenant commander for her, for bravery under unusual circumstances. Which indeed is justified by her admirable courage under trying circumstances."

Despite being sleepy, Nimisha had caught the edge in his voice, mentioning this Captain Meterios. But he would be senior to her no matter the nearly twenty years he'd been stranded on Erewhon.

"Globan Escorias had just joined the *Acclarke* for his ninth tour of duty on her," Jon went on, sliding under the furs beside her and settling her comfortably against him. He chuckled softly. "He'd only time to report in when Helm sounded the alert. Officers get high-risk pay for a four-month tour, so he's never minded the duty. And finally got what he'd been waiting for—and more than he expected. He'll fit in; so will the other *Acclarke*s. Mixed crew, praise be."

"The scientists who survived the station disaster?"

"Dr. Qualta was brought over here for our Doc's second opinion. She had severe internal injuries. Mid-sixties, but her general good health and fitness are a big asset right now. Doc did a little more internal work, since he's grades higher than the one on the *Acclarke*—that was always only for the usual shipboard injuries and ailments—and she'll recover with rest and care. The Sh'im have assigned one of Doc's best trainees to her, and I must say, she's adjusted to the aliens better than anyone else."

"What sort of specialist is she?"

"Astrophysics, but old enough to have plenty of sense."

He really had tangled with Meterios then. "And the others?"

"I could wish for a broader range of specialties among 'em," he said with a grimace, "but they're all welcome. Then, too," he added in a thoughtful tone, "I don't think anyone's going to want to turn around and do another four- or five-year trip back home right away." He gave a little grin and rubbed his hands together, rolling his eyes in an outrageous expression of chicanery. "Who knows how many'll want to stay on. Especially since I know some of the people coming on the Fiver B," he added quickly. "The Chief Engineer's wife is a semantics expert. Nazim Ford-Coattes—"

"My test pilot!" She wriggled a little in his arms to hear such good news.

"Apparently he also tested the Five B, so he was a natural backup in a mixed crew. Gaitama Rezinda got special training from Hiska to be sure nothing went wrong."

Nimisha laughed. "We'd never have got Hiska aboard, but I know Gaitama, and if Hiska trained her, she'll be topflight. Oh, both will be tremendous assets, Jon. Who else?"

"All too young for me to know by name, except Caleb Rustin." He gave her a quick look, and she laughed and patted his side in reassurance. "His XO is Kendra Oscony, tops in communications and mathematics, so Escorias assured me. Ensign Mareena Kawamura, who's got botany and biology; Chief Hadley will be yet another astronomer; and Cuiva's companion, Perdimia Ejallos, from a service family, has good martial arts skills."

She could hear something he wasn't saying. "And . . ." she prompted him.

He wiggled his long legs and squirmed.

"They came along to be sure your daughter and body-heir was properly instructed during the long journey."

"Oh!" Nimisha smiled proudly over that achievement before regarding Jon again with some suspicion. "I could understand her wanting to accompany a mission with the goal of rescuing me, but how did they talk my dam into letting Cuiva go on a four-year-long trip?"

"I didn't think we'd fool you for long. According to Escorias, Lord Vestrin was trying to get possession of the Yard because you were lost, presumed dead."

"The pulse that was received should have dismissed that notion."

"I'm sure it did. The Five B carries mail for you, and there's a rather large lockbox of letter packets awaiting your pleasure. Your mother used your family's private code, so you should have no trouble opening it. Mail could only be slipped in, not removed."

"I still do not understand why my dam would allow Cuiva to take such a long journey. And you know why." She gave his jaw a mock-punch.

"Granted Escorias has friends in the First Family circles, so possibly his gossip is accurate. Certainly the fact that Cuiva was sent along substantiates it."

"Substantiates what? Tell me, Jon. It's my right to know." She felt anger surging within her. She didn't want to be angry with Jonagren Svangel.

"There were two very clumsy attempts to harm Cuiva." His arms tightened to keep her from rearing up in outrage. "They failed because your friend Caleb had the sense to double surveillance as soon as the Mayday was received. Lord Vestrin had been loud in his complaints about how his father's estate had been divvied up."

"More like Lady Vescuya disliked it," Nimisha murmured angrily.

"Her possible connivance was definitely rumored. Then there was the derelict freighter full of explosives approaching the Yard on a trajectory to crash into the Five B's gantry!"

"What!"

"Ssssh, you'll wake someone. The spare cabins have station personnel in them." He waited until Nimisha relaxed. "By then the Fleet and the Yard had tripled security, so the missiles took out its engines and a tug netted it tightly before the explosives on it could detonate. That would have caused a real mess, flicking fragments all over. Both Fleet and APG were investigating all possible leads. Two other devices were discovered before they could be activated."

"And naturally Lord Vestrin was on a hunting party," Nimisha muttered sourly, "and who knows what that virago of a mother of his came up with as an excuse."

"Precisely, so your dam sent Cuiva to safety."

"But, if she's away from Rondymense . . ."

"I think your dam solved that in her devious fashion. We know that Cuiva is on her way here, but a Cuiva has been seen in company of Lady Rezalla. At least until she should have been Neck-laced."

Nimisha felt tears of relief and joy trickle down her cheeks. "I'm a leaky ula-ooli-la," she said, burrowing her face into Jon's bare shoulder.

She could feel his chest shake with the chuckle. "My dear sweetheart, you are never a ula-ooli-la. Not that there is a Basic synonym for that particular Sh'im device."

He stroked her hair and very shortly, warm and infinitely relieved with that especial news, she slept again.

When she finally met Captain Nesta Meterios three days later, Nimisha found it even more difficult than Jon to like the woman. She had had occasion to know many career navy officers from the Yard's proximity to the Vegan Fleet Headquarters. There were some, competent within their specialties, who were worthy folk and about as much fun to be around as a wet towel. They also never seemed to notice their lack of social graces, or even that they lacked the wit and competence that would put them in line for rapid promotion. Meterios was from a service family with several relatives who had had distinguished careers. Quite likely, her performance during the wormhole passage would receive a commendation. That was only because, as Jon said, the preprogrammed AI had kicked in with its femtosecond reflexes, removing Meterios from command—and from making any fatal error. Escorias did mention that the crew was certain that the Helm had saved all on board the *Acclarke* as well as Meterios's butt.

Jon and Doc had kept Nimisha quiet and in bed until they, and she, were certain her strength was sufficient.

"I'll warn you, hon, she thinks a Necklaced First Family female ought to restrict herself to a body-heir, end of sentence," Jon told her, his eyes twinkling with amusement. "She's hot on rules and regs, and is uptight because we donated a lot of what we stripped from the *Poolbeg* to the Sh'im. Gave me the old 'misuse of naval property' line until Syrona showed her that their home is furnished entirely by recycled 'navy property.' Recycling is also very Nav. Frankly, Erehwon is beyond her. You destroyed her faith in you by having five children here and a grown one on her way. I can't imagine why someone with her basic inflexibility was given command of the *Acclarke*."

"I can," Syrona said later when she was visiting Nimisha. "I did my first tour under her uncle, Captain Georgius Meterios, and he was no joy either. He never got command of anything more than a light destroyer, usually assigned to convoy duty."

"Then posting her to the *Acclarke* is damned near an insult," Jon said, irritated.

"I'd consider it one," Casper said with a snort. "Except that, with Helm to take over the moment an emergency occurred, she couldn't mess up with indecision, could she? Dr. Qualta said that no astronomer or astrographer expected the bloody wormhole to reappear any time short of another ten years."

"So she was shunted to a minimal command like Uncle Georgius?" Nimisha gave a sniff, not sure she liked the implications. "Guess she got the biggest surprise of her life."

"And had nothing to do anyway," Jon said with a snide grin. "Helm was programmed to take over the instant the wormhole opened."

"Oh, yes, so it was," and Nimisha felt less like a lost parcel no one really wanted to find.

"So it didn't matter to the result of the rescue if she, or someone more ambitious and capable, was captain."

"Globan says most of his friends applied for the duty in the hope that they'd be lucky enough to be there when the hole opened. Pay was good and the tour short enough so no one died of boredom," Casper added.

"Boredom wouldn't bother a Meterios," Syrona said, giggling. "They thrive on it."

When Jon and Syrona escorted Captain Meterios for an official visit to Lady Nimisha Boynton-Rondymense, Nimisha took instant refuge by imitating her dam, deftly putting the captain in her place. The others had a difficult time restraining their amusement. Meterios was properly obsequious, appropriately apologetic for bothering a First Family scion, and during the refreshments offered, she sat bolt upright on the very edge of the chair as if she were still a first-year cadet. Syrona bustled about fussily as if this were her normal way of attending Lady Nimisha and only once lapsed into a less formal manner. Jon did his rendition of admiral-on-the-bridge, punctilious in his crisply pressed dress uniform, another of the items that had been brought back when the *Poolbeg* was stripped of any useful items and equipment.

No matter what Captain Meterios privately thought of Nimisha's fecundity, no mention was made of it. In fact, conversation flagged very quickly until Nimisha decided to fade away, pretending exhaustion. Meterios flushed unattractively at this tacit reference to her maternity. So the captain, bowing far more respectfully than Lady Nimisha's rank required, finished her formal visit and that was, fortunately, the end of any social intercourse with her. And Nimisha returned to the task of reading five years of accumulated reports from her dam and from Jeska Mlan in her role as managing director, as well as notifications from Admiral Gollanch and other general notes that had been forwarded. One note from Lady Rezalla mentioned sending on the Necklace so that Nimisha could officiate at that ceremony.

"For the benefit of those who might think it odd if we didn't do something on Cuiva's minor major day, we shall conduct a very private affair, complete with a paste imitation of Coskanito's Necklace. He is so discreet and understands the necessity for safety's sake. No one has realized that it is not Cuiva living here with us. The child is a nice little thing and, although I have had to reprimand her several times for conduct unbecoming even her supposed place in our society, she does resemble your body-heir sufficiently to fool almost everyone. Certainly my dam is deluded. But then, Lady Astatine is half blind and almost completely deaf. Her rejuv treatment was one of the first, and she really ought to have waited until the procedure was thoroughly tested. But your grandam never took advice from anyone." Nimisha chuckled over that remark.

Nimisha had wondered how her dam had dealt with such an auspicious day as Necklacing in First Family society, but Lady Rezalla had contrived admirably. Since Nimisha was definitely alive and able to send pulses back to Vega III, and her body-heir was residing in Acclarke, any spurious claim by Lord Vestrin Rondymense-Waleska to reclaim the disputed patrimony would be disregarded.

Once Nimisha was genuinely physically fit enough to attend to such delayed tasks as erecting a new hoist for the iron mine in the hills above the town, and a second lift for the copper mine deeper in the eastern mountain range, she limited her encounters with the *Acclarke*'s captain to the minimum. Especially after she witnessed Meterios's totally egregious attitude toward their alien allies.

"She's a xenophobe," Nimisha said, voicing an opinion shared by everyone else. "One of those Humanity Supremacists, though the fact that she attained a commander's stripes proves that there are gaps in the screening, Jon."

He agreed. "But then, while she was capable enough to command a ship with an AI program, aliens were not an obstacle she was likely to encounter."

The Sh'im would not understand a person disliking them because they were not human. Especially after they had been treated on such an equal footing with the ones they had already encountered—after the initial and short-lived misunderstanding. Before Meterios's xenophobia was revealed, Ay and Bee—who had the best command of Basic, assisted though it was by the translator units they wore—had been assigned to guide the captain anywhere she wished to go. She didn't wish to go anywhere after her first visit to Clifftown—La-ull-losss, in Sh'im. She said she hadn't understood a word of the gabble she'd been subjected to. Unfortunately she saw enough of Clifftown to notice bits and pieces of recycled metal parts that could only have come from the wreck of the *Poolbeg*. She logged in a long and detailed report of such illegal use; Globan heard part of it and crept away. But since she had encrypted it, there was no way the entry could be altered, and she had forwarded it by pulse message. Eventually it would reach Vegan Fleet Headquarters, where it might be totally disregarded.

"Let it stand," Jon said, shrugging. "I doubt I'll ever stand a court-martial over it. For that matter, I've racked up so much back pay, I could pay for twice as much as we recycled."

When Meterios did, reluctantly, have to venture outside, she had an armed escort. Whichever crewperson had that duty was patently unhappy about it. No one else of either her crew or the wormbusters was troubled with xenophobia. Some might not give the Sh'im as much credit for the intelligence they continued to display as others, but most took to them and their ingratiating ways.

"On the one hand, xenophobia wouldn't affect her commanding a ship," Casper said, still the optimist. "It isn't as if she'd be likely to encounter aliens on picket duty. Since we were FSP Explorers' branch, we had very in-depth screening on attitudes toward 'others.' " He bracketed the word with his index fingers. "How would anyone suspect she'd get her knickers in a twist meeting such amiable and kindly folk as the Sh'im?"

The scientists, whatever had been their specialty, were quite willing to muck in with the Sh'im, learning as much as they could from the dark-coats and noticing how tools had been adapted for their three-fingered use. They had suggestions of their own to increase manageability for some tools. In her dash to her assigned escape pod, Dr. Qualta's assistant, Valina Kelly, had grabbed two small telescopes, the most portable of the equipment to hand. She'd strapped them into the second shock pad in her pod. Dr. Qualta owed her injuries to the fact that she had been trying to secure her data disks and her scanner rather than herself. Being tightly netted in, the equipment had suffered no damage at all while she had nearly died of her injuries.

Qualta, Globan, and Kelly, with the enthusiastic assistance of fascinated Sh'im, set up an observatory on the far side of the cliff above the town, in an area still protected by the repeller shields. They were busy mapping and evaluating the visible stars every evening, with the help of five ululating dark-coats.

"Had we had more warning," Dr. Qualta said, "we'd've brought along the sort of equipment to do an in-depth spectral analysis of such unexplored territory."

"Lordee, Qualta," Valina replied, "we were lucky to escape with our lives. I couldn't find even a small microscope, or the main computer. We're lucky we can read what disks we managed to scoop up," she added. "I'm very glad we could pilfer astrogation equipment from the *Poolbeg*."

"That's not enough," Qualta said scornfully. "That system is so obsolete we're better off using what we managed to save. But," she added with a sigh, "it's better than nothing. Is Globan absolutely sure that there's nothing left of the space station that could be salvaged? The Sh'im are such clever metalworkers."

She had admired the mining operations and the repeller-protected farm crops—which she sampled, raw and cooked—and watched with keen interest when young Sh'im started training boks. Luthen Drayus and Tezza Ashke of the *Acclarke*, her radial completely knitted, happily accompanied hunts with Casper, Tim, and his Sh'im cronies.

About the only thing Meterios did right was use the *Acclarke's* missiles during an avian raid. It had the fringe benefit of scaring the captain out of much of her disgruntlement with the unauthorized use of *Poolbeg* weaponry. She had been standing outside when the raid began and the sight of the immense raptors had sent her scurrying inside the *Acclarke*. She had the gall to boast that she had saved the settlement.

Globan had another side to relate with a grin. "I took the liberty of programming defensive action into Helm after you told me what those avian monsters could do," he said. "So it was Helm who bagged the nineteen beasts in that raid, not Nesta Meterios."

"It's probably too much to ask that she'll start believing us when we tell her other minor victories," Jon said with a weary sigh. He'd suspected as much from the excellent marksmanship the *Acclarke* had displayed in destroying so many of the attackers—though he and Nimisha had accounted for almost as many, and the Sh'im manning the cliff batteries had taken out those that had come in too low for the ships' guns to bear on.

Globan grimaced. "I don't think she realized just how much the AI can do without her direct commands. I think we should keep it that way."

"Wasn't she briefed on its capabilities?" Nimisha asked with justifiable rancor. "I mean, even if I didn't consider the Four up to my expectations, she makes a grand courier ship as she is."

"I did study the specs, Nimisha," Globan said. "Gave me something to do on my tours. Not all the captains assigned to the

Acclarke have been as narrow-minded as Captain Meterios," he added to cheer Nimisha.

"That's reassuring," she replied.

"How often do those attacks happen?" Globan asked casually.

"I'm sorry to say, less often, Globan," Jon said, rightly assuming the young officer would have liked to man the *Acclarke*'s gunner station. "But they do come in more numbers as if they could overpower us with sheer mass, so you may still get a chance."

"One more thing, Jon: I think she's trying to turn Helm down. I saw her under the main control board, but I don't think she saw me. She's a control freak, you know."

"Control freak or not," Nimisha said with some heat, "she can't dismantle Helm without losing all control of ship function. Stupid git of a woman. However, I can fix that." She rubbed her hands together with anticipation. "Just get her out of the Four for half an hour so I can add a certain little chip and she can fiddle with the program as much as she likes but she won't disconnect him. D'you remember where I put my tools, Jon?" she asked.

"I stashed them in the garage locker under your private code."

"Good idea."

"Of course, the problem will be getting her *out* of the *Acclarke*," Globan said, not at all optimistic.

The addition of 'a certain little chip' was accomplished just before Captain Meterios took it in her head that Svangel had exceeded his authority in allowing the *Poolbeg* to be dismantled for the benefit of the Sh'im. Or "them," as she insisted on referring to the Sh'im, a habit that irritated even the equably tempered Dr. Qualta.

"They have a name for themselves, Captain," Dr. Qualta said, "and you will be good enough to use it. Sh'im. Sh'im. Sh'im. Very easy to say. Very nice folks when you get to know them."

Meterios was visibly shocked at such vehemence from Dr. Qualta and kept out of her way. Since she was already avoiding

Lady Nimisha whenever possible, Qualta and Nimisha had some relief from the woman's company.

Jon, Casper, and Syrona were not as lucky, since they were, after all, naval officers. Jon cited his seniority in both command and length of service and was punctilious in all his dealings with her. Casper and Syrona were not as lucky, but fell back on the fact that they were Jon's crew, not hers.

With calculated reluctance, Jon finally gave permission for her to visit the hulk of the *Poolbeg*.

"Once she sees the gouges in the hull, she should be able to realize that the ship could never have been repaired this side of the main Mars Yard," Jon said.

"Especially since we couldn't even get the cladding off to be used where it would do some good here," Casper added.

"It'll be a relief to have her out of the way," Nimisha said. "She's beginning to get on everyone's nerves."

Meterios had gone through the Broken Bird wreck with Brad Karpla—or rather those areas of it humans could access. Karpla had been keen to see what sort of weapons the ship had mounted. Jon had explained that, according to the Sh'im, they had carried only asteroid deterrents, but Meterios and Karpla had to make a hands-on verification. Since the "cannon" had been situated in the now-broken nose of the ship, they were inaccessible. Karpla could find no other defensive or offensive gear and came back rather grumpy after a hot day's climbing through the wreck.

"She got real dirty," Tim announced with a massive grin on his face. What he didn't say, and which the adults knew from other sources, was that he and his particular Sh'im cronies had shadowed the pair.

"Captain Meterios? Dirty?" Nimisha said, feigning surprise. "That would have been worth seeing."

"No," Tim replied. "She was real angry, too, and we kept out of her way."

"Just as well, or you'd be in for another chewing out," Nimisha said. In Meterios's opinion, children should be seen and never heard. Tim usually ordered his Sh'im gang about in a voice that a drill sergeant would have envied.

"I don't know how she keeps her uniforms in such impeccable condition, but she always turns herself out properly," Syrona said, trying hard to find something positive to say about the woman. Nesta Meterios was not a tall woman—just making the height required by naval regulations—and skinny, rather than thin. She might have been attractive if she'd tried to emphasize a finely textured skin and rather large eyes and if she'd chosen a more flattering hairstyle.

"Does it herself, I'm told," Casper said. "Not that those uniforms would last long if she were working the way we are."

"Not that she'd ever demean herself to do so," Nimisha said.

Meterios had elected to go on the mission to the *Poolbeg*, reassembling the entire crew complement of the *Acclarke* at a time when Jon, Nimisha, and Casper had been counting on the extra hands to help raise a windmill to power a new well. The only person who went willingly, in fact, was Valina Kelly, who wanted to scan the night skies on that side of the planet. Meterios had been difficult about including a "civilian" on a naval expedition until Dr. Qualta intervened and reminded Meterios that after all, Valina's official and top-priority clearance to be a member of the Wormhunter space station guaranteed that she was cleared for a minor reconnaissance operation.

When the *Acclarke* lifted at dawn, Nimisha happened to be up, soothing a fractious son. Bouncing him on her shoulder, she hurried into the pilot compartment.

"Helm, are you in constant contact with the *Acclarke*'s AI?"

"Yes, Lady Nimisha. We have established a permanent link. I can screen their progress for you, if you wish."

"I do. Keep it up at all times on the B screen and please inform me of any untoward occurrence you two may notice."

"Yes, ma'am."

Later that day, Nimisha cornered Jon for a quiet conversation with him over the disruptive presence of Captain Nesta Meterios.

"I want her out of here before Cuiva arrives," she said.

Jon raised his eyebrows in surprised query. "Why then?"

"I'd have to invite her to Cuiva's Necklacing, and I'll be damned if I'll give the woman that satisfaction."

Jon chuckled. "We don't like her, do we?"

"No," Nimisha said flatly. "This is our adventure, venture, colony, world, whatever, and her attitude could affect our relations with the Sh'im. They're not stupid."

"We can't just send her off on the *Acclarke*," he protested.

"Why not? Helm would get her back."

"True enough, but her XO doesn't think she received any new orders in the packet he handed over."

Nimisha considered that. "And she's not the personality to do anything without orders to cover her butt. I'm surprised she went to the wreck."

"I'm not," Jon said with a wry chuckle. "She's going to do all she can to find fault with me or Casper or Syrona. She's welcome to. We are different branches of service, and what holds for a courier does not hold for an explorer."

"Then how is she trying to fault you?"

"Misuse of naval property."

"You used it to survive, didn't you? Which you once told me was your second operational procedure."

"I did and it is, and on those grounds she cannot fault me. But that sort of personality has got to try."

Nimisha let out an exasperated sigh. "Well, we have to do something about her. I'm not having her at Cuiva's Necklacing."

"I agree, luv," Jon said. "Too bad the rest of the crew is so nice—with the exception of that flat-faced toady, Karpla. He takes an altogether unholy delight in hunting. Tim says his wholesale slaughter goes against Sh'im notions."

"That's what Casper said, too."

"May I suggest a way out of the difficulty?" Doc said.

Nimisha swung round. "You have one?"

"If you're looking for answers, you find them," he said at his most sententious. "What exactly were Captain Meterios's orders?"

Jon and Nimisha regarded each other. "Helm, ask *Acclarke's* Helm the exact wording of Meterios's original orders."

"Yes, ma'am," was the quick response. "I quote 'Captain Meterios, Naval ID—' "

"Skip the heading, Helm, and get to the essence of the orders," Nimisha said.

" 'Is to maintain the *Acclarke* courier vessel, 4CG 2440, in constant readiness at all times. To launch the specially constructed probe the instant the wormhole should appear. To instantly pulse a message of its reappearance Flash Override to Fleet Headquarters on Vega III. To maintain the beacon and all drone beacons in the assigned patrol area. To assist as required the scientific personnel on the space station. If feasible to traverse the wormhole and acquire sufficient stellar spectrum analyses to establish proper coordinates in the space grid. To establish, if at all possible, the current location of Lady Nimisha Boynton-Rondymense. To return at top speed with all pertinent information regarding the wormhole for analysis and dissemination.' Those are the orders. Shall I prepare hard copy?"

"Yes, but I think we have the one we want," Jon said, rubbing his hands together with a gleeful expression on his face. "She has not 'returned at top speed with all pertinent information for analysis and dissemination' and is therefore delinquent in her duty. We've got her."

"Undoubtedly, because top speed is going to take her four years," Nimisha said.

"Unless she plans to go back the way she came in the next five, that'd be my assessment."

"Four years is not so long," Nimisha added, delighting in the prospect of how bored Meterios would be. "But I'd hate for her crew to have to go with her."

"They needn't," Doc said. "*Acclarke*'s Helm is as capable as ours in getting her back to Vegan space. She wouldn't need the crew."

"Yes, but she is their captain."

"Hold it right there," Jon said. "Helm, what orders govern the rest of the crew? Didn't Globan say something about short tours of duty?"

"He did, he did," Nimisha said.

"Technically speaking, they would be off duty at the end of those tours, whether or not they have been returned to base and a new assignment," Jon said, rubbing his chin. "I'd have to check regs on that."

"If you'll pardon me, Commander," Helm said, "you are correct in your assumption. Globan will have served the full four-month tour in another three weeks and five days. The others, with the exception of Brad Karpla, who is serving a year's tour as he is checked out on the special piggyback probe, would all shortly have been replaced. Several, in fact, are overdue for reassignment."

"Meterios could argue that they are not in a position to be rotated in the normal fashion," Jon said, thoughtfully, "and are therefore still nominally under her command. I outrank her, and Exploration has the right to draft additional naval personnel to assist in emergency situations, but I don't fancy trying to argue the matter with her. She can stump me on some unknown paragraph in a footnote in new regs that I couldn't contest."

"I could, sir," Helm said. "The latest updates were added to my memory banks by Commander Rustin on the orders of Admiral Gollanch."

"That's good to know," Nimisha said.

"That would be useful if Meterios happened to admit the infallibility of Artificial Intelligence."

"She denies it?" Doc said, indignantly. "Maybe I can help out here."

"So Globan says, and I'd hate to lose him. He's fitting in here so well. And we need more colonists. Almost none of the science crew want to leave—not with all these undocumented primaries and systems to be listed." He grinned. "Qualta's in heaven and hopes her rejuv will last long enough for her to complete the maps."

"*My* orders," Doc began firmly, "are to assist Lady Nimisha in all matters."

"Even to shanghaiing an officer off-planet?" Nimisha asked, chuckling.

"If need be."

Jon rubbed his chin again. "Orders would work best. She can't quibble with direct orders."

"She's already ignoring one of the specific orders she was given, Jon." Nimisha said.

"True . . ."

"It won't be long before Rustin's here," Jon said. "He can say he intercepted new orders for her at the pulse beacon."

"Any information reaching the beacon is supposed to be forwarded to both Helms," Nimisha reminded him.

"But, if you tell Rustin what's been going on here, wouldn't he help?"

"Does he know Captain Nesta?" Nimisha asked.

"Whose side would he be likely to pick? Yours or hers?"

"Point." Nimisha said, eyeing him askance. "I'd rather we covered that before Caleb reaches Erehwon."

Jon cocked his head at her and she shook hers.

"We were very good friends," she said, "but having met you . . ."

"Propinquity is a decided advantage," he said, pulling her into his arms and grinning at her.

"And five children," she added.

"Will you hold that against me forever?" he asked with a chagrined expression.

"Now and then, perhaps," she admitted. "It's just as well we have the Sh'im to take over, or my attitude would be considerably different."

"You do have your implant operational, don't you?" he asked.

"As of the day I delivered the triplets."

"Then shall we?"

"I was wondering when you were going to get up the nerve to ask again."

"Jon," she began later, "speaking of orders, can you be ordered away from here?"

"Hell's bells, luv, I was on an exploratory mission that, with due modesty, I can say I have acquitted to the best of my ability. As well as taking a cursory look at two other M-type planets in the immediate vicinity. I'm certain that we have a case for making Erehwon the center for further investigations. Since my knowledge of the area is intimate, I might even get bumped up in rank to administration. Which would suit me admirably."

"You want to be an admiral?"

"That'd keep me in administration, which wouldn't hurt my feelings. Depends on how my initial reports and performance are received."

"Another good reason for getting Meterios out of the picture and on a long and uninterruptible trip back," she said.

"I agree. I like Erehwon. I like the life we've been carving out here. I love you."

She stood up and curled her arms about his neck. "I rather thought you might, but d'you realize that's the first time you've admitted it?"

"Out loud." He curved his lips in a very tender smile. "I rather thought you'd've guessed as much."

"I did, but I'd rather hear you confirm the situation."

"Then, Lady Nimisha, I respectfully request a similar confession from you," he said softly into her ear, holding her very tightly.

"I do love you, Commander Jonagren Svangel," she said softly, "though I certainly never expected to."

"Well, you have designed the perfect long-distance yacht: You are free to set that inventive mind of yours to new challenges."

"Hmmm. What a good idea."

Jon gave her another long and deeply stirring kiss before he swung his feet over the bed and reached for his discarded coverall. "I want to have a private word with some of Meterios's crew. And Dr. Qualta."

"And I think I'll just dash off a little note to await Caleb's arrival at the beacon. Something about orders he's received for the *Acclarke*."

"They'd have to be at the beacon," Jon said, stamping into his boots. "Headquarters would have had word by now of the loss of the space station and the *Acclarke*, but he wouldn't have any pulses while on IS drive. So make it clear he's stripped them from the beacon now that it's been repaired and we can get messages to and from."

"Dear heart, don't worry. I come from a very long line of devious women."

Her first instruction to Helm used the cipher she and Caleb had set up for private messages. He'd know to accept and read it by himself. In the opening paragraph, she suggested that the Five B Helm beam orders directly to Captain Meterios on Four's comunit. That would be less suspicious than for him to have documentation to give her. While a pulsed beam message carried no signature, Caleb did know one of Admiral Gollanch's private codes to give authority to such new orders. By citing Meterios as a xenophobe, she'd gain Caleb's understanding of their need to rid the planet of her presence. A pulsed explanation would reach the admiral well in advance of the *Acclarke*. She also asked Caleb how to keep the useful crewmembers on Erehwon. The long trip home under such a captain was likely to cause severe disciplinary problems. Since the original tour of duty had been four months, not much attention had been paid to matching psych profiles. With a Helm to guide a ship through IS drive, no human watch was actually required, and Helm could always rouse the captain for any emergencies requiring human intervention. Not that Nimisha had much faith in Meterios's ability to handle real emergencies. She must have exhibited some initiative to get to be a courier captain but Nimisha couldn't imagine it.

When Jon returned, unable to check with all the people he wanted to speak to, she showed him her message.

"In any case, we have her for not attempting to return back to base as her orders specifically state," he said. "Send it."

She did, and marked off yet another day until she would see her daughter again. The waiting was worse now that Cuiva was so close. While she had been busy, while she had been making a new life here on Erehwon, and with Jon, she had been able to censor painful thoughts and the realization that she had missed so much of Cuiva's youth. And the Necklacing. That was such an important moment in a girl's life. It had been in hers, when she was suddenly about to take her place in Society and be allowed to talk to adults without waiting to be spoken to: to be grown-up! She only hoped that her dam had not constricted Cuiva to what Lady Rezalla thought was proper for a First Family body-heir to learn. And in that, Nimisha would be to blame, having such an unusual interest as ship design. Cuiva would have had no one like Lord Tionel to stand up for any individual interests she might have developed. Well, Lady Rezalla was fair . . .

CHAPTER 11

<< ● >>

"We are emerging into normal space, Captain Rustin, in precisely nine minutes at my mark," Helm said. "Mark."

"About bloody time," was Caleb's soft murmur.

He had risen well before time and enjoyed a leisurely breakfast before translation could occur. Kendra had joined him; since she was such a light sleeper, she woke no matter how carefully he had tried to slip out of the bed. He devoutly hoped that Nimisha would accept his new alliance without rancor. He suspected she would be sensible, but she'd been alone a long time. Would Kendra understand? Probably. They'd developed a very good rapport. Although the Five B's initial orders had only covered a three-month trial run, he had been careful to match the psych profiles of all aboard the Five B to form a good environment for Cuiva's benefit. The result had been felicitous, if startling, when Mareena favored Gaitama and Nazim and Perdimia had paired off. He wondered how Cuiva would take to that, but Perdimia had made it clear to Nazim that Cuiva remained her first order of business. Since he was a Rondy-mense employee, he accepted that equably.

Kendra joined Caleb in the pilot compartment, slipping into the second seat and netting in. Translations out of Interstellar Drive were not likely to be as rough as entering, but this was totally unknown space. There had been bets that Nimisha, discovering herself alone in a strange section of the galaxy, had taken the obvious out and gone into cold sleep. So the Fiver would be nearby. Knowing

Nimisha better, Caleb wagered that she'd been exploring—if that had been an option—since she was not the sort of person to avoid a challenge. They'd soon know, and Caleb had Helm plot reentry well away from the beacon so that, if the Fiver were there, they'd not run into her.

Nine minutes can seem a long time. Kendra was tapping her fingers on the armrest by the final second countdown. By then, the entire crew had gathered in the main lounge in the couches that had security straps.

"Eight . . . seven . . . six," Helm's voice counted down, and then exactly on "one" they were out of the dark gray interspace and back into black space and a bewildering mass of unfamiliar stars. Helm went into instant evasive action, veering away from a tumbled mass of twisted metal.

"Jasassssusss," Kendra said, tightening her hold on the armrests. "That can't be the Fiver!"

Caleb's heart had twisted violently at the fleeting view he'd had of the object, but a second's sober thought steadied his heartbeat. Nimisha had managed to send pulsed messages. So what was that tangled mess of wreckage?

"Messages are pouring in from the beacon, Commander, and analysis suggests that the debris is the remains of the Wormhunter Space Station, not the Fiver."

"What the hell would the space station be doing on this side of the fragging wormhole?" Caleb demanded.

"Latest messages first, Captain," Helm said. "From Captain Meterios—"

"Meterios?" Kendra's voice squeaked in dismay.

"—of the *Acclarke* courier stationed on the other side of the probable site of the wormhole."

"She shouldn't have been drawn into it," Caleb said. "Her position was a hundred thousand kilometers from Nimisha's beacon."

"How do we know that that wormhole has a stable point of entry?" Ian Hadley asked. "The space station wouldn't have stood a snowball's chance in hell if the wormhole opened within even fifty thousand kilometers of it. Can Helm check to see if there are any pods in the wreckage?"

"Later, later," Caleb said. "Let's get the latest reports."

"I shall screen the earlier ones in the lounge, sir," Helm said. "The *Acclarke* reports that it saved eleven out of twelve pods, chief astronomer Dr. Qualta having sustained the worst injuries."

"How did the *Acclarke* weather the passage?" Nazim asked excitedly. He had helped build the Fours that Vegan Fleet had ordered.

"Later, later," Caleb said again, shushing them. "Go on, Helm."

"Messages in the beacon indicate that the *Acclarke* proceeded immediately to the coordinates left by Lady Nimisha for the first of three M-type planets."

"Nimisha went exploring?" Caleb grinned, having won that bet.

"There are reports of her investigations, with Commander Jon Svangel, of the other two M-type planets relatively close to the initial one. She has named it Erehwon."

"Erehwon?" Kendra exclaimed.

"That's nowhere backward," Cherry Absin-Hadley said with a grin. "Appropriate."

"There is also an encrypted message for you, Commander, which I will forward to your cabin," Helm said. "Numerous pulsed messages have been sent back to Vega, sir. Including the latest from Captain Meterios, dated five days ago, Vegan time."

"What's she still doing here?" Caleb demanded in a rhetorical tone. "I know what orders the *Acclarke* was given. In the event the courier got drawn into the wormhole, she was to ascertain if Lady Nimisha was alive and then proceed with all possible speed back to Vega."

"She would first have had to deposit the space station sur-vivors wherever Lady Nimisha is," Kendra remarked. "The *Acclarke* could not manage eleven more passengers."

"In cold sleep it could," Caleb said grimly. Because the entire complement of the Five B's crew was listening, he did not voice his private thought: Whatever had possessed anyone at Vegan Fleet Command to give Nesta Meterios a tour of duty on the *Acclarke*? He answered himself: It was possibly one of the few places in which she could do the least damage, excluding the sudden ap-pearance of the wormhole, which it should have had the speed to outrun. The *Acclarke* Helm had been programmed to take com-mand in any emergency, including the reappearance of the worm-hole. Nesta the Nothing would have been merely a passenger.

While Helm kept trying to present a coherent report, everyone had questions, especially about the world Erehwon. Caleb wished to know who this Commander Jonagren Svangel was. Mareena handed him hard copy access from Fleet files, and consequently he learned that *Poolbeg* had been the last known ship missing in this general area. Captain Panadus Querine had been captain of rec-ord, with Lt. Commander Jonagren Svangel listed as executive offi-cer. The *Poolbeg* was an exploratory service vessel with a crew of ten. Caleb experienced intense relief that Nimisha had not been alone for nearly six years. Not that she wasn't capable of surviving by herself, but to have had company—and the *Poolbeg* had had a mixed crew—would have made her life there more agreeable.

"Captain," Kendra said suddenly, "they have made contact with aliens also shipwrecked."

"Aliens!"

Kendra grinned at the vehemence in his voice. "Sapient ones, too, since their ship crashed on Erehwon."

"Ship? Space-farers? How fascinating! Work for you, my sweet," Ian said to his semantics-trained wife.

"Well, I never," was her astonished response, her green eyes sparkling with anticipation. "Oh, dear, I'd better see if I can locate the translators. I brought them along sort of as an afterthought. Never for one moment thought I'd need them."

"You signed Cuiva off on their use, too, you know," Ian called after Cherry, who was running across the lounge. "We'll have plenty of time, honey . . ." He shrugged as she continued on her way to find the equipment.

"Pretty good detail on the pulsed reports," Gaitama called out, as she was the only one watching the screen in the lounge and the earliest reports. "Planet has some real nasty life-forms. Mareena, come take a look."

Mareena joined the biology ensign in the lounge and gulped when she saw the size of the avians and the immense shaggy creatures. Nimisha had added a human figure to the image to show comparative size.

"Nimisha found other wrecks, not as lucky as the *Poolbeg*," she added, rewinding the tape to show those.

"That's ancient," Nazim said. "Must have been First Diaspora."

"All right, crew. Helm has stripped the beacon of formal messages," Caleb said, half an eye on the screen as he delivered orders. "Helm's sending a pulse beam indicating our ETA at Erehwon. They've put up an operational comsat so they'll know we've made a safe translation. I'm assuming that the *Acclarke* has informed them of our imminent arrival."

"An operational comsat?" Kendra repeated with a respectful gleam in her eye. "Well done."

"Any crew member wishing to add a message to a pulse going back to Vega III should have it ready in twenty minutes," Caleb went on. "I don't intend to hang about here. We'll be resuming IS drive in twenty minutes."

"Hey, that's not long enough, Caleb," Nazim protested.

"Write your reams during IS drive, Nazim, and Helm will relay them when we reach Erehwon. Our first priority is to deliver our sleeping beauty to her mother as fast as possible."

"Aye, aye, sir," was Nazim's prompt reply, and he bolted down the corridor to his own cabin.

"Twenty minutes, Nazim," Caleb called after him.

"Helm, is there anything worth saving from that space station?" Caleb asked.

"The metal and perhaps smaller objects," Helm replied.

"I shot a warning and light beacon over to it, Captain," Kendra said, "to ward off any possible collision."

"Good idea," Caleb said, as he netted in for translation. "Though why Meterios neglected to do so is something I shall have a word with her about. I suspect there'll be more traffic rather than less if Nimisha's planet has aliens. Just like her to find some."

"Some people do have a knack of turning disaster into triumph," Kendra said with a mischievous grin.

"Nimisha certainly does," he agreed, and gave her hand on the armrest an affectionate squeeze.

Her ability to maintain a light touch was one of the qualities about her that Caleb particularly enjoyed in their relationship. He'd never been quite sure when Nimisha was being humorous or subtly sarcastic; being able to relax with Kendra had been an especial boon on this long voyage. She was also assiduous in separating their personal life from their professional.

"Fifteen minutes," Caleb said over the com. "Sent your pulse, Kennie?"

"First in," she said.

"If you'll be good enough to send the official pulse to Fleet Headquarters, I'll have time to send Lady Rezalla reassurance."

She nodded and began to key in the obligatory notice while Caleb, pausing to word his note carefully, sent a privately encrypted message to the Boynton House. He discreetly commented that Lady Cuiva was enjoying excellent health, had completed all the lessons and tutorials sent for her instruction, and was looking forward eagerly to rejoining her mother.

"Translation in thirty seconds," Helm announced and in the main lounge, Caleb and Kendra heard the scurry of people making for secure seating.

"I don't know what it is, Karpla," Doc said, and Nimisha had an image of Lord Naves stroking his chin and shaking his head in perplexity as he regarded the state of Brad Karpla's naked body under the plastic canopy. She could see the dust that oozed in little gouts from the pustules.

He had been complaining of a skin irritation for several days and, although he had seen the *Acclarke* medic, when the irritation began to spread with alarming speed to cover even the soles of his feet, Captain Meterios had insisted that he consult the more sophisticated system. They had been a ludicrous pair on their entry, the smaller captain supporting the taller, heavier gunnery officer up the steps and to the diagnostic unit. Traces of the gray powder that the irritation exuded clung to her uniform, and she had asked permission to use the Fiver's facilities to wash and brush it off.

"Use the farthest cabin, Captain," Nimisha said. "The children are presently asleep in the two closer ones."

"Where have you been, Karpla?" Doc went on, his extendibles busy brushing the powder onto slides, disclosing the odd boil-like pustules covering Karpla's body.

"Hunting," Karpla said, squirming on the couch in an attempt to ease the intolerable itching on his back. "Took a gang of the Sh'im kids—with permission, sir," he added, craning his neck around to address Jon, "to hunt in the mountains."

"Did they warn you about any of the vegetation?" Doc asked.

"Well, I guess they did, but it was much quicker to go through the thickets. We'd spotted a covey of a-alli and you know what good eating they are. 'Sides, these coveralls are pretty impervious to most of the thorns and prickers this planet grows. Would you for mercy's sake stop the fraggin' itching, Doc?" The gunnery officer's plea came out as a nearly hysterical invocation.

"I've already given you a broad antihistamine, Karpla. It should be working," Doc said. "Let me get some idea of what causes it, and I'll knock you out until we come up with a remedy. You'll skin yourself if you keep on doing that." Karpla was writhing violently.

Jon could now see how Karpla had scratched all over himself in an effort to ease the discomfort. His fingernails were bloody and broken, with the gray powder caked under them.

"That fragging thicket caused it. Nothing else on this fragging planet's bothered me. Has to be that."

"Describe the plant?"

"Jasssus, will you stop the itching!"

"I must be sure no one else is caught out as you've been."

Karpla wailed in anxiety.

"I suspect the Sh'im tried to make Karpla avoid the bushes. Surely you've enough for analysis now, haven't you?" Jon didn't have much use for the dedicated hunter, but the man's suffering need not be prolonged.

"*Pullease.*" Karpla was patently in anguish.

Jon didn't see the hypospray, but abruptly Karpla's arching body relaxed, eyes fluttering shut in the next instant.

"Don't come any nearer, Jon." The extendibles within the diagnostic unit were spreading a sheet over Karpla's inert body right up to his ears. The pustules, which had crept up his throat to his face, had stopped on his chin, giving him a vile gray lumpy "beard" along the jawline.

Suddenly the air circulatory system came on full blast, plastering Jon's coverall to him.

"Nimisha, stand near Jon and let the vents clear any possible spores that might have reached you, too," Doc said. "I suspect the powder is airborne. Whether it's infectious or contagious, I haven't yet decided. But you don't want to run the risk."

"The children?" Nimisha realized she'd sent the captain down the passageway past the doors to their cabins.

"Good tight seal on those doors, and Helm's already ordered a complete vacuuming."

"But what is it?" Nimisha asked, hand on her throat in her anxiety. Jon started to put a comforting arm about her and canceled the action.

"Should we shower?" he asked.

"I'd advise it, and I'm preparing a thoroughly stinky but quite effective gel to use."

"How do you know it's stinky?" Nimisha asked, irritable with anxiety. "You have no olfactory organs."

"Because my program tells me the components stink."

"Oh."

"Go shower."

Quite a breeze whipped through the ship since Doc had Helm open the garage hatch and all doors but those on the children's cabins.

"What is going on?" Captain Meterios demanded, leaning into the wind as she returned. It abated just as she reached one end of the medical unit. A quick peek proved to her that Karpla's body was now decently covered.

"Clearing the air, Captain," Doc said.

"What's the matter with Karpla? You've sedated him?"

"The irritation was quite unbearable, Captain. If you will call a stretcher team, he can be returned to his own quarters on the *Acclarke*."

"Your diagnosis?" Meterios stood hands behind her back, looking quite provoked.

"An extreme allergic reaction to vegetation. I have found no comparison for either the dust or the pustules in my exotic disease data banks. An empirical treatment to relieve his extreme discomfort was necessitated."

"Allergy?"

"Karpla, on his most recent hunting expedition, apparently plowed through bushes which the Sh'im avoided. I suspect he would have been wiser to follow their example," Doc said at his mildest.

Meterios was severely irritated as she spoke into her wrist com and ordered a stretcher team on the double. "How long is he likely to be afflicted with this . . . this local allergy?"

"I am running tests on it at this moment, Captain, and will forward the results to you at the *Acclarke*."

"I shall have to set up a watch on him, I suppose."

"That won't be necessary, Captain. I've put him in cold sleep."

"You *what*?"

"Medical necessity. Can't have him infecting anyone else until I've discovered what antidote can prevent its spread."

"Its spread?"

"It could, you know," Doc said. "But you had the good sense to wash immediately when you arrived, Captain. I would suggest that you shower with this gel as soon as you return to your ship." A vial of a dark brown liquid rolled into one of the unit's apertures.

Jon and Nimisha exchanged quick glances, and just then the gurney team arrived. Doc's extendibles had by then encased Karpla in a full cold suit.

"Put him in your medical unit in the *Acclarke* and advise it to monitor him. I'll send what information I discover directly there," Doc told Meterios.

She gave a sharp nod toward Parappan and Amin, who had brought the transport, and left without further comment.

"What happened to him?" Ace Parappan asked as he and the yeoman, Fez Amin, loaded Karpla's body on the gurney.

"Went where the Sh'im told him not to," Jon said succinctly.

"Yeah, he liked hunting with the little guys," Ace remarked.

"Good shot all right, but won't listen to anyone," Fez said.

"You put him in cold sleep, Doc?" asked Parappan.

"Only safe place for him right now. Don't touch the body bag again. Roll him into the cold sleep unit and when it's closed, take a thorough, long shower with this gel." Two vials rolled out of the dispenser drawer.

As Fez put the vials in his thigh pocket, he turned to Jon and said casually, "We got our four-month resupply, sir, just before the wormhole ate us. In case there was something you might need."

"C'mon, Fez," Parappan said, but he winked at Jon as they guided the anti-grav gurney out of the hatch.

Doc waited until they had left.

"Into the shower with you, too. Grab the gel in the dispenser and scrub yourselves well. I'm closing the ship and will add a powerful detox to finish cleaning the air."

"The children . . ." Nimisha started toward their rooms as Jon scooped up the large bottle of brown liquid.

"They're in no danger. I instigated emergency closure and oxygen the moment I had a good look at Karpla's condition," Doc said. "Get scrubbed."

They did, with none of the foolery that often accompanied their showers.

"We didn't need this," Nimisha said, dressing in fresh clothing. She could see that their cabin had been vacuumed, and the air had a decidedly medicinal taint to it. Fortunately when they reemerged into the main lounge, the air there smelled once again of Erehwon's summer aromas.

"Doc, Meterios was in close contact with Karpla. Will that detergent keep her from getting it?"

"Too late for her, I fear," Doc said. "The dust is contagious. She had it on her hands and face and then tried to brush it off when she came in here. Helm informs me there is no trace of powder now in this ship."

"Fraggit!" Jon muttered.

"I don't think I'd wish that sort of allergy on anyone, much as she makes me dislike her," Nimisha said. "How long before she starts scratching?"

"I can't tell, Nimi, but I suspect by tomorrow, she'll be showing signs."

"Then tell her crew to stay the hell away from the *Acclarke*," Jon ordered.

"Helm has already done so since I declared a medical emergency," Doc said.

"I have warned everyone," Helm said.

"What about those poor guys carrying the stretcher?" Nimisha asked.

"They'll be fine," Doc said easily. "That's why I put him in a body bag. No further danger of contamination. Hopefully the cold will also wither the powder, since it thrives in heat." The medical AI made a throat-clearing sound. "It occurs to me, Lady Nimisha and Commander Svangel," he went on formally, "that treatment for this condition may only be available back where exotic diseases have been studied. And often cured."

Jon and Nimisha exchanged glances, and Jon began to chuckle. "You didn't have a hand in this, did you, Doc?"

"Me, sir? No, sir," Doc said with what sounded like a genuine indignation. "But it does give us a legitimate reason to send the *Acclarke* back to Vega as fast as Helm can take it. Karpla is, and Meterios will shortly be, dangerous to both humans and Sh'im. Their condition is unlikely to deteriorate once they are both in cold sleep . . ."

"Especially since those were Meterios's original orders," Nimisha said drolly.

"And they can be dealt with by medical authorities on their arrival. I strongly urge you to take my advice in this matter."

"Doc?" Nimisha began, her expression severe.

"One grabs occasions as they arise, Lady Nimisha," he said at his most courteous and cryptic.

"What was it they used to say about gift horses?" Jon asked, raising an eyebrow as he gave her a charming lopsided grin. "And whatever they got in that four-month resupply should be appropriated as fast as possible."

"Jon, we shouldn't," Nimisha said, aghast.

"Why not? Those two won't need it, and if there's some fresh homegrown produce—"

"There is," Doc interrupted. "I had Helm check with Four's Helm. D'you want the manifest?"

"We can make sure the crew it was designed for get it, love," Jon said, touching her elbow. "Sure won't last four years back to Vegan Headquarters. And we'll be having visitors who'll have run out of the supplies they came with."

"Yes, we will, won't we?" Nimisha wavered.

The next few days were fraught with nervous tension, begun when Captain Meterios informed Captain Svangel in a tone bordering on hysteria that she had awakened to find herself itching unmercifully.

"Your Doc can handle it," Jon said, "but if you have anyone else in the *Acclarke*, get them out!"

"As you well know, Commander," she said, her voice dripping venom, "my crew—" She paused to emphasize her displeasure. "—prefer the native accommodations."

"As mine do, for that matter, Captain. Get into the medical unit. We'll be over—"

"You shouldn't risk it," Nesta Meterios said, her voice frantic.

"Once you're in the medical unit, our Doc will tell yours the procedures to instigate, Captain Meterios," Jon said firmly. "As I am senior serving officer, I hereby formally relieve you of your command, Captain Meterios, and it will be noted that your illness came about in succoring a member of your crew. Please proceed immediately to the medical unit."

When there was no outraged refusal, Jon and Nimisha exchanged surprised glances.

"You heard Karpla," Doc said. "She can't be as bad off as he was when she brought him here, but that doesn't mean she isn't suffering a lot."

Jon strode down the passageway.

"You will, of course, not go in there without full decontam gear," Nimisha said.

"Damn sure," was his reply as he hauled open the storage units.

"That won't be necessary," Doc said soothingly. "Helm'll decontam the entire ship once Meterios is in the medical unit. And she's wasted no time either."

Nimisha crossed her arms over her chest and, foot tapping, regarded the medical unit. Somewhere it should have eyes that she could pin with her glance when necessary, like right now. She could almost appreciate those who did not like dealing with AI units on the grounds that there were no eyes to contact or anything humanoid about them except their programmed voices.

"How often do you AI's talk to each other, Doc?"

"Only in emergency situations, my dear Nimisha. And this *is* one, you'll grant."

"Yes."

Jon came back into the main cabin, properly accoutered, masked, and wearing an oxygen tank.

"I told you that it won't be necessary," Doc said, sounding peeved. "As if I would risk anyone else."

"You risked Meterios," Jon reminded him.

"I did not. Karpla did. The contagion had already passed between them when she assisted him here. I even give Meterios full credit for that act of mercy."

"She probably couldn't stand Karpla's complaints," Nimisha said unkindly.

"Lady Nimisha!" Doc said in a chiding tone. "Surely that good deed must redeem her in your estimation."

"I'll try to let it," she replied.

"Helm, muster the *Acclarke*'s crew at the skiff hatch," Jon said. "We can get those supplies off now that the captain's . . . being taken care of."

Nimisha was almost shocked at the malicious twinkle in his eyes as he waved her a farewell.

As soon as Jon left, Nimisha went to the bridge of the Fiver and watched him trudge across the sun-baked dusty landing field to the other vessel. Fortunately, decontam suits used air-conditioning, so he wouldn't be too uncomfortable in today's heat. On the way, she saw first Globan, then Drayus and the other crew members, fall in beside him. Whatever explanation he gave them stopped them in their tracks. Then Globan started giving orders, and Ace Parappan and Fez Amin, with Tezza Ashke right behind them, found an empty four-wheeled cart, which they pushed to the stern hatch of the *Acclarke*. Some of the Sh'im came along to either investigate or help.

"Now hear this, Nimisha Boynton-Rondymense speaking," she said, using the traditional hail. "Captain Meterios has become infected by whatever allergen Brad Karpla brought back from his latest hunt. The *Acclarke* is officially in the strictest quarantine. If anyone is experiencing a body-wide itching, please report here immediately. You there of the *Acclarke* crew, do exactly, and only, what Commander Svangel orders."

"That includes the Sh'im, Nimisha," Doc said sternly.

"Including Sh'im. We'd like to speak to those who accompanied Brad on his most recent hunt, to determine which plant caused his condition. Karpla and Captain Meterios are resting comfortably while an antidote or a treatment can be found."

"Which I can't find without the full resources of a naval medical facility," Doc added sourly.

Jon had barely returned from his several duties on the *Acclarke*, telling Nimisha that Captain Meterios had been put into cold sleep, when Helm announced a contact.

"Fiver, this is Fiver B calling." Nimisha gulped at the sound of Caleb Rustin's unmistakable baritone.

"Fiver B, this is Nimisha receiving you loud and clear. Where are you?"

There was a brief pause that told both Nimisha and Jon that the Fiver B was still a long way off.

"We have just translated to Insystem drive at heliopause and are reducing our speed preparatory to landing at the coordinates on record."

"Is Cuiva with you? May I speak to her?" Nimisha said, knowing she didn't need to shout but doing so in her excitement. Tears ran unheeded down her cheeks, and she felt Jon's hand gripping her shoulder in comfort.

She thought she'd expire during the time it took for her message to reach the incoming ship and the answer to get back to her.

"She's in cold sleep. I promised Cuiva not to wake her until her birthday morning, Nimisha," Caleb replied. "She's also a junior officer now. She put her travel time to good use."

"Then she has her necklace with her?"

"Yes, and yours, too."

Nimisha could not restrain her sobs then. "Oh, the dear, dear girl. Oh, my darling Cuiva!"

Jon edged into the second seat and took over.

"Lieutenant Commander Jonagren Svangel speaking. Lady Nimisha is temporarily overcome with joy at your message."

Pause.

"Svangel? Delighted to know that Nimisha has not been alone on that planet."

"Not half as glad as we were, Captain, to see a fresh face, and have the advantages of such a well-equipped ship."

Pause.

"Best ship ever built for this type of duty. Has Meterios departed for Vega III?"

"Captain Meterios and a crew member, gunnery officer Brad Karpla, have been stricken with an unknown, virulent allergic reaction to local vegetation. Medical advice has put them in cold sleep until they can receive treatment."

Pause.

"How long has Meterios been in sleep?"

"Since this morning, Captain Rustin."

Pause.

"She had orders to return immediately to Vega as soon as she had found Lady Nimisha and established her well-being, Captain."

"Lady Nimisha pointed this out, but Meterios felt obliged to remain until you had arrived."

Pause.

"Too bad. What of the rest of her crew and the surviving space station personnel?"

"They have all been accommodated in other quarters since their landing here and were not in contact with the affected personnel."

Pause.

"That's fortuitous." Even the distortion of their relative distances did not quite rob the remark of its drollness. "Captain Svangel, I am sending you the necessary data for the *Acclarke* Helm to return immediately at the fastest possible interstellar speed to

Vegan Fleet headquarters. Under the circumstances, it's reassuring to know we have that capability in the Fours. They are much in demand."

"I shall so enter that order in the log and dispatch the *Acclarke* within the hour."

Pause.

"We shall send a pulse message, announcing the ship is in a quarantine status and must so be regarded. Have Helm answer any hail with that warning."

"Yes, sir. Complying."

Pause.

"Is Lady Nimisha still there, Captain?"

"She is." With that, Jon tactfully removed himself from the cabin to allow them privacy. Nimisha had got over her initial reaction to the long-awaited news, although the brilliance of her eyes told him how excited she was.

"I'm told she has the Necklace with her, is that right, Caleb?"

Pause.

"Yes, it is. Lady Rezalla was determined that Cuiva's own mother would do the honors, and Cuiva voluntarily went into sleep to be sure you were able to follow that tradition."

"Has she changed much since I last saw her?"

Pause.

"You'll notice it." Caleb replied and Jon—though he tried not to listen—heard a chuckle. "She's not a little girl anymore. But I need to know more about the aliens, Nimisha. There's some consternation about that situation, to judge by the messages at the beacon."

"They must be relatively new," she said, "but then, I have to admit we've been pretty busy and don't strip the beacon as often as we should. Then the *Acclarke* XO told us the beacon had suffered damage so we actually didn't receive earlier messages." She felt a little miffed at Caleb for changing the subject. "The *Poolbeg*'s an exploratory ship, with appropriate crew, and the three survivors had enough training so that we could make a proper contact, according to FSP protocols, when we encountered the Sh'im. That's what they call themselves. Their ship was also caught by the wormhole while they were on an exploratory voyage, hoping to find a new colonial world. So they fall into the same classification humans do. We've managed to adapt speakers to catch their language; some of their sounds are out of our auditory range, but we have established very good working relationships."

Pause.

"We have a semantics expert on board who will be most disappointed," Caleb said and chuckled.

"I doubt it. We haven't got more than basic words, action verbs, and general ethical ideas. No abstract philosophy or much history yet. We're beginning to need better communication on the mechanical level, so they can learn how to manage some of our equipment."

Pause.

"They're that intelligent?"

"They probably have had space travel a lot longer than we humans have," Nimisha said.

Pause.

"Accepted, Lady Nimisha. Now get that quarantined ship off your planet."

Jon slipped back in. "Helm has programmed the *Acclarke*, Captain. You will be able to see her in the night sky in approximately two hours from my mark." He watched the bridge chronometer. "Mark."

Pause.

"Over and out for now. Check with you later." The speaker went dead.

"How'd you program the *Acclarke* Helm from here?" Nimisha asked Jon, surprised.

He pointed to his wrist unit. "Actually, I did most of it when I went to check on Meterios. She was out of it already, so what she didn't know wouldn't give her a chance to complain."

"I could almost feel sorry for— There she goes." The *Acclarke* was making a stately vertical liftoff, her thrusters stirring up dust from the landing area. Nimisha flicked off a salute. "Bye, bye, Nesta. Oh, fraggit, Jon, did the crew have time to get their gear off?"

"Crew have already had their gear off a long time, luv," he said with a chuckle. "Longer than Meterios knew."

They went to the hatch to watch and saw that many were observing its departure, its crew saluting until the main engines kicked in with the telltale flare from the rear tubes.

As Jon pulled Nimisha back into the Fiver and into his arms, they both heard the muted wakening cries from the open comunit in the babies' cabin.

"You're not anxious, are you, luv?"

"Of Cuiva's coming? No, no. I've longed for the sight of her." She jerked her thumb at the babies' cabin. "She'll be surprised, but I think she'll be glad to have brothers and sisters."

"I hope so because she's got a passel of them."

"Passel? Where do you get such language, Captain?"

"I was raised wrong." He kissed her to prove it before they went to see to the needs of their offspring.

As the Five B neared its destination, conversations became easier, pauses shorter. Syrona conferred with Kendra Oscony on how she had constructed the comsat she had sent up, and Kendra approved. It would certainly suffice until the pulse message load increased. Oscony informed Syrona that there had been advances in pulse messaging: The current pulse time to this area of space had had two months shaved off the original year and four months. Jon and Casper spoke at length to Chief Engineer Ian Hadley, who was able to offer advice on the mining operations. Much botanical data was uploaded to bring Mareena Kawamura up to speed on those parts of Erehwon that had been investigated in any depth. There was plenty left to be explored and documented.

Nimisha had conversations with Perdimia Ejallos about her daughter and was much reassured that Cuiva had coped well when the voyage had been extended past the initial three months. Perdimia told her how hard Cuiva had worked to get her Junior Practical Officer's rank and had "signed off" in all she had studied. She spoke also with Gaitama and with Nazim, who was disappointed that the *Acclarke* had already left. It was one of the ships that he had personally test-flown and he was sorry to miss her. Nimisha did not remark that he was the only one who did. Hadley had long discussions with Dr. Qualta and Valina Kelly concerning their progress in charting the new stars. He didn't wish to duplicate their efforts, since there was so much to be analyzed and documented.

Fiver's Cater was informed of the need for special dishes for Cuiva's Necklacing ceremony, slightly complicated because it would have to be held outdoors so that the Sh'im might witness the event. Tim explained to his friends that it was a sort of coming of age for a dark-coat's eldest child.

"I am *not* a dark coat," Nimisha said, pretending to take umbrage and tossing over her shoulder the thick braids in which she kept her luxuriant dark hair. "Not by a century or so, but the analogy is basically correct," she added, relenting when she saw that her teasing remark had startled Tim.

"The Sh'im are cooking up a storm and I've got to go hunting, Nimi," Tim said, settling around his waist the heavy belt to which he attached his various weapons. He was tanned, well muscled, and looked more like an ancient primitive hunter than a modern space-age ten-year-old. "Oh!" He turned back at the hatch. "Can I go on calling you Nimi? Will I have to start with the lady bit?"

"We're all in this together, Tim, but it might be proper for you to be formal during the Necklacing ceremony, when we'll all observe strict protocol as tradition decrees." She'd said the last in a very haughty tone.

"Oh, of course, Lady Nimisha," he replied in a plummy voice, having a keen ear for mimicry. He leaped from the hatch to the ground, giving the liquid-tongued call to assemble his fellow hunters. He was the best Sh'im speaker of all the youngsters: but then, as they grew older, they'd acquire a more useful vocabulary, too.

The hunters would be after a-alli today, the small treehoppers of Karpla's last hunt. They used their wings only to glide from one branch to another in the forested slopes east of Clifftown. Their dark flesh was very tender and succulent, so the creatures were much prized as a protein source, but they were not easy to catch. Hunting them was reserved for special occasions and could occupy several days before sufficient numbers were acquired. Their feathers were of various hues, helping them blend into the blossoms or leaves of their roosts, and were used as adornments in the crowns, or wreaths, the Sh'im wore on special occasions. The down could be stuffed into winter robes for extra warmth, the offal used as bait in fishing, the tendons dried for thong ties, and bones crushed for fertilizer.

With so much to do, even with everyone organized to help, Nimisha did not have much time to worry about the long-awaited meeting with Cuiva, or the problem of explaining so many siblings.

In planning the actual landing, Caleb decreed that it should be dawn, to keep his promise to Cuiva that she'd be awakened on her birthday. Every human was awake well before sunrise that day, making last-minute preparations. Caleb had suggested a private breakfast for mother and daughter on board the Five B.

"The crew will want to be out and about and as far away from the B as possible the moment we land," he said, chuckling. "And I need to have some time to speak to the other naval personnel before the ceremony begins."

"That sounds ominous," Nimisha said, wanting to be present at the first meeting between Jon and Caleb.

"Why should it? It's to their credit that the three of them survived as long as they did," Caleb replied. "Anyway, one of the pulses I collected from the beacon are commendations and promotions for them, which I will take great pleasure in presenting."

"Oh, why weren't they forwarded to us then?" Nimisha asked. A promotion for Jon would have given him more clout in dealing with Meterios.

"Navy regs," Caleb said.

As the Five B settled gracefully onto the landing field at Clifftown in the predawn light, Captain Jonagren Svangel, Lt. Commander Casper Ontell, and Lieutenant Junior Grade Syrona Lester-Pitt, sweating in their dress blues—the only uniforms they had left—formed an escort for Nimisha, stylishly dressed in a cool tissue gown, one of a closetful of elegant outfits she'd never bothered to use once she landed on Erehwon. She and Syrona had altered the dress to fit Nimisha's new dimensions.

The main hatch of the sleek golden ship opened, the steps were lowered, and the crew emerged, fanning out and trying not to break their attention stance to eyeball their new environs. All of them were in dress whites, the naval contingent saluting while those not in uniform placed their right hand on their hearts, a gesture that caused Nimisha's heart to jump. Jon pressed her arm against him and then brought them both to face Caleb Rustin.

"Sir, Lieutenant Commander Jonagren Svangel, welcoming you and your crew to Erehwon," he said, with a crisp salute.

"So good to see you, Caleb," Nimisha said. She stepped forward

and greeted him with the four cheek kisses of long-term friendship.

"It is very good to see you, Lady Nimisha," Caleb said, bowing
formally. "May I present the crew and its civilian members?"

"You may, of course."

Then Caleb bent toward her and added in a murmur, "Cuiva is
not quite awake yet, so we're stalling a bit until she is." He gestured toward the woman first in the lineup. "My executive officer,
Lieutenant Commander Kendra Oscony, Lady Nimisha."

Between Oscony's smart salute and then her acceptance of
Nimisha's handshake their eyes met, and Nimisha's smile broadened. She need not worry about Caleb. Kendra had paired with
him on the voyage. Relieved on that score, Nimisha concentrated
on meeting the other naval personnel. To both Gaitama and Nazim,
she gave the two kisses that acknowledged their long acquaintance
and her pleasure in seeing them again. Perdimia was last in line,
and although Nimisha did not know her, she accorded the bodyguard two kisses and warmly shook her hand.

"I owe you much, Perdimia Ejallos, for protecting my daughter
so diligently."

Perdimia, flushing with pleasure at the accolade, dipped in a
respectful curtsy. "She has been a pleasure to serve, Lady Nimisha."

Then Jon introduced his shipwreck companions and the *Acclarke*
navy personnel who had remained behind, as well as the Wormhunter contingent. He introduced Valina Kelly, Roscom Granjor,
and Adjudic Kwan, explaining the absence of the others by saying
that Dr. Qualta had done a long night's duty with her staff and they
were sleeping late this morning.

"If you've granted shore leave, Captain Rustin, I think our
group would be very happy to show your crew around a bit.
The Sh'im aren't up yet." Jon gestured to the tip of the sun just
showing over the forested eastern slopes. "Tim's here to help

with translations until your units can be programmed to Sh'im speech."

"Ready when you are, sirs and ma'ams," Tim said, lifting his translator from his chest in demonstration.

"Let me add that Tim is an indigenous human resident of Erehwon, having been born here," Jon said, "as well as our most valuable translator."

"I may ask for an hour or so of your time later, then, Tim Lester-Ontell," Caleb said without any condescension.

"Happy to oblige, sir," Tim said, beaming broadly.

Caleb turned to Nimisha then. "Now that we've acquitted the formal courtesies, Lady Nimisha . . ."

"Let's ditch the titles, shall we, Caleb?" Nimisha said, an edge to her voice. She kept finding the return of formality annoying. Without further delay, she marched up the steps. At the top, she stopped and turned.

"Permission to go aboard, Captain Rustin?" she asked in a meek tone.

"Permission enthusiastically granted, La . . . Nimisha," Caleb said, grinning as he waved her up the steps.

Though she could hear the others breaking ranks at Caleb's "Dismiss!" and Tim renewing his willingness to translate, she was stricken with sudden hesitation as she stood in the hatchway.

"Go on, Nimi," she heard Jon say, softly, supportively.

So she did and stopped because, although the dimensions of the Five B were the same as her Fiver, it was subtly a navy ship, and furnished as such without the more homey touch she'd managed on hers.

"She's just rousing, Lady Nimisha," Doc said, startling her. The AI's voice was that of Lord Naves, which she hadn't expected.

Her "oh" of surprise elicited a chuckle. "Well, I am the best they have in medical AI's, you know, Lady Nimisha. Captain Rustin chose me because Lady Cuiva would recognize my voice and be comforted. Come around to the unit. Speak to her. That will complete awakening."

Nimisha felt her eyes fill with tears as she walked around to catch the long-awaited sight of her daughter. Cuiva was stretching sleepily, arching her back and pulling her knees up. Nimisha indulged herself with a long look at the rousing child who was a child no longer, having developed a slender womanly form during their separation. Cuiva was subtly Rhidian with the line of her brow, but more Boynton than Farquahar-Hayakawa in coloring and form. She'd been dressed in a knee-length tunic the same color as her eyes, the neckline leaving the body-heir tattoo on her neck uncovered. Nimisha drew in a long breath, trying to slow her joyfully beating heart and shaking hands so eager to embrace her daughter. Her eldest daughter—and that mental correction settled Nimisha's nerves. Of course, without Lady Rezalla to glare disapproval for a totally unacceptable display of excess emotion, Nimisha could do what she damn pleased, but she did not think she should confront her waking daughter with a tearful mother, and took firm control of her emotions.

"Cuiva dear, happy birthday," Nimisha said lightly, joyfully, and dropped a kiss on a sleep-flushed cheek. Cuiva smiled, still not fully awake, and hearing a dream voice.

"She's in excellent condition, Lady Nimisha," Doc murmured. "We've been careful to maintain muscle tone during her sleep, so she should have no ill effects. She's to have small meals to reacquaint her stomach with food, but Cater knows. And she can have judicious portions of her Necklace banquet food."

"Thank you," Nimisha murmured. Then, in a stronger, teasing tone, no longer able to delay, she said, "Cuiva, you sleepyhead. Wake up. It's your fourteenth birthday and there's a lot to be done before your Necklacing."

The gentian eyes flew open, caught sight of her mother's grin—

which Nimisha hoped was neither doting nor dopey—and then the girl was clasping her mother to her with strong young arms, cheek against cheek.

"Oh, Mother, Mother, Mother," Cuiva cried, standing up and then whirling her mother around and around in an exultant dance.

"Easy does it, Cuiva," Doc said.

"Oh!" Like a child caught misbehaving, Cuiva put one hand to her mouth and grinned mischievously at her mother. Nimisha felt the girl's body quivering and deftly upheld her, walking them both to the nearest chairs.

"And it is my birthday? Caleb kept his promise?"

"He has indeed. It's just dawn on Erehwon—that's what I named the planet," Nimisha hastily explained.

"Nowhere?" Cuiva's fingers squeezed tightly on Nimisha's hand, which she had not released. She giggled. "Just the name you'd pick, isn't it?"

"It has seemed appropriate," Nimisha agreed. "Whatever, subjectively, this is the morning of your fourteenth birthday."

Cuiva looked around. "Where is Caleb?" she demanded, seeing no one else. "And Perdimia?"

"Did I hear my name?" Caleb said, poking his head through the open hatch.

"And Perdimia!" Not that Cuiva had released her firm hold on her mother.

"Perdimia," Caleb called out the open hatch, "your presence is requested."

Perdimia, with a respectful bow to Nimisha, stepped into the lounge, at which point Cuiva lost all formality and, jumping up, hugged the woman, kissing her cheeks four times in the formal manner before she started effusively thanking her for all her care.

"I think food might be the next order of the day, Cuiva," Doc said firmly. "Cater, I do believe you have organized the appropriate sustenance for Lady Cuiva?"

"But where is everyone else?" Cuiva demanded, looking about. "I can't start my birthday without Gaitama and Nazim and Cherry and Kendra and Ian and Mareena. That wouldn't be proper, would it, Mother? They all cared for me. As you did," she added, raising herself on tiptoe to kiss Caleb's cheek. The way she hung on his arm made Nimisha wonder if she had a young girl's crush on the attractive man. Caleb had developed quite an air about him, new to Nimisha; a subtle improvement.

"We thought to give you a little private space with your mother, Cuiva," he said.

Cuiva stood upright, reminding Nimisha so much of herself at that age and on the day of her Necklacing that she thought her heart would burst. "It is *my* birthday and I've waited long enough for it. So I do the choosing, now that I'm legally old enough to have a say in what I want to do."

Caleb scratched the back of his neck. "Then I apologize for not discerning your wishes first, my dear, because I dismissed the crew. Some of your mother's friends are showing them about."

"Oh, how selfish of me," Cuiva said, remorseful.

"Not at all," Caleb said quickly. "Very thoughtful to wish to include them. Give them a little walkabout time and then I'll recall them for elevenses. This is a glorious planet at dawn."

"They *have* all been cooped up longer than I was," Cuiva said, still repentant.

"We'll join you while you eat, dearest," Nimisha said, going for the dish that had just appeared in Cater's dispenser. Returning to Cuiva's table, she spotted Jon lurking outside. "Well, there's one who hung about to meet you. Jon, please come in and meet my daughter."

"Permission to come aboard, Captain Rustin?" Jon asked formally in the hatchway.

"Permission granted, Captain Svangel."

Deciding to make it plain where Jon stood in her regard, Nimisha met him, linked her arm in his, and led him to the table. "Cuiva, this is Jon Svangel, one of the three survivors of the *Poolbeg*, which had the misfortune to meet the wormhole that snatched me, too. He and the others have been my very good companions."

Cuiva gracefully held out her hand, but at the angle to be shaken, not kissed.

"My congratulations on achieving your minor majority, Lady Cuiva," Jon said, shaking her hand first and then turning it to drop a light kiss on it. "This is just as much an occasion for us as it is for you."

Cuiva smiled back at him and shot a mischievous glance at her mother and a quick sideways one at Caleb.

"I am most relieved to know that my mother had companions." Her formal phrasing was accompanied by a radiant smile of relief.

Jon shot a quizzical look at Nimisha and then at Caleb, who shook his head.

"There's a lot more you'll need to know, my love," Nimisha said, slipping into her chair again. "I could stand caffeine, Cater, and something more substantial for breakfast. Caleb, Perdimia?"

"I'll get it," Jon said, giving her shoulder an affectionate pat that he intended everyone present to notice.

Perdimia didn't know where to look.

"What more should I hear first?" Cuiva asked, though her eyes followed Jon to the dispenser.

"You weren't awake when we arrived at the beacon, Cuiva," Caleb said, "Your mother and her friends have also made contact with aliens. Sapient aliens."

"Oh, Mother, you didn't! How marvelous! What are they like?"

"We haven't seen any either," Caleb said with a laugh.

"I have," Perdimia said. "They're small, gray, furry, I think—" She looked to Nimisha, who nodded. "—and there seem to be a great many of them."

Nimisha laughed. "We're in the largest of their six settlements.

This is the main one. Their wrecked ship is on the other side of the cliff."

"Oh, Mother, how wonderful. Sapient aliens! But, if their ship crashed, then they're not indigenous, right?" Cuiva's curiosity did not allow her to make much progress with her bland breakfast.

"Eat," her mother said. "Quite right, they're not indigenous to this planet, but they are space-farers, so we can treat them as equals." Nimisha settled a stern look on Caleb and Cuiva. "We— or rather Tim Lester-Ontell—have acquired a fair amount of basic terms and verbs. We've managed to program translators, but we're nowhere near understanding abstract terms yet."

"Cherry Absin-Hadley will be glad to hear that," Caleb remarked with a grin.

"The main point I'm making," Nimisha continued, "is that we haven't compromised the evolution of a new species. That would be a major breach of FSP regulations."

"They couldn't exactly expect you to hide in a cave for five years, could they?" Cuiva asked indignantly.

Jon laughed. "No breach, and as my ship was on an exploratory mission anyway, we followed protocol. In fact," he added, turning to Caleb, "we've been adapting the *Poolbeg*'s gig for three-fingered hands, so they can learn how to fly it. That is, Captain Rustin, if you have no orders to the contrary. We've found the Sh'im to be intelligent, quick to assimilate and learn from demonstration . . ."

"They're allies," Nimisha said firmly.

"No reason not to continue on that footing," Caleb said, raising his hands in accord. "They've obviously impressed you."

"We've mining operations under way, since we've exhausted what we found in the freighter—"

"Freighter?" Caleb asked, surprised. "Your initial report mentioned four wrecks. Where did that come from?"

"First Diaspora, from the design of it," Jon said. "Most of its pods survived the rough landing and we put them to use."

"Meterios took exception to that," Nimisha began.

"To your use of jetsam?" Caleb frowned. "Survivors have the right to use any material to hand."

"We felt that included recycling whatever we could use of the *Poolbeg*," Jon went on.

"Of course it would," Caleb said firmly. "Don't worry about Meterios. She's in trouble anyhow for delaying her return."

"Actually, her delay worked to our advantage, Caleb," Nimisha said, grinning. "We couldn't send the rest of her original crew back on a quarantined ship. And most of them were on short-term tours, so . . ."

"So, as senior serving officer, Captain Rustin, I take responsibility for keeping them here until proper orders could be transmitted. Were there assignments in the messages at the beacon?" Jon asked.

"Not yet," Caleb replied with a slight grin, "considering the time it takes for a pulse message to get where it's going and return. Frankly, Svangel, I doubt Headquarters would fault your decision to retain them here when you can use their skills to advantage."

Jon started to shake his head in the Sh'im manner, but Nimisha's nudge had him change it to the appropriate human one.

"A tip on local protocol," she said, leaning across the table to Caleb. "The Sh'im have reversed the meaning of nod and shake. When they shake their heads, they mean yes. A nod implies the negative. We're used to it now, but you'll need to know."

"Sorry to mar your birthday breakfast with naval matters, Cuiva," Caleb said.

"I don't mind, Caleb. It made this goo go down without me noticing that it doesn't taste like much at all," the girl said, regarding the final spoonful with no great enthusiasm. "And it's so good to be awake. You don't dream in cold sleep, you know. And now I'll have to catch up on all that's happened. So confer away."

Caleb acknowledged the invitation. "Since Headquarters does know from your flow of pulses that an alien contact has been made, you couldn't be in better odor with Fleet and the Federated Sentient Planets right now."

"That's a relief," Jon said.

Caleb started to shake his head—then nodded, practicing the Sh'im fashion, grinning as he switched. "Forget Meterios. She had her head so far up her ass her eyes were brown."

They all laughed at that, though Cuiva's laugh was more tentative, having never before heard that particular phrase.

"I beg your pardon," Caleb said hastily, bowing to both Nimisha and her daughter.

Nimisha was laughing too hard to do more than shake her head.

"*Incoming avians,*" Helm announced, startling everyone at their leisurely meal. "The Fiver forwards the alarm. How do I respond?"

"Caleb, tell your crew to seek immediate shelter and do not, I repeat, do not attempt to return here," Nimisha said, as she and Jon leaped out of their seats and toward the bridge. Jon grabbed her arm before she automatically took the pilot's chair. "Your permission, Captain?" Jon said.

"Helm, Lady Nimisha and Captain Svangel share the conn," Caleb said, and then spoke urgently into his wrist com.

He was no more than a step behind them into the bridge as they slipped into the seats, Jon touching in orders for the missile launchers as soon as he could reach the pad.

"Helm, Nimisha Boynton-Rondymense here. Accept orders from Fiver on emergency procedures."

"I am accepting emergency procedures from the Fiver," Helm replied.

"Magnify main screen to northwest at eleven of a clock port side," Jon said. "Arm missile launchers. Targets are coming in fast in uneven deployment. Fire when locked on."

The forward screen magnified the advancing waves of avians, looking so evil that both Perdimia and Cuiva, standing out of the way at the entrance to the bridge, gasped at their appearance.

"Aren't we going airborne?" Caleb asked.

"No need," Nimisha said. "Lordee, they've got some big ones today, haven't they, Jon?"

"Are they all that size?" Caleb sounded properly awed.

"I mean the boulders they're carrying to drop on us," Nimisha said. "It's not the size of the predators that makes them so dangerous. It's their payloads."

"Why?" Caleb asked. "Repellers should be able to cope with rocks."

"Screen's giving you a false picture of their actual size, Cal. Some are bigger than the Fiver from that armed tail to the nasty snout," Nimisha said. "The Sh'im are as good marksmen as we are, but we've learned to shoot down as many as possible before they get in too close, because any hits over the repeller shields leave an awful mess to scrape off. Not to mention a stink in the summer."

"I think we'll catch most of these before they get anywhere near the perimeter of the shields," Jon said, making a minute correction in trajectory just as the Fiver opened up. "Good man, Casper."

"Not if Globan got there first," Nimisha said, her expression gleeful.

"Not this time. Globan's manning the gig, don't you remember? Syrona's in the skiff." He turned his head slightly toward the three observers. "We managed to fit the Fiver's skiff with homemade rockets. And our allies are operational, too," he added as the batteries on the heights began bracketing the still distant avians. "Used the *Poolbeg*'s ordnance—what hadn't been destroyed by scraping along the wormhole. That's proof enough for me of the wisdom of having AI helms for emergencies."

"I gather that the *Acclarke*'s AI took over when it was sucked into the wormhole?" Caleb asked.

Nimisha gave a wicked laugh. "I got the distinct impression that Meterios went paralytic."

"Then wasn't it fortunate that the AI was preprogrammed," Caleb said wryly. "I gather the *Poolbeg* was not?"

"Captain Querine was a damned good pilot, and Peri Swanick was the jig on helm and had taken us safely through two asteroid belts earlier on—" Jon nodded Sh'im-like. "—but no human reflexes are fast enough to handle a transit as treacherous as that wormhole. You'll see that from the state of the other wrecks."

"Fiver got off with only minor scrapes and Helm is still apologizing," Nimisha said.

"I think I see what you mean about the attackers." Caleb pointed to the screen as they all watched avians disintegrating in the air, their disparate parts leaving bloody trails as they dropped to the plains well before the spread of the settlement. "Your confederates are good marksmen."

"More avians attacking from starboard, coming in over the hills," Helm said.

"Order Globan and Syrona to intercept," Jon said. "Hoping to catch us with the sun in our eyes, are they?"

"The avians have that much intelligence?" Caleb asked, surprised.

"Whatever they use for brains is sufficient to make them a real nuisance," Nimisha said. "We'd hoped that Doc's little ploy would work."

"What was that?" Caleb asked.

"Leaving out treated bait that would inhibit yolk-formation in the females," Nimisha said. "We haven't had a raid in so long I was hoping that had done the trick. In the last two spring seasons we've cleared out as many nests as we could find."

"Don't you hunt them?" Caleb asked.

"Constantly," Nimisha said.

"You never hunted at home, Mother," Cuiva said in a scared little voice. She was standing right up against Perdimia, who had a comforting arm about her.

"Hunting here is not a sport, Cuiva dear. It's a necessity—both for food and survival, as you are witnessing," Nimisha said.

"I perceive the distinction, Mother."

"We'd've spared you this, believe me," Jon said, his fingers busy on the touch panel to adjust the launchers' trajectories. "The avians have an uncanny instinct for appearing at precisely the most inappropriate moments . . ."

"Like when our crops are ready to be harvested," Nimisha added, desperately trying to find some way to alleviate Cuiva's distress. "You don't have to watch, you know."

"If this has been part of your life, Mother, and will be part of mine, I must learn to accept it."

"Well said, Cuiva," was Caleb's accolade.

Cuiva stood up straighter, gently disengaging herself from Perdimia's support. She watched for a few more moments while the Five B's missiles joined the hails from the smaller ships, cutting down the avians as they tried to swoop down on the eastern side of the settlement.

"Aren't aerial displays often put on to welcome visitors to new planets?" Cuiva asked, trying for a lighter tone.

"Not quite this kind," Nimisha said, but she gave her daughter a grateful glance. Then a heartbeat later, she added, "I think that might have been their last fling. At least today. We certainly have decreased the numbers they can put in the air. Fiver?"

"Yes, ma'am?"

"Do the cliff batteries see any more incoming from the east?"

"Casper here, Nimisha. Syrona, Globan, and I are going to make sure. Reset the trajectories to lob shots over the hills, will you? Just in case?"

"Will do," Nimisha said, glancing over to see Jon's fingers busy on the touch controls.

"Reset," he said, his hands poised to hit the toggle at the first hint of more trouble.

"Any ground casualties?" Caleb asked with understandable concern.

Nimisha started to nod, then switched to shaking her head, and asked Helm to bring up the side screens to show where his crew, the other humans, and the Sh'im had taken refuge well under the repeller shield that protected the settlement. A siren blared out the end of the emergency. Those in the Five B could see the excited reception of the all clear, with humans dancing around with the much smaller Sh'im as if they had established friendly relationships during the air raid.

"There's no ill wind that doesn't blow some good, is there," Nimisha said, rising and stretching the tension out of her shoulders before she embraced her daughter. "Better now than during the Necklacing."

When Jon saw the stricken look on the girl's face, he added hurriedly, "They're dawn or dusk attackers, Lady Cuiva. Your ceremony's safely scheduled for noon."

"So my birthday fireworks were a little early," Cuiva said and, though her voice was a little shaky, she managed a fairly humorous grin.

"Attagirl!" Jon grinned approvingly at her.

"D'you have any more surprises like this on your Erehwon?" Caleb asked in a dry tone.

"None quite as dangerous as those," Jon said. "As Nimisha mentioned, we haven't had a raid in a while. Either they saw you landing and thought to catch us off guard . . ."

"If they're clever enough to think of such a thing," Nimisha put in.

"Which I doubt," Jon replied. "They should have got the message that now we've got ships, the cliff batteries and enough ammunition to keep hammering them until they leave, that maybe they should give up."

"Or," and Nimisha didn't like to voice the suspicion, "they've called in reinforcements from the other continents and that means they're more intelligent than we've suspected."

"Fiver's Helm wishes me to inform you that the number of avian casualties are the largest so far on record," reported the Five B Helm.

"I can't say I'd be sorry if the species does commit mass suicide," Nimisha said. "Oh, I shouldn't say such things, love," she added when she saw the stricken look on Cuiva's face. "But those monsters killed so many of the *Poolbeg*'s crew."

"My deepest apologies, Captain Svangel," Cuiva said with formal but sincere remorse. "I had no idea you had suffered any casualties from those dreadful creatures."

"How were you to know, Lady Cuiva?" Jon said kindly.

"Briefly, are there any other predators of that ferocity that we have to guard against while we're on-planet?" Caleb asked.

"There's a smaller continent," Jon said, "that has some very large grazers that can be dangerous if something stampedes them but we tend to stay clear of their herds whenever possible. The smaller grazers are easily frightened and very fast in making strategic retreats. We haven't seen any of the slime slugs on this continent . . ."

"Which is just as well," Nimisha said with a grateful sigh.

"Plenty of scavengers, usually small and ground burrowers that are attracted by the smell of blood. In fact, I suspect they're already at work on this morning's carnage," and Jon gestured to the hills from which the last attack had come and then the distant area beyond the repeller screen, "cleaning up the . . . remains. Lakes and rivers, other than the ones we have seined out and made safe here at Clifftown and the five Sh'im towns, are not suitable for bathing. I'd warn your crew, sir. We have domesticated deer-like creatures to use as a farm and draft animal and the Sh'im are trying to get some other types that might be stronger for such things as hauling heavy loads."

"Sir—" Kendra Oscony, Ian Hadley, and Nazim were all trying to get through the hatch at the same time. Kendra, being the slimmest, slid in sideways, saluted. "Reporting for duty."

"Good of you, XO," Caleb said, "but I'm given to understand that the natural . . . denizens of the planet will remove the . . . remnants of the recent air attack."

"They will?" Hadley asked, his eyes wide. "Some of those—" He cleared his throat hastily and rephrased what he had been about say. "—monsters are the biggest things I've ever seen alive."

Jon explained about the scavengers, and Caleb issued the warnings with the advice to pass them on until he could post the notice as well as vids of the indigenous wildlife.

"Those Sh'im are dead shots," Hadley said, shaking his head in approval.

"With only three digits to work with, too, on controls built for five," Nazim said.

"I gather you had a chance to become acquainted with our allies?" Jon asked, grinning.

"Hell's bells—sorry, ma'am," Ian interrupted himself with a grimace at his rough speech. "Before your com message reached us, we'd been tackled and sat on, so we couldn't make a dash back here to assist."

"Whoever was flying that gig is some pilot," Kendra said approvingly.

"Globan Escorias, formerly of the *Acclarke*," Jon said.

"Escorias has a reputation for being a clever pilot," Kendra said with a grin. "Then who was manning your Fiver, ma'am?"

"Please address me as Nimisha, Kendra," she said firmly, and Kendra made a grimace of apology. "Helm handles the Fiver's offensive."

"And the Five B's, as well," Caleb said, forestalling Kendra's next question.

"Sort of makes gunners redundant, doesn't it?" Hadley said with dismay.

"Only if you're shy of personnel, Ian," Nimisha said. "We need marksmen when we hunt for food here on Erehwon, so if that's an interest of yours and your commander has no objections, I'm certain you can join a hunt."

"Young Tim tells me he leads them," Ian said, still slightly miffed.

"Young Tim?" Cuiva asked.

"Syrona's ten-year-old," Jon said. "He's our resident language specialist."

"He was displaying his skill during the raid," Kendra said, grinning. "And taught us a few words and when to nod and when to shake our heads," she added with feeling.

"That's where Cherry is," Ian Hadley said. "She's got units she'll want to adapt but she's vowel deep in the sounds the Sh'im make. You never mentioned their size or their three fingers."

"There's a lot we haven't had time to mention," Nimisha said, thinking of the other surprises in store for her daughter.

"I think Lady Cuiva's feeling a bit faint, Lady Nimisha," Perdimia began.

Even as Nimisha rushed to help get Cuiva to the nearest chair, she added, "Nimisha, please, Perdimia. And Cuiva. We don't have my dam to scowl at us for dispensing with formalities. Sometimes we've precious little time to worry about protocol on Erehwon. Cater, what's Cuiva to have next?"

"Broth and it's ready."

"Oh. Would you get it please, Perdimia?"

"Is it just dizziness?" Caleb asked, anxiously.

"I'm fine, really I am," Cuiva replied, but the hand she tried to use to dismiss her problem was noticeably shaking.

"What do you expect, overloading the girl with so much excitement barely out of sleep?" Doc said. "Cater's put the necessary additives to the broth."

"Perhaps if you took her to the relative quiet of the Fiver," Caleb suggested.

Nimisha and Jon exchanged guilty glances. "Relative quiet" with young triplets depended entirely on their whimsical feeding times.

"Casper's?" Jon suggested and immediately cancelled that idea. "No, Hope and the twins will be there."

"What's the matter with the Fiver? It's only a step away. I'll carry her," Caleb began.

"Let's let her drink the broth first, shall we?" Nimisha said brightly.

"She can stay here, of course," Caleb said, "but we thought you'd like her with you."

Kendra cleared her throat. "I think that perhaps there are others staying in the Fiver?"

She managed to avoid direct eye contact with Nimisha by striding over to the dispenser and asking for two coffees. She brought one back to hand to Caleb, who absently thanked her.

"Yes," Nimisha said, still not quite having the moral courage to deal Cuiva yet another shock, "that's right, Kendra."

"We have children," Jon said bluntly. "We had no way of knowing how long any rescue mission might take," he went on, addressing Cuiva more than the others.

"Understandable," Caleb remarked amiably. "First duty of the marooned explorer is to survive."

Nimisha was relieved at how well Caleb reacted to the initial announcement. If only he doesn't fault Jon when the full truth is known.

"It is one reason exploratory crews are mixed," Jon added, carefully choosing his words and still looking straight at Cuiva.

"You mean, I have a brother or sister?" Cuiva asked.

"Not slow on the uptake, is she?" Kendra remarked drily.

"Twins, in fact," Jon said very brightly. "They run in my family. I'm a twin."

"Oh, Mother, if you knew how I yearned for siblings . . ." Cuiva had recovered sufficiently to hug her mother enthusiastically. "Boys or girls?" she asked Jon.

"Actually, both." He cleared his throat, and rattled on, trying to get to the critical part—the recent arrival of the triplets. "Tim was the only child who survived our initial attempt to increase the human population. There was a pretty nasty fever we couldn't seem to reduce with what medicines we had left. Just before Nimisha arrived, Syrona got pregnant with Hope, who's four now. Then Syrie had twins, too."

"She did?" Cuiva replied, blinking.

Caleb was beginning to wonder at the curious recital of Erehwon genesis, but all Cuiva heard was the last.

"Twins?" She exclaimed, her eyes round, "Mother, you had twins?"

Nimisha gave a nervous laugh.

"Two sets of twins did much to increase the esteem in which the Sh'im hold us humans," Jon continued laboriously.

"More than your ability to destroy those avians?" Caleb asked, more confused than surprised. "And erect repeller shields?"

"I think it's a species sort of thing," Nimisha put in. "Sh'im females start breeding at two years, have two to three offspring every year for the next ten."

"But we're humans," Caleb said in objection.

Kendra cocked her head and then ducked away, grinning.

"Oh, please, Mother, could I meet our twins right away? How old are they?" Cuiva asked eagerly.

"I'd say about three years," Kendra said. "They were with Dr. Qualta and Valina Kelly when the attack started. Your sister resembles Lady Rezalla. Don't know who the boy looks like."

"Then will you kindly tell me exactly what's bothering the pair of you?" Caleb asked in a command tone. "You've acted with common sense and practicality, considering your situation."

"What bothers us—" Jon began again, and stopped.

"Is that our Doc"—Nimisha rushed in with the rest of the explanation—"is of the opinion that there's some element in the soil of this planet that encourages fertility. Grazers and even the boks have multiple births, too."

"So who's on the Fiver?" Cuiva asked.

"Triplets," Nimisha said and pointed a finger at Jon and then at herself. "We've named them Tionel, Tyrone, and Teresa."

Cuiva stared, shocked, for a long moment at her mother, gulped and then burst out laughing. "So I'm big sister to *five* brothers and sisters?"

"I'm afraid you are, dear heart, but don't for an instant think that diminishes my love for you, my firstborn and body-heir."

Cuiva embraced her mother so tightly that Nimisha gave a little squeak. "Of course not, mother mine. Only we'll have to figure a way to keep such news from Lady Rezalla. She'd be appalled!"

The tension that had been growing during that drawn-out recital evaporated in laughter and congratulations.

"I must say, Mother, you have certainly provided me with a spectacular birthday," Cuiva said, standing and urging her mother to her feet. "I must see them. I really must." She turned to the Doc. "And don't you dare deny me."

"Joy is a far greater stimulant than any I could give you, young Cuiva."

CHAPTER 12

To suggest that the rest of that auspicious birthday was anticlimactic would be inaccurate. Once the skiff and gig had returned, Caleb ordered that the Five B's stored gig and the disassembled shuttle be put into service as quickly as possible. However, the *Poolbeg* gig, piloted by an eager Nazim, would accommodate quite a few, if they didn't mind a little crowding on the short hop to the Broken Bird. Ool and Ook indicated that they would be guides for a tour of their ancient vessel. There was space to accommodate the senior officers of the Five B: Caleb, Kendra, Chief Engineer Hadley, and Tim to act as interpreter. The officers were fascinated and frustrated at the number of sections of the crushed ship that couldn't be accessed.

"The Sh'im don't know much about the ship really, sirs," Tim said. "Jon thinks it came down about a hundred and fifty of our years ago, and the Sh'im life span is only about thirty, so it's dim, dark history to them."

"Would they mind me poking about?" Hadley asked, seconded by Nazim.

Tim made the request. "No, not since you arrived in such a fine ship with no marks on it at all." He grinned.

"I gather they came through the wormhole," Caleb said, "but the ship doesn't appear capable of making a surface landing. Not the right design."

"I got into one of the cargo holds, Commander. They did have landing craft, but they're all messed up. And, sir," Tim went on, grinning with mischief, "don't tell 'em you didn't come through the wormhole. They were real impressed with the Fiver having only a few scratches. Since there're none on the Five B, it'll raise you in their eyes if they think you did even better."

"Good point, Tim," Caleb said while the others grinned. "Think Cherry'll be able to sort out her translators, Ian?"

"She won't have any trouble, Captain," Tim said. "I showed her a lot already, so she could get right to work."

They had reached the gig and now went aboard.

"I'd like to see more," Caleb said, taking the seat beside Nazim and peering out the wide front screen at the sun-parched landscape, "but I think we'd better return to the settlement and file an initial report."

"Yeah, there's a lot to be done," Tim said with a grin. "But your being here is the best. Of course, you wouldn't be here if the Necklacing wasn't to be done, would you?"

"Not entirely, Tim. We came to rescue Nimisha once we knew where to find her. However, the Necklacing is an event we have looked forward to now for a long time," Caleb remarked. Then he and the others took the short trip up and over the cliff, observing the battery installations where busy Sh'im were servicing the tubes, and down to the landing strip. "I see that the gig is missing."

"I think Globan promised to take Cherry and Mareena to see the avian corpses," Tim said. "They're xeno and biologist, aren't they? That's what they told me during the raid. Right now's a very good time for them to record the scavengers." He gestured directly east and then to the north where most of the avian corpses would be.

When they landed and disembarked, Tim said something to the dark-coats, who shook their heads.

"If you'll excuse us now, sir," he said. "They've got to go, too."

The dark-coats, shading their eyes, bowed formally to the

humans and set off at a good pace beside Tim, heading for the settlement. That there was great activity was obvious by comings and goings and the construction of some sort of a circular edifice, being garlanded by colorful summer foliage and blossoms.

"That's a nice lad," Hadley said. "Not at all self-conscious and certainly knowledgeable."

"Makes a nice change from the kids in the restrictive upbringing in some of our planetary societies," Kendra remarked.

"I'd say that the most amazing aspect is that the four of them survived as long as they did," Caleb said. "I'll want to learn more of their history. Later. Right now, we have reports to make."

As soon as the officers had left on their tour of the Sh'im wreck, Nimisha escorted Cuiva to the Fiver. Jon accompanied them, and Perdimia followed a short step behind, carrying the long Coskanito Necklace case and the dress box.

"See the scrapes, Cuiva dear." Nimisha pointed to the marring on the port side. "Helm kept damage to a minimum."

"Quite a feat, as you'll be able to appreciate," Jon said, "when you see the condition of the other wrecks on Erehwon."

"So we came the safer way," Cuiva said, not quite concealing an eager nervousness. "This is a very pretty valley," she added, glancing beyond the landing field and its hangar to the Sh'im cliff and its settlements. "Is that large house over there where your friends live?" she asked.

"Yes, thanks to the prefab units in the freighter pod we found—"

"You found, Nimi," Jon corrected her.

She rolled her eyes at his qualification. "All of us," she began in a starchy tone, "were extraordinarily lucky that so much of its cargo had been destined for a colony. We could use everything there was."

"Weren't there any survivors?" Cuiva asked softly.

"None we ever found," Nimisha said gently, patting her daughter's arm. "We think it originated in the Second Diaspora, so it's quite old. I don't know how they managed to fly such a crate, much less expect it to reach its destination. Which it didn't. Oh, dear," she added, for muted howls could plainly be heard through the open hatch.

"They're in good voice today," Jon said with a chuckle as Nimisha hurried up the stairs ahead of them.

"They're hungry," Nimisha explained in a slightly apologetic tone. "Ah, food is on the way," she added as a Sh'im female, clasping three feeding bottles to her furry chest, made her way from Cater to the first cabin. The Sh'im shook her head at Nimisha and kicked the half-closed door open. Nimisha caught sight of Tezza Ashke inside the room, jiggling Tyrone, who was always loudest when hungry, his face contorted and red with outrage.

With an inaudible mutter, Perdimia pushed past the others and hurried into the room, closing the door on all the hungry voices.

"That's good of her," Jon said with a sigh of appreciation. "D'you think she might take over? Or is that outside of her expertise, Cuiva?"

"I suspect not, considering the alacrity with which she reacted," Nimisha said, grinning and turned to look at her daughter.

"As I'm now fourteen, if not yet Necklaced, and I'm certainly not anywhere near Lady Vescuya or Lord Vestrin, I don't think I need a bodyguard anymore." Cuiva caught and held Jon's eyes.

"Not with both your mother and me to be sure of your safe-keeping," Jon said with a courtly bow.

"Thank you, Jon," Cuiva said with gentle dignity. "I'll need to know a lot more about this world. Before I went into cold sleep, Caleb explained that, once we found you," Cuiva put her fingers firmly around her mother's arm, "he never doubted we would, you know." Nimisha nodded. "Even when we got here . . . 'nowhere'—" Cuiva giggled while the other two grinned at her amusement. "—he said we'd have to send a pulse—which they have managed to speed

up by"—another giggle—"three months and then wait for its answer. Because what happens next depends on what's been found
here. And you certainly have found a lot. All exciting, too!"

"Tomorrow your mother and I demand the honor of showing
you around, Lady Cuiva," Jon said with a wink at Nimisha.

"But it's been an exciting morning, young lady, and if I may be
so bold as to interrupt your reunion, I think a short nap might be
advisable," Doc said.

"I was about to suggest one," Nimisha said, "but we could use
another snack. Cater, have you something savory on hand? This
morning's raid shorted me on breakfast."

"I do, Lady Nimisha, and Helm has informed me of Lady Cuiva's
special needs. May I welcome you to Erehwon, ma'am?"

"I'm very glad to be here, I assure you, Cater, and happier to be
awake again. But Mother," Cuiva said, turning appealingly to Nimisha, "how long do I have to eat that awful stuff?"

"I have prepared a broth and toast, Lady Cuiva," Cater said
with bright encouragement.

"I'll leave you, then, since you have Perdimia to help now. I've
got some checking to do." Jon bent to kiss Nimisha's cheek, gave
her daughter a quick bow and a grin, and then strode away.

Cuiva waited only until she could no longer hear his footsteps
and then she smiled joyfully at her mother. "Kendra will be so relieved, Mother."

"Ah, I thought that was the way the wind blows," Nimisha said.

"She's nice, and a very good mathematician. I learned a lot
from her."

"I'm told you qualified as a Junior Officer. And signed off very
high in all the specialties." Nimisha gave Cuiva a big hug for her
achievement.

Cuiva flushed. "Well, I had to learn all I could if we were to find you, my mother, so I thought learning about astronomy, mathematics, physics, and all that might prove useful."

"Which it still can, since it would appear that we're stuck here for at least two years—unless they've also made significant changes in how to speed up pulse messages. Now eat, my pet," Nimisha said.

"Then can I meet my siblings?" Cuiva asked, looking over her shoulder at the closed cabin door.

"Yes, and then you may all have a morning nap."

When Casper and Syrona got back to their quarters, they found neat packages awaiting them.

"Now that's real thoughtful," Casper said as he saw the tropical-weight dress whites. Since the hat was on top, he settled it to his head at the proper angle. "Someone's clever at guessing sizes."

"That tunic's a new cut," Syrona said. She fingered the material. "Much lighter, too. You won't know you're wearing it." She held up trousers that had a crease almost sharp enough to cut a hand. "I guess I've got the same," she said with a sigh. She and Nimisha had fashioned a very elegant sarong-length skirt and sleeveless top for the Necklacing. Nimisha could design clothing as well as spaceships.

"We can change once the ceremony's over, but we *are* Navy," Casper said, appreciating her reluctance after spending so much time making the special outfit.

"Are we, Casper? Still?"

"Until otherwise notified." Then he added, in quite a different tone of voice, "I don't know about you, Syrie, but I'd hate to have to leave here. We've made such progress, and there's so much I want to see done."

"Me, too," she agreed softly, turning away to open her parcel. "Well, at least we won't swelter," she said, tilting her uniform hat at a civilian angle on her head. "I'll have to do something with my hair after all." She'd let it grow long and usually wore it in a braid.

"Braid it up, like you used to. I'd hate to see you cut your hair, dear. But I sure need a trim if I'm to be correct in uniform again," Casper said, regarding himself in a mirror that had been retrieved from the *Poolbeg*.

Syrona was doing that for him when Tim burst in, full of his successful escort duty.

"Chief Engineer Ian wants to see as much as he can of the Broken Bird and the freighter and that ancient wreck that Nimisha found and Nazim's one *o'olio* of a pilot. Ook and Ool said so. With two gigs, the skiff, and two Fivers, can we do more exploring now, huh?"

"I shouldn't be at all surprised," Casper said, grinning at Tim's ebullience.

"Hey, Casper, looks good," Tim added, then frowned as he peered into the open parcels. "Don't I get new clothes, too?"

"You will also notice that these are uniforms, and ten is too young even to be a cadet," Syrona said with mock severity. "You'll be a lot cooler in the clothes I made you than we will come noontime. We'll be changing out of uniform as soon as we can, I assure you. Now go shower. You've got rust on your legs and arms again. Showing off in the Broken Bird, were you? You be sure to put antiseptic on any cuts under all that dirt, hear me?" She listened for acquiescence delivered in a disgusted tone of voice.

Then she ran one hand over the smooth fabric of the dress whites until Casper, changing into his uniform, noticed her apathy.

"What's the matter, Syrie? You're not annoyed by the whites, are you? I think it was a damned nice gesture so we wouldn't have to wear the only proper attire we have left."

Syrie sank on to the end of the bed, her face at once sad and angry.

"When I think of what we went through . . . never knowing . . . and all our friends dying, the children . . ." Tears leaked from her eyes, and Casper immediately settled beside her. She tried to push him away. "I'll get your brand-new tunic all wet."

"And it'll dry in five minutes outside. Now what's the matter? This isn't like you."

"Why, if Nimisha hadn't got trapped by that wormhole . . ."

"Oh, Syrie, darling, that's not fair. You *know* that searches were made for us. But Nimisha managed to get a Mayday out. We didn't. No one knew *where* to look for the *Poolbeg*. Anyway, Globan told me while we were rigging the tarpaulin that Navy listed the *Poolbeg* at the top of its 'look-for' list, and every Explorer ship went out with its specs and crew complement. They even had details rooting through junkyards now and then, in case parts of the *Poolbeg* could be located. And an undercover agent in that pirate gang that occasionally raids in the Sirius sector. We'd've been found, sooner or later." He chuckled, catching her chin with gentle fingers and making her look at him. "Cherry told Globan that Cuiva was so determined to find her mother that everything she learned on board the Five B was aimed at doing just that. Cuiva pestered the life out of Hadley, who's the astronomer on the Five B. And drained Kendra Oscony of advanced maths. And signed off on all the major specialties as a Junior Officer. That girl would have searched for her mother for the rest of her life. For that matter, so would Captain Rustin, even after he paired off with Kendra. Seems he said he owed Nimisha and he was going to pay her back if it took his lifetime, too."

Syrona began to sniffle again. "I didn't think I could *have* such mean thoughts about Nimisha after all she's done for *us*! But when the uniforms came . . ."

"That wasn't *her* idea, Syrie," Caleb said with a chuckle. "Rustin didn't miss us sweating in the dress blues."

"No matter what I just said, Casper, I don't want to *leave* here. Tim's First Family on Erehwon. Back in any of the colonies he'll just be a—nothing."

Caleb gave an amused snort. "I doubt our Tim will be a nothing anywhere, Syrie. You know how smart Jon and Nimisha think he is, and I know he's already proved it to Caleb Rustin. Look how he's helping their semantics officer adjust her translator units."

"But what if we're *ordered* to leave Erehwon, Casper?" she asked in a muted wail.

Casper pulled her to her feet and into his arms, where he held her tightly, smoothing back the short hairs that had escaped her braid. "If it comes to that, Syrie, I'll resign. You can, too, and we'll all be colonists. We have that right under Exploratory Service regs."

"I'd forgotten that," she said, and began to cheer up. She rubbed her cheeks dry. "I won't take long to change, dear. That's one advantage with uniforms," she added, carefully picking up her new one and making for the bathroom she had designed for their private use. "No problems about what to wear and when to wear what."

Jon had had a chance for a private conversation with Caleb Rustin in his cabin, though Caleb dodged most of the initial questions about his current orders and if there were some pertaining to the shipwrecked crew.

"There are two points that I didn't mention in any of the pulses, Captain—"

"Caleb, Jon."

"Thank you, sir . . . thanks."

"And what could you have failed to mention in the full reports I'm still reading?" Caleb asked, gesturing to the disks on his desk.

"The first oddity is that, when I computed the vector of the wreck we found in space on our way to Secondo, it had not—" Jon paused. "—come from the same area of space in which *our* wormhole ejected us. Of course, as we know now, that wormhole moves about on the other side; after all, it caught the space station *and* Meterios, who were both supposed to be well beyond its range. So—" Jon hesitated again, dubious. "I wonder if there could be more than one wormhole emptying into this general vicinity."

Caleb considered that for a long moment. "We know so little about wormholes that you could be right."

"I'd rather not be," Jon said ruefully.

"Hmmm, yes, I agree. You said two points?"

"Yes, and maybe it is part of the first. On our way back from checking out the third M-type planet, the one Nimisha calls Tertio, I answered a muted alert from Helm. Nimisha was sleeping a lot just then, pregnant with the twins. I certainly didn't want to wake her unnecessarily. What alerted Helm was an old emission trail."

"It was?" Caleb sat up straighter, elbows on the armrest, his fingers linked. "How old? What sort of fuel trace?"

"That we couldn't establish with any accuracy, but several months old at the least. The course just brushed the heliopause of Tertio. We diverted to see if we could pick up stronger traces. It was heading off our port side. Helm took readings of the stars in that direction, but none of them were close enough to be an immediate destination."

Caleb leaned back in his chair and steepled his fingers thoughtfully.

"That's extremely interesting, Jon, because we found traces not that far from the beacon."

"You did? Meterios mentioned nothing."

Caleb snorted. "She only saw what she expected to see, although I'm willing to give her the benefit of the doubt in this instance. She was probably too busy catching loose pods and dodging the space station debris to notice anything as nebulous as that was, even three months earlier. But it's there. And we have it on record. Did Nimisha mention seeing anything on her way in?"

"No, and Helm would have mentioned a previous sighting. The one we saw was probably months old. Helm's a lot more sensitive than other ships."

"I think we might do well to set up a few drone-eyes," Caleb said. "And possibly a discreet installation on the farthest moon. As I'm sure you've gathered, we're here until further orders can be pulsed through to us. I hope you don't mind."

"*Mind!*" Grinning like an idiot, Jon shook his head in the human fashion. "Having new people here?"

"I rather thought that would be your reaction," Caleb said drolly. "In any event, we've enough equipment and certainly the skills to produce a good early warning system, even if we have to manufacture some things here on Erehwon."

Jon turned serious again, too.

"Two sightings might mean a reasonably regular shipping lane through this area of space. On the other hand, maybe the trail was from a ship heading away from another wormhole exit. I think I prefer shipping lines."

"I think I do, too," Caleb said with a grin. "But shipping what and by whom? M-type planets are rare enough. Since the Sh'im were caught by the wormhole, those traces might not be from their colony ships. I think we need more evidence before we put it on the worry list. I'll include your observations in my report."

Jon nodded. "Then, too, the Sh'im would prefer a dimmer primary than this one, or those of the other two M's. Sh'im eyes need shading. That's why we borrowed the tarpaulin." Jon gave a droll smile. "For an unpopulated area of space, this sector shows more traffic than certainly *I* thought there'd be."

"We'll just keep optics up there to spot the next batch of traffic. Did you ever see any exploratory probes while you were here?"

Jon gave a bark. "Not so much as a con trail. Though we were scarcely in a position to do any signaling once the shuttle was crocked. Sure had the surprise of my life when Nimisha flew in to our site on the *Poolbeg's* gig."

"Yes, but then she's been surprising people since she was Necklaced. Which reminds me, Jon . . ." Caleb rose and picked up a neat package from his bed. "Think these might come in handy for today's ceremony. And they've improved tropical dress whites while you've been gone."

Jon didn't waste any time opening the parcel and grinned with real pleasure to find the hat fit his head perfectly. "I appreciate this, Caleb, more than you know. Those dress blues are *not* for this climate."

"Got to preserve all the naval traditions we can. When the fun's over, let's get our com experts together and see what we can come up with"—Caleb held up a warning hand—"without exactly explaining why we want the equipment."

"Since when did the Navy explain more than need-to-know?" Jon asked with a cocky grin. Then he noticed the wall clock. "I'd better go get dressed. Thanks again."

Jon ended up showering and changing in the only empty cabin. He was buckling the white web belt—an item of uniform that had never altered—when there was a quick knock at the door and before he could say anything, Syrona, exceedingly correct in her whites, entered and closed the door behind her.

"I'm here to trim your hair, Captain Svangel."

Jon's right hand went to the damp hair well below his shoulders. Syrona grinned and held up scissors and comb.

"Casper didn't complain, and you better not."

"You haven't cut your hair, have you, Syrie?" Jon demanded anxiously.

She turned her head so that he could see the intricate braids that extended below the back of her hat.

"Sit," she said, pointing to the stool and draped his damp towel over his shoulders. "It won't take long. And may even look better than the job I did on Casper, now I've got the hang of it again."

"Hey!" Jon protested when he heard the first snip.

"Oh, relax. I've never cut anyone's ears, and you simply have to look as good as you can to match Nimi and Cuiva. That is, when her mother and Perdimia finally made her stop playing long enough with her brothers and sister to *get* dressed. You'd think they were more important than her Necklacing."

Jon chuckled, careful not to move his head. "Got over that one easily, didn't we?"

"Cuiva's a nice person. Everyone on the Five B—and we have got to do something about proper names for those ships, you know—thinks the world of Cuiva. D'you know she intended to keep looking for her mother if it took her entire life?"

"Dedication seems to be a Boynton trait."

He felt her comb through much shorter hair. "Sit still. I need to clip . . . just . . . one or two. There!" She gathered up the towel carefully from his shoulders to keep the cuttings from escaping.

Jon blinked twice in the mirror at his new elegance and grinned. "Thanks, Syrie."

"Now finish dressing. It's nearly time to take your seat."

Placing his hat correctly under his left arm, Jon made his way out of the cabin and into the main lounge of the Fiver. There he stopped short, his jaw dropping as he saw Lady Nimisha Boynton-Rondymense and Lady Cuiva Boynton-Farquahar looking every inch the First Family scions they were. Nimisha was now clad in the filmy delicately blue gown, no doubt from the box Perdimia had brought over from the Five B. Her luxuriant hair had been plaited into a high coronet on the crown of her head, with jeweled pins that picked up the colors of her Necklace, making the hairstyle truly regal. The Necklace was magnificent in its intricacy, covering exactly the heir tattoo beneath it as Cuiva's Necklace shortly would.

He had trouble breaking his eyes away from Nimisha, for he'd never seen her in her role as a First Family body-heir, despite knowing every whorl of her tattoo. She smiled gently, as if she understood his confusion at her transformation.

Reassured by that smile, he took time to regard Cuiva, dressed in a subtle, not quite formfitting white gown that flowed about her slender body, outlining young breasts, slender waist and hips, reaching to her ankles, her feet in white sandals. Her hair was also dressed high on her head with ringlets that cascaded down but were somehow held on a level with her delicate ears. The neckline of her gown had been designed to show the body-heir tattoo that would soon be covered by her Necklace. She was as radiant as her mother, but she dropped her eyes shyly as he stood there, mesmerized.

"I gather we pass inspection," Nimisha said, breaking the spell.

"I've never seen you look so beautiful, Nimi," he said in a rough, low voice, and then laughed softly when she blushed. "And you, Lady Cuiva, must be the most radiant minor major body-heir ever seen in the entire galaxy, including this sector." He accorded her his deepest bow.

Perdimia entered the room, her shorter hair somehow more elegantly arranged. She was clad in a long pearly gray gown, its elegance understated. She carried the Coskanito box that held Cuiva's Necklace.

"May we," Doc began, "the AI crew of the Fiver, congratulate you, Lady Cuiva, and salute you on your first step into maturity. May you live long and be happy."

"Here! Here!" chimed in Helm's tenor and Cater's alto.

"If you'll just get out of here now, Jon," Nimisha said with a wide grin to take the edge off the order, "we can begin."

The automatic bells signaled noon, and Jon strode as fast as he could out of the Fiver and toward the circle where the ceremony would take place. He couldn't quite shake off the amazing visions of mother and daughter until he was suddenly engulfed by the sun-warmed fragrance of the blooms that had been gathered to enhance this outdoor affair. The tarpaulin did provide shade for Sh'im sun-sensitive eyes, but it also kept in the floral aromas, intensifying them. Bleachers that had been erected to accommodate the hordes of spectators were already crammed. He saw Syrona taking her seat by Casper and Tim, and noticed there was an empty place on a chair—not a Sh'im stool, for which he was immensely grateful—beside Caleb, with his first officer just beyond him. So he made his way there. Opposite the naval contingent was a special raised section, designed so the view of the smaller Sh'im would not be impeded by the floral decorations massed to create a circle. Many of the humans were seated on couches and chairs, Jon absently noted. Safer than those wretched stools.

The circle was broken by a few strategically placed gaps for exits and entrances. In its center stood a three-tiered podium. That was where Nimisha would formally Necklace her daughter.

Over the liquid vowel sounds of the Sh'im, he heard music. The musicians might have been professionally inferior to the fine orchestra that Lady Rezalla would have hired for the occasion, but the strains of old Earth tunes were, to his thinking, far more appropriate to rustic Erehwon. As he took his seat, he thought maybe they should call the Fiver "Erehwon." Not accurate, though: That ship would always know where she was!

A hush settled. The soft music faltered a moment and then bravely started a triumphant march, not quite martial but vaguely familiar to him and in the proper tempo for a sedate progress. He turned his head, as everyone did, to see Nimisha, leading her daughter by the hand down the slight slope to the shaded arena. Sunlight sent shafts of light from the jeweled Necklace Nimisha wore. There were oohs and aaahs from the humans and the Sh'im liquid sound of approval, certainly the most beautiful sounds they made and far more evocative of joyfulness than human exclamations. Cuiva kept her eyes down, not so much in modesty as to be sure of her footing on the uneven, sun-baked ground. Behind them came Perdimia, looking as if she held back tears by sheer willpower.

Nimisha led Cuiva into the garlanded circle through one of the openings, where Perdimia halted. Mother and daughter continued around its circumference: mother on the inside. This was the point of the ritual, the presentation of a daughter to the mature spectators invited to a Necklacing ceremony that signified the daughter's right to set childhood behind her. That none were relatives or highly respected family connections did not matter. Cuiva's only other near kin were fast asleep or being amused elsewhere, since even the twins were much too young to behave during this formal part of the day's ceremony.

Jon felt himself almost bursting with pride as Cuiva inclined her head to him as well as to Caleb. Having completed the circle, Nimisha led her daughter to the central podium and Perdimia advanced slowly to them. Nimisha stood on the highest tier with Cuiva on the one below, facing her mother. Perdimia held up the opened case. Slowly and gracefully Nimisha lifted up the exquisite Necklace by its ends, the jewels sparkling from the glare of what sun did penetrate tiny holes in the tarpaulin.

"With this Necklace, Cuiva Boynton-Farquahar, I, your mother, Nimisha Boynton-Rondymense, confirm that you have reached your fourteenth birthday and your minor majority. I confirm you unequivocally as my body-heir and eldest daughter."

Then Cuiva turned her back on her mother while Nimisha carefully draped the beautiful jewelry about Cuiva's slender throat, making certain that it fitted exactly over the tattoo that it replicated in gemstones, size, and design. She clasped it so that the drop sapphire exactly covered that part of the tattoo on Nimisha's back.

Nimisha stepped down to the same level as her daughter, signifying Cuiva's new level in First Family social ranking, and kissed her six times. Tears of joy streaked, but did not mar, their cheeks.

Cuiva stepped to the ground and gave Perdimia the four kisses of deep friendship before she made her way toward the naval contingent and the space station personnel. They rose as one body, the Navy saluting. Cuiva gave Caleb the six kisses of kin relationship that plainly astonished him. Jon could see Nimisha's smile of approval. But when Cuiva accorded him the same degree of relationship, he had to blink away tears of surprise and unexpected pleasure, and swallowed against a huge lump in his throat. What a graceful way to accept a stepfather! She winked at him, her eyes full of mischief for a moment before she stepped to Kendra, embracing her warmly and with two cheek kisses. She gave similar salutes to all those who had been on the Five B. She warmly embraced Syrona, Casper, and Tim, which Syrona later told Tim was more than they could have expected since they had only just recently met Cuiva. She shook hands with the *Acclarke* crew members and the space station personnel before she made her way across the arena to curtsy deeply to Ook and Ool, graciously bowing to the others.

Then Caleb Rustin stepped into the arena, hat under his arm, walked toward the podium where Nimisha stood, and surveyed the crowd.

"Let us all give a rousing cheer for our Lady Cuiva on this auspicious occasion."

He led the cheers, punctuated by the ululations of the Sh'im, who jumped up and down and waved their hands high above their heads, spinning round and round in place until it was a wonder none fell. With a word to Nimisha, who looked surprised, he led her to his chair and gestured for Cuiva to take the one Kendra Oscony immediately vacated, snugging a long black case under her left arm. The XO entered the circle, one step behind Caleb as he strode to the podium. Caleb took the top level and pointed his finger at Tim and Cherry, who ducked quickly around the circumference of the arena to where Ook and Ool sat. There they crouched beside the couches so they did not obstruct the Sh'im view of the next event.

"Lieutenant Commander Jonagren Svangel, Lieutenant Casper Ontell, Ensign Syrona Lester-Pitt, front and center."

Marching abreast and immediately in stride, the three came forward and halted.

"At ease," Caleb said in his most official voice.

The silence was broken by two light voices doing their best to translate unknown rites into a culture that might have nothing similar at all.

"I received a pulsed message at the beacon that I may now read," he said. He took from his breast pocket a handful of the parchment on which commendations and special orders were printed; various colored ribbons and seals adorned the documents. "Ensign Syrona Lester-Pitt."

She took one step forward to break rank, turned an exact forty-five degrees to port, took two more steps, and smartly turned to face the commander, saluting.

"I have the pleasure to announce your promotion to Lieutenant Commander, retroactive to your landing here on Erehwon twenty years ago." He handed her the promotion document, and Kendra handed him the small box with the proper rank collar tabs. He stepped down and attached them to her uniform. Then he saluted her with a broad smile. "Well deserved, Commander. Don't move," he added as Syrona started to turn away. "It is also my distinct pleasure to award you the Galactic Medal, Gold Class with two clusters, for courage and devotion to your service above and beyond the call of duty."

Syrona's eyes widened and she blinked against tears. Kendra passed over the beautiful medal on its multicolored bar so that

Caleb could pin it above Syrona's breast pocket. This time his salute was held moments longer than necessary.

"Your courage is exceeded only by what you and your fellow survivors have managed to achieve in the most dangerous and primitive conditions. Your Service has asked me to extend their deepest respect. Your name is already listed on the Honor Board at Headquarters."

Syrona somehow managed to return to her place in rank and paid no attention to the tears still trickling down her cheeks or the fact that she had to sniffle.

Casper Ontell was promoted to full Commander and received his Galactic Medal, Gold Class with two clusters, and a repeat of the citation that Syrona had been given.

"Lieutenant Commander Jonagren Svangel, I have the great pleasure of confirming your rank as Captain, retroactive to the date you assumed command on the death of Captain Panados Querine of the *Poolbeg*." Caleb's grin was broader than ever as he pinned on Jon's new rank pins and handed over the promotion document. "I am also directed by Federated Sentient Planet Exploratory Service to award you the Galactic Medal, Platinum Class with four clusters."

"I don't deserve that," Jon murmured.

"Shut up," Kendra muttered back. "You bloody well do."

"Quite right, XO," Caleb said, and attached the medal with its iridescent ribbon bar to Jon's chest, saluting him with extra precision and length. He waited until Jon had taken a backward step to fall in line with his companions before he held up the final sheet.

"If you are in accord, Lieutenant Commander Lester-Pitt, Commander Ontell, and Captain Svangel, it is the wish of your Service as well as that of Fleet High Command and the Senate of the Federated Sentient Planets that you accept the administrative management of this planet and continue the fine work you have already done with your—with *our* alien allies. Such a decision, so far from your home planets and family, may not be an easy one to make and I am directed to allow you to consider the proposition until we have received further, or different orders sent by pulse messages. Additional support units are on their way—though we know they will take approximately four years to reach us—but any and all of them are subordinate to your commands and such titles as seem relevant to enforce the policies of mutual cooperation and development of equable Human-Sh'im relations."

The audience, including those nearest the translators, erupted into cheers, hoots, hollers, calls, whistles, and other sounds that made some humans cover their ears in protest.

Caleb stepped down from the top level. "You'll have to draft a plan for development and exploration of this sector of space, you know," he said quietly to the three newly promoted and honored officers. "But we can take our time on that."

"Who owns this planet then?" Jon murmured, his face expressionless.

"The indigenous personnel," Caleb said with first a nod and then a shake of his head. "Which I interpret as those born here." He looked directly at Tim, so earnestly translating to Ook and Ool. "And the Sh'im. Your lot, too, Jon. D'you think Nimisha will stay on?"

"You couldn't drag Nimisha away from here with a space gantry," the Lady answered for herself, having quietly joined them. "How did you manage to blackmail so many people into agreeing to all this?" she asked.

"I didn't do anything," Caleb said, holding up his hands in mock defense. "I was on my way here." Then he relented with a big grin. "Now your esteemed mother, Lady Rezalla, made certain that neither High Command nor FSP Senate was going to slight *her* body-heir, since it was your ship and inimitable wit and courage that precipitated the discovery of this brand-new sector of space. And rescued our lost officers."

"Nimisha deserves a medal, too," Syrona said, blushing a little when Caleb gave her an odd look.

"Civilians don't get medals," Nimisha said. "They get greater responsibilities, but since I can pick mine—again—I'd rather stay on Erehwon with all my friends." She touched Syrona's cheek, then Casper's, before linking her arm in Jon's and standing close to him. "You've some time to kill here then on Erehwon, Caleb? Kendra?"

"That's open-ended," Caleb said with a grin and a quick glance at Jon. "I'm still your naval attaché, Nimisha. I can't seem to get relieved of that duty."

"Onerous as it is," she said, pretending long-sufferance.

Tim burst into the small circle of them, hugging his mother around the hips and then pulling her down so he could see her medal, and then Caleb's and Jon's.

"Just how much did the Sh'im understand of the honors ceremony, Tim?" Caleb asked, hunkering down so he was on a level with the ten-year-old.

"Well, we know they knew that Cuiva's now an adult. They know that you got honors, and they were very impressed with the way you did it all, Caleb," he said. "Looked right *o'olio* to them. But the best part is that we're all staying. They really didn't want us to leave."

"As if we would," Nimisha said indignantly. "We still have to find their home world and see if Tertio's M-type can be made habitable and— What are you laughing about, Captain?" she demanded of Jon.

"Lady Rezalla knew what she was doing," Jon said.

"Lady Rezalla always knows what she's doing," her daughter said firmly. She kissed him enthusiastically while the others cheered.

"So it's just as well, isn't it," remarked Caleb at his drollest, putting his arm about Kendra's waist and pulling her close to him, "that Lady Rezalla does not know the half of what her daughter's been up to."

"Mother?" Cuiva's soft voice interrupted. "Can we start the dancing now?"

"And the eating?" Tim asked plaintively.

"Just a moment, if you will, Timothy Lester-Ontell," Jon said firmly. He pointed to where the Sh'im had been seated, on couches and chairs. Without their occupants, it was plain that these were naval issue. "How did the Sh'im end up with *Acclarke* furnishings?"

Syrona gasped, Casper gulped, and both stared at their son in amazement.

"Well," Tim replied, not at all dismayed by Jon's or his parents' reaction, "Captain Meterios and Brad Karpla wouldn't be needing them, since they're asleep. And I thought Ook and Ool should have something more . . . important looking . . . than their stools." Then he cocked his head questioningly at his adults. "I didn't do anything wrong, did I? We're always recycling stuff here, aren't we?"

The adults exchanged glances and then Nimisha burst out laughing.

"We are indeed always recycling stuff here," Jon said, trying very hard not to break into a smile. "But the *Acclarke*'s furniture falls in a different category, since she's going back to her base for reassignment."

"Oh." It was obvious that Tim did not quite understand the distinction Jon was trying to make.

Casper and Syrona both started apologizing at once until Jon held up his hand.

"We can't give him examples and then complain when he follows them, can we?" he said. "We all have enough back pay to refit the entire ship if anyone complains."

"No one will," Caleb said firmly. "After all, the furniture was only bolted to the floor to keep it from sliding about in turbulence."

They all began to laugh at that, while Tim kept looking from one face to another, clearly mystified.

"Is it okay for me to go eat now?" he asked.

"Yes, go on, Tim," Jon said and gave the boy a little push toward those crowding around the refreshment tables. "Only I want to be around when you two explain the difference to him," he added, cocking his finger at Tim's shocked parents. "And he's got the right idea about eating. My lady?" He held his arm for Nimisha to take and led the procession to the Necklace feast.

EPILOGUE

"How do they keep going?" Jon asked in a weary voice, flapping a hand in the direction of the music still coming from the arena. That there were unusual sounds made by alien instruments and alien throats adding to the volume seemed only appropriate.

"You know how they love celebrations," Nimisha said, leaning her head on his shoulder. Her bare right foot touched his. She had long since removed her finery, including her Necklace, and her hair, though still braided, hung down on either side of her shoulders.

"It could go on all night," Casper said, glancing down at Syrona, who was fast asleep, head on his shoulder, both hands curled about his upper arm. They were dressed in the more comfortable summer gear and occupied one of the two long couches.

They had all changed out of their formal dress uniforms, and found enough extra sarongs for Kendra, Caleb, Ian, and Cherry, who were the other occupants of the Fiver's main compartment.

Although the table near Cater still displayed celebratory viands, most of the debris of a fine feast had been cleared away.

"Night's nearly over," Kendra remarked into the silence that had followed Casper's observation.

"So the celebration goes on all tomorrow—or today, since it's already today," Casper said, lifting a hand briefly and letting it fall back across his leg. Syrona murmured sleepily and snuggled in.

"I should try and get some sleep," Nimisha said in an apathetic tone.

"Why?" Jon turned his head toward hers. Her face was tilted against his shoulder; they were stretched out on the other long couch. "The Sh'im ladies are on duty. They cope. In fact," he added, fatigue slowing both thought and remark, "from what Cherry there said, they consider it a very respectable occupation."

Cherry opened her eyes. "Tim helped, but I got a lot of good detail of how they run their communities. Two years growing up, ten years producing, and the males are just as involved in the process as the females. Then, with any luck, they've got another fifteen or twenty to do what they want to: hunt, develop skills, build, and decorate . . . I crawled into one or two of the caves this afternoon and they have murals—they make all their own pigments, you know." She paused, sighed, and picked up her narrative. "Seems like there was some kind of competition that Ook, Ool, Ay, and Bee referred as to which females would be allowed to assist the *i'l 'iliti*."

"I thought that referred to the shaggy grazers," Casper said, rousing slightly in surprise.

"It now applies to you as well, but it's said in a different pitch and with much affection," Cherry said with a slightly smug smile.

"I thought I recognized several different Sh'im going in and out," Nimisha said, trying to focus tired eyes on Cherry across the lounge.

"Probably. There were so many applying for the job that I guess they've been split into shifts," Cherry said. "I'll have to check with Tim tomorrow, but that's how I figured they must have worked it out."

"Casper," Syrona roused enough to ask, "where *is* Timmy?"

Casper inclined his head. "Outside."

"He is dancing," Helm said, "with young Sh'im."

"Oh," Syrona murmured. "Thanks, Helm." She resettled herself against Casper. "I still can't get over him appropriating the *Acclarke* furniture."

Jon and Caleb both chuckled.

"Escorias has taken most of the blame for that," Jon said. "Tim evidently asked Globan to explain what he'd done wrong. He and Tim had been working on the platform for the Sh'im to use at the Necklacing before the *Acclarke* left. Tim thought the couches would be nice. So Escorias showed the Sh'im how to undo the bolts."

"That's a relief," Syrona said. "I'd hate to think we had encouraged him in—" She paused.

"In taking ways?" Nimisha asked, grinning.

"Colonial recycling," Jon said firmly, waggling a finger at her.

"The boy shows great initiative," Kendra said approvingly. "We could always give him Junior Officer training."

"With Cuiva showing him the ropes?" Jon asked.

"The very person to do so," Caleb murmured.

There was a companionable silence for a few moments, until Nimisha spoke again.

"You know," she began, "while it's good to know my dam has taken charge of Rondymense—" She couldn't help a giggle over that. "—we are going to have to figure out some way to shorten the long haul from here to there. Is that why they're letting you stay on here, Caleb?"

Caleb grinned sleepily. "You figured it out, did you?" But he turned his head just slightly to catch Jon's eye and Svangel nodded with a little smile.

"Finally. Does she have an attaché, too?"

"Well, he's there more to assist Jeska, who's got a good grip on design, too—"

"She should," Nimisha interjected with a snort. "I taught her all I knew, and Hiska likes her. So did all the other department heads once they figured out how smart she was."

"Didn't take them long," Caleb said, "once they saw how she rushed Five B through to completion."

"And that reminds me," Nimisha said. "It's confusing to have two Fives. They need names."

"They do," Syrona said, rousing again. "Said so this afternoon to Jon."

"Do I still own them both, Caleb?" Nimisha asked.

"You certainly do. Lady Rezalla had to give me official permission to remove Five B from the Ship Yard to make our getaway."

"Good. That settles that," Nimisha said. "I'd like to name this one"—she pointed one finger downward—"the *Querine-Weleda*."

Syrona sat up, wide-awake, and Jon turned to regard Nimisha with bemused admiration.

"Oh, that would be such a fitting tribute to them," Syrona said, her voice thickened with emotion. "They were a very dedicated pair."

"And what name have you decided on for the Five B?" Caleb asked, though by the expression on his face, Nimisha rather thought he'd guessed.

"It's not just filial respect that's involved, but gratitude for all she's connived at behind the scenes to be sure we get to keep what we've made. It's also letting my mother as she so often does, have the last word." Nimisha grinned. "I officially declare that the Five B is now the *Lady Rezalla*."

About the Author

ANNE MCCAFFREY is one of the world's most popular authors. Her first novel was published in 1967. Since then, she has written dozens of books, of which there are more than twelve million copies in print. Before her success as a writer, she was involved in theater. She directed the American premiere of Carl Orff's *Ludus de Nato Infante Mirificus*, in which she also played a witch.

McCaffrey lives in County Wicklow, Ireland, in a house of her own design, Dragonhold-Underhill, so named because she had to dig out of a hill to build it. There she runs a private livery stable, raising and training her beloved horses for horse trials and show jumping.